Her Brooding Duke

The Worthington Legacy
Book Seven

Marie Higgins

ARE YOU SIGNED UP FOR DRAGONBLADE'S BLOG?

You'll get the latest news and information on exclusive giveaways, exclusive excerpts, coming releases, sales, free books, cover reveals and more.

Check out our complete list of authors, too!

No spam, no junk. That's a promise!

Sign Up Here

www.dragonbladepublishing.com

Dearest Reader;

Thank you for your support of a small press. At Dragonblade Publishing, we strive to bring you the highest quality Historical Romance from some of the best authors in the business. Without your support, there is no 'us', so we sincerely hope you adore these stories and find some new favorite authors along the way.

Happy Reading!

CEO, Dragonblade Publishing

Additional Dragonblade books by Author Marie Higgins

The Worthington Legacy
Her Perfect Scoundrel (Book 1)
Her Dreamy Deceiver (Book 2)
Her Adorable Cad (Book 3)
Her Irresistible Charmer (Book 4)
Her Captain Enchanter (Book 5)
Her Sweetest Rogue (Book 6)
Her Brooding Duke (Book 7)

Love's Addiction Series
A Wallflower to Love (Book 1)
A Governess to Protect (Book 2)
A Maiden to Remember (Book 3)

Chapter One

England, 1823

Louisa Hamilton moved with purpose, her sharp eyes locked on her unsuspecting target. She slowed her steps, careful not to draw attention as she zeroed in on the gentleman's overcoat. Luck seemed to favor her today—the coat's large, loose pockets promised easy access. A pocket watch, a money clip, anything of value could be hers in seconds. He stood on the bustling street, engrossed in conversation with another man, the crowd offering her the perfect cover.

A gust of wind whipped through the narrow alley, biting at her skin and sending a shiver down her spine. Early spring was her least favorite time of year—the cold always found a way to seep into her bones, especially when lurking in the shadows.

With one hand, Louisa clutched her threadbare coat tighter against her chest, the missing buttons leaving her vulnerable to the chill. Every shilling she earned was stashed away in secret, hidden from Macgregor's prying eyes. He still controlled her, his grip as suffocating as ever, and she knew she'd need every penny if she ever hoped to escape his gang of thieves and scoundrels.

She should have been scanning her surroundings for watchful eyes or signs of trouble, but her mind wandered. The bustling streets of Richmond, the quaint shops, and the uneven cobblestone roads were so different from the city she remembered from six years ago. So much had changed, yet here she was, still trapped in a life she longed to leave behind.

Memories brought on heartache, and she didn't dare think of the time her family died. Didn't dare think of everything she'd gone through—suddenly being orphaned and placed in the wrong hands.

Shaking off the unsettling memories, Louisa refocused and edged closer to her mark. Just one more step and she'd be close enough to act. If she could lift something valuable from the gentleman on the corner, it would be more than just a small victory—it would be her first real step toward a new life, a life she had only dared to dream about for years. Freedom was within reach, and all she needed was one successful swipe to set her plan in motion.

The sweet scent of sticky buns drifted through the air, momentarily overwhelming her senses. Louisa closed her eyes, inhaling the mouthwatering aroma, her empty stomach twisting in protest. It had been two days since her last meal, but hunger was a small price to pay for her freedom. Breaking away from Macgregor's grasp mattered more than satisfying her appetite— especially now that he aimed to drag her down even further, from a thief to a prostitute. Bile rose in her throat at the thought. Macgregor never made idle threats, and she knew he'd stop at nothing to bend her to his will. But she wouldn't let that happen—not now, not ever.

Taking a deep breath, Louisa concentrated on the gentleman and closed the space between them until her ragged dress brushed against his trousers. The man didn't turn, and the person he conversed with didn't seem to realize his friend was about to be relieved of his pocketbook.

Her heart pounded so hard it felt like it might crack a rib, threatening to betray her nerves before she could finish the job. This should be easy. She'd done it countless times over the past six years. Macgregor always called her one of his best, which was likely the only reason he hadn't started selling her to men yet.

But today, the usual confidence was clouded by something else: hope. The hope that this could be her last job, the one that would finally buy her the freedom she'd been secretly planning for the past two years.

Taking a slow, deliberate breath, Louisa steadied herself, forcing her trembling hands to still. Her fingers inched toward the gentleman's coat, movements practiced and precise. The fabric brushed her fingertips as she deftly began to search the pocket. Yet, even as her hand remained steady, she shifted her eyes across the crowded street, sharp and vigilant. Every passerby, every shadow, every flicker of movement felt like a potential threat—a witness who could ruin everything with one shouted warning. Her heart raced in her chest, but her focus remained locked on the task. Almost there... Just one more second, and she could taste the freedom she'd been dreaming of for so long.

From behind, a man's voice rang through the breeze. Her target turned and looked over his shoulder. Snatching her hand back, she closed her eyes and froze, hoping she hadn't been caught. Instead of the angry voice she expected to hear, her target greeted yet another friend.

Slowly, Louisa peeked through her lashes at the group of three. The newest man's hearty laugh sent a jolt through her, triggering an unsettling rhythm in her chest. His voice—so achingly familiar—stirred memories she'd long buried, as if a crashing wave of the past had suddenly overwhelmed her. Narrowing her gaze, she focused on him, and bit by bit, fragments of her old life came into sharp, chaotic focus.

She blinked, her breath catching in disbelief. A ghost? It had to be—yet there he stood, her once-betrothed, laughing and chatting with the two other well-dressed gentlemen. Could her mind be playing tricks on her? After all, she was back in Richmond, the town where she'd grown up, the place where her life had unraveled. But this... was completely impossible.

Scenes and voices from the past crept into Louisa's mind, a

haunting reminder of the day her world fell apart. *I'm sorry to inform you, Miss Louisa, but your family and betrothed died in a house fire.* The shock had been overwhelming, shaking her to her core as she stood outside the girls' school, clutching her best friend Eliza's hand. Their tear-filled eyes had met, both too young to fully understand the depth of the loss.

Eliza had promised that her uncle, Percy Featherspoon, would take care of Louisa. Trusting in her friend's words, Louisa had gone with him, only to be whisked off to Scotland within days. She never saw Eliza again. Six long years had passed, and the truth of that dreadful day remained elusive, always lurking in the back of her mind. She'd spent those years wondering what really happened—how could everything she loved be taken in a single moment?

Now, standing in Richmond, her heart pounded crazily, each beat laced with disbelief. Could it be true? Had her fiancé been alive all this time? The thought sent an icy wave crashing through her, shattering everything she thought she knew. How could he have survived? Why hadn't he come for her? Her mind spun with questions, each more painful than the last, unraveling the fragile sense of reality she'd built over the years.

She shook her head, stumbling back from the group of men, her vision blurring with confusion. If Frank had been alive, Eliza would have told her. He would have found her—he *should* have found her. But no, it had to be a cruel trick of her mind, a stranger who just happened to resemble the man she had loved so deeply. The thought gnawed at her, and her knees buckled beneath the weight of it. She leaned heavily against the side of a building, struggling to catch her breath, but it wasn't hunger that made her dizzy now. It was the devastating possibility that the life she had mourned, the love she had lost, had never truly been gone at all.

With shaky fingers, she wiped back the stringy hair hanging in her eyes, looping the strands over her ears. Louisa didn't want anything to distract her from studying the man who resembled— and sounded—so much like Frank.

Quite strapping, she must admit, and he did resemble the young man she remembered as a thirteen-year-old. His hair wasn't as white-blond as she recalled. Then again, neither was hers. She couldn't make out the color of his eyes from way over here, but if he were indeed her betrothed…

An ache throbbed in her forehead, and Louisa pressed her fingers to the spot, trying to chase away the rising pain. No, it couldn't be him. Her entire family had been lost that terrible day. Frank—her cousin, her father's only male heir—had come to stay with them after his graduation from Eton. He had been in the house when the flames consumed it, taking everyone she loved. She had clung to that truth, as unbearable as it was, for so many years. It was the only way she had been able to survive the grief, the only certainty in the chaos that followed.

But now, the man standing before her unraveled that certainty, and the thought clawed at her, reopening old wounds she'd thought had scarred over. Could it be possible that Frank hadn't perished in the fire after all?

The man flipped his hand through the air and chuckled. Her heart leapt. Frank had always had a twittery kind of laugh.

"Will you be at White's tonight, my good man?" One of the others clapped her fiancé look-alike on the shoulder.

"But of course. Only the company of a beautiful woman could keep me away."

"I'm assuming your fiancée does not know?" the other man replied with a smirk.

"She does not *care*, and neither do I." He laughed again, but more harshly.

Tears burned at the corners of Louisa's eyes, blurring her vision again as the familiar voice echoed in her ears. Why did he sound so much like Frank? And… engaged to another woman? The very thought twisted her heart painfully. Frank had always wanted to marry for love, just as she did. They had both come from parents who were wildly in love, the happiest people she had ever known. It was something they had talked about often—

how they wanted a love like their parents, full of joy and passion, not some cold, arranged union.

Her betrothal to Frank had made perfect sense. As her father's heir, it was expected he would marry her, securing both the title and the family legacy. Even at the age of twelve, Louisa had believed in that future. She had dreamed of the day their youthful bond would blossom into the kind of love their parents had shared. But now, everything felt twisted, broken, as though the past she had clung to no longer made sense. Could this man truly be Frank? Or was it all just a cruel illusion, sent to torment her already shattered heart?

"Then I bid you farewell until tonight, Wellesley."

The name hit her like a violent gust of wind, knocking the air from her lungs. If the building hadn't been behind her, she would have collapsed. *Wellesley.* The title that had been awarded to her cousin before his supposed death.

She watched in stunned silence as Wellesley—Frank—walked toward a waiting carriage and climbed inside. Tears stung her eyes and blurred her vision. Her heart pounded so fiercely that each breath felt like a struggle. He couldn't be alive... could he? If Frank had survived, what else had been hidden from her? Could her family, too, have escaped that devastating fire?

She had to know. She had to follow him. With trembling hands, she pushed off the wall and began to move, watching as the carriage rolled away, heading toward the very place where her home once stood. Every step quickened her pulse, a desperate hope rising within her. Could it be possible after all these years? Could the people she had mourned for so long still be alive?

Forgetting her gnawing hunger and the weakness in her limbs, Louisa bolted from the crowd, heading toward the road that led into the countryside. Instinctively, her feet found the path she had known so well as a child, the shortcut through the trees that connected her home to the town. But the thought gnawed at her—he couldn't possibly be going to *that* house, could he? The home she remembered had burned to the ground six years ago.

She had never seen the wreckage with her own eyes.

When Mr. Featherspoon had ripped her away from school, he'd taken her straight to Scotland, denying her any chance of return, and sold her to Macgregor. That dark chapter of her life felt distant now, as though it belonged to someone else. She hadn't set foot on English soil until a mere fortnight ago, yet here she was, racing toward the shadow of a past she thought had been destroyed. What if everything she'd believed about the fire— about the deaths—had been a lie?

The possibility sent a surge of adrenaline through her, over-powering her exhaustion and hunger. Her legs, though weak, moved with a newfound determination, fueled by the desperate need for answers. Was her home still standing? Had she been wrong all this time? Unanswered questions thudded in her chest alongside her frantic heartbeat, propelling her forward, despite the fears that clawed at her, threatening to drag her down. She had to know the truth, no matter what awaited her.

The farther she ran, the more the sun dipped lower in the sky. The closer she came to the place she'd known as home for the first thirteen years of her life, the more her throat tightened with emotion. She'd had such happy memories here. It was too painful to remember how much she had back then, only to have nothing now.

Out of breath, she stopped by a bulky tree and fell against the large, chipped trunk. Her chest burned as sharp breaths tore from her throat. Off in the distance, the clip-clop of horses' hooves pounded on the ground. She stumbled toward the sound. Through the trees, the carriage carrying Wellesley pulled in front of a structure.

She sucked in a quick breath.

The large, gray two-story manor stood before her, untouched by time, exactly as she remembered it. The small flower garden near the wide, two-step porch still bloomed with vibrant colors, as if the years had never passed. The golden knockers on the grand double doors gleamed in the sunlight, polished to perfection, just as they had been in her childhood.

As a young girl, she had often imagined herself as a grand lady of the manor. Servants in burgundy coats and white gloves would open those heavy doors for her, bowing low as she swept inside, dressed in the most exquisite gown. Her faithful puppy, Shadow, would come bounding toward her, tail wagging, showering her with affection and slobbery kisses. And in her fantasy, her perfect suitor—tall, kind, and full of love—would be waiting for her by the hearth, arms open, ready to embrace her with warmth and devotion. It had been a simple, innocent dream, filled with hope and the promise of love. Now, standing before the very home that once held those dreams, reality felt far more complicated.

In seconds, the dream went up in flames and immediately turned ash black. Her dream would never happen now. Not with all she'd been through with Macgregor.

None of this should have happened. Louisa shouldn't be standing here, lost in dreams of the life she could have had, instead of consumed by the disgust for the life she'd been forced to endure. But here she was, her heart pounding furiously in her chest, the weight of it almost unbearable. The sight of her childhood home, still standing so pristine, tore through her like a knife. The flood of memories—the innocence, the hope—was overwhelming, a stark contrast to the harsh reality she now faced. Seeing this place, untouched by the devastation she had lived through, felt like it might break her all over again.

Stopping near another tree, she placed her cold, clammy hand to her throat as she glanced around the grove. Evening's shadows play with her tear-blurred vision, making her think she'd been followed. She listened for the sounds of crunching leaves and broken twigs, but all that surrounded her was her own heavy breathing.

Why had Featherspoon told her she hadn't a shilling to her name when the grand house standing before her suggested otherwise? At the time, she had no reason to doubt Eliza's uncle, trusting him in her grief and confusion. She'd stayed with Featherspoon for only a few short weeks before being handed over to Macgregor's so-called *care*.

His assistance had been anything but. She had been sent to hell. The children in Macgregor's home had mocked her, refusing to believe she had once been born into a life of privilege. They called her names and taunted her relentlessly, shattering what little remained of her identity. It hadn't taken long for Louisa to understand—lying was her only means of survival. The truth about her past had become a distant, dangerous secret, buried beneath the layers of deception she had built to protect herself from the cruelty of the world Macgregor had thrust her into.

Taking a deep breath, Louisa glanced around the thicket, trying to ground herself in the present. The frogs croaked by the nearby pond, and crickets filled the night with their steady song, but her heart was heavy, twisted with the weight of unanswered questions. None of it made sense. Why would Eliza's uncle, a man she had trusted in her darkest hour, lie to her? What could he possibly have gained by hiding the truth?

She felt as if she were standing on the edge of a cliff, with only half the puzzle in her hands, the crucial piece still missing. Without it, everything remained a confusing blur, and the ache of not knowing gnawed at her, pulling sobs from the deepest part of her soul. Something was being kept from her—something vital— and until she uncovered it, she could never truly understand the life that had been stolen from her.

As Frank disappeared inside, Louisa crept closer to the house, her heart racing with a mix of fear and hope. She kept low, moving carefully, every step deliberate as she navigated the familiar flower garden—her mother's pride and joy. The sight of the blooms brought a lump to her throat, and before she could stop them, tears slipped down her cheeks. For the first time in years, a fragile hope stirred in her chest. Could it be possible? Could her parents still be alive? She had dreamed of being in their comforting arms again, hearing their familiar voices soothe away the pain of the past.

Peeking through the window, she spotted Frank standing in the hallway, his face twisted in a scowl, his voice raised in a heated argument with someone inside the sitting room. Louisa couldn't make out whom he was speaking to, but it hardly mattered. All she wanted—more than anything—was to see the two people she had longed for every single day since that awful day. Her parents. If there was even the slightest chance they were still here, she had to know.

"You. Scamp! Get out of here!"

Someone yelled behind her as a pointy object poked into her back, making her jump. She swung around. A gardener held a shovel as loathing glinted in his old eyes. She didn't remember him as a child.

Her heart dropped. "No, please. I—"

"Leave now or I'll call the constable."

"You don't understand," she pleaded in frustration.

The gardener signaled to two burly men standing behind him, both dressed in rough, workmanlike clothing. Louisa's heart sank—she didn't recognize either of them, and they certainly hadn't worked for her family when her parents were alive. Before she could utter a word of explanation, the two men seized her by the arms, their grip unyielding as they dragged her toward the main gate.

Panic surged through her, her mind racing with protests, but the words died in her throat. She struggled against them, but they were too strong, and all she could do was watch as the house— the last connection to her past—faded farther from her reach.

She squirmed as their beefy fingers dug into her arms. "I demand you release me!"

The two oafs laughed and ignored her wish.

"Please listen to me. I live here." She wiggled and tried to kick them, but they walked too fast for her efforts to be of any consequence.

Upon reaching the gates, the men tossed her roughly onto

the dirt road, the iron gates slamming shut behind her with a resounding clang. Louisa winced, pain shooting through her knees from the hard impact, and when she glanced down, her palms were scraped and raw. Tears stung her eyes, but it wasn't just the physical pain—it was the humiliation, the helplessness of being thrown out like a trespasser from the home that had once been hers. Her chest tightened with the weight of sorrow and frustration as she lay there, the hopes she had clung to unraveling with every painful breath.

"Don't come back, or we'll inform the constable of your trespassing," the shorter one snipped.

The constable. The thought sparked a flicker of hope in Louisa's chest, giving her a reason to breathe again. If she could find the constable, she would demand he take her home—or at least to Frank. Her cousin would surely recognize her. Wouldn't he?

She glanced down at her ragged, tattered clothes, a deep frown forming on her face. Despite her appearance, she knew one thing for certain—she had to get back into that house and confront Frank, no matter the obstacles.

With frustration bubbling inside her, Louisa tore herself away from the iron gates and broke into a run toward the village. Her heart pounded in time with her hurried footsteps as she fought to shake off the sadness and the confusion that had plagued her since arriving.

She needed answers today—answers to the questions that had haunted her for years. And she wouldn't stop until she had them.

Chapter Two

TREVOR WORTHINGTON, FIFTH Duke of Kenbridge, clenched his jaw, his grip tightening on the reins as frustration burned through him. The relentless gossip, the incessant whispers about his late wife, were enough to drive him mad. If he heard her name uttered one more time, he'd be hard-pressed not to throttle the speaker. The weight of betrayal still pressed heavily on his heart, making the already difficult mourning period nearly unbearable. Why couldn't people just let the past die?

He urged the horse to quicken its pace, wishing he'd opted for his steed rather than the curricle. The stiff formality of the dinner party he'd just left had called for appearances, and against his better judgment, he had attended, thanks to his mother's insistent prodding. She had been adamant—now that his year of mourning was over, it was time for him to reenter Society. But Trevor had no desire to return to a world that reminded him of everything he'd lost.

The more Trevor thought about his deceased wife, the angrier he became. He didn't want her ghost haunting his thoughts, didn't want to dwell on the betrayal that still twisted like a knife in his chest. All he longed for was a normal life, free from the chains of the past. But one thing was certain—he would never trust a woman again.

A cloud drifted over the moon, casting deeper shadows across the road, mirroring the dark thoughts swirling in his mind. Whether it was the night's creeping darkness or the gloom within his own head, both were equally maddening, and he silently cursed them, wishing they'd vanish as easily as they came.

Trevor slowed his horse as he rounded the bend, easing the reins slightly. He wasn't about to risk flipping the curricle just because someone at the dinner party had uttered Gwendolyn's name, stirring his anger. The last thing he needed was to lose control now, despite the storm of emotions raging inside him.

As the clouds parted and moonlight spilled across the road, something caught his eye—a shadow shifting along the edge. His heart lurched. Before he could react, a figure darted out from the darkness and straight into his path. Trevor shouted, yanking hard on the reins, but it was too late. His horse clipped the person, sending them tumbling to the ground.

Cursing under his breath, Trevor brought the horse to an abrupt stop. He leapt from the curricle, heart pounding in his throat, praying he hadn't killed anyone. He frantically scanned the area, but the figure was nowhere in sight. How could they have vanished? He was certain he'd felt the impact.

Straightening, he scratched his head in confusion, certain the body had to be nearby. Off to the side, the road dipped into a small gully. Trevor crouched low, squinting through the heavy shadows, hoping to find some sign of the mysterious figure.

"Is anyone there?" He waited, and then said, "Please answer me. I need to know if you are all right."

The moon's light vanished behind a thick veil of clouds once more, casting everything in near-total darkness. Trevor, moving carefully, slid down the steep hill into the gully, the damp earth making his descent treacherous. His heart pounded, dread building with every step. As he reached the bottom, his foot struck something soft—something that wasn't moving.

He froze, a surge of panic gripping him. Bending down, he extended a shaking hand, his fingers brushing against the warmth of a body. He recoiled, his breath catching in his throat. *Good heavens.* It was a girl!

Without wasting another moment, Trevor dropped to his knees beside her, his mind racing. His hands trembled as he gently ran them over her arms and legs, searching for any sign of broken bones, blood, or injury. The girl was so still, her body limp beneath his touch, and a deep sense of responsibility weighed heavily on him. Had he killed her? The thought was unbearable.

His fingers brushed her face, feeling the softness of her skin, then moved downward to her slender neck. He held his breath as he pressed his fingers to her throat, desperate to find a pulse. For a moment, he feared the worst, but then—there it was. A heartbeat. Faint and fragile, but still there. Relief flooded him, though it was quickly replaced by fear. She was alive, but barely.

Hastily, Trevor scooped the girl into his arms, her limp form barely stirring. A soft moan escaped her lips, but she didn't wake. As he adjusted his grip, his fingers brushed against something warm and sticky on her arm. His heart sank—blood.

Groaning inwardly, he knew he didn't have much time. She needed a doctor, but his manor was closer than the village. He'd have to get her there and send for his physician immediately.

With careful urgency, he carried her up the slope, his muscles straining as he climbed out of the gully. Once he reached the curricle, he gently laid her on the seat and climbed in beside her. As he urged the horse forward, her fragile body shifted, rolling toward him. He braced her with his arm, trying to keep her steady, though her awkward position made maneuvering difficult. Every bump in the road sent a jolt through his spine, but he kept a firm hold on her, focused on the path ahead.

The horse and road, thankfully, cooperated, and soon enough the familiar sight of his manor came into view. Relief washed over him, but he knew the real work was just beginning. He slowed the horse to a stop before carefully lifting the girl once more, cradling her close as he hurried up the steps. Bursting through the door, he shouted for his servants, his voice echoing through the grand foyer.

Within moments, his butler appeared, eyes widening at the sight of the unconscious girl in Trevor's arms.

"Fetch the physician—immediately," Trevor ordered Hobbs, his voice firm but tinged with urgency. The butler nodded quickly, disappearing to carry out the command, while Trevor stood there, his heart still racing, silently willing the girl to hold on. Her dirty face held a mixture of smudges, scratches, and blood.

Without another thought, he rushed up the stairs. He carried her to the closest guest room and toward the bed. Mrs. Smythe, the housekeeper, bustled in only seconds behind.

"Oh dear," she exclaimed, wringing her hands against her middle. "What do we have here, Your Grace?"

"There was an accident. I hit her with the curricle."

The older servant gasped and covered her mouth. "Oh, dear Lord."

Trevor gently laid the unconscious girl on the bed, stepping back as Mrs. Smythe pulled down the covers. Now, with better light and a chance to look more closely, the full extent of her condition became painfully clear. She was covered in grime from head to toe, her hair matted and filthy, its color impossible to discern after what must have been weeks, if not longer, without a proper wash. Her skin was layered with dirt, and her clothes— little more than rags—hung loosely from her thin, frail frame.

He shook his head, his heart sinking. A vagabond, clearly, likely an orphan. The gauntness of her face, the way her bones jutted out beneath her skin—she was half starved. A wrenching pain gripped his chest as he gazed at the pitiful figure before him. Poor thing. And to think *he'd* been the one to run her over. But she was alive, and as long as she breathed, there was hope.

Trevor's thoughts shifted from guilt to resolve. He could help her, not just by saving her life, but by giving her a chance at something better. He would see to it that she was well fed, cared for, and clothed properly. And once she recovered, he'd find her a position—perhaps as a maid or cook in a decent London household. Anything to ensure she never returned to the streets, never again had to endure the life she had clearly suffered through. He couldn't bear the thought of her continuing to starve, shivering in tattered clothes for the rest of her days.

"Mrs. Smythe, please clean her up before the doctor arrives."

"Yes, Your Grace."

"And take care not to disturb the wound on her shoulder."

His housekeeper gave a single nod before hurrying out of the room, her short legs moving as fast as they could carry her. Trevor bent over the girl, gently brushing the tangled hair away from her face. His mind whirled with questions. What had brought her to this state? How long had she lived like this? And then a darker thought crossed his mind. Could she be dangerous?

But as he studied her again, taking in her delicate, almost frail features, the idea seemed absurd. She couldn't possibly be a threat to his household. Her slim arms and legs showed no signs of strength, and whatever life she had led, it clearly hadn't prepared her for violence or mischief. She looked more like a girl who had been worn down by the harshness of the world than someone capable of harm.

The sticky feeling of blood on his hand and sleeve caught his attention, snapping him from his thoughts. He glanced down, realizing he was still covered in it. While waiting for the physician, he would need to clean himself up. Before he could move, hurried footsteps echoed down the hall. Trevor turned just in time to see Mrs. Smythe return, followed by two maids, their arms laden with towels, bandages, and a clean nightdress.

They moved swiftly and efficiently, prepared to tend to the injured girl. Trevor stepped back, grateful for their assistance, though the sight of the blood reminded him of the urgency of the situation.

"I shall leave now that the girl is in good hands."

"Not to worry, Your Grace," Mrs. Smythe promised. "We'll take special care of her."

Nodding, Trevor let out a long, weary sigh and strode from the room, his mind heavy with frustration. None of this would have happened if he hadn't gone out tonight. His mother had insisted that the evening's dinner party was a *must-attend* event, the perfect way for him to reenter Society after his period of mourning. Dowager duchesses often knew such things, but even she couldn't have foreseen the streak of bad luck that had shadowed him ever since his ill-fated marriage three years ago.

As he entered his chambers, he gave his valet instructions to prepare a bath. Wearily, Trevor sank into a cushioned chair, running his fingers through his hair and closing his eyes. The exhaustion wasn't just physical—it was a deep, gnawing weariness that seemed to settle into his bones. He couldn't keep the girl here, no matter how much he pitied her. She was young, probably just past adolescence, but far too young to fit into any role in his household. He had no position for someone like her, and keeping her here would only complicate things further.

Yet, despite his rational mind insisting he should send her away, a nagging guilt tugged at him. He couldn't shake the image of her frail body, half starved and bleeding, lying helpless in the road. What had her life been like for her to end up in such a state? As he sat there, the weight of responsibility pressed down on him, harder than ever.

Thomson, his ever-efficient valet, rushed through the door with buckets of steaming water, two more servants trailing behind, carrying additional loads. Trevor began to undress, trying to push away the haunting memories of Gwendolyn that always seemed to resurface at the worst times. The ache of betrayal throbbed in his head like a dull, relentless drumbeat. If only he could forget her—forget the past that had left him so scarred. Gwendolyn's actions had altered him, darkening his once-optimistic outlook and leaving behind only cynicism and mistrust.

Perhaps that isn't entirely a bad thing, he thought bitterly. After all, women could not be trusted, and learning that lesson early was a hard-earned advantage. It would serve him well in the future, preventing further heartbreak.

Trevor hurried through his bath, scrubbing quickly as if he could wash away not only the grime but the unwelcome thoughts of Gwen. He needed to focus on the present—on the life he was determined to rebuild. His new life, free of past mistakes, started today. Yet, in one disastrous evening, he had nearly ruined it by running over a girl, leaving her on the brink of death.

A heaviness settled in his chest as he recalled her pale face and fragile frame. *She could still die,* he realized, and the weight of that thought made his heart sink. What should have been a fresh start now felt tainted by guilt and uncertainty.

Thomson had already laid out fresh clothes for Trevor, making it easy for him to dress quickly. Once he'd pulled on his crisp shirt and trousers, he ran a comb through his damp hair, smoothing it into place. Without wasting any more time, he strode out of his chambers and hurried back to the guest room, his mind fixed on the injured girl.

As he approached the door, Mrs. Smythe and the maids were just stepping out, their arms filled with bloodied towels and soiled garments. They paused briefly to nod respectfully as Trevor approached, their expressions a mix of concern and quiet efficiency. Trevor's heart quickened as he stepped past them, hoping for a sign that the girl's condition had stabilized.

"How is she?" he asked, stepping inside the room.

"She's still unconscious, Your Grace." Mrs. Smythe frowned. "Poor woman has scrapes and bruises all over her."

Trevor blinked in surprise. "Woman? She's not a young miss?"

"No, Your Grace. I'd say she was at least in her early twenties, perhaps a mite younger."

"But she's so tiny."

"That she is. She's nothing but skin and bones. We'll need to fatten her up, I'd say."

He nodded. "My thoughts exactly. As soon as the doctor has

checked her over, I want some soup brought up. Will you see to that, Mrs. Smythe?"

"Of course, Your Grace." She kept silent as the other maids brushed past them before the older woman leaned in closer to him. "I think you should also know, the woman has scars on her back."

He narrowed his gaze on the housekeeper, and then to the woman lying on the bed. "Scars, you say?"

Her voice lowered. "Yes. Like she's been… whipped."

His stomach churned. "Someone whipped her? As small as she is?"

"That's what I'm thinking, yes. And they are not new scars, either."

"If I get my hands on whoever did that…"

Anger simmered within Trevor as he approached the bed, directed not at the unconscious woman but at the unknown person responsible for her injuries. Yet, the moment he laid eyes on her, his breath caught. The girl he'd brought home earlier had transformed, as if by magic, into a striking woman. The maids had washed away the grime, revealing long waves of blonde hair that cascaded over her shoulders, still damp from the bath, resting against the soft curves of her fully grown figure. Her pale face, now clean, contrasted starkly with the thick, dark lashes that swept over her high cheekbones, casting delicate shadows across her face.

She was quite beautiful. He had to admit it, though the realization unsettled him. This woman, with her tattered clothes and air of mystery, was no one he knew. She belonged to a world far removed from his—someone of a class he wouldn't have associated with under normal circumstances. Yet here she was, lying in his home, her vulnerability and beauty impossible to ignore.

Voices from the hallway snapped him from his thoughts. Stepping toward the door, Trevor peeked into the corridor to see Hobbs, his butler, leading the way for a familiar figure. Relief washed over him as he recognized the physician. Finally, someone who could help.

"Thank you for coming on such short notice," Trevor told him.

An older man, Doctor Bryers's white hair thinned on his head, showing more spots of baldness than not. His spectacles perched on a long, straight nose as he opened his black medical bag. "Your servant tells me there was an accident."

"Indeed there was, doctor. I hit her with my curricle as I traveled home this evening. She's still alive but has a faint heartbeat."

Doctor Bryers walked to the bed. "Mrs. Smythe? I shall need your assistance while I check her." He glanced at Trevor. "Your Grace, would you be so kind as to wait outside?"

"Certainly." Trevor left the room and shut the door behind him.

For the next hour, he paced the length of the maroon carpet in the hallway, his impatience mounting with every step. He hadn't felt this restless since the births of his son and daughter—or rather, he corrected himself bitterly, Gwen's son and daughter. The nagging uncertainty over their parentage weighed heavily on him, as it had ever since that fateful discovery. He still didn't know if the twins were truly his.

A groan escaped him as he rubbed his forehead, trying to banish the painful memory. Time would reveal the truth soon enough. Worthingtons were known for their dark hair, striking blue eyes, and tall stature—traits that ran through his family for generations. Even his mother towered over most of her childhood friends. But the twins... Their gray eyes and lighter hair unsettled him, never quite fitting the mold he expected. And then there was Gwen's lover, a man with unmistakable red hair. If the children shared that trait, it would confirm his worst fears.

The thought gnawed at him, leaving a bitter taste in his mouth. He would find out the truth soon enough, but until then, the doubt hung over him like a dark cloud, just as it had for years.

The bedroom door creaked open, bringing Trevor from his thoughts. Mrs. Smythe motioned him to enter. He hurried to the doctor, anxious to hear how the injured woman fared.

Doctor Bryers rolled down his shirt sleeves. "She's most fortunate, Your Grace. I could not find any broken bones. She has a large wound on her shoulder, which I assume came from the impact of the horse slamming into her or when she hit the ground. She has a sizable goose egg on her head, which will disappear within time, as well as the scratches received from the fall." He shrugged on his overcoat before meeting Trevor's stare. "Until she awakens, I will not be able to tell if she received any internal injuries."

"Internal?"

"Mainly head trauma." He scratched his chin. "Please send for me when she comes to, and I shall check her again."

"Certainly, doctor."

"I request you not move her for a few days to give her time to heal. She will be stiff and sore from the accident and will have a few bruises."

Trevor nodded. "I shall keep her here as long as necessary."

The doctor patted his shoulder. "You are a good man, Your Grace. This woman fell into the right hands."

Trevor wanted to believe anyone would have acted the same way and shown similar concern, but he didn't speak his mind in front of the doctor. He managed a small smile and shook the older man's hand.

"Thank you again for your hastiness into this matter."

"You are most welcome, Your Grace. I'm only pleased to be of assistance."

"Would you like Mrs. Smythe to get you a cup of tea and biscuits before you leave?"

"Thank you, but no. I was on my way to another call before I came. If you will excuse me."

"Of course."

As Hobbs escorted the doctor down the stairs, Trevor turned

back toward the bed, his gaze settling on the woman lying still as death, though her chest rose and fell with steady, gentle breaths. The doctor had suggested she stay at the manor to recover, but Trevor couldn't help but wonder if her fate would be any better under his roof. After all, he seemed cursed when it came to women—they always seemed to die in his presence.

The thought gnawed at him. If this woman didn't pull through, it would be yet another cruel reminder of the tragedy that seemed to follow him. He could almost feel the weight of it bearing down on him, that inescapable belief that his very presence brought death. Gwendolyn's passing still haunted him, even if the truth was far more complicated than he allowed himself to admit.

It was simple—he had killed his wife, even if not by his own hand. And if this young woman didn't survive, it would only confirm what he feared most: that his fate was sealed, cursed to bring death to those who came too close.

Chapter Three

P AIN PULSED IN Louisa's head with every beat of her heart, radiating through her entire body as if she'd been crushed beneath a heavy weight. Even her eyelids ached as she struggled to open them. When she finally managed a squint, confusion set in. Had she died and gone to Heaven? Why else would she be in such a luxurious room, dressed in warm, clean nightclothes and nestled between soft sheets on a bed that felt like a cloud? The scents surrounding her were foreign—everything smelled too clean, too fresh.

A low moan escaped her lips as she closed her eyes again— the simple act of breathing sending sharp stabs of pain through her chest. What had happened to her? Her mind was a fog, offering no answers, only a heavy emptiness where memories should have been.

Suddenly, a soft, soothing voice broke through the haze, accompanied by a gentle touch on her fingers. The kindness of the moment lulled her into a brief, peaceful sleep, but she was soon stirred awake by a new sensation—a tantalizing scent wafting through the room. *Food.*

Her stomach growled hungrily, the smell of fresh bread teasing her senses, reminding her just how long it had been since she'd last eaten anything at all. "Come now, dearie. Open your eyes," the kind voice prompted her.

Louisa blinked and slowly opened her eyes. The room wasn't as bright as it had been earlier, thank goodness. The older woman leaning over her wore a servant's black-and-white attire, with a white mobcap covering her brown hair.

"Let's sit you up, shall we?" The servant helped to adjust Louisa by stuffing pillows behind her.

Louisa clenched her teeth, trying to suppress the wave of sharp pain that surged through her with each movement. But once the pillows were adjusted beneath her, offering much-needed support, the intensity of the pain eased just enough for her to take a shallow breath. As her body relaxed slightly, she glanced down at her arms, momentarily transfixed. The delicate sleeves that covered them were pristine—whiter than anything she had worn in years—and adorned with intricate lace embroidery that seemed far too beautiful for her reality.

This has to be a dream. Her mind struggled to accept what her eyes were seeing. It couldn't be real. How could she, a ragged, starving girl, be swathed in something so fine, so elegant?

"How are you feeling, dearie?" the older woman asked, amber eyes narrowing with worry.

"I—I—" Louisa cleared her dry throat a couple of times before the servant brought up a cup of tea for her to sip. She closed her eyes and savored the taste. *Wonderful.*

When the servant took the cup away and set it on the stand next to the bed, Louisa cleared her throat again. "I ache all over."

"That's to be expected from the dreadful accident, or so the doctor explained."

Louisa's head throbbed harder. What accident? She didn't remember any accident. "I do not understand, ma'am. What accident are you referring to?"

"Why, the accident you had last night when His Grace hit you with his horse and curricle."

Fright surged through Louisa, tightening her chest and making her head throb with unbearable intensity. Why couldn't she remember?

Panic clawed at her insides as she squeezed her eyes shut, pressing her fingers to her aching forehead. Try as she might, she couldn't recall being struck by a horse and carriage—or anything else, for that matter. Her mind was a void, terrifying in its emptiness. Who was she? The weight of that question was crushing.

Her gaze drifted toward the unfamiliar woman standing beside the bed. Desperation took hold as Louisa raised her cold, trembling hands to cup her own cheeks, as if trying to ground herself in the present, trying to find something real. Tears brimmed in her eyes, blurring her vision, while a thick knot of emotion swelled in her throat.

Her voice, broken and raw, finally escaped. "I—I—I don't remember," she whispered, her voice quivering as the enormity of her fear settled over her like a suffocating blanket. The sense of loss—of not knowing who she was—was more than she could bear.

"Hush, dearie." The servant sat on the edge of the bed and stroked Louisa's hair. "The doctor mentioned you would be disoriented a bit when you awoke. There's nothing to worry about."

Louisa shook her head. "You don't understand. I cannot remember *anything.*" A tear slid down her cheek. "I've no memory of what I did last evening, or before that, or the day before that." Her voice rose in panic.

"Shh… Not to fret, my dear. Calm yourself, and I'm certain your memory will return."

Louisa lowered her hands to her lap. "Do you truly believe so?"

The servant nodded. "Yes, I'm certain. My name is Mrs. Smythe. I'm the housekeeper here at Kenbridge Hall. I shall take care of you until you are better."

Louisa nodded, trying to take the woman's advice and calm her fears. "It's a pleasure to meet you, Mrs. Smythe. My name is Louisa…" Her memory stopped. Once again, fear flared inside her, bringing a state of panic with it. "Oh, no. I—I do not even recall my name!"

"Good heavens, child." Mrs. Smythe took Louisa's hands. "You do not remember your own name?"

She shook her head. "Just Louisa."

Mrs. Smythe rose from the bed, wringing her hands against her middle as she switched her gaze from the door to Louisa. The older woman's amber eyes widened. "I need to inform His Grace about this unexpected turn of events. I think we should have the doctor return posthaste."

As the servant hurried out of the room, moving as if snakes were snapping at her heels, Louisa's fragile composure shattered. Tears spilled freely down her cheeks, each drop heavy with the fear and confusion that overwhelmed her. The older woman had been her only source of comfort, gently soothing her rising panic with soft words and kind gestures. But now, even that small reassurance was gone.

Louisa's chest tightened painfully, a new ache blooming beneath her ribs. This time, she was certain the pain had nothing to do with the accident—it came from something deeper, an unbearable weight of isolation and helplessness. The tears kept falling, and with them, the terrifying realization that she was truly alone in this strange, unfamiliar world, with no memory of who she was or how she had gotten there.

Within minutes, heavy footsteps echoed down the hallway, each thud growing louder, until suddenly, a large figure filled the doorway. Louisa's breath caught in her throat. The man's towering height stunned her, but even more striking was the concern etched across his chiseled, handsome face.

As he approached the bed with purposeful strides, the fabric of his crisp white shirt stretched across his broad shoulders, highlighting his lean, powerful frame. His black trousers hugged muscular legs, making him appear every bit as imposing as he was graceful.

She had never seen anything—or anyone—so captivating in

her life. Then again, maybe she had, but she simply couldn't remember. Even so, something deep in her heart whispered that she wasn't accustomed to looking at men like this one—men who exuded such strength, confidence, and quiet intensity.

Her pulse quickened, not just from his imposing presence but from the unsettling realization that she had no idea how to feel about him.

He stood above her, and she sank into the pillows, staring at him. "Your Grace?"

He nodded. "Mrs. Smythe tells me your name is Louisa."

"It is."

He pulled a wooden chair next to the bed and sat. Slowly, he stretched his arm out to touch her, then—as if changing his mind—quickly withdrew. "Louisa, please do not be frightened. We will take care of you."

She managed a small nod.

"Mrs. Smythe also tells me you cannot remember anything."

"All I can remember, Your Grace, is my first name... and that I don't believe I have been in a room as grand as this or worn a gown so expensive."

The lines around his mouth softened. "Be that as it may, the doctor told me you had a goose egg on your head. I can only surmise that is the reason for your unclear memory."

Cautiously, she lifted her fingers to her scalp and brushed them across her head until she found the lump. She winced. "I trust the doctor knows what he's talking about."

"Yes," he said. "I would not put my care in the hands of anyone else. Doctor Bryers is very good."

She licked her dry lips and lowered her hands. His stare calmed her, and a warming blanket of comfort surrounded her. Strangely enough, the emotion seemed foreign. "Thank you, Your Grace."

He smiled, but somehow it didn't quite reach his eyes. "Until your health and memory have been fully restored, I think you should stay here and let us take care of you. Mrs. Smythe will have some delicious soup brought up. I assume you are hungry, correct?"

She nodded. "Famished. I think I could eat a horse… or two."

Chuckling, he stood and motioned for the older servant to draw near. "Please keep me informed of her progress."

"I certainly will, Your Grace."

Just then, another maid walked into the room, carrying a tray with a bowl of soup and a glass of milk.

His gaze switched back to Louisa. "Please rest until you are feeling better."

"I shall. I thank you for your hospitality."

He nodded, turned, and walked out the door.

Louisa's heart softened, warmth spreading through her chest. What a fine man. A man who didn't just help strangers—he went out of his way for them, without hesitation or expectation. But beneath that generosity, she sensed something more, something that tugged at her curiosity. He seemed to carry a quiet vulnerability, a hesitance that went beyond mere politeness. He'd avoided touching her, which she first attributed to gentlemanly restraint, but there was an unspoken depth to it. An invisible barrier, like he was holding back, guarding something within himself that she couldn't quite grasp.

"Now, let's sit you up a little more so you can eat." Mrs. Smythe helped Louisa with lifting herself up until she could have the food tray placed on her lap.

"This smells wonderful." She smiled, fairly salivating over the bowl of soup.

"It's not a full course, mind you, but when you are feeling better, we shall serve you more. His Grace wants us to make you healthy." The older woman tsked. "I fear you are nothing but skin and bones."

Louisa glanced down at her thin wrists and fingers. "I wish I could remember why."

"You shall in time, dearie."

"Mrs. Smythe, you have all been so kind. I don't know how

to repay you."

"Oh, tosh. Not to worry, my dear. His Grace is very kind, and he will not ask to be repaid."

Louisa glanced toward the door, hoping he'd come back and make her feel protected again. Strange how the loss of his presence left her empty inside. "Tell me about him," she asked before shoveling some soup into her mouth. *Ahh... chicken and dumplings.*

"His Grace, the fifth Duke of Kenbridge, is the most caring man I have ever met." Mrs. Smythe smiled widely. "I have known his family for many years. They are the best of the best."

Louisa swallowed what was in her mouth before asking, "Is he married?"

A frown changed the housekeeper's expression, and her amber eyes clouded with pain. "The duchess passed on nigh twelve months ago, I fear. The duke has not been the same since. Poor man, trying to raise his children without a mother." She shook her head. "It takes a man with a big heart, to be sure."

Perhaps that was the emotion Louisa had glimpsed in his eyes: mourning his wife. "Thank you for telling me. I shall not bring up the subject again." She took a sip of her milk and silently sighed with satisfaction.

Although Louisa had promised the housekeeper she wouldn't bring up the subject of the man's deceased wife, her curiosity gnawed at her. She couldn't shake the urge to probe further, to ask the servants until her questions were answered. Besides, it would give her something else to focus on—something to distract her from the haunting memories of her own past. Those memories, if she let them in, would consume her, driving her toward the edge of madness. She needed something, anything, to keep her mind busy, something external that wouldn't unravel her from within.

She eyed the soup again, its warmth and richness calling to her with an intensity she hadn't anticipated. Each sip seemed to ignite a deeper hunger within her, a desperation that quickened her pulse. It wasn't just the taste—it was the gnawing fear that this meal, as perfect as it was, might be her last. A forbidding sense of scarcity gripped her, as if the food could vanish at any moment, taken away without warning. Despite her rational mind knowing the duke would surely feed her again, her body refused to listen. With a surge of urgency, she lifted the bowl, tipping it to her mouth, as if she could protect herself from a world that had denied her too much for far too long.

"Oh, my…" Mrs. Smythe quickly slapped her hand over her mouth, her wide eyes watching in judgment.

"What's amiss?" Louisa asked with her mouth full. A portion of the soup dribbled down her chin.

Quickly, the housekeeper brought a linen napkin to Louisa and wiped away the liquid before it fell to her clean nightgown.

"I fear… you are *very* hungry, my dear. But"—Mrs. Smythe pointed to the utensils—"there is a spoon for you to use."

Louisa glanced at her hands dripping with soup. Embarrassment washed over her and she snatched the linen cloth to wipe away the proof of bad manners. "Forgive me for acting like I'm half starved." Perhaps she *was* starved. Her thin arms definitely proved she needed to eat more, and if her stomach—which rested on her backbone—was any indication of how regularly she ate, she would have to fatten up a bit.

Mrs. Smythe's expression changed from one of shock to humor as she winked. "You just have a healthy appetite. But I think if I ever find the person who was starving you, nothing will keep me from beating him with a whip." Once again, the servant gasped and slapped her hand over her mouth. This time, however, the color disappeared from her face.

Louisa arched an eyebrow, her curiosity piqued. Why had the housekeeper acted so strangely? By all accounts, no one seemed to know her—so why did Mrs. Smythe give her the distinct impression that she did? There was something in the woman's eyes, a flicker of knowledge, perhaps even suspicion, that Louisa couldn't ignore.

Wiping her mouth hastily with the back of her hand, Louisa used the sleeve of her gown, an action she immediately regretted. Mrs. Smythe cringed, her disapproval evident, and quickly handed Louisa another linen napkin.

"Oh, I'm sorry," Louisa mumbled, feeling awkward as she dabbed the napkin to her lips. She then attempted to blot the stain from her sleeve, and a flush of embarrassment heated her cheeks. What else had the housekeeper noticed?

"So, Mrs. Smythe?" She lifted her gaze to the servant. "Since I do not remember who I am, do you know me? Do I look familiar at all?"

"No, I'm sorry. I'm really the wrong person to ask. If anyone will know, it'll be His Grace."

Frowning, she nodded. "True. I certainly hope someone will know me because I most definitely do not. And not having anything to think about all day will drive me absolutely insane."

"I cannot even imagine. His Grace will provide you the best medical care available, and I shall assign a maid to stay by your side and keep you company."

"Thank you, Mrs. Smythe. Your assistance is much appreciated."

Once the food settled warmly in Louisa's belly, a deep, bone-weary fatigue crept over her. Her eyelids grew heavy, and each blink became slower than the last. The exhaustion that had been tugging at the edges of her mind now crashed over her in waves. All she wanted was to sink into the soft, inviting bed and let the comfort of the covers wrap around her, shielding her from the world. Sleep beckoned her like a gentle whisper, and she could no longer resist its pull.

"Here now, Miss Louisa." The housekeeper removed the tray of food. "I think rest is the best medicine."

Louisa yawned. "I believe you are correct."

Even though her body ached with exhaustion, Louisa rolled onto her side and closed her eyes, hoping sleep would finally claim her. But it didn't come easily. Mrs. Smythe had dimmed the lamps, casting the room in a soft, shadowy glow, yet Louisa remained wide awake, her mind restless. Try as she might, the Duke of Kenbridge occupied her every thought. It wasn't just his striking appearance that intrigued her—though he was undeniably handsome—it was the sorrow the housekeeper had hinted at, the sadness that seemed to cloak his very being.

Had she always been this curious? This need to unravel mysteries, to understand the hidden depths of others—was it simply in her nature? Perhaps. But there was something different about the duke. This time, her curiosity wasn't just intellectual; it was something deeper, more personal. He fascinated her, not just because of the enigma he presented, but because of the way his presence stirred something within her.

As she lay there, eyes closed, her imagination began to wander. She envisioned him not just as a figure of mystery, but as someone strong, someone who might one day hold her with those capable hands. The thought brought a warmth to her cheeks, and before she could stop herself, her mind slipped into fantasy. It was a tempting reason to let herself drift, to dream of something—someone—who made her heart race in ways she hadn't felt in a long time.

Chapter Four

"WHAT ARE YOU to make of this, Mother?"

Trevor paced the length of his study, his footsteps echoing in the stillness as his mother sat on the edge of the couch, absentmindedly fingering the pearls around her neck. He had just finished recounting the horrific details of the accident and, more troubling still, the girl's complete memory loss. The weight of the situation pressed heavily on him, far more than he had anticipated. Never before had he been faced with such a dilemma. He hadn't slept at all the previous night, turning over countless scenarios in his mind, each more uncertain than the last.

What was he supposed to do now? If Miss Louisa wasn't a respectable woman—and how could he know, given her amnesia—he could hardly justify keeping her in his house. Yet, he couldn't bring himself to cast her out either. It was, after all, his carriage accident that had nearly claimed her life, and now, because of him, she wandered through a haze of forgotten memories. The thought of abandoning her to fend for herself, with no recollection of who she was or where she belonged, felt unconscionable. But allowing her to stay? It risked scandal.

He glanced at his mother, hoping for some wisdom or clarity, but all she did was offer a thoughtful hum, her eyes distant. He knew no easy answer existed. The question loomed over him, growing heavier with each passing hour—what kind of man would he be if he turned his back on her now?

"Oh, dear." The dowager tsked and shook her head. "I must say, Trevor, this is upsetting news. I think what we need to do is discover who amongst the *ton* has lost a daughter." She fluttered her hand against her throat. "Although, I think that might be hard to do since you don't know if this girl is of Quality or not."

Blowing out a frustrated sigh, he dug his fingers in his hair. "Oh, Mother, I highly doubt she is of noble birth. You should have seen her. The dress she wore was small, like a young girl's, and tattered badly. The oversized coat she wore was a man's garment, and very old with several missing buttons. Her hair looked as if she had not washed it for quite a while."

His mother's face turned white as she grimaced. "How utterly disgraceful."

"She speaks as though she has some education, but I don't believe she is of Quality."

"Oh, Trevor. I don't know how we will find the girl's parents then, assuming she has any."

He nodded. "That is my concern as well."

"What are you going to do with her once she heals?"

He stopped pacing in front of a window overlooking the land sloping over the hillside. The sun shone over the green grass, and highlighted the flowers by the fence. "I'm responsible for the accident, and if she does not regain her memory, I shall have no other choice but to offer her employment here."

Gasping, his mother stood and rushed to his side. She clutched his arm. "You cannot be serious. You do not know where she's been or what she's done. She could steal from you."

Over his shoulder, he met his mother's stare. "What would you have me do? Send her out on the streets to care for herself? If this was what she had been doing, it's obvious she failed miserably." He shook his head. "If anything, having her work here will give her experience so she can find employment elsewhere. If she steals from me, I shall handle it the way I would with any of my other servants."

A small smile touched his mother's worried face as she caressed his cheek. "You are a very caring man, my dear, and I'm proud that my son has a big heart."

Rolling his eyes, he turned away from her and peered outside again. Out in the yard, flocks of birds flitted from one tree to another as in a rhythmic dance. His mother didn't know what she was talking about—him having a *big heart.* "I appreciate your sentiments, Mother, but I assure you, I do not deserve them."

She took a step back. "Would you like me to go see the girl and talk to her?"

He shrugged. "I do not think it will do any harm. I'm certain she would enjoy the company." He strode toward the door. "Come, I shall take you to her room."

"After my visit with the girl, I hope you don't mind if I take a peek at my precious grandchildren. I have not seen the twins in a fortnight."

"Do as you wish, Mother. I'm certain they will love to see their grandmamma."

He clenched his jaw as he marched into the hallway and toward the stairs, balling his hands into fists at his sides. He dared not tell his mother he doubted he had sired the twins. His mother had thought the sun rose and set on Gwendolyn, and he didn't have the heart to give his mother such disturbing information that his wife was not the pure, sweet woman she'd led everyone to believe.

When he reached Miss Louisa's room, the door stood open. Mrs. Smythe chatted with the stranger as if they were the best of friends. Louisa didn't notice him, so he was able to study her for a few moments. Color bloomed in her cheeks today. Her blonde hair held a healthy shine and even had a slight curl to it. The white nightdress emphasized her slender figure, and it bothered him to see her looking so gaunt. The housekeeper said something and Louisa laughed, which brought a smile to his face. At the same time, he realized there was a sad quality to the tone of her laugh. Indeed, this woman's past would remain a mystery to him until her memory returned. A strange emotion stirred within him, and it pierced his heart.

Finally, her gaze shifted to him and she smiled brightly, sitting up in bed a little straighter. "Your Grace. What a surprise it is to see you."

He nodded and strode into the room. "Miss Louisa, may I present my mother, the Dowager Duchess of Kenbridge."

His mother stepped inside and walked straight to Louisa's bed. The young woman's eyes grew wide as she gazed upon his mother.

"A pleasure it is to meet you, Your Grace." Louisa bowed her head and lowered her eyes. "Forgive me for not getting out of bed, but I'm still quite weak."

"That is to be expected, my dear. My son told me about the terrible accident. May I say how relieved I am to hear you are doing better?"

Louisa met his mother's gaze and smiled. "Thank you, Your Grace. I do feel better today, although my body still aches."

"I'm certain you will feel that way for a few more days."

"Indeed."

Trevor found it hard to keep from watching Louisa. Even weak and thin, she was quite a lovely woman. It surprised him that he'd once mistaken her for being a mere girl. Her eyes twinkled—a remarkable green color—whenever she looked at him, and he worried about her actions. She didn't have a memory, so would she look to him as a hero even if he was the one responsible for her accident in the first place? He couldn't allow her to peer at him with such admiration. Having her thinking of him in that way wasn't a good thing, but for some reason he didn't want to discourage her just yet. It'd been a long time since a woman gazed at him as if she were utterly infatuated. He shouldn't, but he quite enjoyed it.

His mother squared her shoulders and turned his way. "My dear son, your servants should be commended. Miss Louisa looks quite well for someone who nearly lost her life."

He smiled and gave his housekeeper a nod. "Mrs. Smythe has been a godsend."

The older servant giggled as her face lit up like a beacon. "Your praise is most heartwarming."

Trevor stepped closer to Louisa. He couldn't stop his attention from roaming over her wide green eyes, pert nose, and delicate lips. Once more a twinkle sparked in her orbs before she lowered them to her folded hands on her lap. Long, thick eyelashes swept her cheeks before she lifted her gaze and met his.

"Tell me, Miss Louisa, have you remembered anything about your life?"

She frowned. "No, Your Grace. I fear my mind is still closed to the past."

Unease filled him when a thought nagged at his subconscious. Could this woman be lying to him? What if she did this as a means of staying in his house and being cared for? After all, most of the women he'd known in his life—save for his mother—had deceived him. Surely, he would have to keep a close watch over this one.

He swept his attention over the slender column of her neck. "I'm certain your memory will return with time."

When he met her sparkling eyes, he couldn't turn away. They entrapped him, lured him, and if he looked deeper, he'd see into her soul. What kind of past did she have? Did she hold secrets? He suspected she had a few since his housekeeper informed him about the girl's scars. If she lied to him about her memory, could he blame her? She would definitely not want to return to her former life. Being whipped was certainly not a life at all, and he couldn't allow her to go back to such circumstances. In just the few times he'd spoken with her, he'd been besieged with an overwhelming need to protect her.

Confused by the compassion trying to surface inside him, he pulled away and smiled at his mother. "Well, I believe we should allow Miss Louisa to rest now. Don't you agree?"

"Certainly, my dear."

Louisa nodded. "Thank you for coming to see to my welfare, Your Grace, and it is a pleasure to meet your mother as well."

Both he and his mother left the room and he closed the door behind him. When they were far enough down the hallway, his mother turned and grasped his arm, stopping him.

"Trevor, I think I may know her, or her family."

He arched an eyebrow. "Indeed? Why would you think you know her? She's clearly not from our class."

"Clearly, but she resembles the Earl of Danvers's wife quite a bit. I took tea with Lady Danvers and the future Lady Wellesley the other day with a few other ladies, and Louisa's big green eyes are just like Lady Danvers's. Eyes like that are hard to ignore."

Trevor folded his arms as he tapped a finger on his forearm. "Danvers, you say. I don't believe they have a daughter."

"No, I don't recall them ever mentioning one, but there's an uncanny resemblance between Louisa and Lady Danvers. Are you not friends with Lord Danvers's nephew, Wellesley?"

"We were briefly introduced a few years ago, but I wouldn't say we were close." He squeezed his mother's hand. "Do not fret. I'm quite certain if Louisa is of any relation, we shall hear about her disappearance soon."

"As always, you are correct." She sighed heavily. "It's just devastating to think that her family could be out there some-where praying for her safe return. I know I prayed day after day for word about your brother, Tristan, when we thought he had died. Because his body was never found, I hoped that perhaps he lived and was lost somewhere."

Trevor's heart clenched, remembering the tragedy of his brother's death, only to discover two years later he was alive and had lost his memory. "Yes, that was a joyful day when Trey brought him home alive. I wish the same fate for Louisa, but Mother, please don't think she will be as fortunate. Those scars on her back tell me her life has not been good. She may not have a loving family to return home to as Tristan did."

Tears gathered in his mother's eyes. "I have been kept in a

sheltered world, I suppose, and it's hard for me to image anything so disturbing."

"It is hard. All I'm saying is don't mention anything to Lady Danvers or her nephew. Don't even speak a word of this to your friends. Miss Louisa may become a servant in my home eventually and I would hate to have gossip going around about her."

His mother lifted her hand to her throat, toying with her pearls again. "You really intend to make Louisa a servant here?"

He nodded. "Don't you agree it will be a better life than what she may have come from?"

"Of course it would be a better life. I just worry about you and the twins and I would hate to see anything bad come out of all this." She leaned in and kissed his cheek. "You are such a thoughtful man." She pulled away but hooked her hand around his arm. "Now, take me to see my beautiful grandchildren."

"As you wish." He gritted his teeth as he walked with his mother toward the nursery. It had been a few days since he'd seen the twins himself, and he geared for the heartache that would slam through his chest when he looked upon them.

Until he discovered their true parentage, which might never be possible, he held his emotions inside. The twins were only two years old, and it would be easy to love them with all of his heart. But he refused to give them his love until he knew the truth. Their mother had broken his heart, and he feared any more damage might do him in for good.

He tried to focus on his mother's chatter about her other grandson—Trey and his wife, Judith's first child. A boy that looked exactly like Trey—poor lad. Trevor hoped his nephew would inherit Judith's sweet nature instead of Trey's stubbornness. Trevor loved his brother, and thanked the Lord his brother had changed for Judith, but Trevor still felt his nephew would do better in life if he took after his mother.

They reached the nursery and his mother opened the door and walked in. Trevor forced himself to move behind her. Mrs. Jacobs sat in a chair reading a book. Amanda lay, tummy side down beside her on the floor, concentrating on her small wooden farm animals. Adam sat next to his sister playing with blocks. When the little girl's head bounced up to meet her grandmother's, Amanda's cherubic face bloomed with color. She jumped to her feet and squealed, throwing her arms out. Adam smiled wide and ran into Trevor's mother's embrace.

"Oh, look at how much you two have grown." His mother picked them both up in her arms and kissed their chubby cheeks. "Grandmamma has missed you terribly."

Mrs. Jacobs set her book down, stood and bowed. "Your Grace. What a pleasure it is to see you again."

His mother set the twins down and took each of their hands. "So, what have my wonderful grandchildren learned today?"

As Mrs. Jacobs told his mother about the twins' accomplishments, Amanda snuck a peek at Trevor around her grandmamma's skirt. Big, wondrous eyes, so much like Gwen's. In fact, Amanda looked a lot like her mother. Both children did. If only they'd have a hint of Worthington show through, Trevor would give his twins the world on a silver platter. As it was, Amanda peered at him as if she would cry at any minute. Another piece of his heart broke again—just like what always happened when he came into the nursery.

He tried to give her a pleasant smile as he nodded. She quickly buried her face in his mother's dress. As much as he wanted Amanda and Adam to be his blood, he didn't dare hope.

Betrayal mixed with overwhelming guilt began to suffocate him, and he knew he needed to escape. "If you will excuse me," he interrupted the two women. "I have business matters to attend."

"Of course, my dear." His mother smiled warmly as she stroked each child's head. "My grandchildren and I will spend some time together."

He gave a small bow before turning and leaving the room. Pain speared his heart, bringing back the same ache he'd experienced when he first discovered Gwen with another man.

Trevor had longed for a child to call his own, and his wife snatched that from him by sharing herself with others. Was it any wonder he stayed away from the nursery? The suffering was too great to bear.

Hurrying to his study, he cursed his weakness and vowed to harden his heart once more.

Chapter Five

L OUISA SAT ON the window seat with bent knees against her chest as she peered outside. The sun's descent painted the palest-pink hues and a burnt orange on the horizon. Coolness from the window relaxed her a bit while the hearth held a roaring fire. Although she still couldn't remember her life, she sensed her body wasn't used to such warmth.

She glanced at her toes peeking out from underneath her nightdress. Why were her limbs so thin? She'd been eating like a starved person, and thanks to Mrs. Smythe, the food kept coming. Louisa also had the impression she had never eaten such scrumptious meals, either.

As the housekeeper busily tidied up the room, Louisa stared in bewildered silence. This wasn't right. She couldn't allow the servant to wait on her. Louisa jumped to her feet and straightened the blankets on the bed.

Mrs. Smythe spun around and gaped. "Miss Louisa, what are you doing?"

"I'm helping you."

"But why?"

"I don't think I'm used to being waited on." Louisa stilled for a moment. Deep inside she had the horrible feeling that she'd had no one to look after her. The realization left her hollow and cold.

Mrs. Smythe shooed her with her hands. "You are still very

weak. Please sit back by the window while I finish up here."

Louisa nodded and did as requested. Boredom fell over her quickly, and she realized something else about herself. She couldn't stay idle.

From the corner of her eyes, a lovely jewelry box sat on the small table closest to her. Carved with swirly gold lines and red hearts, the wooden box was decorated with chips of colored glass. Curiosity pulled her nearer. Those chips weren't just colored glass, but... *rubies*.

She glanced at the housekeeper who wasn't looking, and then quick as lightning, Louisa snatched the object and hid it under her leg, knowing this would bring a tiny sum to her pocket.

Wait... What was she doing? There was no reason she needed to steal this. Unease spread through her as if she'd just been bathing with the pigs. What on earth had made her want to take such something, especially from the people who were nursing her back to health? Cautiously, she withdrew the jewelry box and placed it back on the table.

The housekeeper picked up the tray of empty dishes and turned to Louisa. "I'm happy to see you have a healthy appetite. His lordship will be relieved to hear that as well. Do you need me to get you anything before I leave?"

Slowly, Louisa blew out a relieved breath that the older woman hadn't seen her take the expensive item. "You have been so thoughtful, Mrs. Smythe. I feel I should be doing that instead of you."

"Oh, nonsense. You need to gain your strength."

"Indeed, I do. Even with all the food I have eaten, I feel weak as a kitten."

"I must say, you have more color in your face this evening."

"That's good to know." Louisa smiled. "Before you leave, I do have one small request, if you please."

"What is that, miss?"

"Would you find me some books to read? I have become bored today and wish to indulge my mind with stories since I don't have anything to think about."

The housekeeper's eyes flew open wide. "You can read?"

Louisa scrunched her forehead. *What an odd question.* "But of course. Why would you think otherwise?"

Mrs. Smythe shrugged and gave a light chuckle. "Forgive me for doubting your ability, but when his lordship brought you here, your clothes were ragged beyond reason. I figured you to be an uneducated vagabond."

Shame weighed heavily in Louisa's mind. She had ragged clothes? Perhaps she couldn't read. Yet, she felt she knew how. "How very observant of you, Mrs. Smythe. I understand your reasoning. I wish I could tell you why I was dressed that way."

"No need to fret, miss. You must have been raised properly, because you are very well spoken. I'm certain His Grace will give you a better life here as one of his servants."

Hope blossomed in Louisa's chest and she smiled. "Do you really believe so?"

"Yes, I do. He's a good man, I assure you. Kenbridge Hall is going to feel like heaven compared to where you came from. At least his lordship does not beat his servants, like yours did."

Louisa lost her smile. What was the old woman talking about now? "I'm afraid I don't quite understand. Why do you think my master beat his servants?"

Mrs. Smythe frowned and shook her head. "Oh, my dear. I should not have said anything. Obviously you don't know."

"Know what?"

"Your back… you have long crisscross scars on it, as if you had been whipped."

A slow ache pounded in her head and she massaged her skull. Whipped? For the love of all that was holy, why would anyone do that to another human being? "I wish I could remember, but perhaps it's a good thing I cannot."

"Yes, dearie. I suspect it is a good thing. I shall fetch some books for you right away." The housekeeper waddled toward the door.

"One more thing, please," Louisa called out to the other woman. "Could you ask the duke if I might have a moment with him? I have some questions to ask about the night of the accident."

"Certainly." Mrs. Smythe hustled out, leaving the door open.

Louisa released a sigh and rested her forehead on her bent knees. From the way the older woman described Louisa's appearance, she wondered what had happened in her past. She didn't want to remember. Perhaps it was something terrible and traumatic, and her mind blocked it out. As much as she didn't want to remember anything bad, she did want to think about *something*. Currently, all she could think about was the duke and his caring heart and the passion she'd witnessed in his gaze—if even for a brief moment.

Since she'd first laid eyes on him, she couldn't stop thinking about his kindness. This morning when he'd visited, his expression seemed hollow at first, as if he were just going through the motions of being concerned about her welfare. His mother appeared genuinely worried, but the duke… It was as if he stared right through to her soul, until he'd stepped closer. Once her eyes locked with his, she couldn't look away. His mesmerizing blue eyes captivated her, held her prisoner. She didn't mind at all. He was quite handsome, and the more she stared, the more she wanted to be held in his big strong arms, and drown in the warm compassion of his captivating cobalt eyes. She suspected he didn't offer this expression very often.

This wasn't a proper way to think about someone who might become her employer, especially if Mrs. Smythe was correct and he planned to hire her. Surely Louisa only felt this way because he was her rescuer. If not for him, she would have died. Perhaps she admired him for saving her life and not for the person he really was. Then again, she didn't know what kind of person he was.

Heavy footsteps thumped up the stairs and she jerked up her head. Stalling at the door, the duke's gaze swept over her. Even with the distance separating them, his eyes burned a path over her body. Realizing she was out of bed without her wrapper, she blushed and pulled her knees closer to her bosom.

"Mrs. Smythe mentioned you wished to see me?"

The duke's deep voice stirred flutters in her chest and she nodded. "I would like to talk to you about the night of the accident, if you don't mind."

He meandered into the room toward her. This evening he dressed casually. His white lawn shirt stretched across his broad shoulders, and his tan breeches appeared almost too snug on his thighs. The black knee boots he wore made her wonder if he'd been out riding earlier. She let her gaze travel back up his wide chest and noticed his collar and cravat were missing, giving her a glimpse of his bare neck. When she caught herself gawking, embarrassment washed over her, yet her heartbeat quickened. Why did she act as if she'd never seen such a robust man before?

Then again, she still didn't know if she had or not. In reality, this very well could be her first time.

He perched next to her on the window seat, which was large enough for both of them to sit without any part of his body touching hers. Although she wouldn't mind having his leg brush hers—even if it was accidental.

As soon as he leaned against the window, he pulled away and threw a quick peek at the glass as he rubbed his arm. "Aren't you cold sitting here?"

"No. The room is toasty warm and here by the window it's refreshing."

He glanced at the hearth's roaring fire. "Indeed, it is quite warm. I'll have Mrs. Smythe dampen the fire."

"I appreciate it, Your Grace. You have been more than generous and I cannot thank you enough."

A small smile tugged on the corner of his mouth—a nicely shaped mouth that was hard not to stare at.

"It is the least I could do since I nearly killed you," he said.

"Can you tell me what happened? I have so many unanswered questions, and with my mind blank, getting a few of them answered would be most valued."

Nodding, he shifted on the seat. "I will tell you what I know, which I fear is not much." He braced his palms on the edge of the seat and leaned slightly forward, still keeping his eyes on her. "I was returning home from a dinner party, when I hit you. Clouds hid the moon, and I didn't see you until too late."

"Where was I?"

"You ran out from a group of trees into my path. I have no clue where you were coming from. And you must have been running fast because all I saw was a shadow before my horse struck you."

She rested her folded arms on her knees and leaned her chin on her forearm. "Mrs. Smythe says my clothes were tattered and dirty."

"Terribly so. And it appeared you had not bathed for a month."

She cringed. "Do you think I'm a vagabond?"

"I did, yes, but then your appearance suggested you had fallen on hard times. However, I realize how well you speak, and it makes me wonder what really happened to you."

"Mrs. Smythe said there are scars on my back." The duke nodded as though he knew exactly what scars she spoke of. A thrill rushed through her, wondering if he indeed saw her bare back. "D—did you see them?"

"No. I left the room before she bathed you."

Releasing a heavy sigh, she slid her legs to the floor and stood. Threading her fingers through her hair, she walked toward the fire, her mind whirling with confusion as the pound in her head continued to grow. "Oh, I pray I will remember soon. I don't wish to be a burden on you."

When she turned and caught his gaze, her mouth dried. His attention wasn't on her face as she'd expected, but on her body, sliding over every inch, especially between her neck and knees. His slow perusal made her heart hammer a foreign rhythm and caused her to burn from embarrassment. Once again, she'd forgotten she wasn't wearing a wrapper.

Quickly, she folded her arms in an attempt to hide herself. He rose and walked toward her at an unhurried pace. She couldn't move, although she should fetch a shawl or something to cover herself. After all, she was a woman, and he was most certainly a man.

"Miss Louisa," he said in a deep voice as he lifted a lock of her hair lying on her shoulder. "You are not a burden to me or my staff." His gaze moved briefly to her mouth before bouncing up to her eyes again. "I feel responsible for the accident, since my thoughts had wandered and I was not watching the road as I should have been."

"Please don't blame yourself. It wasn't your fault. Obviously, I was not in my right mind when I ran into the street."

He cupped her chin with his other hand as he gently stroked her cheek with his thumb. "As it were, I feel responsible, which is why I shall keep you here until you are well."

His tender touch melted her insides, her limbs would soon follow, she was certain—unless she removed his hand, which she was reluctant to do. An invisible pull encouraged her to lean forward and snuggle against his palm, which she did very subtly.

"What if I never regain my memory?" she whispered.

His stare danced between her eyes and her mouth once again—but longer this time. Cotton took up residence in her throat, making it impossible to swallow.

"Then I suppose I shall have to keep you on indefinitely," he answered in a low tone.

Somehow, he'd put her in a trance—one she did not wish to leave. She could stare into his blue eyes all night, just as long as he would continue looking at her as if he couldn't get enough.

But he pulled away, and his quick movement jerked her back to reality.

"As a maid, of course," he finished.

Her body shook from either the accident or the hold he'd had on her a moment ago. "Of course, Your Grace." She smiled. "But I wonder what it is I can do?"

"Not to worry, dear Louisa." He stepped back. "When you are able, we will discover which area of the estate you are best suited for."

She tightened her arms around her chest, suddenly chilled. "You don't know how happy that makes me."

He nodded toward the bed. "Rest well, and on the morrow you will feel better, I assure you."

He walked out the door, closing it behind him. Although excitement bounced in her chest, so did a different feeling. She'd never—that she could remember—felt so helpless than she had a moment earlier. His overpowering presence had caused her body to weaken in the worst way. If she stayed as his servant, she'd most certainly have to get rid of these ridiculous yearnings for his affection. Although she didn't remember anything, she knew servants did not fall in love with their employers—especially dukes.

Chapter Six

*T*HE YOUNG WOMAN *is infatuated with me.*

Trevor groaned and covered his face with his hands as he leaned his elbows on the desk. Yesterday in her room had been a mistake. He should not have gone to visit her without one of the other maids present. He should not have sat so close, and he definitely should not have watched her walk in front of the hearth. The shadowy shape underneath her nightdress displayed a woman who was full grown.

'Twas his own fault for being without a woman for so long. He'd been betrothed to Gwendolyn for over a year while her father and brother traveled abroad to settle business dealings, and so Trevor became celibate during that time to prepare for marriage. Once that moment came, he was disappointed. Gwen hadn't been passionate, nor had she given him the smallest inkling that she enjoyed his kisses.

It crushed him to think he'd chosen a wife who couldn't participate in the marriage bed. He'd longed for a passionate woman to share his life with, and disappointment soon became his lonely companion. Gwen was not the woman he'd dreamed about.

Shaking his head, he pushed the bad memories aside and tried to concentrate on his estate accounts. The ledger book open in front of him didn't hold any interest, not when the mysterious stranger in his guestroom wouldn't leave his mind.

After he'd left her room yesterday, he'd felt like such a fool. Why had he looked at her like a love-starved man? And why had he touched her? Her hair was like satin against his fingers, and she smelled like roses. Of course, it was the way she gazed at him with such admiration in her eyes that was his undoing. Never had a woman looked at him this way.

Having any kind of feelings for her was impossible, especially if he intended to keep her on as a servant. He was not—nor ever would be—the kind of man who dallied with servants. His father had been that sort of scoundrel, and at a young age, Trevor had vowed he'd never become like his sire. Trevor should dismiss Louisa once she gained her strength, but he didn't want her to return to her former life. It wouldn't be honorable to send her off into a world like that. Anyone who would whip a woman should be shot through the heart.

Yet he couldn't have her here to torment him. Her innocent eyes that sparkled whenever she smiled would be hard not to stare at, and her pouty heart-shaped lips were entirely too sensual for a mere maid. Once she became strong again and her body nourished as it should be, she'd become a temptation. There was only one thing to do in a situation like this… train her well and help her find employment elsewhere.

Plain and simple, he could *not* have her disrupting his life.

A knock on the door brought Trevor alert. "Enter."

Hobbs opened the door and stepped inside the room. "You have a visitor, my lord." He handed the card to Trevor. "Viscount Putney is waiting in the drawing room."

Trevor gnashed his teeth and at the same time tried to keep from displaying his anger. Bile rose to his throat as his fingers tightened around the calling card. He wanted nothing to do with *that* man, except to shoot him between the eyes and pretend he'd never met him. Unfortunately, Trevor was a duke and needed to act accordingly.

After taking a deep breath, he answered calmly, "I shall be

there momentarily, Hobbs."

The butler nodded, turned and left the room. Trevor stared at the open door. What could Putney possibly want to talk about? It would be easier to wrap his fingers around the viscount's throat and choke the very life out of him than tolerate his presence.

Shaking his head, he recalled how his mother thought he had a *big heart*. She would faint dead away if she knew what wicked thoughts ran amok through his head now.

Trevor stood and kept his balled hands at his side as he strode from the room. The sooner he discovered what the man wanted, the sooner he could kick him out of his house once and for all.

When he entered the drawing room, the tall, red-headed lord turned away from the large window and pierced Trevor with his stare. He almost laughed at his visitor's expression—as if this were Viscount Putney's home instead. Trevor wished the man would not covet everything in Trevor's possession. Wasn't it enough Putney was the last man to sleep with Gwen?

Folding his arms across his chest, Trevor lifted his chin stubbornly. "Speak your piece and leave."

Putney squared his shoulders and narrowed his gaze. "I want to know why you treat the twins so poorly."

The comment caught Trevor off guard, and he almost laughed. Instead, he arched a critical eyebrow. "Why do you care?"

"Are they mine?"

Trevor marched toward the man, ready to throttle the creature. He stopped in front of Putney and scowled. "I wish I knew."

"One of my servants informed me yesterday that you are not certain that you are their father."

"And pray, how should *your* servant know this?"

"She's friends with Mrs. Jacobs, your nursemaid."

Bloody gossiping staff! "What I do or will *not* do with the children is no concern of yours."

"It is if they are mine."

Trevor's hands itched to slam his fist into the man's nose.

How could Putney even think such a thing? "Has it slipped your mind that Adam and Amanda were born to *my* wife? Under the laws in England, that would mean the twins are my children, not yours."

"But you do not want them," Putney sneered. "Clearly, by the way you have ignored the poor children; you wish they had not been born." He lifted his chin as if to challenge Trevor. "On the other hand, I want them both. I want to be their father since I loved their mother so much. Amanda looks just like Gwen and I want to see her daily and be reminded of the love we once shared." His eyes misted. "Gwen was not supposed to die."

"You are correct. She was supposed to live and care for her children. Unfortunately, there were other things that seemed more important to her, like carrying on an affair behind her husband's back." Trevor grumbled under his breath. Being reminded about the past literally churned his stomach, and looking upon Putney as if he deserved the twins' love made Trevor want to vomit. "As it is, until I know who sired them, Adam and Amanda will remain in my home as my children. Is that clear?"

"Abundantly, Your Grace." Putney turned, and charged out the door.

Inhaling deeply, Trevor tried to calm the anger and betrayal threatening to kill him. If he could have changed places with Gwen and been the one to die, he would have. Living a lie and knowing the scandal might ruin those children wasn't worth this heartache. Trevor knew well what scandal does to children, since his own father had punished his family until his dying breath.

Trevor stormed out of the room. Several of his servants lingered in the hallway, pretending to be doing something constructive. They didn't meet his gaze, which told him they'd heard every word. Nevertheless, it wasn't them he wanted to lash out on right now.

"Mrs. Jacobs," he hollered up the stairs.

Up the staircase he ran, skipping every other step until he

reached the second level. His legs ate up the space as he made his way to the nursery. Mrs. Jacobs was reading the children a book when he walked inside. The older woman's eyes widened and her face paled.

"Might I have a word?" he growled.

She nodded and looked at the twins. "Play with your blocks until I return."

Amanda switched her gaze between him and her nursemaid, nodding slowly. Adam followed instructions quickly without blinking an eye. Trevor stepped out of the room, not wanting the children to hear what he had to say. When Mrs. Jacobs closed the nursery door behind her, she looked at him with frightened eyes.

"I will make this quick, so listen well. If I ever hear of you gossiping about my family or what goes on in this household again, I will dismiss you without a reference. Is that clear?"

"Yes, Your Grace."

"Those two children in there—" he pointed to the room— "should not have to be the ridicule of gossip. I will not have them growing up to have their peers whispering nonsense behind their backs. It does them more harm than you realize, and the last thing I want is for them to be hurt. Do you understand?"

Mrs. Jacobs nodded again, flexing her hands by her side. "I understand."

"Good. See that you do not open your mouth unwisely again."

He turned and stomped back to his study, knowing he needed a strong drink very soon. As he passed Louisa's room, he thought the door cracked open a bit, but he didn't stop to look. Instead, a bottle of scotch was what he needed to calm his ire.

When he entered his room, he slammed the door. The pictures on the wall shook. He cursed his life, hoping he would get so foxed that all the ache and pain would leave him to peace.

"WHAT DO YE mean she's missin'?" Richard Macgregor shouted at the insipid child in front of him. "Didn't ye both leave for the same area the other night?"

David cringed and shook his head. His dirty brown hair stuck to his ears and didn't move at all. "That we did, sir—as we've done before—but we've never come back at the same time." His Adam's apple bobbed once. "I waited and waited for Louisa to come home, and when she didn't, I went looking for her. I asked everyone, I did, and nobody seen her, not even once during the evening." He shrugged. "She's up and disappeared, I tell ye."

Anger rose inside Richard's head and he bunched his hands into fists. "I highly doubt she was stupid enough to get herself caught by the police. She's better than that."

"Aye, Mr. Macgregor. She's a slippery as an eel, and she taught all of us how to hide or run away from getting caught."

"Just in case, I will have the gaol checked." He flipped his hand through the air, causing David to flinch. "Now be off with ye. Time's a wastin' and you won't be makin' any money standin' around talkin' to me."

"Aye, sir." The gawky youth fled out the door as fast as his worn-out shoes would carry him.

Richard grumbled curses as he strutted into the room where all the children slept on bedrolls. All rolls were neatly folded and placed against the wall—even Louisa's—but the children were gone to do their daily earnings. If Richard hadn't been entertaining a certain harlot last night, he would have noticed when his prized pupil didn't return home.

"Augh." He slammed his fist against the wall. He should have known Louisa would soon become a problem. After all, the older they grew, the more they gained a conscience and realized thieving for him was wrong.

Richard had been in this business long enough to know the attitude pattern of those who worked for him, so he should have realized that Louisa was being more compliant... friendlier, and more eager to make him happy. She must have also assumed what he wanted to do with her. Girls her age were too old to pickpocket. Especially the pretty girls. They were better use to the older gents, the ones who would pay handsomely to have a willing wench in their bed for a night of pleasure. Even a few madams were eyeing Louisa as someone they could add to their brothels.

Richard needed her back immediately. Louisa brought in more money than the others. He couldn't allow her to leave. He didn't think she'd been caught. The girl was too clever for that. No, she was running, to be sure.

Scurrying out of the room, he snapped curses on his way to the front door. He'd instruct the children to watch for her. He'd ask his friends as well. Richard would find that girl if it was the last thing he did—and when he found her, he'd punish her severely. She'd think twice about leaving him again.

Chapter Seven

"I HONESTLY DON'T think I have ever been given a dress of such quality, Mrs. Smythe." Louisa stared at herself in the full-length mirror. The black-and-white servant's dress fit her body like a glove, and the soft material caressed her skin. Something told her she'd never owned such a dress. Happiness bubbled in her chest, for she was the luckiest girl in England. Truly, fate had smiled on her to put her in the Duke of Kenbridge's path.

Mrs. Smythe grinned wide as she watched Emma comb Louisa's hair and wind it into a bun before placing a white cap over it. "Is this not so exciting?" Louisa asked the housekeeper. "I'm so very privileged to be a servant in such a household." Louisa switched her gaze to Emma. "And I thank you for showing me how to fix my hair."

Emma bobbed her head. "My pleasure, Louisa."

"His lordship gave me the responsibility to find a place for you here." Mrs. Smythe beamed. "We shall start you in the kitchen for now." Her gaze ran over Louisa's body. "Since you are so fond of the food, I believe that would be the place for you to start."

Louisa giggled and patted her stomach. "The food here is most delicious, I assure you."

"You have gained a little weight in a week's time, I might

add, which tells me you were certainly lacking."

"Indeed I was." Louisa turned from side to side as she studied her body through the mirror. Why didn't anything look familiar? Not even wearing a servant's dress could shake her hidden memories.

"Come. I'll take you down and introduce you to the kitchen staff."

Mrs. Smythe led the way, out of the bedroom and down the stairs. Louisa's steps weren't as hurried as the other woman because she couldn't stop admiring the decorations, statues, and paintings along the way. The duke certainly had a lovely home, and so very large. As they passed a room with an open door, she took a quick peek inside. The room stood empty, except for a few furnishings along the walls. *A ballroom.*

Her thoughts came to a halt as did her footsteps. Yes, indeed this was a ballroom. In fact, even now she could hear the orchestra playing as her mind imagined couples dancing and sweeping around the room like a flutter of colorful butterflies.

She closed her eyes as the vision grew. A little girl, standing back, watching…dreaming. The deep laughter of an older man as he picked her up in his arms and swung her around, making her feel like a princess. The image of his face was fuzzy, but he had curly blond hair and a square jaw. The little girl's voice whispered the word, *Father.*

Louisa snapped alert, her heart beating frantically. A throb in her forehead began, and the harder she tried to remember, the worse the pain became. Had she remembered something from her past?

Realizing she'd been daydreaming, a sharp stab of panic pierced through her. *Imbecile! Stop laggin' behind and get to work or ye'll be sorry!* The warning echoed through her head, but it didn't come from her voice. The man's raspy tone chilled her bones and quickened her step to catch up with the housekeeper. She knew as sure as she breathed that daydreaming was not an option.

But why would she think about being in a ballroom? Apparently, she must have been a servant for a wealthy family and had witnessed the father dancing with his young daughter. She frowned. If only she could remember her own family. Perhaps it wasn't wise to remember. Because of the scars on her back, she knew she hadn't had a life of luxury—or a happy one.

Determined to make His Grace proud, she squared her shoulders and quickened her pace.

As she turned a corner, still trying to reach Mrs. Smythe, she walked into the muscular figure of a man. His large hands grabbed her shoulders to keep her from falling and she looked up into the startled eyes of Kenbridge. His rugged appearance and more-than-handsome face caused her to gasp. She hadn't seen him since he'd visited her that night in her room, and she sorely missed looking at him these past several days.

He ran his gaze over her as he stepped back. A smile pulled at his lips. "Louisa, it's good to see you looking so well. I'm relieved to know you are up and about."

Quickly, she curtsied. "Forgive me for not seeing you—until I ran into you, that is." She grinned. "Mrs. Smythe is taking me to meet the kitchen staff. That is where she wants me to start working."

"Splendid. I'm happy to see you are starting off right." He motioned his hand toward the end of the hallway. "Do not let me keep you."

She curtsied again. "Thank you, Your Grace." Although she didn't want to take her eyes off him, she must. Pining away for the lord of the manor wasn't healthy.

Pulling herself away from his company was hard. She'd miss talking to him and seeing his sparkling eyes, and a smile tug at his tempting mouth. Yet it wasn't her station in life to become his friend...only his servant. Whatever was in her past, she did know this—he would never be more than her employer.

She hurried down the hall and met Mrs. Smythe just as she entered the kitchen. As the housekeeper made the introductions, Louisa listened closely to catch everyone's name. Most had a

French name. She should have suspected the duke would only hire French cooks. Francois, the head chef, stuck his nose in the air as if he didn't want to be bothered by Louisa. She wanted to slap him for his rudeness.

"Nice to meet you, Monsieur Francois," she greeted as politely as she could.

The overly large cook grumbled and turned away from her, back to the stove. *"Petite sotte. Pourquoi c'est moi qui doit être sa nourice?"*

She hitched a quick breath. For the nerve of that man! How dare he think he'd have to watch over her like a governess? Louisa huffed and planted her hands on her hips and replied, *"Peut-être c'est moi qui est assignée de garder des coquins insipides."*

Gasps exploded around the room, especially from Mrs. Smythe. Louisa had actually spoken in French... hadn't she? Yes, she had!

Snapping her mouth closed, she glanced around at the other servants who looked at her with wide, questioning eyes. Heat crept up her face and she knew some of them had understood her words. She'd actually called the cook an insipid fop. Oh, the humiliation...

"Land sakes, my dear, you spoke French." Pure wonder shone in Mrs. Smythe's eyes.

"I know." Louisa hiccupped a laugh. "And what's even stranger is that I know what I said." She met Francois's accusing glare. She was not about to apologize, either.

"I'm now wondering if you worked for someone who spoke that language," the housekeeper added.

"I don't know, Mrs. Smythe. But it does have logic. Perhaps that is how I was able to learn it."

The tense moment passed slowly, but soon the others had returned to their duties. Mrs. Beauchamp took over instructing Louisa after Mrs. Smythe left. The French woman appeared to be in her early forties, still quite lovely with a buoyant personality. Louisa warmed up to this lady quickly, which was good since the others seemed to shoot daggers at her. Especially Francois.

She listened closely to what Mrs. Beauchamp taught her, but nothing made sense. It was as if she couldn't fit the pieces of the puzzle together. The names of the spices confused her even though she tried to memorize their names and what they were used for. And why was it so important to take out the eggshell pieces that fell into the bowl when cracking eggs? Another thing that didn't make sense was why the dry ingredients had to be separate from the liquids? They would eventually go into the same bowl when they were done.

Through her hazy memory, she tried to recall everything as she helped prepare His Grace's dinner. Time passed quickly, and soon the meal was ready. As she waited to hear the butler announce the duke's meal, Louisa causally leaned against the table, knocking her elbow against a pan. The object fell to the floor with a roaring crash, and whatever was inside glided quickly across the floor as if in a race to reach the stove.

A kitchen helper walked by and slipped on the gooey substance. Down she went, whacking her bottom on the hard floor. By now, several others had rushed over to see what the commotion was all about. When Francois bent and touched the thick liquid, he rattled off curses in French that would make an intoxicated man high on spirits blush, and then the chef issued commands as if they were all in the military instead of the kitchen.

With dishcloths in hand, everyone scrambled to clean up the mess—after slipping several times on the slick floor, of course.

Mrs. Beauchamp threw Louisa an accusing glare before switching her attention back to the task. She grabbed a hand towel and moved to help, but Francois looked directly at her and shook his head. Embarrassed, Louisa stepped back to the corner of the room by the door, her heart wrenching with disappointment.

"Mademoiselle, do not come closer. Ve vill clean zis up without yur help."

Ashamed, Louisa nodded. From out in the hall, the butler's call announcing dinner echoed. Nervously, she nibbled on her fingernails, moving her gaze from one servant to the next. Who was going to serve?

In a flash, she knew… as if she'd always known. The footman served. So where was he? And why wasn't he doing his duty?

She finally spotted him on the floor arguing with Francois. If she tried to interrupt, she was certain they'd both yell at her. At this point, she didn't think she'd be able to handle such verbal abuse.

There was no other choice. She must serve His Grace. Excitement welled inside her as she picked up the tray of food. She anticipated him gazing at her with those smoldering eyes while he praised her for a job well done, as long as she didn't tell him about the mess she'd just made in the kitchen. That would decidedly deflate her enthusiasm.

She thought about the conversation she'd overheard the other day between him and Mrs. Jacobs. Although she wasn't one to listen to other conversations, his voice had raised so loud she couldn't help but eavesdrop. She'd cracked the door open just enough to watch. Whatever Mrs. Jacobs had done left him in a fit of anger. After he'd walked by Louisa's room, her heart broke for him, wishing there was something she could do to soften his mood. Since she was still new at his household, she didn't dare ask too many questions. But the suspense nearly killed her.

Louisa wanted so badly to impress the duke. He'd done so much for her and she didn't know how to repay him.

When she stepped into the dining room and saw him, her heart dropped. His wide, strong shoulders sagged as he stared with empty eyes at the green leaves of the centerpiece. She'd do anything to change his expression to a happy one.

She stopped by his side and he raised his gaze to her. She curtsied. "Your Grace."

His eyes widened as she set the bowl of soup in front of him. "Louisa? Where is my footman, Mr. Stevens?"

"Well, you see, Your Grace… there was a disturbance in the kitchen, and Mr. Stevens started arguing with Francois. I did not dare interrupt." She shrugged. "I knew your meal needed to be served quickly and so I took on the responsibility myself. You don't mind, do you?"

He gave her a small smile, which lightened her mood considerably.

"Louisa, I must say, you have taken well to this position. I'm impressed you acted so hastily, and I commend you for that." He dipped his spoon in the bowl and brought the liquid to his mouth.

It surprised her that she had thought of that as well. Now she really believed she'd been a servant in a place such as this. How else would she know such things? "Thank you, sir. It is my wish to please you—as well as the others."

"I'm quite certain you will." He set the spoon down. "Might I inquire about the other day?" he said softer.

"About what, sir?"

"When you overheard me talking to Mrs. Jacobs in the hallway."

Heat rose to Louisa's cheeks and she glanced at the white tablecloth covering the table. "I fear, Your Grace, I didn't hear much, and what I did hear I could not understand."

"Which is how I would like it to be," he said with a hint of sternness to his voice as he leaned closer. "Just know I am a man who does not tolerate gossip."

"And you should not have to, sir. Gossip is a vile tool, only meant to harm people."

He smiled and lifted the spoon to his mouth again. "Indeed."

She curtsied again, and left his side. She ought not to converse with him while he ate, even though it still bothered her because she didn't understand what gossip had so upset him with the children's nursemaid.

Just as she reached the doorway, he choked. Swinging around, she gasped, wondering if she should go assist him. He lifted his glass of wine and practically gulped it. On instinct, she hurried back to his side.

"Your Grace? Is something amiss?"

His eyes watered as he took another drink before setting his glass down. "It's the soup. There's something…wrong."

Worry climbed through her, tightening her chest. *I helped make the soup.* "What is it?"

"Something does not taste right." He dipped his spoon in it then placed it in his mouth. Once more he choked and quickly lifted the drink. Flipping his hand, he motioned for her to take it away.

She did; her heart sinking as she carried it back to the kitchen. What had she done? She was almost certain this disaster was her doing as well.

The kitchen help still scrambled about trying to clean the floor. She stepped as carefully as she could and retrieved the next plate then carried it back into the duke who watched her through hooded eyes. *He knows this is my fault.* "Here is your next course."

"Thank you, Louisa."

This time, she stepped slowly back toward the door as he cut into his venison dipped heavily in creamy sauce…which she made. She held her breath, watching him. After a couple of chews, she thought it safe to exhale, but then he gagged and spit out the food onto his plate.

"Good heavens, what is this? Did nobody taste this in the kitchen before serving me?"

Tears stinging her eyes, she hurried back to him. "Is there something wrong, Your Grace?"

He cut another piece of meat and sniffed it. "This tastes horrid." He held up his fork to her. "Take a bite and see."

Nodding, she slowly leaned in and opened her mouth. He slid the piece of meat in and she bit down. A strong taste coated her tongue, and she knew what she'd done wrong. It served her right for not remembering which herb to use when most of them looked alike. Tears slid down her cheeks as she forced herself to eat. It was the least she could do for ruining his meal.

"Really, Louisa. You don't have to eat it."

He held up his linen napkin, which she gratefully took and spit out the food. After wiping her mouth, she shook her head, her tears falling faster. "You don't understand, Your Grace. I was the one who helped make this. Clearly, I didn't know what I was doing." She ended with a sob and covered her face with her hands. Wasn't it bad enough she didn't have a memory, and now...she made someone sick from her own cooking!

He stood. Warmth melded into her as two strong arms wrapped around her, pulling her next to his hard body. The feeling was foreign, yet she enjoyed it and wanted more. Turning her head, she snuggled against his chest, taking the comfort he offered. His scent of spice enveloped her and she breathed slowly, deeply, taking it all in. She could close her eyes and stay this way forever.

Forever ended abruptly when he stiffened then jerked away from her as if she were hot coals. She met his angry eyes and swallowed hard. *What have I done now?*

As she searched his expression, it looked as if he struggled with an inner demon himself. At first he appeared angry, but within seconds confusion creased his face just before he gave her a smile—one that looked entirely too forced.

"No need to fret, Louisa. Clearly your talent does not lie in the kitchen. I shall have Mrs. Smythe find another place for you on the morrow."

Nodding, Louisa wiped the moisture under her eyes. "Your Grace, you are too forgiving."

He chuckled and returned to his seat. "Now, if you will, please send Mrs. Beauchamp in here so I can have my chef fix me something else."

"As you wish." She curtsied and hurried into the kitchen. By this time the mess had been cleared. As she explained what happened, a few of the others snickered behind their hands, and Francois's higher-than-thou attitude grated on her nerves. At least she wouldn't have to work with them after this.

Sadly, Louisa walked toward her new bedroom. Earlier, Mrs. Smythe had shown her the servants' quarters, which was where Louisa would be living. They were not as large or as decorated as the guest room, but she still considered herself most fortunate to be here in the first place.

From the end of the hall, giggling erupted. She stopped, not thinking she'd heard right, but then two voices whispered through the stillness from behind a closed door. Louisa crept closer to the sound, realizing it was children's voices coming from within the linen closet. Cautiously, she pulled the door open. Two sets of eyes, almost identical, stared up at her. A little boy and girl—twins—cuddled together on the floor. The little boy lifted a finger to his lips as to shush her.

Louisa glanced up and down the hall then crouched to their level. "Whom are you hiding from?" she whispered.

"Mrs. Jacobs," he answered.

"Are you Adam?" She looked at the girl. "And Amanda?"

They nodded their curly honey-blonde heads. Such beautiful children. "All right, I shall not tell." She glanced up the hallway again then back to them before winking. "If you need me, I shall be right over there." She pointed to her door.

Adam nodded and shut the door even before Louisa could move. Walking back to her room, she chuckled. As she opened the door, the sound of booming footfalls jerked her around. Mrs. Jacobs wore a stern expression as her tree-trunk-shaped legs carried her large body toward the linen closet. By the look on the older woman's face, Louisa could tell the twins were going to get a scolding soon.

The nurse yanked open the door and grabbed the boy and girl by the arm, whipping them out of the closet. Amanda sobbed and tried to pull away. Adam struggled and kicked, which only succeeded in making Mrs. Jacobs more upset.

"Hold still, will you." The nurse growled and pulled Adam's arm harder. "You little twit, listen to me," she snapped.

When Amanda cried out, Mrs. Jacobs smacked the girl's face.

Something fierce snapped inside Louisa and she flew from her room and ran toward the three. She pushed the nurse away from the sobbing children and folded them both in her arms. "How dare you raise your hand to her?" Louisa glared. "They were doing nothing wrong but playing a game."

Mrs. Jacobs folded her arms smartly across her chest. "They were hiding because it's their dinner time, and they always resist when I try to feed them. They complain that they do not like the food."

Louisa glanced at the two in her arms, their faces streaked with tears. She stroked each head and held them against her bosom. "They are just children, for heaven's sake. They are going to be picky eaters."

Mrs. Jacobs arched an eyebrow. "Do you think you can do any better? I heard you could not even help with His Grace's dinner tonight. What use are you if you can't even perform household duties correctly?"

Anger shot through Louisa and she pierced the older woman with her stare. "This is *not* about me, but these two darling children."

"Listen, little missy, if you do not keep your nose out of my affairs, his lordship will hear about this."

Louisa lifted her chin stubbornly. "I hope he does because I have something to tell him about the way you are punishing his children."

"He doesn't care a fig about his children."

Blinking in unbelief, Louisa shook her head. "Would you care to wager your career on that?"

Defeat made Mrs. Jacobs's shoulders sag. She shook her head. "As you wish, I will not say a thing." She held out her hands for the children to take, which they didn't. "Come along children. If you are good, I shall have Cook fix you some pudding."

They both looked up at Louisa with questioning eyes. She smiled and motioned her head for them to go with their nurse. Hesitantly, they took Mrs. Jacobs's hands and walked down the hall with her.

Louisa growled as she marched back to her room. She should inform his lordship of the treatment the woman showed his children. It was uncalled for. No wonder those poor things were scared.

From out of nowhere, a sense of dread grew heavy inside her…as if she'd experienced those frightened feelings before. Without a doubt, Louisa knew what Adam and Amanda were feeling—what fear clawed through their hearts, freezing their limbs. And especially the sadness of knowing there wasn't anything to be done but return to the person who caused all the terror.

Shadowy scenes rushed through her head. She was young. Frightened. Her body weak. A large man stood above her, holding a whip. He threatened to beat her if she didn't do as he said.

Tears pricked her eyes and she sank on her bed. Was she remembering something about her past? If this was indeed part of her memory, she had no wish to bring it back.

Chapter Eight

AT TWO O'CLOCK in the afternoon, Trevor poured himself a drink. Still too early to drink spirits, he knew his nerves needed the company only port would provide. Especially since his brother Trey and their mutual friend Lord Hawthorne would be joining him shortly for a ride around the estate.

Trevor rolled his eyes. Somehow his brother had gotten it into his head that Trevor needed male companionship. What he needed was peace and serenity. More than that, he needed people to stop pitying him.

Gossipmongers still circulated stories about Gwen's affairs. Trevor had heard people whispering when they thought he wasn't there. Thankfully, though, there had been no gossip about the twins. He might doubt who sired them, but he didn't need Society following him around to discover the answer.

"Excuse me, Your Grace."

Trevor turned his attention to the door. Hobbs stood with a solemn expression—as always—and without a wrinkle in his uniform. "What it is, Hobbs? Have my guests arrived?"

"Yes, sir. They are waiting in the drawing room."

"Splendid." He swallowed the last of his drink, placed it on the liquor tray, and strode out of the room. Perhaps visiting with his brother and Hawthorne would lift his spirits…more than the alcohol.

When Trevor entered the drawing room, both Trey and Hawthorne stood waiting for him, dressed in their riding clothes. Trey chose darker colors while Hawthorne wore lighter. Trevor wanted to chuckle since the two men were usually so much alike in their tastes.

"Good afternoon, Trey. Hawthorne." Trevor bowed to both men and they returned the greeting. "Are you ready to ride?"

"Indeed I am," Hawthorne began, "but before we go, will you tell me who that charming creature is." He pointed out the window. "I confess I do not usually converse much with servants, but she looks familiar."

Trevor moved to the window that looked out over the flower garden. Louisa stood with Mrs. Fitzwilliam as they plucked dead leaves from the bushes. "That is my newest servant, Louisa."

Trey rushed between them, peering out. "Is that the vagabond Mother told me about the other day?"

Leave it to Mother... Trevor wondered what part of *don't tell anyone* his mother didn't understand when they had discussed this subject. "I know not what she told you," Trevor replied, "but she is the girl I nearly killed when my vehicle hit her." He prayed Louisa wouldn't turn toward the house and witness the three of them gawking like spectators watching a horse race.

Hawthorne shook his head while rubbing his chin. "I swear to you she looks familiar, but I cannot decide where I have seen her before."

Trevor clapped his hand on Hawthorne's shoulder. "I doubt she is who you think. By the way she was dressed that evening when I hit her, I can assure you she had probably made Seven Dials her home."

"How utterly sad," Hawthorne mumbled. "She does not have the appearance of one of those varmints. In fact, by the delicate way she moves and her tiny build, I would have assumed she was born of Quality."

Trey chuckled. "Dominic, my good man, I know you are desperate to find a willing maid, but really, you need not look at my brother's servants." He motioned his hand toward the flower garden. "I'm quite certain you can find them anywhere."

Trevor rolled his eyes. Trey would always think this way, even though he had a lovely wife at home. Thankfully, Judith kept Trey under her thumb—which was where Trey wanted to be anyhow. Unfortunately, Dominic Lawrence was still a confirmed bachelor.

"Gentlemen," Trevor began, "I think we can forget this matter and begin our ride—"

"Is it true she lost her memory?" Hawthorne asked.

Silently, Trevor groaned. "Yes, it is. The girl has yet to remember anything. Not even the accident."

"Amazing, don't you agree?" Trey ran his fingers through his dark hair as he narrowed his gaze out the window. "I cannot fathom what it could possibly be for that girl not to remember anything."

Trevor folded his arms. "Believe me, the girl cannot even remember her last name. My housekeeper had her help in the kitchen last evening, and Louisa messed up her duties terribly. I'm quite certain it was because she just could not remember her upbringing. The girl does not even know how to cook."

Dominic grinned and tapped his finger on his bottom lip. "Gentlemen, we are forgetting one thing. Louisa is *not* a girl."

Although Hawthorne ogled her like a sweetmeat, Trevor couldn't stop gaping at the way the servant's dress fit snug against her. Now that her hair had been wound into a bun, he could see more of her slender neck. He didn't need to close his eyes to remember what she looked like standing in her nightdress with her hair long and flowing over her shoulders and down her back. Interest stirred inside him and he wished it hadn't. In fact, it had been stirring inside him quite a bit lately, even at night in his dreams.

Blowing out an irritated breath, Trevor turned away from the window and walked toward the door. "Gentlemen, are you coming? I'm in the mood for a ride around the estate. I do not want to stand in front of a window all day ogling a servant girl." When Hawthorne whipped an accusing scowl Trevor's way, he retorted, "Forgive me. I mean *woman*."

Finally, Trey and Hawthorne pulled away from the window and followed Trevor outside. As he headed toward the stables, Dominic ventured toward the flower garden. Trevor groaned. What was wrong with that man? He couldn't be *that* desperate for a wench.

As Trevor approached Lord Hawthorne, Dominic had just introduced himself to Louisa, and raised her hand to brush his lips across her knuckles. Inwardly, Trevor seethed. *The rake.* Was his friend seducing Trevor's servant right here in front of everyone?

"And this is Lord Trey, His Grace's younger brother," Hawthorne finished introductions.

Louisa smiled and curtsied. Thankfully, Trey didn't kiss the woman's hand like Hawthorne did, or Trevor would have reprimanded his brother.

Trevor took a deep breath and exhaled, trying to calm his impatience. When Louisa's gaze met his, her green eyes twinkled. Her eyes hadn't done this when her attention had been on Hawthorne or Trey. Trevor wished she'd stop looking at him this way...and he wished his heart didn't leap with excitement when she did.

He smiled. "Louisa, it does me good to see you out in the garden today."

"Well, Your Grace, Mrs. Smythe thought I needed to be outside and enjoy the fresh air and sunshine, so she turned me over to the good graces of Mrs. Fitzwilliam and the gardener."

He tilted his head, studying her complexion. "Mrs. Smythe is correct. You do need a bit more color to your face. I trust you are feeling better today?"

"Yes. Much better."

Trey nudged him with his elbow. "Oh, Trevor, old boy, clearly you can see how well she looks. Her face is positively glowing."

Her smile widened, making her amazing eyes glisten more.

"Splendid, now if you will excuse us Louisa—"

"Miss Louisa," Hawthorne cut him off. "I must say, you do look a bit familiar to me. Have you ever been in Mayfair, by chance?"

Her cheeks turned pink. "I cannot say, my lord. Even though I'm recovered from my accident, my memory still has yet to return." She stepped closer and hesitantly laid her finger on Hawthorne's gloved hand. "But please, tell me if you know who I am. I feel so lost without my memory."

"I fear, I cannot say whether I know you or not. You just look familiar."

Frowning, she dropped her hand and stepped back.

"Come now, Hawthorne," Trevor spoke up. "You have upset the woman. Let us adjourn on our ride and let her be."

"Forgive me, Louisa." Hawthorne smiled. "I hope your day improves."

"I'm certain it will, my lord."

As the men walked away, Trevor found himself sneaking a peek back at her. Sadness lurked in her expression, but when her gaze met his, she smiled. He gave her a polite nod and turned away, once again wishing she wouldn't react in this manner. Yet, he nearly encouraged her behavior. Why couldn't he stop?

The men mounted their saddled horses and began their ride. At first it was quiet, which gave Trevor a moment's peace. He'd always enjoyed riding, and it didn't matter if he had company or not. It surprised him that his visitors weren't talking like loose-lipped women. Glancing back, Trevor studied their expressions. His younger brother appeared deep in thought, and poor Hawthorne...that man couldn't stop looking back toward the house. Could the man really have met Louisa somewhere in Mayfair? Yet if the young woman were indeed of noble birth, wouldn't her family be looking for her by now? And that certainly didn't explain the scars on her back.

"Trey?" Trevor finally broke the silence. "How is that lovely wife of yours?"

His younger brother grinned wide. "Perfect, as always. She loves being a wife and mother."

Trevor nodded. "Judith is certainly a gem. The best thing that ever happened to you, if I might say."

"I agree," Hawthorne chimed in. "I have never seen you happier."

Trey chuckled. "And with our long-lost brother, Tristan, home again, life is definitely good."

"Indeed, it is," Trevor agreed. "I just wish Tristan would not stay cooped inside the house with Mother so much. If he's not there, he's wasting away in his London townhouse. He needs to get out and meet new people. And for sure, he needs to forget about Lady Hollingsworth."

"Oh, that reminds me," Hawthorne's voice grew loud. "Have you heard the startling news? Lord Hollingsworth died late last night. From what I have heard, the police do not know what to make of it."

At the same time, Trevor and his brother pulled their horses to a stop. Hollingsworth was not a name either of them wanted to hear...especially the lord's wife. She was the very reason Tristan had nearly lost his life.

Trevor scowled. "Dead, you say? Are you jesting, Hawthorne?"

Trey murmured a curse and shook his head.

Lord Hawthorne leaned forward on his horse and stroked the mane. "It was a shock, to be sure. Lady Hollingsworth found him passed out drunk in the stables that night. The man was not wearing a stitch of clothing. She was so disgusted with her husband, she left him there, but a few hours later the stable boy found his lordship dead."

"What is this news going to do to Tristan?" Trey asked.

Trevor hardened his jaw, fearful to say anything at this moment. The Worthington family hated Lord Hollingsworth. All of them wished the man dead. But now... Indeed, what would this kind of news do to Tristan's well-being?

Taking a deep breath, Trevor prayed his anger wouldn't show. "I shall have a talk with him. Let us hope this news does nothing to our brother. I would think after two years Tristan has gotten over that fiasco and is well on his way to living a normal life again."

Trey urged his horse into a walk, which the others did as well. "I would like to think Tristan is over that, but sometimes…" He shrugged. "Sometimes he grows quiet and I wonder if he does not still think about her."

"Well, I pray he does not get any wild ideas now that she's a widow." Trevor adjusted himself in the saddle. "That woman broke his heart once, I would hate for her to have the chance to do it again."

The other two men nodded. Trevor pushed his steed faster. He'd definitely take the time to talk to Tristan now. His brother's head injury from two years ago had brought trauma on the family and Tristan took a long time to recover. Finally he seemed normal again, and Trevor couldn't let anything disrupt his brother's life. Especially now.

An hour later, the men stopped by a pond to rest their horses. Dominic and Trey had been chatting back and forth during the ride, but seldom did Trevor join in. Now the two seemed remarkably quiet. Trevor prayed the two would remain this way until they left the estate.

"I cannot stop thinking about Louisa," Hawthorne broke the silence.

Silently, Trevor groaned.

"You know," Trey said, "Mother was telling me she thought Louisa might be Lord and Lady Danvers' daughter."

Trevor shook his head and moved away from the pond, closer to his brother. "Trey, would Louisa really be their daughter? I would think by now her family would be missing her. Am I correct? Besides that, I do not think they have a daughter."

Trey shrugged.

"Actually," Hawthorne said, "I recall a conversation I had with Viscount Wellesley a few years ago. He mentioned having a younger cousin who drowned when she was twelve years old." He met Trevor's eyes. "How old do you suppose Louisa is? If I remember correctly, the drowning happened six years ago. That would make his cousin nineteen."

"She does not look that age." Trevor shook his head.

Trey scratched his chin. "Yet, in a way she does. There is something in her eyes that speaks of a hard life."

"Are you saying Louisa could be the Danvers' daughter and never drowned?" Trevor asked.

"That's what I'm saying." Trey nodded.

"Then why has she not been with her family all these years?" Hawthorne wondered.

Trey shrugged. "Perhaps she lost her memory all those years ago instead of when you hit her with the carriage?"

Blowing out a frustrated breath, Trevor rolled his eyes. "If that were the case, she would not have acted so distraught when realizing she did not have a memory." He grumbled and turned to mount his horse. This was how gossip began, and he wouldn't have any more of it. "Gentlemen, I grow weary of this discussion. I'm heading back to the manor with or without you."

Chapter Nine

LOUISA CLIPPED A few more dead leaves before turning her gaze in the direction where the men had ridden off. She didn't expect them to return anytime soon, but still...it was nice to watch nonetheless. Lord Hawthorne seemed very friendly, but not at all familiar. He thought he knew her, but she doubted he did. Although handsome, he didn't spark her memory at all. It surprised her to think he actually flirted with her, yet it was still Kenbridge who held her attention.

Trevor.

His brother had called him by his given name, a name she hadn't heard until today. Now she couldn't stop repeating it in her mind. What a glorious, masculine name. Dreamily, she sighed. If only she were a true lady, he might look at her as a woman. Instead, all he saw was a servant—or the vagabond he'd rescued.

When she caught herself not focusing, she snapped her attention back to the rose bush. *Dawdling is not tolerated.* Yet, the raspy voice from the dark recesses of her mind that disturbed her from time to time slowly diminished and peace settled over her. Although she received the impression she hadn't been allowed leisure time in her past, she was given more freedom to do so now. Her work still had to be done, but at least her mind could create another world for her dreams.

Still, it didn't stop her from wishing she were someone else. The vision she'd had about being at a ball as a young girl—or at least witnessing it—seemed so real. She'd love to have that kind of life, even if she were the personal maid for the lady of the house.

So lost in her dreams, she didn't realize what she was doing until Mrs. Fitzwilliam gasped. Louisa jerked alert and glanced at the woman whose wide eyes were directed on the flower bush in front of Louisa. She swung her attention to what she'd been cutting. A sob gushed from her throat. All around her feet littered the beautiful flowers she'd cut to shreds.

"What have you done?" the other woman shrieked as she yanked the clippers out of Louisa's hands.

She groaned. "Please, forgive me. I—I—I wasn't watching. I didn't pay attention—"

"Obviously." Mrs. Fitzwilliam rolled her eyes. "I'm relieved you only destroyed one bush instead of the others in his lordship's garden."

"As am I."

"What in heaven's name were you thinking?"

"I was not thinking, which is clearly my problem. I daydream so often."

"Daydream?"

"Yes, and I'm sorry. I shan't do it again."

Mrs. Fitzwilliam placed hands on her beefy hips. "Woolgathering should not be done while we are working. This is probably why you ruined his lordship's meal last night."

"Actually, it was because I confused the herbs."

"If you are ever going to prove yourself to us and his lordship, you have to focus."

Louisa nodded. "I understand. Again, please forgive me."

The other woman handed the clippers back to Louisa and nodded at the next bush. "See if you can trim that without cutting every last flower."

"Thank you." She walked around the shredded rose bush to

find another one. Against her legs rubbed something soft and furry. Startled, she jumped away and looked down, thinking she'd see a rodent. Instead, a gray kitten mewed and gazed up at her.

"Oh, look what I found." She scooped the kitten in her arms. The animal purred and rubbed its face against her arm. She turned to the other woman. "I didn't know his lordship had cats."

Mrs. Fitzwilliam narrowed her gaze on the kitten. "They are all kept in the stable, to keep the mice away from the grain. This animal is probably one of those."

Louisa petted the soft fur. "The kitten does not look as if he's been fed properly."

"Well then, perhaps he isn't one that's kept in the stables. I will have Murray take it away."

"Oh, no." Louisa stopped her. "Why can we not keep it?"

The other servant crinkled her nose. "Keep it? You cannot be serious. You are a servant, Louisa, not a child."

How she wanted to snap at the obtuse woman for that comment. Of course Louisa wasn't a child. Just because she wanted a kitten didn't make her youthful. She continued to pet the animal, the soft fur soothing her temperament. "Adults have had pets before, have they not?"

"Yes, but you have no place to keep it, and Murray is not going to want another varmint in his stables. He cleans after horses all day; he's not going to take care of a pet for you as well."

Shrugging, Louisa turned her back on the other lady and slowly strolled along the stone path toward the lawn. Kittens were such helpless creatures, needing someone to take care of them. They were perfect for children.

Just then a stern voice boomed through the silence coming from over by the house. Mrs. Jacobs marched with the children toward the lawn. Louisa gasped. *Marched?* Both Adam and Amanda's faces were drawn into frowns as their stiff bodies marched in time with Mrs. Jacob's calls. *Two-year olds don't march.*

"I shall return momentarily," Louisa called over her shoulder as she hurried toward the twins. When she neared, they looked at her and slowed their pace. When their eyes rested on the kitten in her arms, they stopped and turned toward Louisa. She smiled. "Would you like to pet him?"

She crouched as they ran up to her. Grins lit up their cherubic faces, and the sun glinted off their golden hair, almost giving it a strawberry tint. Adorable children.

"What is the meaning of this?"

Inwardly, Louisa groaned. How did she forget about Mrs. Jacobs? She met the old nurse's glare and smiled politely. "I'm letting the twins pet the kitten."

"How dare you interrupt us? Could you not see we were marching?"

"Indeed, I did see it, but I thought you were playing a game."

"A game?" Mrs. Jacobs shrieked. "Marching is *not* a game."

Louisa shrugged. "Well, it should be if you ask me, since marching is *not* for children. So I thought the twins would enjoy petting a kitten instead."

"Oh." The older woman huffed. "You dare to go against my activities for the children?"

Louisa tilted her head. "Actually, that thought did not cross my mind, but now that it has, I must say how appalled I am that you are making these children *march*."

Red blotches colored the woman's face as she opened and closed her mouth as if trying to catch flies. "I am their nurse, not *you*."

"That you are, but I would think you could find something better for them to do besides *march*. They are only two years old, for heaven's sake. They are not in training for His Majesty's Forces."

Mrs. Jacobs lifted her chin in a challenge. "This is the age to start shaping them to walk like ladies and gentlemen."

Louisa snorted a laugh. "Pray, Mrs. Jacobs, how many ladies have you seen marching down the street in Town? For that matter, how many gentlemen? Although I have only been in this house a little over a week, I cannot say I have seen his lordship march at all."

The twins giggled.

"Oh, this is utter…nonsense." The nurse threw up her hands as she glanced around the yard. "Where is His Grace? He shall know of this at once."

Louisa handed the kitten to Adam before standing. "Splendid idea. We shall wait for him to return from his ride with his brother and Lord Hawthorne, then you can explain why you made his children march—for no reason at all, mind you—when they really wanted to play with a kitten."

Mrs. Jacobs stepped in front of Louisa, with a glare that pierced right through her. "I really do not like you."

Louisa shrugged. "And I do not approve of the way you treat the twins. They are not…" She glanced at the two, trying to think of what she wanted to say. "They're not miniature adults." She threw Mrs. Jacobs a scowl. "They are small children, you imbecile. They should not march all day long and be forced to do things they do not wish to do. They are young and should enjoy life before it gets snatched away."

An ache grew in Louisa's heart, and with it came pressure in her head, making it throb. Tears gathered in her eyes. "Children are not slaves, and should not be treated as such." She stepped closer to the old hag, staring her down. "Know this, Mrs. Jacobs, what you teach these children now will stay with them until they are grown. They need space to play and be free, instead of the toy soldiers you want them to become."

"Forgive me for intruding, but what is going on?"

Trevor's deep voice caught her off guard and she spun around. He didn't appear angry, just curious. She quickly wiped her eyes, but she suspected he already noticed she'd been crying. She curtsied, as did the nurse.

"Well, your lordship," Mrs. Jacobs started, "Miss Louisa and I were just discussing…"

"Papa." Adam stepped closer to Trevor and held up the animal. "See? Kitty."

Trevor's face softened as he knelt to his son's level and petted the cat's fur. He lifted his gaze to Louisa. "It did not sound like you were talking about an animal."

"At first we were, sir," Louisa muttered.

The duke's gaze switched between his son and daughter. "Where did you get the kitten?"

Amanda pointed to Louisa. "Her, Papa."

He looked back at Louisa and she blushed. "If it's all right with you, of course."

He smiled and nodded. "I cannot see a reason why not."

Beside her, Adam and Amanda cheered and jumped up and down. Louisa's grin stretched wide. She also noticed the duke's face brightened a bit more.

"Thank you, Your Grace." Louisa curtsied then turned to her duties in the garden.

"Louisa?"

She stopped and looked at him over her shoulder. "Yes?"

"I would like to have a talk with you. In my study, if you please."

Dread washed over her and she gulped. "Yes, sir."

She dragged herself back to Mrs. Fitzwilliam's side and pulled off her gloves. "His lordship needs to see me."

"I think we may know why..."

Louisa didn't meet the other woman's gaze when the other servant made that comment. Yes, Louisa knew why. She couldn't follow instructions, and she argued with most everyone she worked with. What was wrong with her? Had she been like this before she lost her memory? Perhaps that's why she'd been whipped...for not following orders.

By the time she entered the house and walked to the duke's study, he was waiting inside. She moistened her lips with her tongue then knocked on the open door.

"Come in, Louisa, and close the door behind you."

Chapter Ten

HEART THUMPING OUT of control, Louisa took calculated steps inside, shutting the door closed as she passed. The duke stood leaning against the corner of his desk. She walked up to him and stopped, not daring to meet his eyes. She couldn't for fear she'd crumble.

"Now, would you kindly explain to me what you and Mrs. Jacobs were really discussing?"

Swallowing another hard ball of fear, she nodded. "How much did you hear?"

"I heard enough to tell me how upset you were with the nurse's actions."

Louisa took a deep breath and lifted her eyes to his. Instead of the anger she expected to see, his soft expression let her know her fears had been all for naught. At least for now.

"When I first saw Mrs. Jacobs and the twins, she was having them march up and down the walk—arms and back straight, chin up—like trained soldiers."

His eyes widened, and finally she detected a hint of anger. "They were *marching*?"

She nodded. "Yes, Your Grace. I asked why she was having two-year-olds march in such a way. I could not abide her tactics, mainly because they made no sense to me. Children should not have to act in such a manner, especially when they are so young.

Their nurse treats them as if they are hers to command to do whatever she wants. The twins' eyes were drawn with sadness, and it tugged on my heartstrings."

"Now I want you to tell me," he said, pulling away from the desk to stand in front of her, "why you are so emotional about it?" He lifted his finger to wipe a tear from her cheek.

It was all she could do not to collapse against him and sob. She wished she knew why it bothered her so much. She hiccupped a laugh and shrugged. "I don't know, Your Grace, only that I could feel what those children must be feeling."

"Have you remembered something about your past?"

"No…at least I don't think I have. All I know is how frustrated I became to see Mrs. Jacobs treating your children with such lack of respect." Her voice broke. "They are still babies. They should not be scolded, or slapped, or commanded…" A sob tore from her throat and she covered her face as tears poured down her cheeks. Once again, her heart broke knowing—actually *knowing* what those two had been feeling.

The duke's arms wrapped around her as he brought her against his hard chest. Although she shouldn't, she pressed herself against him and continued to cry. This sense of comfort was foreign, and she knew without a doubt it had been a long time since she'd experienced it.

Her head fit just under his chin, and she hadn't realized he was so tall. Still, she was reluctant to leave his soothing embrace. Slowly, his hands slid up her back to her neck, and when his fingers connected with her skin, he caressed her. The sensation warmed her, yet at the same time hot tingles shot throughout her body.

She lifted her face to look at him. Tender eyes stared at her. Leisurely, his gaze moved over her face in interest, and she nearly melted.

His hands slid further up her neck until his thumbs toyed with her earlobes. The touch was so personal, so stirring, that she wanted to close her eyes and snuggle against him. Her breathing grew deeper. Faster. And by the quick rise and fall of his chest, something was affecting him because his ragged breaths matched hers.

"Louisa," he said so very softly. "I get the impression you had a difficult past, and that is what has brought all of this on."

She licked her dry lips again. "I wish I knew, but... I do feel like my past is one I don't wish to revisit. Sometimes I get feelings—or fears, actually—that seem to come out of nowhere."

When his gaze landed on her mouth, she froze. The color of his eyes turned a different shade of blue—like rain clouds covering the sky. Yet anger was not the emotion he held, not when his face appeared so soft. Not when his mouth parted and his face drew nearer...

Oh dear. He was going to kiss her. And she was going to allow it.

His lips hovered over hers and she closed her eyes, waiting. But within seconds, he pulled back.

On shaky legs she stepped away from him and sat on the edge of the couch. Dare she say anything about it? Had he really meant to kiss her or was that her imagination playing tricks on her? Knowing the way she liked to woolgather, this was probably all her doing.

Breathing slower, she wiped the moisture from her face before looking at him again. His hard expression didn't tell her anything about his thoughts as he stared at the floor. Silence stretched between them, but she couldn't think of anything to say.

"So—" He cleared his throat. "What else has Mrs. Jacobs done to my...the twins that you have witnessed and not approved of?"

She linked her fingers together tight in her lap. "I should not say, Your Grace."

"Why?"

"I—I do not think it's my place to gossip."

"Did you witness this firsthand?"

"Yes."

"Then it's not gossip." He came toward her, stopped, and knelt on one knee in front of her. His eyes were dark again, but not with desire. Far from it, in fact. "Tell me what she did."

"The other night they were hiding from her, and when she found them, she slapped Amanda across the face. I scolded Mrs. Jacobs then."

He took a deep breath and placed his hand over hers. "Thank you for your assistance."

Louisa nodded. "I could not let her treat your children so disrespectfully." She disentangled her fingers to clutch onto his hand. "But please, Your Grace, don't say anything to her on my account. I'm having a rather difficult time making friends in your household, and I fear I have already made Mrs. Jacobs my enemy."

"Not to worry, my dear." He gave her a half smile. "I shall keep an eye on her from now on. The twins should not be treated as such by her or anyone else."

Relief poured through Louisa and she relaxed her shoulders. "No, they should not."

He stood, pulling her hand so she rose with him. "I appreciate your candidness. You may leave now."

She curtsied and walked to the door. As she rested her hand on the doorknob, she looked over her shoulder at him. He was back to leaning against the corner of the desk again, his gaze riveted to hers.

"Before I leave," she said, "I must apologize."

"For what?"

"Destroying your rose bush." She shrugged. "I fear we have discovered yet another talent I do not possess."

He tilted his head back and laughed. The richness of his laughter weakened her legs and she feared she'd soon be mush on the floor. This was a normal feeling she received while around him and she quite enjoyed how it made her heart light.

TREVOR DISMOUNTED AND tied his horse to a post in front of the tavern his brother, Tristan, frequented. Trevor didn't have to ask if his brother was here, it was common knowledge anymore. Since Tristan had returned to the family two years ago, he'd been hiding from the world, but not from his friends at the tavern.

Tristan was only a year younger than Trevor, but twenty-eight was still too old to be acting like a young, foolish man fresh out of school—like Tristan enjoyed displaying quite often. Because Trevor was almost thirty, he took life a little more seriously, and of course being the oldest brother, he felt Tristan needed someone older and wiser who took on more responsibility to assist him in times of peril.

He walked into the dimly lit tavern. Standing just inside the door, he waited for his eyes to adjust to the lighting. Strange how most taverns he'd been inside didn't have windows so were dark no matter what time of the day it was. Six tables with worn chairs filled the dirty room. Two barmaids scurried from one table to the next, carrying drinks for their patrons. The scent of alcohol permeated the air with a nasty stench, and if Trevor didn't hurry and leave, his stomach would protest the stench.

But talking to Tristan was most important. The younger brother had been on his mind since Trevor heard about Lord Hollingsworth's murder.

It was easy to spot Tristan. He sat in the corner with a mug up to his mouth as foam coated his upper lip. When he saw Trevor, he motioned with his hand to come closer.

Trevor neared the table and smirked. "For some reason, I knew I would find you here."

Tristan chuckled. "But of course, my good brother. Do you not know this is my home away from home?"

"Indeed, it is." Trevor sat and leaned his elbows on the table. "How much have you consumed thus far this evening?"

"I am only on my second drink. Why? Would you like me to order you one? I have a close and personal relationship with the barmaids. I'm quite certain they would bring me anything I need."

"Please, do not trouble yourself on my account."

"So why did you decide to grace me with your presence tonight?" Tristan lifted the mug and took another drink.

"I have been worried about you. It has been quite a while since we have talked on a serious level."

Tristan flipped a hand in the air. "If you are going to give me one of your *big-brother* lectures, save it for when I need it. I assure you, my good man, I do not require it tonight."

Trevor shrugged. "As much as I hate to disappoint you, I fear tonight will have to be the night for that talk."

Setting the mug hard on the table, Tristan rolled his eyes. "As you wish." He blew out a frustrated breath. "Say what you came to say and then leave me to sulk in my misery."

Trevor would like to help his brother, but didn't know how. Trey was actually the brother better at knowing how to help Tristan since Trey had relied on spirits a lot before he married Judith. "I just want to know if you have heard about Hollingsworth."

Tristan nodded. "Of course. All of London knows by now. The constable has even graced my doorstep with his presence. He wanted to discover my whereabouts the night the *good lord* was killed." He pushed his fingers through his wheat-tinted hair. "Can you believe people actually think I killed Hollingsworth?"

"Where did they get such an insane notion?" Trevor answered sarcastically.

His brother leaned on the table, closer to Trevor. A day-old beard had grown on Tristan's face, and he scratched his while his gaze narrowed.

"As much as I hated the man, I had plenty of chances to end his life in these past two years. I did not kill the bloke, even if I wanted to."

"And should I be worried about the widow Hollingsworth?"

Tristan snorted a laugh. "Worried? Pray tell, why would you be worried about her?"

"Because she is no longer married to the lout, that's why." Trevor arched a critical eyebrow. "And I worry that my brother might get it in his intoxicated head that he wants to talk to her again."

Letting out a brash laugh, Tristan sat back in his chair, shaking his head. "What a wild imagination you have, dear brother. Can you not remember what she did to me four years ago?"

"I remember. I just pray *you* remember."

"No need to fear. That memory is something I shall never forget again."

"Splendid." Trevor pushed away from the table and stood. "My work here is done." He smiled. "Please, do not be a stranger. You know where I live, and you are welcome to visit any time."

"And—" Tristan waved his hand through the air, motioning toward the room—"you know where I live, as well."

"Have a good evening," Trevor muttered as he walked away.

"I plan on it."

Chapter Eleven

"I WILL COUNT to three, and if you have not come down from there, you will regret it."

Trevor paused on his way to the library. He crinkled his forehead and listened closer, wondering who could be saying that…and why?

He glanced up the hallway then down from whence he came. The female voice echoed through the silence he had requested his servants keep during the morning hours while he worked in his study. So who could be ignoring his wish?

"I mean it. Blast it all, get down. Now." The voice lowered into a grumble. "Spooks, you are the Devil's own animal."

Trevor took soft steps toward the library, hoping not to alert his servant, although he had a sneaky suspicion who disrupted his quiet morning, anyway. *Louisa.* She seemed to disrupt a lot of things in his life lately.

When he reached the door, he stopped and peeked inside. Standing on a stool, Louisa teetered as she reached the top shelf on tiptoes. What was the foolish woman trying to accomplish besides tempting fate and perhaps breaking her neck?

Wearing her maid's black dress and white apron, he realized he'd have to instruct Mrs. Smythe to find her another dress…one that wouldn't fit her body so well. The material stretched across her back and tiny waist, reminding him she was *not* the young girl he'd thought he'd ran over with his carriage, but a woman full grown. From this vantage point, her slender ankles and calves flashed at him.

Louisa growled and stretched farther. The stool tipped and she gasped. Arms failing about as she searched for something to grab hold of. He rushed to her side just as she slipped off. Before she hit the floor, he caught her.

A whoosh of air escaped her throat, and she wrapped her arms around his neck, clinging to him. Closing his eyes, he enjoyed the moment, even if it was only for a few seconds. The scent of roses drifted around her and he held himself back from burying his face in her neck and inhaling deeply.

"Oh, heavens."

She gripped his shoulders and looked at him. Her gaze touched every inch of his face, resting a mite longer on his lips than necessary. How could he look away when she tempted him so? He'd admired her lips yesterday afternoon in his study before almost kissing her. Indeed, he should have had better restraint. She was off limits. Yet, even in his dreams, she tormented him.

Once again, the urge to follow through with what he'd started yesterday became strong. He wouldn't mind feeling her lips rub against his in a passionate kiss. He longed to have her arms wrapped around his neck as she leaned into him, participating fully.

Bringing his thoughts to a screeching halt, he reminded himself of her status in life—a servant. He steeled himself. *I am not my father.*

She inhaled sharply and scrambled out of his arms and curtsied. "Oh, good heavens. My apologies, Your Grace. I—I didn't see you."

He chuckled. "How could you when you were not looking my way?"

Moving another step back, she fidgeted restlessly.

"What I would like to know," he said, pulling his thoughts away from the desire stirring inside of him, "is why you were talking to my books? More importantly, I fear for your frame of mind because you spoke as if you expected an answer."

Her eyes widened then she giggled. "Oh, no. I was not speaking to your books. I was trying to coerce the cat down from the shelf." She pointed to the bookcase. "Spooks did not want to come down, so I was convincing him otherwise."

"Spooks?"

"Yes, sir. He's the cat I gave the twins yesterday."

Trevor nodded. "And what is he doing in my library?"

She shrugged. "He's either trying to further his education by reading, or he's hiding from me."

He chuckled again. Louisa certainly had a quick wit. Lately, he found himself laughing more than he had before when she was around. He also realized he'd begun to desire a woman. Gwen had somehow taken that ability away from him since he married her, but slowly, Louisa was bringing it back.

He glanced to the top shelf. "It appears as if your attempts of coercing him down have failed. I suppose I should try."

"Oh, no, Your Grace. Let me do that."

He ran his gaze over her petite frame. "You, my dear, do not have arms long enough." Trevor's gaze slid playfully toward the stool. "Obviously."

Carefully, he climbed on the stool and peeked on the top shelf. Spooks curled in a ball and slept like a baby, which made it easier to slip his hand under the animal and carry him down. Once Trevor's feet were firmly on the floor, he handed the bundle to Louisa.

"Honestly, Louisa, I don't know why you thought this animal belonged to the Devil. I had no problem with him."

Grinning, she shook her head. "Then Spooks must appreciate your gentle hand more than mine."

Without thinking, he cupped her fingers and caressed them. "Actually, your hands are considerably softer." He winked. "I think the cat didn't like the names you called him."

She laughed. "Perhaps. I don't know what I would have done

if you had not happened by. I would probably be chasing that animal all afternoon."

How he wanted to lift her fingers to his lips and rub her softness against him. The urge to take her in his arms became overpowering, and he knew she'd somehow enchanted him. Her smoldering eyes nearly had him on his knees begging for her affection.

Heavens, what's wrong with me? He wasn't desperate like Lord Hawthorne. So why did Trevor feel he must have Louisa?

He released her hand and stepped back. Being this close wasn't wise or healthy. Hooking his hands behind his back, he wished he'd stop thinking about her in such a personal way. Yet it was such a pleasant change to have his thoughts wander in her direction, which always made him smile.

"So what does Mrs. Smythe have you doing today?" he quickly asked.

"I'm tidying up in the rooms." She took the feather duster out of her apron pocket. "Until she finds me something else to do, this is what will keep me busy."

"Seems like an easy enough task."

"I certainly hope so, Your Grace. I would hate to think I mucked up another position."

"Rest assured, Louisa, Mrs. Smythe will find the right fit for you."

She shrugged as her hand petted the sleeping kitten in her arms. "The housekeeper will not allow me into the kitchen. Neither will Francois. And Mrs. Fitzwilliam refuses to give me anymore rose clippers." Louisa took a deep breath. "I fear at this rate, Mrs. Smythe will run out of things for me to do before too long."

He leaned back on his heels and crossed his arms. "Do you remember anything about your past?"

"Well, I have had a few visions. I believe I had worked for a wealthy family before. The other day when I looked into your ballroom, I saw one in my mind. It was crowded with people, and there was a little girl who wanted to dance, so her father picked her up in his arms and swung her around. And then, of course, I remembered the things I did in the kitchen about the footman and the butler." She smiled. "I also believe this family I worked for might have taught me French."

He arched an eyebrow. "You speak the language?"

"Yes. When Francois made a rude comment to me the other day, I replied back in French. It surprised everyone in the kitchen, especially me."

Trevor couldn't stop watching the way her hand moved across the animal's fur in soft strokes. And for the life of him, he wanted to feel her tender touch. "That is very interesting." Before he could stop himself, he reached over and petted the animal curled against her. When the tip of his fingers brushed her fingers, fire shot through him. Although he didn't want the incredible feeling to leave, out of propriety, he withdrew.

"Indeed it is, Your Grace."

He cleared his throat—and hopefully his mind as well—and stepped back. "Well, I shall leave you to your duties. What are you going to do about the cat?"

"I need to return Spooks to the nursery… unless you would like to do it."

He blinked, surprised. Why would she think he'd want the chore?

"You could check on the children," she continued innocently.

Their eyes locked and Trevor stilled. Those huge, round green eyes peered straight through him—right into his soul. Did she know? Could she actually *see* his insecurities regarding the children? *Impossible.* Yet, there was something all too intuitive—worldly—in her arresting gaze. This woman was a mystery, and not just in regard to her memory. No, something innate drew him to her. Something carnal and deep. It would behoove him to be wary.

"I would not wish Mrs. Smythe to think I'm shirking my duties." She smiled and gently dropped the kitten into his arms.

Grudgingly he took the animal. "Would you do this for me, please?"

Staring into her lustrous eyes, he knew he couldn't possibly turn her away. Not with her pleading gaze locked to his. "No, we… um… do not wish Mrs. Smythe to think that about you when, um… it's far from the truth." His heart pounded crazily the longer he looked at her, and he couldn't believe how tongue-tied she made him.

A smile stretched across her mouth and her lovely eyes twinkled. Slowly, she curtsied, holding his stare the whole time. When she turned to continue tidying up the room, it took all of his willpower to pull away and leave.

Strange to think, but she had bewitched him.

He hurried up the stairs toward the nursery. He opened the door to the children's room and walked inside. The twins stopped playing and looked up at him with wide eyes. When their gazes fell to the cat, they cheered and jumped to their feet. His heart melted as they came to him holding out their hands to take the animal. Even Amanda didn't seem frightened of him. How he prayed the children were his and not another man's offspring.

Mrs. Jacobs waddled toward him, smiling. "I see Miss Louisa found the kitten."

"Yes, she did."

The older woman clucked. "I almost wish she hadn't. Having the animal in the nursery distracts the children."

"From what, Mrs. Jacobs?"

"Well…from their studies, of course."

The conversation he'd had with Louisa the other day about the children resurfaced. He frowned. "Considering the twins are only two," he said sternly, "I do not see how a cat is going to distract them from their studies when they should not be studying at all. And if they do, it should only be at limited times during the day."

Mrs. Jacob's narrowed eyes laced with malice, and as she opened her stiff lips to speak when a crash shook the walls. The mysterious boom had come from downstairs. His heart dropped. He darted out of the nursery and down the stairs. Servants filtered from the other rooms to see what had caused the sound.

Then came Mrs. Smythe's shriek. "Louisa!"

Fear lodged in his throat, and he ran faster. Had something terrible happened to her? Yet the closer he came to the library and could hear the housekeeper's irate grumbles, a different fear took over. *What did Louisa do this time?* He almost didn't want to know.

Chapter Twelve

SERVANTS PEERED INTO the doorway of the room where he and Louisa had talked only moments ago, wide eyed with hands over their mouths. Trevor pushed past them to enter. Then halted.

Mrs. Smythe paced the floor, in between the books on the floor and the overturned bookcases, mumbling incoherently as she made wide gestures with her hands. Trevor took in the scene carefully. How had his bookcases—two of them, anyway—fallen over?

"What is wrong with that girl," Mrs. Smythe said to nobody but herself. "I have only so much patience..." She bunched her hands into fists. "There's only so much I can do." She stopped and faced Trevor. The older woman's face crimson with fury. "I've tried, Your Grace, but she is unteachable. I cannot train her. She just..." She motioned her hand toward the mess on the floor. "Obviously, she has no skills at all. I have never seen anything like this in all my years." She breathed deeply, rubbing her forehead.

"Where is Louisa?" he asked.

The housekeeper threw up her hands. "I don't know, Your Grace."

"Your Grace, if I may?" Hobbs moved beside Trevor. "I saw Louisa run out the side door toward the west end." He pointed in the direction.

Trevor inhaled deeply, hoping to calm his ire before he went after the girl. "I shall find her and have a talk with her."

A few of the men lifted the bookcases as the maids scurried around, picking up the books. A slight pound started in Trevor's forehead as he left the house in search of the reckless woman. He tried to convince himself it wasn't her fault...that because her loss of memory she really couldn't be blamed for causing such havoc. Yet he wondered why she hadn't found what she was good at. Obviously, she had worked for a wealthy family. Her vision of the ballroom and the way a meal should be served suggested she had. So then why couldn't she do anything right?

He walked a good distance, wondering if he should have taken his horse. She couldn't have gone too far. Then again, she'd been running, and probably scared of punishment. And rightly so...since she could have destroyed his library. At the same time, she could have hurt herself, and his gut churned with the knowledge. He couldn't bear to see her injured any more than she had been.

When he neared the pond hidden in the grove of trees, her sobbing echoed through the stillness and he slowed his steps. On her knees, she faced the pool of water and rocked back and forth, her arms wrapped around her waist. Locks of hair had fallen from her bun, and dangled around her shoulders and face. Pity tugged at his heart. Poor confused girl.

She sniffed and wiped her hand under her nose. She'd yet to face him. "I cannot help it. Nobody understands." She sniffed again. "What's wrong with me? It's no wonder I was starved half to death, I never do anything right."

Did she know he was so near? Yet she made no indication she was aware of his presence. Taking soft steps, he moved closer. Her rambling didn't make sense. When she saw him, she flinched. Wide, terrified eyes peered up at him, her mouth and shoulders quivering.

"Oh, please forgive me." A fresh batch of tears streamed down her cheeks. "I don't know what's wrong." She sniffed.

"Please don't take away my meals for punishment. I promise I will try harder."

He stopped short. Stunned. Why on earth would she think he wouldn't feed her? Her too-slender frame from when they first met haunted him and horror dawned, sending a wave of nausea through his gut. *Dear God!* He moved toward her. "Louisa, I—"

Still on her knees, she jumped away from him. "Please, don't hurt me. Don't withhold my food. I will do better, Macgregor—" Suddenly she stopped. Her face paled as her arms fell to her sides.

Clearly, she had remembered something. He knelt in front of her and cautiously grasped her shoulders. "Louisa? What do you remember?"

"I—I—" She sucked her bottom lip into her mouth.

"Who is Macgregor?"

Her body shook as the color in her face faded quickly. "I don't know," she whispered. "All I know is he was mean to me. When I didn't do his bidding, he starved me."

Confusion twisted inside Trevor's head, wrenching his heart. He wanted to pull this poor woman into his arms and wash away those vile memories. For certain, she was still disoriented. Had she been hit in the head during the accident in the library?

"It's all right." Ignoring the warnings in his head, he followed his urges and tugged her into his embrace. She wrapped her arms around his middle as hard, wrenching sobs shook her. Her face pressed into his chest and his shirt quickly dampened from her tears.

"Shhh…" He stroked her satin locks flowing down her back. Resting his cheek on top of her head, he closed his eyes. The scent of roses he'd always detected whenever she was around enveloped him. Comforting her felt too nice and brought a little peace to his own troubled life. She'd made him laugh when he thought he'd never do it again. She made him smile and peer at the world from a different angle. More importantly, she made him feel needed—like he'd never felt before.

Without thinking first, he placed a kiss on her head, lingering before pulling away. "Please don't cry." Literally, her sobs were tearing him apart—as was holding her so closely. "I would never punish you in such a way. Never."

Slowly, she shook her head, still against his chest. "Why can I not remember?" she whispered.

He touched his lips to the skin below her hairline. "The doctor said your memory would return in its own time."

She lifted her head, meeting his eyes. "Honestly, I cannot recall this Macgregor. In my mind, all I see is a shadowy figure of a man. A beastly man with a raspy voice. But..." Her mouth quivered again. "I can feel how frightened he made me. I truly believe he's very dangerous."

"I swear to you, Louisa, I will not allow him to come near you." He stroked his thumb across her cheek, removing her tears. "Do you trust me?"

"Yes."

Her gaze dropped to his lips, and suddenly, his mouth turned dry. Long, wet lashes fluttered against her cheeks as she licked her lips. Her green eyes darkened and desire leapt inside him. She slid her hand up his chest slowly. His muscles flexed beneath her fingers. By the time her palm rested on his neck, his heartbeat had quickened considerably. Heaven help him, but her touch was so sweet he wanted more.

"Trevor Worthington, you have such a giving heart. You are the kindest man I know."

It was the first time she'd said his given name, and the words breezed from her mouth like an angel's kiss. He enjoyed the way his name sounded from her musical voice, and he realized he wanted to hear it more often.

He couldn't fight it any longer. Perhaps if he kissed her just this once it would satisfy his craving...it would appease his curiosity so he could put her from his mind—and dreams—once and for all.

"Why," she whispered as her fingers brushed fire into his skin, "are you so wonderful to me?"

How long had it been since a woman's sweet words had stirred such emotion inside him? Her intoxicating eyes melted his resolve, and he wanted to hear more of her words whispered in kindness.

His breathing turned ragged as he slowly brought his mouth down to cover hers, still moist from her tears. He kissed her gently, first the top lip and then the bottom. A sigh escaped her throat as she leaned closer. Cupping her face, he pressed his mouth more firmly against hers until she relaxed. As he continued the kiss, heat seared through him and explosions erupted in his ears.

Letting out a little sigh, she clutched his shirt. He moved a hand down her back, urging her against him more. Finally, he was able to touch her back and waist the way he'd craved earlier when she stood on the stool in his library. As she returned his kisses, he swept both hands over her, stroking her blonde hair, her slim shoulders, strong back, and tiny waist.

It had been too long since he had kissed a woman who responded so quickly. Hesitantly, he withdrew. Happiness filled her expression through her closed eyes and parted grin. Her cheeks were pink, her lips moist and swollen. He loved staring at her this way. But more than that, he loved partaking of her sweet lips and melting kisses and wanted this feeling to last... forever.

Unfortunately, forever was a shorter time span than he'd liked because off in the distance, her name was called.

Dash it. He pulled away. By the dazed look in her eyes, he knew she hadn't heard. "Someone is coming," he said.

She gasped and turned away from him, swiping her hands through her hair frantically. How he wanted her back in his arms.

What they had done should never happen again. Breathing deeply, and slowly, he willed the yearning pain to leave his heart and never return. He stared at the pond, wondering if he should jump in. After all, the cool water would bring him back to reality.

Before the voices reached them, he felt confident enough to walk beside Louisa out of the grove of trees. Mrs. Smythe and another maid came their way. Louisa's frown had returned and she wiped under her eyes, giving the impression that she'd been crying.

"Oh, thank the Lord, His Grace has found you." Mrs. Smythe rushed to Louisa and took her in a hug. "I worried where you had run off to."

Louisa sniffed, keeping her gaze on the ground. "Please forgive me for causing such trouble."

Trevor stepped closer, forcing himself to act like a duke and not a seducer of distraught young women. That was what Hawthorne was good at—not Trevor. "Louisa, I told you not to worry. We know you cannot remember much, but your memory will return in due time."

She lifted glassy eyes to his for a brief moment before looking back at her feet. "I thank you, Your Grace. You are certainly a man with a big heart to forgive so easily."

He met Mrs. Smythe's eyes. "Please let her rest. She's had a difficult morning."

"As you wish, Your Grace."

They walked back to the house, and with each step, he scolded himself. What had he been thinking? Obviously he'd not used his brain, but his lonely heart instead. The sad thing was he couldn't stop thinking about that kiss…about how she sighed his name, and most importantly, how she felt in his arms. Finally, he was able to feel like a desirable man, and heaven help him, he wanted to feel this way all the time!

It didn't matter. This could never happen again. He must see to it that Louisa was trained in something and then sent to another household to live.

Chapter Thirteen

RICHARD MACGREGOR RODE his horse hard. Frustration built inside of him like a festering infectious wound, threatening to kill him within time.

He'd lost money already due to Louisa's absence. He threatened all the children to find her. And every night as they returned to the house and had no information for him, he took out his anger on them, whipping them soundly. Someone had to know something!

Louisa had disappeared into thin air. Literally. There was no trace of her whatsoever. This was *not* acceptable!

Since her disappearance, he'd searched completely through three towns. Any woman he came upon who resembled Louisa, he stopped. None of them were the thin, pretty girl with wavy blonde hair. And as each minute passed without finding her, he became that much angrier.

As he neared the town he was headed for, he slowed his animal just a mite as not to draw attention to himself. Although he furiously searched for Louisa, he couldn't alert the police to his panic. He'd kept himself—and his thieves—away from anyone suspicious. Whenever the police started sniffing around and asking questions, Richard had taken his band of miscreants to another town to set up camp.

He rode slowly through town until he spotted an inn. His

throat was dry and he needed something to moisten his mouth—and alert his mind. Richard stopped his horse, jumped down, and tied him to the post before entering the establishment.

Only a few gents lingered in the smoke-filled room. The scent of alcohol hung thick through the air as Richard made his way toward a table. When the familiar looks from a nearby man caught Richard's attention, he turned and hurried to that table instead. The gent was heavily into his cups already this early afternoon, and Richard realized the scent he'd detected when first entering the inn came from this table alone.

"I should've figured ye'd be in here," Richard snapped as he sat across from the other man.

Percy Featherspoon jumped in his chair and nearly toppled over, but grasped the table to keep himself from falling. His wide, glassy eyes latched on to Richard. After a couple of blinks, the other man nodded.

"Macgregor. What do I owe this hon-nor of your pres-sence?" he slurred.

"I thank ye for recognizin' me considerin' how foxed ye are." Richard drummed his fingers on the table. "But nonetheless, I'm happy to have found ye. I need to talk with ye about an important matter."

Featherspoon straightened in his chair, but still swayed as if the room were spinning. "Whot about?"

Richard rolled his eyes. "What do we usually discuss?"

The other man bobbed his head once. "You want another child."

"Indeed, I do," Richard said softly. "And soon. One of my best has run away, but I'll find her."

Featherspoon's forehead creased. "Your best, you say? Which one?"

"Louisa."

It took only a moment before Percy's eyes widened and color left his face. "Oh, dear. This is *not* good at all."

"Of course it's not, but..." Richard scratched his chin as he studied the lanky man with thinning hair sitting across from him. "Why do *ye* think this isn't good?" He leaned closer. "What do ye know about this chit that ye haven't told me?"

"If memory serves, I think Louisa Hamilton grew up around this area."

A different kind of anger hit Richard, exploding in his head. "Ye *think* she grew up around here? Ye brought Louisa to me in Scotland. Ye told me she was orphaned."

"Uh... well, you see..." Percy ran his long fingers through his receding hair. "I'd only told the girl she was orphaned when in reality, I... um... kidnapped her."

Grumbling a steam of curses, Richard leapt across the table and grabbed the other man's overcoat. "What kind of insipid fop are ye, man? Do ye know what kind of problems could arise now?"

Percy peeled Richard's fingers off his garment. "You don't understand. I did it for my... um, a family member. Several years before I took Miss Hamilton, I was disowned by my family. By taking Louisa, I found a way to get back into their good graces."

Richard righted himself in the chair and scrubbed his face. This couldn't be happening. Macgregor did *not* make mistakes, and he killed those working for him who did.

He jumped to his feet and lifted Percy with him. "Then I suggest ye sober up quickly, because Louisa is missin' and ye are goin' to help me find her."

Percy nodded quickly. "Indeed, I will. I assure you, we'll find her quickly."

LOUISA HAD BEEN woolgathering. Again. Yet what else could she do? All she had to think about was the wonderful, kind, and loving man who had kissed her so passionately.

She'd wished Trevor hadn't asked Mrs. Smythe to give her

some time off because she needed something to keep her mind and hands occupied. If she worked with her hands, then her mind wouldn't relive every minute, every incredible second she had been in Trevor's arms at the pond. He'd kissed her with such gentleness it took her breath away, and when he'd touched her so tenderly…it was all she could do not to swoon.

What would have happened if Mrs. Smythe and Beth hadn't come to find her? Would Trevor have taken things further—and would Louisa had allowed it? Not once did she think about what they were doing as being wrong. In fact, it was the greatest feeling she'd ever experienced. Her body told her no man had kissed her like that before, and for certain no man had touched her in such a way that made her toes curl and her mind float as if on an endless cloud spinning toward paradise. Every time he touched her it had been so sweet and endearing.

All night she had dreamed about Trevor…dreamed of what kind of life she'd have as his wife. Although utterly ridiculous, she needed to dream—to feel alive.

In the morning, confusion settled in her head and she wondered if she'd ever kissed a man before. She seemed to know how. For some reason, her past held this secret, and she didn't know if she wanted answers. It was easier to be oblivious.

Today Mrs. Smythe put her in with the laundry maids. Determined to learn something without messing it up, Louisa listened to instructions and followed their example the best she could. Occasionally she caught herself slipping into a fantasy about Trevor, but before too long, she pulled herself out. She must impress Trevor's household staff. She must not disappoint him again.

Louisa really had to watch herself in the laundry room. Touching Trevor's clothes, she wanted to close her eyes and run the cloth along her cheek, but she refrained—although it was extremely hard to do. She tried to act as if her heartbeat didn't pump out a crazy rhythm every time she touched an article of his clothes, and could practically picture him wearing them.

As she turned to move, she accidentally bumped into the hot stove. Her palm burned and she jerked away from the heat. Through the thick fog still in her mind, a memory formed.

She was a small child around five years of age. She had touched the hot poker from the fireplace and burned her finger. Her father lifted her in his arms and soothed her while her mother spread some kind of ointment on her skin.

Louisa couldn't see faces, but in her heart, tenderness grew from this memory and she realized she must have had a loving childhood. Odd, but her parents weren't dressed in servants' clothes or rags. Instead, they were dressed similar to Trevor and his mother.

Within seconds, the memory faded and another replaced it. She was frightened. Terribly so. A bulky man stood over her with a poker from a fireplace—much different than her earlier memory. This man was angry. Threatening her. "If ye slip up one more time, I won't hesitate to use this."

All at once, a place on her leg began to throb. This man had burned her on purpose before as a form of punishment. Louisa bent as she lifted her skirt and touched the very spot he'd harmed her. She'd noticed the puckered section of skin the other day and wondered about it. Now she knew.

An ache pounded in her head and she squeezed her eyes closed and willed the pain away. Questions swam in her head. Where were her parents—and how did she end up with that terrible man?

Time slipped by quickly since there was a lot of work to be done with the laundry. By the end of the day, Louisa's arms were as heavy as wet rags. Not only was her body exhausted, so was her mind since she hadn't been able to remove those two confusing memories from her head.

Thoughtful Mrs. Smythe had a hot tub of bath water waiting for Louisa in her room. She quickly undressed and then sank in the water, sighing aloud as it relaxed her. Before she became too weak, she washed her hair and piled it on top of her head as she finished scrubbing the rest of her. She laid back and closed her eyes, enjoying the peacefulness.

She pushed aside the bad memories and an image of Trevor surfaced…the library…and being in his comforting arms. Especially the wonderful kiss by the pond. Unfortunately, something else niggled at her mind. Why had she pleaded with him not to withhold her meals as punishment? What had happened in her life to make her say that? And who was Macgregor? She didn't want to think about the shadowy vision she'd had before Trevor had taken her in his arms and comforted her beyond belief, yet the man Macgregor was a mystery that needed to be solved. Although she couldn't picture his face, she knew she feared him. She also knew he was somebody she did not want to remember.

Fear like never before encompassed her, and she wanted to hide away forever. If Trevor hadn't arrived when he did, who knows what might have happened in her frame of mind.

Suddenly, Macgregor's voice rang clear in her head as she remembered the threatening man with the poker in his hands. Gasping, she sat up straight. Chills ran through her body, testifying that the man with the poker was indeed Macgregor.

She quickly climbed out of the tub, dried her body, and threw her night rail on. Taking the brush, she slowly walked to the fireplace to warm herself, dry her hair, and think. Within minutes, footsteps boomed on the floor down the hall, marching up toward her room.

Her heart dropped. *Oh, no. Not again.*

Chapter Fourteen

OUT OF ALL the garments for her to shrink, why did it have to be his favorite shirt?

Trevor marched toward Louisa's room, anger filled him with each step. Yesterday, he'd promised not to blame her for messing up, but this was where he drew the line. Did she even realize how much he'd spent for that shirt?

He hadn't realized it was a size smaller until readying himself for a dinner party tonight. When he pulled the shirt over his head, he knew right away something was amiss. The material hugged his shoulders and chest more than they should. The sleeves were not billowy or long, but snuggling against his arms and ending just below his elbows. He didn't have to ask Mrs. Smythe where she'd put Louisa today. His ruined shirt told him enough.

He reached her bedroom door, stopped, and pounded. "Louisa, I would like to speak with you, if you don't mind," he snapped.

"Uh…" Bare feet padded on the floor. "As you wish, but—"

Trevor didn't wait to hear the rest of her thoughts before he swung open the door and stepped inside. "Do you realize what you have done—"

Near the fireplace, wrapped in a night rail as damp hair hung down her shoulders and arms, stood Louisa. She took his breath away. Oh good heavens… Why hadn't he waited for her answer?

Gazing at her made it hard to breathe, and if his throat kept tightening, he wouldn't be able to swallow, either.

She stood clutching a towel to her bosom with wide eyes. Her mouth parted as if she wanted to speak, but only quick breaths escaped.

Inwardly, he groaned. "Forgive me, Louisa. I should have waited for you—"

She gasped and pointed to his shirt. "Did I do that?"

It took him only a moment to realize what she was referring to—the very reason he came here in the first place but seemingly forgotten about. Before he could respond, she hurried to him and clutched his arm. Tears swam in her eyes.

"Forgive me, Your Grace. I honestly thought I had followed directions in the laundry room." She sniffed and wiped away a stray tear. "But I fear I have no skills at all."

Trevor released a heavy sigh and silently cursed his temper. He'd made her cry again. "Louisa, forgive me. I shouldn't have—"

"Indeed, you have every right." She threaded her fingers through her hair and pushed back the damp strands from her face. "I will leave first thing in the morning to find other employment. Although, at this point, I have no idea what kind of employment to search for." Her voice broke and she bit her trembling, bottom lip.

Shaking his head, he stepped closer to her. "That is utterly ridiculous, Louisa. I'm not sending you away."

She sniffed. "You should. I cannot do anything but destroy things."

"I'm quite certain you can do something, but we haven't found it yet."

"You have so much patience, Your Grace. By the time we discover what it is I can do, you may not have a house left standing." She swept her hand, indicating his attire. "Or any clothes to wear."

Her comment—as serious as she tried to make it—made Trevor grin. "Oh, Louisa. I believe I have just discovered your skill."

She arched an eyebrow. "You have?"

"I enjoy having you around because you make me laugh, which is something I haven't done for a long time."

Her face cracked a smile as she wiped away a stray tear. "You are being very humorous, Your Grace. But there is no possible way I can find work as a jester. It just isn't done in this century."

He laughed again. "No, my sweet. You will not find work as a jester." Sighing heavily, he glanced down at his shirt. "Well, I suppose I should change. I have a dinner party to attend this evening."

"I hope I have not made you late."

"Of course not. Are you not aware that a duke is never late?"

"So true. Out of respect, they cannot serve the food unless the duke—or someone with the highest title—is there."

"You are correct." He tilted his head. "I truly believe now that you have worked at an estate at one time. You know your way around a manor, even if you don't know how to work the different positions."

She nodded. "I think you are correct. In fact, earlier this evening, I did remember something."

Excitement shot through him as he grasped her hands. "Please tell."

"I burned myself on the stove," she said, lifting up her palm, "and I remember being a young girl and burning myself. My parents cared for me. Although in my memory I couldn't see their faces clearly, I could tell they were dressed as you and your mother are. I don't know what might have happened to them to make me live like a vagabond, but I do feel these were indeed my parents."

"So you feel like you were raised in a good home with noble parents?"

"I do."

"Very interesting. I would love to test a few theories on you to see what you know. One I could probably do right now."

"What is it?"

"I would like to see how many dances you know."

Louisa stared wide eyed at him for a brief moment before snorting an unladylike laugh he thought was adorable.

"Me? Dance?" She shook her head. "I think not, Your Grace. Although I don't remember my life, I would certainly know if I have ever danced before."

"Come now." He held out his hand. "Let us see for ourselves, shall we? Have you danced the Scotch Reel? We shall try that out first."

"But…" She acted as if she would say more, but then paused a few moments before shaking her head. "We don't have enough people. We need at least four more dancers."

Trevor grinned. "Very good. You do know about that dance. Can you now show me what you would do if we had that many more people with us?"

Staring at the floor, she stood in silence, then slowly her feet began to move in the right direction. The fancy footwork required would be difficult if one had never attempted this dance, but Louisa moved through the steps perfectly. Every second that passed, her eyes grew rounder and her smile wider.

"Splendid," he praised. "What about the Cotillion?"

She started to shake her head, but soon she took his hand as he led her through the beginning of the dance. Excitement jumped in her eyes as she realized she could dance. His heart also accelerated. For certain, Louisa was no vagabond at all. The happy expression on her face warmed his heart.

"Very good, Louisa. Now there is one more I want to see if you know."

Her head bobbed in a quick nod. "Oh, yes. Let's see what else I remember."

He hesitated with this dance. Although scandalous, the waltz was still played in some ballrooms across England. Napoleon had tried to make this dance socially acceptable, but most of Society was appalled at the closeness of the dance. However, if Louisa had indeed been raised by parents of Quality, she would have known this—either scandalous or not.

And this gave him the perfect excuse to hold her close.

Trevor took her hand in his and placed his other around her waist, slowly pulling her to him. "Do you know the waltz?"

Her buoyancy dulled considerably as a slight tremble took over her smile. But her feet moved with his as he led her around the small bedroom floor. Suddenly, her exuberance changed, and a different expression crossed her face. He'd seen this one before—the most recent was when they were by the pond and right before he'd kissed her.

"I do know this dance," she whispered. "Not many people will dance the waltz."

"Indeed. To some, it's considered scandalous."

"You are correct."

"But you are dancing with me now," he said in a soft voice as his heartbeat knocked crazily against his ribs.

Her gaze flitted between his eyes and his mouth as the color in her eyes darkened. His throat turned dry, and he couldn't swallow even if his life depended on it. The more they danced, the closer he pulled her as if it were natural to want her so near. To make matters worse, she didn't try to stop him like a proper girl would have done.

Together, their footsteps slowed as their gazes collided, and held. Although kissing her the first time had been a mistake, kissing her twice would be a death wish. It wasn't right; propriety tried to reason with him in his head, yet the quick beat of his heart argued.

Her chest moved just as quickly as his did; her ragged breath fanned his face. It wasn't until the front of her body touched his when he realized he'd pulled her that close. Miraculously, though, their feet had stopped.

All he could think about was the sweet, tender kiss they'd shared at the pond. In his ears, the only sound he heard was her fast breath and the crashing of his own heart. He should say something to break this incredible spell, but a part of him didn't want it broken, and that part of him was the one in control right now.

He dropped his mouth to hers in a passionate kiss. Her fingers dug into his shirt, clinging to him as if she was afraid to let him go. Her lips met his demanding ones and responded as if she couldn't get enough. He knew he couldn't.

Pressing her against him harder, his hands wandered over her back, threading through her silky hair, and sliding down all over her gown that clung to her where her hair was dampened. Beneath his fingertips, the welts on her back were pronounced because now she had nothing to hide them but her thin, damp gown.

She's been whipped! The thought jerked him back to reality. Why would a gentle-bred woman have been whipped like a common thief?

He broke the kiss and slowly pulled away, not wanting to make her aware of why he'd stopped. When her eyes fluttered open a blush stole across her cheeks.

"Forgive me, Trevor," she whispered. "Once again, I have lost all my senses when in your arms."

His heart flipped upon hearing his name on her lips—just like what had happened at the pond. "No, it's my fault, dear Louisa. I can't seem to…" He shook his head, stopping himself from admitting his weakness. "I should not have taken advantage—"

"No, don't say that." She brought her fingers to his lips. "I participated fully. You did not take advantage of me at all."

"I see it differently, my dear. I'm probably a good ten years older than you. I should know better."

"You forget, I have my own mind." She shrugged and chuckled. "What I know about it, anyway. But I could have stopped you at any time."

"So you are correct."

"However—" she cleared her throat and stepped back—"I fear I have made you late for your dinner party."

He nodded. "If I hurry, I will not be late, I assure you. Have a pleasant evening." He nearly tripped on his way to the door, hurrying to leave. Cursing his weakness, he silently promised himself he would never do that again. Yet in the back of his mind, he knew he would kiss her if given another chance.

TREVOR STOOD AMONGST a group of men who partook of their brandy and cheroots after leaving the dining room. He smiled and nodded to those around him, but his ears didn't register to what conversation was abuzz at the moment. Instead, he replayed the moments with Louisa. How could he keep himself from thinking of her right now? Not only did he enjoy their kiss, he discovered a little more about the mystery woman.

Indeed, she must have been raised with parents of Quality. How else would she have known those dance steps—and react the way she did to the waltz? Hopefully, she would remember more soon and relieve this burden of doubt he had in his mind before he went insane. Men from Trevor's upbringing did *not* consort with servants in such a way. True, his father may have caused a lot of scandal and brought shame upon the family, but Trevor was not that kind of man—and he was never going to be.

"Your Grace, why are you standing by yourself?" Lord Hawthorne sidled up next to him and faced the glass door overlooking the flower garden in the backyard. "You must be lost in your thoughts, because I cannot see anything outside that could hold your interest for so long."

Trevor smiled at Dominic and lowered his voice. "My good man, you should know me well enough to realize dinner socials like this bore me after a few minutes."

"Indeed, they do." Dominic lifted his goblet of brandy in a salute before swallowing the remainder in the glass.

"How are you faring this evening?" Trevor asked. "I'm surprised to see Trey is not with you."

"Not tonight, no. Trey called off because he wanted to spend some time with his darling wife."

Trevor smiled. "As it should be."

"Indeed, Trey is one fortunate man."

"Agreed." Trevor lifted his glass in a salute and took a quick swallow.

"I hope you don't mind my asking, but"—Dominic leaned closer to make the conversation more private—"how is that lovely servant of yours? I have thought of nothing else since I met Louisa. She had the most enchanting eyes, does she not?"

Trevor rolled his eyes, wishing Nic wasn't such a rake. "Hawthorne, I'm quite certain other things have been on your mind, but Louisa is doing fine. I thank you for asking."

"Has she settled into any position yet?"

"None as of yet, but we will not give up hope."

Hawthorne chuckled and rubbed his chin. "I still believe I have seen her before—or at least someone who resembles her. In fact, let me see if he's still here." Nic stretched his neck as he looked across the crowd of men. "There he is." He waved his hand. "Wellesley, over here, if you please."

Trevor gritted his teeth. He bunched his hands into fists and quickly rested them behind his back to keep from using Nic's face as a punching bag. Trevor had warned Nic not to stick his nose into Louisa's business. But as Trevor watched the other gentleman hurry to Nic's side, unease washed over Trevor. Although Wellesley and the Danvers' deceased daughter were nothing but cousins, the resemblance between this man and Louisa was unsettling.

"Wellesley, my good man, have you been introduced to Trevor Worthington, Fifth Duke of Kenbridge?"

"No, I have not." Wellesley bowed. "A pleasure to make your acquaintance, Your Grace."

Trevor bowed. "Likewise, I'm sure. I do believe I'm acquainted with your uncle and aunt, however I have not spoken with them for quite some time. How are they faring?"

"They are very well, thank you."

"Forgive me for asking," Nic began, "but I cannot recall if you have any cousins, Wellesley."

"Not with the Danvers, I'm afraid."

Trevor released a relieved sigh. Yet, at the same time, he almost wished Louisa had been part of this man's family, just so they'd know who she was.

"They had no children?" Nic inquired again.

"Actually," Wellesley added, "they did have a daughter at one time, but she drowned when she was twelve years of age."

"Indeed?" Trevor asked quickly. "What was her name?"

As much as he didn't want Dominic to keep prodding into this man's life, Trevor did want some answers to the mysterious woman he couldn't keep from wanting to kiss and hold. He must know why this woman confused him so.

Chapter Fifteen

TREVOR WAITED, HOLDING his breath for Wellesley's answer.

"My cousin's name was Bessie. That was the nickname I called her, anyway."

"Her name was Elizabeth?" Hawthorne asked.

"Yes."

Sadness crept upon Trevor as his whole body relaxed. He hadn't realized until now how tense he'd been. "I'm very sorry to hear this, Wellesley. I thought one of my brothers had died a few years back, but thankfully he was found alive." Trevor clapped his hand on Wellesley's shoulder. "I do understand your loss."

"I thank you, Your Grace. I must admit, when I heard about Tristan being alive, a part of me wanted something like that for Bessie. Not only was she my cousin, but we were betrothed at a young age. I had prayed that somewhere—someone would find her alive and bring her back home. However, after six years, I know that can never happen."

"Forgive me for asking," Nic interrupted, "but am I to presume your cousin's body was never found? Is that why you had hoped she would still be alive?"

Wellesley nodded. "You assume correctly, Hawthorne. She was at school when it happened. Her body was never found."

"Perhaps there is still hope—"

"Hawthorne," Trevor barked. "Do not give the man false

hopes. I do know how that feels, as well."

"Quite right, Your Grace." Nic looked at Wellesley. "Forgive me for speaking out of turn."

"Not to worry, my good man." Wellesley smiled. "As I mentioned before, we are all past the stage of hoping. We have come to accept her death."

Before long, Nic and Wellesley started a new topic. However, Trevor couldn't stop thinking about Louisa. A part of him had hoped she would be Wellesley's cousin. That would explain so much. If the girl had been raised by noble parents, Trevor would definitely consider courting her. He already adored her unpredictable sense of humor, and she made him laugh too many times to count. He thoroughly enjoyed being with her and talking and dancing.

He smiled wide. How could he not after what they'd shared in her bedroom? It had been so long since he'd been that comfortable in a woman's presence. He couldn't even remember being that way with his wife. Yet being with Louisa seemed so natural.

So perfect.

Unfortunately, everything was *not* perfect. He was a duke, for goodness' sake, and there were certain rules he had to follow when courting a woman. Servants were not included in those rules.

Dominic's belt of laughter brought Trevor out of his thoughts. Nic and Wellesley were still talking about something mundane, and Trevor needed to be alone with his thoughts.

"Gentlemen, if you will excuse me." Trevor bowed before turning and leaving, heading straight out of the room to find the butler. Leaving posthaste was necessary, since he couldn't possibly be good company with his turbulent thoughts.

Before making his departure, he apologized to the hosts, then hurried out to his awaiting buggy. Just as he reached his vehicle, two gentlemen standing by the stairs broke away and came toward him. Trevor didn't know them personally, but had been introduced years ago—and of course knew them by reputation.

"Hold up there, Kenbridge," the Earl of Langston called out.

Out of politeness, Trevor stopped and waited for Langston and Sir Johnstone to join him on the bottom step. "Good evening," Trevor said and bowed. The other two men returned the gesture.

"I'm glad to have caught you before you left," Langston said. "Johnstone and I were just discussing the sudden and tragic death of Lord Hollingsworth."

Confusion washed over Trevor. "And why did you need to talk to me about it?"

"Because of the rumors."

"What rumors?" Trevor shrugged. "I fear I have not heard anything besides his servant found him dead in the stables."

The other two men traded nervous glances. Sir Johnstone rubbed his chin. "You have not heard about your brother?"

Fear crawled up Trevor's spine. "Which one?" he asked, but pretty much knew the answer already.

"Tristan, of course."

Trevor knew what the men were trying to get out, but he wouldn't give them the satisfaction of gossiping. "What about him?"

"I have heard rumors that the police are suspecting your brother."

"Suspecting my brother? Of what, may I ask?"

Once again, the other two men exchanged glances, but this time their expressions were almost perplexed—as if they thought Trevor was the one who'd gone daft.

"Killing Hollingsworth, of course," Johnstone replied.

Trevor rolled his eyes. "You cannot be serious. Have the police nothing better to do than suspect Tristan of murder?"

"Well, he does have a good motive," Langston said matter-of-factly. "After all, he was in love with Hollingsworth's wife."

"That was about four years ago." Trevor scowled. "Tristan has since recovered from the ordeal. I do understand why my brother would think badly of Hollingsworth—the very man who nearly killed Tristan, mind you—but time heals all wounds, and I assure you, Tristan wants nothing to do with Hollingsworth or his wife." He took a deep breath to try to calm his ire. "I can also assure you my brother had nothing to do with the lord's death. I sincerely hope the police find the culprit soon and put all rumors involving my brother to rest. Has Tristan not been through enough already?"

Before either of the other two men spoke, Trevor gave them a quick bow. "Now if you will excuse me, I was on my way home. Good night."

When he was in the buggy and the door closed, he blew out a frustrated breath. He prayed the police would indeed find the murderer and leave his brother alone! Trevor feared what might happen if the police arrested a Worthington. He was certain his life—and that of his family—would never be the same again.

LOUISA HUMMED AS she worked beside Mrs. Smythe going from room to room dusting and straightening—and anything else the housekeeper deemed important. Although Louisa should be paying attention, her thoughts were filled with memories of last evening. Of dancing with Trevor. Of kissing him to distraction. And especially, enjoying every second.

He didn't apologize for kissing her and holding her so close. And she hoped he had the same kinds of stirring feelings in his chest that she had in hers. She wished he was falling in love with her as she knew she was with him.

Her chipper mood was also due to the fact that she remembered those dances. While he walked through the dance steps, she pictured in her mind when she'd been dancing as a young girl. She couldn't have been more than ten years of age. A boy just a few years older shared the dance, and off in the distance the faint voice of an instructor echoed through the ballroom. Louisa couldn't remember anything about the instructor or the boy who'd been with her, but she did remember learning how to dance. Best of all, she remembered wearing a pretty frock with matching-colored bows in her ringlets. She had *not* been a servant.

Until now.

The unanswered question swimming in her head since she realized she couldn't remember, returned. What circumstances brought her to this point in her life? The more she pondered this question, the more she realized her troubled life may be the very reason she couldn't recall now. Perhaps her past had been so horrid she didn't *want* to remember.

"Louisa, I do believe you have accomplished something this morning without it turning disastrous." Mrs. Smythe beamed.

Louisa chuckled. "It's hard to believe, is it not? But the day is still young, and I do not dare feel confident yet."

The housekeeper patted Louisa's shoulder. "If you tell yourself you will fail, it will happen. But if you switch your thinking around, I'm quite certain positive things will come out of it."

Louisa nodded, not wanting to give the housekeeper any false hope—even though Louisa still wondered if something bad would happen today.

"I would like you to work in the kitchen this afternoon. His Lordship is having a small social this evening, and we need all hands in the kitchen to help."

Louisa gulped down the dread crawling up her throat. "Are you certain? Remember what happened last time I helped the chef?"

Mrs. Smythe shook her head. "You will not be working with the food this time. I have already discussed this with the kitchen staff."

"I thank you, Mrs. Smythe. I will do my best today."

And Louisa meant it, even when she walked into the kitchen and noticed the distrustful glances from the staff. She raised her chin defiantly. Although she might not have a skill, she could definitely be a good helper.

After an hour passed and she hadn't broken a dish or had anyone yell at her, Louisa felt more at ease. By everyone's tone of voice when they spoke to her, they were feeling relieved as well. This gave her more courage and determination to make them like her.

Soon she had completed the tasks assigned to her and was given permission to leave—as long as she returned in two hours to help prepare the actual meal. She agreed and left out the kitchen's back door. Earlier today, the spring weather had been slightly chilly, but now the heat in the kitchen nearly suffocated her, so she welcomed the cooler air as she walked toward the stables.

From the hillside near the stable, she spotted the old biddy, Mrs. Jacobs who stood talking to Mrs. Fitzwilliam. Louisa stopped and scanned the hillside again, but did not see the children. Fear crept over her as panic settled in her stomach. Why weren't the children by their nurse? A movement down the hill caught her attention. Adam and Amanda were skipping in merriment toward the gurgling stream.

Louisa snapped her gaze back to Mrs. Jacobs who was thoroughly engrossed in a conversation with the other servant. Would the children's nurse notice they were so far away?

Louisa feared the worst. If the children moved any closer to the stream they could slip and fall in the water. Their nursemaid was too far away to help.

A memory invaded her mind. She was in her twelfth year, and with another girl a few years older. Louisa had been distraught and ran toward a large body of water. She slipped, and fell in, her heavy cloak, taking her under, until her friend pulled her out.

Louisa's heart twisted. The twins had nobody close by to save them as Louisa had when she was young.

The clip-clop of horse's hooves thudded on the ground, pulling her focus to the animal. One of the stable hands led the large animal out of the stable. Immediately, she knew what she had to do. She ran to the boy and yanked the reins out of his hands.

"I need to borrow the horse. I will return him soon, I assure you."

The lad opened his mouth to reply while shaking his head in denial, but she didn't care. She ripped the reins out of his hands and jumped on the saddled horse astride. Kicking her heels into the animal's belly, she hollered a command, and the horse took off toward the stream.

The children were now near the stream, throwing rocks into the water. Louisa knew they didn't have any idea how much danger they'd be in if they fell into the encompassing water. As she directed the horse toward the twins, she prayed they would be safe until she got there.

TREVOR WALKED OUT of the house, down the steps to the lawn. Louisa's high-pitched voice made him pause. When he noticed her atop his horse—the very animal Trevor had instructed to be saddled and ready for him—annoyance grew inside his chest. But then he noticed where Louisa was heading. Mrs. Jacobs's cry of alarm pulled his attention to her as she lifted her skirt to her ankles and dashed down the hill toward…

He hitched a breath. *Adam and Amanda!*

Cursing, he broke into a run, calling out to the stable boy who stood with his mouth agape. "Bring me another horse. Immediately."

By the time Trevor made it to the stables, the lad had pulled out another horse. Not caring if he rode bareback, Trevor jumped on the horse. Clutching the animal's mane, he urged him toward the stream, his gaze fixed on the children.

Just before Louisa reached the twins, Amanda fell into the

stream. Panic washed over him. The little girl couldn't swim. Flaying her arms, she screamed. Adam cried as he backed away from the turbulent water. Trevor pushed his horse faster, praying he'd reach her in time.

Louisa flew off the horse like a long-winged bird, swooped into the water and grasped Amanda by the waist. The sobbing little girl clung to Louisa as she pulled her out of the stream onto the grassy bank, safely.

Trevor yanked the horse to a stop, but jumped off even before the animal had stilled. Trevor rushed to the shivering girl who still held tightly to Louisa's neck.

"What in the blazes happened here?" His voice rose due to the irritation—and panic—flowing through him right now.

"Trevor, give me your coat." Louisa's voice came out sweetly even though worry lines still etched in her face.

Nodding, he shrugged out of his garment and handed it to her. Carefully, she wrapped little Amanda in the coat.

"There now, Amanda," Louisa said in a reassuring tone. "You are safe."

Louisa's lovely green eyes silently pleaded with Trevor as she held Amanda toward him. Understanding her plea, he took the little girl in his arms. Within seconds, she cuddled against his chest, still crying.

Ever since realizing his wife had deceived him, Trevor had not wanted to give his heart to the twins. But as he listened to Amanda's little cries, the wall of ice he'd built around his heart slowly thawed. This little darling needed his comfort—his protection—like never before. And heaven help him, he *wanted* to give it to her. To both of the children.

Louisa moved to Adam and lifted him in her arms. She stroked his head and cooed softly that everything would be all right. The boy snuggled against her bosom as his sobs subsided. Louisa's gaze met Trevor's and she smiled.

A lump formed in his throat and he could hardly swallow. He motioned her closer. She followed his instruction until he slipped his arm around her and the boy.

"All is well now," Trevor whispered, still meeting Louisa's tender gaze.

"Oh, good heavens." Mrs. Jacobs ran up to them, huffing and out of breath, with Mrs. Fitzwilliam trailing not far behind. "I honestly don't know what happened, Your Grace," the nursemaid said.

"I do." Louisa's expression turned firm as she aimed a harsh look at the obtuse woman. "You were not watching the twins as you should have and they wandered away." She took a deep breath. "I shudder to think what might have happened if I had not seen Adam and Amanda so near the stream."

Stubbornly, the heavy-set woman lifted her chin. "You are incorrect. I was watching them."

"Apparently, not closely enough," Trevor snapped before Louisa could rebut the nurse's explanation. "Mrs. Jacobs, this is not the first time you have slacked in your duties—but it will be the last, I assure you. Pack your things and leave my household immediately. You are no longer in my employ."

"Oh no, Your Grace. I assure you, Miss Louisa is mistaken—"

"Leave now, Mrs. Jacobs. I have made my decision and there is no swaying me."

The older woman gave him a curt nod, turned and marched up the hill toward the manor. Mrs. Fitzwilliam stood, wringing her hands against her middle.

"Is there anything I can do?" she asked.

He nodded toward Mrs. Jacobs. "I would like it very much if you could help her pack so she could leave today."

"As you wish, Your Grace." She turned sharply and hurried after the other woman.

For the first time in a long while, Trevor was quite satisfied with his hasty decision.

"We should get the twins back to the house," Louisa said.

He glanced at the woman still by his side and smiled. Her eyes gleamed, and he couldn't keep his heart from melting.

"Indeed we shall."

The clatter of wheels pulled Trevor's attention away from Louisa. His groomsman and the stable boy rode up in the curricle and stopped. The lad jumped down and collected the horses ridden by Louisa and Trevor.

Trevor grinned at his servants. "Quick thinking, Jenkins." He glanced back at Louisa. "Please return with me back to the manor."

Jenkins helped Louisa inside, still holding Adam, and Trevor tightened his hold on Amanda as he climbed in the vehicle.

"Your Grace," Louisa said after the curricle had lurched into motion. "May I take care of the children until you find another nursemaid? I probably don't have much experience—"

"That's a perfect suggestion." He smiled wide. "Louisa, you have shown more interest in my children and concern for their welfare than Mrs. Jacobs ever did. I think you are well suited for this position, and I would be extremely happy if you would take over immediately."

Louisa's face lit up as her smile widened. Excitement danced in her pretty eyes as she nodded. "Oh, thank you very much. You don't know how happy this makes me."

He wanted to take Louisa in his arms and hold her—and yes, even kiss her. Thankfully, his arms were full or he would have done that very thing.

Glancing down at Amanda he pulled her away just enough to lift her face toward his. "How do you like that arrangement, my little one? Would you and your brother enjoy having Miss Louisa as your playmate?"

The frightened look on Amanda's face disappeared and a bright grin replaced it. "Yes, Papa."

"Me, too," Adam chimed in.

"Splendid. I know the three of you will have a pleasant time together."

Cheering, the children clapped their hands.

Relief swept over Trevor the more he watched Louisa and

the twins. Deep inside his chest, an unknown and confusing sensation grew. He didn't want to ponder over the emotions flowing through him at this moment, but one thing was certain. Louisa's presence had blessed his house immensely. He never wanted this pleasure to end.

Chapter Sixteen

"LOUISA? I NEED to have a moment with you, in my study if you will."

Trevor's voice was so soft, Louisa wasn't sure she'd heard him. But thankfully he knew to be quiet in the dimly lit bedroom while she rocked on the chair, humming a lullaby to help the twins settle down for the night.

She met his gaze across the room. He stood by the door opened just enough for him to peek his head inside. The expression on his face wasn't one of displeasure. Of late, she'd come to expect this. Sighing with relief, she realized she might have actually done something right for once.

Quietly, she stood and tiptoed to the door. "The children have just fallen asleep. I fear they will awake and find me gone."

"Mrs. Smythe will sit with them just long enough for me to speak with you."

Louisa glanced behind Trevor at the housekeeper standing not far behind him. Louisa gave Trevor a smile and walked into the hallway as Mrs. Smythe entered the bedroom, softly closing the door behind her.

For an awkward moment, Louisa stood in front of Trevor as their gazes locked. He shifted from one foot to the other while she scratched her arm. Finally, he turned and strode toward the stairs, occasionally glancing at her over his shoulder.

Not a word was spoken between them until they entered his study and he closed the door. "Your Grace," she broke the silence, "I want to thank you for giving me a chance to be with the twins. They are adorable children and very well behaved."

He grinned and walked to his desk, sitting on the edge. "I have watched you today, and I'm impressed with your remarkable ability to handle them. I don't know why I have never paid attention to the way Mrs. Jacobs cared for them before. I thank you for making me aware of her neglect."

Louisa took a timid step closer, as she folded her arms. Happiness grew in her chest. Had she ever heard so much praise in her past? "Was this what you had wanted to discuss with me?"

"Yes, but not fully. I want to tell you how wonderful I think you are taking care of the children."

He'd talked this way about his children before, and it made her curious. Why did he never want to refer to them as *his* children? They were always just *the children* or he called each one by name. Very odd.

"I thank you, Your Grace."

"I wish for you to call me Trevor when we are alone."

His voice deepened, and her heartbeat took on a different rhythm. Her palms moistened and her throat dried. More than anything she hoped he wanted to kiss her again, yet a part of her knew he shouldn't. After all, she knew his dinner party would start within an hour and so she mustn't do anything to distract him. "As you wish, Trevor."

He cleared his throat and straightened his shoulders. "I actually want to discuss a couple more things with you before my guests start arriving. First, I think you need a different wardrobe."

Confused, she glanced down at her servant's uniform. "Why? What's wrong with this?" She picked at the apron.

"Louisa, my sweet, you are not a mere maid any longer. You are the children's nurse, which means you don't have to wear a uniform."

"But Trevor, I have no other clothes."

"This, I realize. So, with your permission, I would like to have a dressmaker come see you tomorrow so she can make you some frocks."

Excitement budded inside her chest. "Indeed? Oh, Trevor. This is so unexpected. I don't know what to say."

He shrugged. "*Thank you* would suffice."

She moved closer and grasped his hands. "Yes. I thank you so much for your generosity. I honestly don't deserve your kindness."

"Oh, I believe you do." He pulled one of his hands away and caressed her cheek.

Her face burned from his compliment, and she was certain the palm of his hand would feel the heat emanating from her skin. Yet he continued to cup the side of her face, and she couldn't resist snuggling against him. She loved staring into his warm blue eyes, yet doing this would make her want things that were impossible to have.

"Well, thank you again. I will repay you."

He shook his head. "Staying on as the children's nurse is payment enough. They love you, and I… I… um, I think you shall make a very capable nursemaid for them."

Why did she have the feeling he was going to say something else? It was probably because her heart wanted him to have the same affectionate feelings that flowed through her. "I will certainly try my hardest."

"As I know you will." He dropped his hand and moved away.

Disappointment sat heavily in her chest. "What was the other thing you wanted to discuss?"

Trevor sat behind his oak desk and rested his steepled fingers in front of him. "Yesterday when you rescued Amanda, you had taken my horse—"

"Oh, forgive me, Your Grace. When I saw how close the twins were to the stream, I didn't have time to think and at that moment, the stable boy was bringing out your horse." She shrugged. "I didn't think—just reacted."

He held up his hand for her to quiet. "Yes, I know this. And please, my name is Trevor." He winked. "But if you had let me finish, you would realize I was not reprimanding you for riding my horse."

"You weren't?"

"No. I wanted to ask you if you remember where you learned how to ride like that."

She blinked her wide eyes. "Pardon me?"

"When you mounted my horse and took off, you rode like an accomplished rider. Did you realize this?"

"No."

He nodded. "Of course I didn't think of that until earlier this evening, but most servants don't know how to ride that way. And most women do not ride astride. I could tell you were a very accomplished rider."

She chuckled and moved to the cushioned sofa near his desk and sat. "Once again, this is something I did out of reaction. I must have known how to ride in order to do it, but I fear I cannot remember."

"I honestly believe that you came from a family of Quality." He leaned his elbows on the desk, dropping his hands palms down. "But the question remains, why would a girl who came from such a family end up on the streets half starved, and... whipped?"

"These are questions I would love to have answered. If only the cloud covering my memory would leave. But the more I try to delve into my past, the more my head pounds with confusion."

"Have you recalled anything yet?"

"Yes. When I saw the twins by the stream, I remembered falling into a deep pond when I was younger, and my cloak pulling me down until I was submerged in water. I couldn't breathe. Another girl who was slightly older than I, was the one who pulled me out."

"Interesting." He scratched his chin. "Do you recall where you were and who the girl was?"

She shook her head. "It was a quick memory, but I remember feeling very distraught. And although I can't see the girl clearly, I think she was a good friend and not a sibling."

"Have you remembered anything more—before that?"

"Not since we danced."

"Are you talking about the memory you had of burning yourself?"

"Well that—and recalling being taught to dance when I was in my tenth year."

His eyebrows rose. "Indeed? What did you remember?"

"I was with a boy older than me and we were both being instructed on how to dance. We were in a grand ballroom, much like yours." She frowned. "But that's all I remember; not any more about the instructor or even the boy who was with me. Although…" She chewed on her bottom lip. "I know I wore a pretty pink frock and had bows woven through my ringlets."

"How extraordinary." Trevor stood, walked around the desk and sat beside her. He took her hands in his. "Slowly your memory is returning. And, the more you remember, the more I feel you were never a servant. That is the very reason you have not been able to do the duties assigned you."

She nodded vigorously. "Those are the thoughts I have had as well. Although"—she lost her smile again—"I don't want to get my hopes high only to discover all of this was a dream."

"No, Louisa dear, I don't believe this is a dream." He squeezed her hands. "If you don't mind, I will ask around to see if anything tragic happened in the past several years, like a family dying or a daughter being taken from her family."

Sighing she smiled. "Thank you, Trevor." She pushed her fingers through his hair. "The Lord certainly blessed me when He put me in your path."

He chuckled. "Even though I nearly killed you with my curricle?"

"Yes. Being hit by you was probably the best thing that happened in my life."

He shook his head. "Don't say that until your memory returns. You may end up hating me after all."

"Never. Hate is the furthest emotion from my heart right now."

Silence stretched between them as his gaze smoldered. She sighed. His blue orbs were so captivating. His lazy smile made her heart flip. What she wouldn't give to have him look at her this way all the time, and for it to be right.

"What do you feel right now?" he asked softly.

She sucked in a quick breath as her heart hammered. Dare she tell him? As much as she'd like to confess her feelings, she dared not for fear he wouldn't return them. Yet, studying his expression made her realize he might indeed feel something for her… something stronger than just an employer and his servant.

"Oh, Trevor." She breathed heavily. "I fear that telling you what's in my heart will be no good for I am but a servant and you, my master."

"What if you are not a servant? What if you are an heiress or your father is titled?"

"Trevor, I don't dare dream of such things, especially if discovering the truth will only break my heart. I cannot give my heart away and have it crumpled when my memory returns."

Nodding, he leaned his forehead against hers and closed his eyes. "I understand completely."

An awkward silence grew thick around them, only their ragged, mingled deep breaths were heard. His breath smelled like the wine he usually drank before his evening meal. As she breathed in his masculine scent, she wondered why he didn't pull away from her. Did he want her to make the first move? She couldn't. Being this close was too nice. So wonderful. She didn't want it to end. Ever.

Finally he moved, but instead of pulling away, his arms slipped around her waist as he pulled her closer. At first she thought he just meant to hug her, but soon his lips brushed over her cheek, heading for her mouth.

Although she knew it was wrong, she wanted this. Wanted him.

Before his lips found hers, she turned her face and kissed him first. A moan tore from his throat as his arms tightened around her. He turned the kiss wild, slanting his head and opening his mouth for more. She answered back just as urgent, winding her arms around his neck. Breaths blended, tongues danced, and lips caressed as if they couldn't get enough. She knew she couldn't. She wanted more. So much more.

He pulled her closer, deepening the kiss. Releasing a deep sigh, she weaved her fingers through his thick hair. Soon the kiss softened and became more meaningful. She responded with all the emotion blooming inside of her. Without a doubt, she loved him. But confessing would not be right. Not until they knew about her past.

Finally, Trevor withdrew and gazed tenderly into her eyes. A heart-warming smile graced his beautiful mouth. A pleasurable moan escaped her lips.

He drew his fingers over her cheek. "I should ask forgiveness, but—"

"None is needed."

He placed a small kiss on her mouth. "I can't stop myself, Louisa. Heaven knows I should, but I cannot."

"Why do you think you should?"

"I'm much older than you—probably a good ten years."

She shook her head. "That's not a problem at all. I'm an adult and you are an adult. I have seen women my age marry older men all the time."

"So true." He chuckled and pulled away. "Unfortunately, if you don't return to the nursery soon, Mrs. Smythe will wonder what is happening between us."

Louisa nodded. "That, she will. And if you stay with me on the sofa like this, your guests are going to see wrinkles in your clothes and wonder why."

He stroked her cheek. "I promise we shall discover your past.

I cannot wait to make this right."

"I hope you are correct, Trevor."

"I am."

Chapter Seventeen

"Good day, Your Grace."

Trevor nodded to his mother's butler as he entered the dowager house the next morning. "It is a fine day, Bentley. By chance, is my mother up for company?"

The old servant smiled wide. "She is always up for your company, my lord."

"Splendid. I shall wait for her in the sitting room. Please have Cook prepare us some tea and biscuits."

"As you wish." The servant bowed, turned, and went on his way.

Trevor walked into the sitting room. Sunlight spilled through the open drapes, bringing light into the sparkling room. This had always been his mother's favorite place to visit with guests, and to read. Even when his father was alive, especially when his father was alive. Most of Trevor's childhood memories were of his father holed in his chambers, sleeping off his drunken spree from the night before. While Trevor's father slept, his mother was a cheerful, fun and energetic woman. When the old lord of Kenbridge was awake, his mother turned into a timid mouse, afraid to speak loudly or to be noticed.

God may look down on Trevor for feeling this way, but the Worthingtons became a better family once the Duke of Kenbridge met his Maker. The old man couldn't do anything right, and he for certain didn't make an exemplary duke. Then again, Trevor wondered if he was messing up his life as well having feelings for a woman who might not be of noble birth.

He walked to the window and looked out across his mother's gardens—her pride and joy. He might not have turned out as bad as his sire, but Trevor had made one mistake after another. The first one being his marriage to Gwen. Because he'd wanted to be a good son and prove to the *ton* the Worthington name should be respected, Trevor married the woman his parents had chosen for him instead of trying to find love.

Groaning, he rubbed his forehead. Some things in his life he did not wish to remember. This was one of them. Yet, the painful reality always hit him in the face—especially when he had to look at Adam and Amanda every day. He wanted to be their father so badly that he hardened his heart for fear the truth would kill him. If those adorable children turned out to have a different father…

"Trevor, what a pleasant surprise."

He snapped around and smiled as his mother entered the room. "Good day, Mother. You look lovely, as always." He met her halfway and kissed her cheek.

"Always the flatterer." His mother giggled. "Were my eyes deceiving me, or did I see you rubbing your forehead." She lost her smile as she stroked the side of his face. "Do you have a headache, my dear?"

"No, Mother. My mind was lost in yesteryear, I fear."

"Ah," she said with a nod. "Revisiting the past would give anyone a headache."

Chuckling, he led her to the sofa. "So right you are."

"How are my precious grandbabies?" She sat, adjusting her gown around her legs.

"They are extremely well. Especially now."

The dowager arched an eyebrow. "What do you mean by that?"

"Lately, I have discovered their nurse, Mrs. Jacobs, had not been caring for the twins as she should. I let the nurse go and have already replaced her."

"With whom?"

"Do you recall that young woman I nearly killed with my curricle three weeks ago?"

The older woman gasped. "You can't be serious. You are allowing *her* to watch my grandchildren? Why, she's a filthy vagabond."

Trevor rolled his eyes. "Mother, do you honestly believe I would allow someone uneducated tend to the needs of the children?" He shook his head. "Since Louisa has been in my employ, I have noticed many things about her, and I truly think her skills are best used as a nursemaid for Adam and Amanda. They simply adore her, and she's such a loving person."

"Well, if you say she is a good person and capable of caring for the twins, then I trust your opinion." Her hands twisted a white, laced handkerchief.

"Louisa is a good person, Mother."

"Has she remembered anything of her past?"

He shrugged. "A few things, and out of those things, I'm led to believe she was raised with noble parents."

"What things did she remember that made you believe?"

He told her about the dances she knew, and riding like an educated horsewoman. He told his mother how Louisa knew how to speak French, and how there was not one thing in his household that she could do, except care for the twins.

"I do understand." The dowager leaned toward him. "Is she Lord Danver's daughter as I suspected when I first met her?"

"No. I spoke to their nephew, Lord Wellesley not long ago, and he said he did have a cousin, but her name was Elizabeth."

"What happened to her?"

"She drowned."

"How very sad."

"Indeed it is, but I'm still wondering who Louisa's parents could have been. There are so many possibilities I wouldn't know where to start." Sighing, he ran his fingers through his hair. "Her parents could have died, and she could have been sent to an orphanage. Or perhaps she was raised with her grandparents, and they passed on. Or, heaven forbid, she could have been kidnapped."

"Quite right, Trevor. And if it happened a while ago, who knows where she came from."

"My thoughts precisely. I do not dare ask around, mainly because I would not know what to ask—or whom to ask."

"So right. And if our search leads us nowhere, that would be very heartbreaking for her."

"Indeed, it would." He sat back against the cushioned chair. "Mother, if you will, please listen for any—" he hesitated, not really wanting to request this from his mother—"gossip you might hear that would be beneficial to Miss Louisa's circumstances. You know how I loathe gossip, but in this case, we need any help we can find."

"I wholeheartedly agree." The dowager smiled. "Let's pray we find something out very soon."

The butler brought in tea and biscuits and set them on the table.

"Thank you, Bentley."

As his mother poured, the butler laid some invitations on the table. "Your Grace, these came this morning."

"Thank you again, Bentley." She handed Trevor a cup before turning back to the invitations and sorting through them.

"Anything promising?" he asked before sipping his lemon tea.

"A few." She stopped on one and her eyes widened. "Oh, here is one from Lady Freeman. She's having a weekend party at her estate." His mother's forehead creased. "So I wonder why she's inviting me?"

Trevor chuckled. "Is the invitation addressed to only you or is Tristan's name on there?"

She turned over the card then laughed. "Oh, I see now. Yes, Tristan has been invited. I'm certain Lord and Lady Freeman are in hopes of getting their daughter married soon."

"I would think so. The poor girl has been out five seasons already."

"Yes, the poor thing. Even with as many people as she's been introduced to, she still cannot find a husband." She paused for a moment then suddenly gasped and faced Trevor. "Oh, heavens. I think I have a solution to Miss Louisa's dilemma."

"Pray, what could that be?"

"I shall have a weekend party myself, and invite everyone and their families. You, of course, will have to bring her to watch the children. But while she's here, she might see someone who looks familiar or who will spark her memory."

For the first time in quite a while, his mother actually made sense. Louisa would not really mingle with the guests, but she'd be able to watch them. Hopefully someone would make her remember.

"Mother, I do believe you are brilliant."

Her cheeks reddened. "You really think it will work?"

"It's definitely worth a try.

She placed her teacup on the side table. "Oh, I can picture the party now. We shall have the lords playing horseshoe by the pond, and their wives and children will be relaxing on the hillside, sitting on blankets, of course."

Trevor stared at her as she continued to plot out the upcoming event, but all Trevor could think about was Louisa. Was he making the right decision in having her see these people? What if something dreadful happened in her past and that was the reason she couldn't remember? But more importantly, if she had a dark past, would he still want to pursue his feelings for her? After Gwen's betrayal, he wondered if he could trust again.

Gwen had ruined his life, to be sure.

When his mother paused with her planning, he quickly stood. "I must be leaving now. I have other things needing to be done today."

"Of course, my dear." She stood and walked him to the door. "Give my love to the twins."

"I shall." He kissed her cheek then left.

His horse hadn't been brought around, but then he expected this since he had made such a hasty departure. Instead of staying by the front steps and waiting, he chose to walk toward the stables... a place that only held bad memories. As much as he tried to tell himself remembering didn't matter any longer, his clenching chest had other plans.

The closer to the stable he came, the more he tightened his hands into fists. This very stable. Nearly sixteen months ago his life had caved in around him. Nothing had been the same since.

As Trevor stopped in front of the stable, his memories rushed upon him as if he had stepped back in time and everything was happening all over again.

TREVOR SAT IN the nursery, holding Adam. The twins were growing so fast, and Trevor feared he wouldn't get to spend enough time with them once they started walking—which would be very soon. Even now Trevor played with the twins more than most dukes did. Certainly more than his own father had.

Trevor's eleven-month-old son laughed and clapped his hands. His heart swelled with love as it always did when he was around his children. Across from him, Amanda sat on her mother's lap as Gwen cooed to their daughter. Amanda's eyes gleamed while watching her mother. Her cherubic face lit up.

It surprised Trevor to see Gwen showing so much love since she hadn't displayed much affection thus far during their marriage. Then again, most arranged marriages were loveless. Even so, Trevor wanted to find love. He wanted what had been missing in his own parents' marriage.

Gwen's hesitant gaze met his then quickly dropped back to their daughter. She cleared her throat. "I have decided to let Mrs. Tillborne go."

Confused, Trevor shook his head. "Why? She's been a wonderful nursemaid for the children."

Gwen threw him a scowl. "You are not up here as much as I, so you do not see what goes on." She heaved a breath. "Do you not trust me in these matters?"

Trevor held his tongue for fear he'd say something irrational. Then again, his wife was the one who had the quick temper, not him. "I didn't say that, did I?"

"You always act like you do not trust me. I'm fearful of saying anything to you anymore and seeing that judgmental look on your face."

Holding his breath, he rubbed his forehead as it began to pound. This always happened whenever he and his wife discussed anything. "Fine. Hire another nursemaid. As long as she makes you happy."

"Augh." Gwen huffed and placed Amanda on the floor near some toys. "You are impossible!" She stormed out the door as if rabid dogs were nipping at her heels.

Trevor blew out an agitated sigh. He'd prefer playing with the children by himself anyway. After he and Adam joined Amanda on the floor, Trevor forgot about his irritation, and gradually his headache dissipated as well.

Time slipped by when he was with his children. They brought so much joy to his heart and to his life. He couldn't imagine what his daily routine would be without them. Soon their beautiful eyes drooped with fatigue, which meant playtime was over. A few times he'd sat beside their cribs as they slept, content to watch them. Such angelic children. They were such a blessing.

The door opened and Mrs. Tillborne shuffled in. Her eyes red and swollen. Trevor frowned, anger building inside of him. Gwen must have delivered the bad news to her already. Sometimes his wife never thought of other's feelings.

"I suppose it's nap time?" he asked in hushed tones.

She nodded without meeting his eyes.

The nursemaid was a sweet woman and tried her best to please him and Gwen. The pretty young woman was newly married, but barren. She treated the twins like her own, and they adored her.

"Mrs. Tillborne, I want to offer my apologies, and I will gladly give you a reference—"

"Please don't, Your Grace." She held up her hand. "If you say any-

more I fear I'll start crying again." Her voice caught and she nibbled on her bottom lip as tears filled her eyes. After a couple deep breaths, she finally met his gaze. "I know you had nothing to do with this." She gave him a weak, shaky smile. "You are a very kind man who deserves better." She slapped a hand to her mouth.

Confusion of a different kind budded in his chest. Something wasn't right. "Mrs. Tillborne, what are you talking about?"

Shaking her head, she bent and picked up Amanda. "It's not my place to say, Your Grace. Forgive me for overstepping my bounds."

As she carried his daughter to her crib, he lifted Adam in his arms and followed. "I wish you would tell me. Your words are most confusing." He handed Adam to her then stepped back. "Please, Mrs. Tillborne. I promise not to get upset."

A strained chuckle came from her as she set Adam in his crib, then turned and looked at Trevor. "You will get upset, I assure you."

Enough was enough. Her words had him very worried now. "I demand you explain yourself, then."

Shrugging she walked away from the babies who were already half asleep. "I suppose the truth needs to come out, and since your wife has released me from my duties, it's only fair I should say something." She took a deep breath, turned and faced him. "Your wife is not being faithful to you."

Chapter Eighteen

H ER STATEMENT TOOK him by surprise and he stumbled as he strolled near her. "Pardon me?"

"I caught her and another man in the stables last night. Because she knew I had seen, she told me she wasn't satisfied with my work and wanted me to leave." A tear fell from her eye. "Forgive me, Your Grace, for being so blunt, but I felt you needed to know about your wife."

He wanted to laugh from the absurdity of the mere idea of Gwen feeling any kind of passion for a man. Yet, before his thoughts ran off on him, he brought them to a halt. Mayhap that was the very reason Gwen couldn't give him her love—because she loved another. And pray, how long had this been going on behind his back? Gwen's lack of passion had been noticeable since they were married.

Good heavens. It couldn't be…

"What were they doing?" he asked, although a part of him didn't want to know.

"They were lying in the hay wrapped in each other's arms. The lord had already started to undress your wife before I arrived."

Trevor gritted his teeth. "She was with a lord?"

"Yes, Your Grace."

Trevor squared his shoulders and nodded. "Thank you for telling me this. I shall look into the matter posthaste."

She curtsied. "I will pray for you, my lord."

He left the nursery and before he knew it, he'd flown down the stairs and headed for the front door. When his butler passed, Trevor stopped him. *"Where is my wife?"* he snapped.

"My lord, she has gone to visit your mother."

Again? Agony gripped his heart. In the past month, Gwen had visited his mother quite a bit, and he'd never questioned why. He did so now.

"I'll be going there as well." He yanked open the front door and stormed out.

"Your Grace, let me have Levi saddle a horse—"

"No need. I shall do it myself."

With each step, Trevor's heart grew heavier. His head throbbed with tension pounding through his veins, and the doubts and unanswered questions weren't helping to ease his burden. When he stomped into the barn and picked up the saddle, Levi was right there to assist.

"Allow me to do it, Your Grace."

Trevor had been ready to argue, but quickly decided it was best that the stable boy saddle the animal. In Trevor's state of mind, he might forget something that would result in bringing injury to him or the horse.

Once the animal was ready, Trevor jumped on and urged the stallion into a run, guiding him toward his mother's estate. This couldn't be right. This had to be a mistake. Gwen wouldn't bring shame to the family. But if she had been carrying on in secret, what would he do? Sending her far away sounded reasonable, but that wouldn't solve his problem of wanting a happy marriage and lots of children.

Then a thought struck him. The twins. Where they his or some other man's babes? Trevor's head pounded harder, nearly making his vision turn dark. He didn't know what he'd do if those adorable children were not his...

As he rode up to the manor, his mother's groomsman came out to collect the horse. "Your Grace, it's good to see you here."

Trevor nodded and turned to dart up the steps, but quickly stopped. "Tell me"—he aimed his question at the servant—"is my wife here?"

"Yes, milord."

"Does she come here often?"

"That she does."

"Is she here now visiting my mother?"

"Um, she's here, but I haven't seen her with your mother as of yet."

"Where did you see her last?"

"*Walking toward the pond, Your Grace.*"

Trevor took off in a run, toward the pond located in back of the stables. As he passed an open window, his wife's giggles floated through the air. Trevor stopped and looked at the structure. Without hearing each word, he detected a man's voice along with Gwen's.

Instead of barging in on the two, Trevor took quiet steps closer to the window. He couldn't see them so figured they were lying on the hay nearby. He moved to the door and slowly pulled it open, hoping the lovers wouldn't hear him. Good fortune had been on his side because he was able to sneak in until he spotted them. She was with the neighbor who bordered Trevor's mother's lands. Just as he'd suspected—she and Lord Putney were in each other's arms, lying on the hay. Gratefully, their clothes were on.

"I wish we did not have to sneak around like this, my love." Gwen's voice came out clearly.

Trevor fisted his hands by his sides but kept still.

Lord Putney stroked Gwen's cheek. "It's the only way we can be together. I do not look forward to the day our secret is exposed. There are too many judgmental people who would never understand our love."

"I don't care if everyone knows. I love you, George. I cannot live without you."

Pain as sharp as a knife ripped through Trevor's heart. How he'd longed to hear his wife say those words to him. Now he loathed them, and especially the woman who said them.

"Did you fire the nursemaid?"

Gwen nodded. "She shall not be a problem we have to worry about any longer."

"It was my fault, entirely. I should not have come to your home, but I just had to see you." His mouth covered Gwen's for a quick kiss before he pulled away. "More than anything, I want you as my wife and Adam and Amanda as our children."

Bile lurched in Trevor's throat. This could not be happening. He squeezed his eyes closed. Please Lord, tell me they are not Putney's children.

"As do I, my wonderful man."

More smacking of lips and groans were heard, making Trevor open his eyes. This had to stop before he emptied his stomach in a nearby stall.

Taking a deep breath, Trevor prayed for courage as he stepped toward them. "Unfortunately, that will not happen as long as I'm alive."

Gwen and her lover jumped apart. Putney's face paled, but Gwen's did not. By the arch of her brow and lift of her chin, Trevor wondered if she was happy he'd discovered them. Slowly, she rose, casually wiping the pieces of hay from her gown.

"So you know," she said matter-of-factly.

"Indeed. Did you honestly think I would be blind forever?"

She shrugged. "I have been able to keep the truth from you since we were married, so I figured a little longer wouldn't harm anyone."

He glared at her. "How long have you been carrying on with Putney?"

"I have loved him since we were sixteen."

"Why didn't you marry him?" Trevor growled.

"Because my parents didn't think he was wealthy enough. And of course, you had the higher title."

Trevor shook his head, raking his fingers through his hair. "It was all about money?"

"Of course. Most marriages are that way, why should yours be any different?"

He found himself laughing, although humor was the furthest thing from his mind. "Well, my dear wife, I can fix that quickly enough. From this point on, you are cut off from my money. Although—God forbid—you shall remain my wife, you will not get a shilling from me ever again. And I shall tell the stores to seek approval from me before you make any more purchases."

Gasping, she ran to him and beat his chest. Trevor stumbled backward toward a horse.

"Gwen, my darling," Putney called to her as he tried to stop her. "No need to fear. I will buy you anything your heart desires. I shall find a way to make more money."

Trevor shook his head. Putney was a foolish dolt and deserved the pitiful woman. "Putney, you might as well give up. Let her have her tirade. Little good it will do her." He shoved the other man away.

"You cannot do that to me," she continued to yell and pound on Trevor's chest, backing him into the stall more. "I am your wife."

"Oh, so now you want to live up to the title. Sorry, Lady Kenbridge,

it does not work that way. Not in my eyes, anyway."

Growling, she lunged at him and raked her fingernails across his neck. He grasped her hand, keeping the viper from striking again. "Gwen, you have now made your bed in the filthy stables. I hope you enjoy your life." He pushed her away.

She stumbled backward and fell against the horse. Startled, the animal neighed and jumped. Gwen continued downward until landing by the horse's back legs.

When the horse continued to stomp and snort, fear sank inside Trevor. Everything happened so fast he didn't have time to react—and neither did Gwen. The horse kicked her in the head, silencing the angry woman quicker than any words would.

How long Trevor stood staring at his mother's stables, he didn't know, but a flock of geese flying overhead brought him out of his devastating memory. When would he forget the past? Putney had blamed Trevor for not saving Gwen when the horse trampled her to death. Even now he wondered if he hesitated from pulling her away from the horse because of his anger for his wife.

Perhaps he had killed his wife.

He released a pent up breath and continued into the stable. Levi quickly brought his horse around and wished Trevor a good day.

A good day? How long had it been since Trevor truly had had a *good* day?

Gradually, a grin snuck across his face. It didn't matter if Louisa brought disaster into his household on occasion, she'd certainly made his days brighter.

As he prepared to mount, another rider came into the stable. Trevor smiled at his brother, grateful to see him since his brother hid himself most of the day and drank with his friends at night.

"Good afternoon, Tristan," Trevor called out.

Tristan nodded and dismounted. His light brown hair ratted in the back of his head as if he'd been sleeping somewhere. A day's growth of whiskers coated his chin. Trevor wished his brother would take better care of himself.

"What are you about this afternoon?" Tristan asked.

"I have been to see Mother. What have you been doing? Or need I ask?"

Tristan shrugged, acting like he didn't have a care in the world. "I don't think you need to ask."

"Very well then. Can I speak to you about other business?"

Groaning, Tristan ran his fingers through his unkempt hair. "Does it have to be now?"

"I'm here and you are here, so why wait?"

Tristan sighed and folded his arms, leaning back against a wall. "Then I beg you, hurry and say what is on your mind."

Trevor moved toward his brother, stopping in front. "I want to know why the authorities are suspecting you of Lord Hollingsworth's death."

Tristan snorted a laugh. "The authorities suspect many others as well."

"Are you trying to tell me I should not be worried?"

"Not as of yet, I'm not."

Arching an eyebrow, Trevor asked, "Is there any reason to seek a solicitor at this time to represent you?"

"No reason I can think of."

Trevor cupped his brother's shoulder and squeezed. "Forgive me for worrying about you. It comes natural, you know."

Tristan chuckled. "I'm quite certain it does with you being the oldest brother."

"Well, keep your nose clean and far away from the Hollingsworth estate. Then I will not have to worry as much."

Tristan narrowed his gaze and scrubbed his unshaven chin. "I know you better than that, Trevor. What's *really* on your mind?"

"I just told you." Trevor dropped his hand and stepped back.

"No, I can read you, dear brother. You are worried that I am going to try to see Lady Hollingsworth, correct?"

"You cannot be further from the truth."

"Well, in case you are worried, let me assure you, I have no plans of seeing Diana. She is out of my life forever."

Trevor smiled, relief sweeping over him. He didn't want to admit it, but his brother could read him well. "I'm very happy then." He nodded toward the house. "Now go in and get washed up before our mother sees your devilish appearance and has the vapors."

"As you wish." Grinning, Tristan turned and walked out of the barn.

Why Trevor still worried about his brother, he didn't know. But he'd put that problem aside for now. There were other things to think about, and Louisa came first and foremost.

LOUISA FELT LIKE a princess in her new dress as she took the twins on their afternoon walk. Today she gave them a tour of the flower gardens on the estate. Every rosebud, and every carnation was in full bloom, and the beauty of the flowers nearly took her breath away.

Another thing that amazed her was the fact that she could name each flower. Certainly she had not been a gardener before, so how did she know each name and what the flower represented and what months they bloomed? She wanted to believe—as Trevor had—that she came from a family of Quality, but she did not dare. Something in the back of her mind warned her to beware and not tread in that direction.

She tried to teach the twins about the flowers, but soon their attention became distracted and they wanted to chase butterflies. Laughing, she joined them, realizing they were too young to learn about the names of flowers anyway.

One thing led to another, and soon she started tickling them. The twins made a game of it—to hide until she found them, and when she did, she'd tickle. Laughter floated through the air and made her heart light. She didn't know why she couldn't remember her past, but the feeling she had right now told her she wasn't used to laughing or her heart being so filled with love.

Soon the twins turned on her and tried to tickle her. She fell to the ground laughing as they jumped on top. Rolling around like this made her hair fall out of its bun, but she didn't care. She loved being carefree and fun.

Within minutes, another voice was heard laughing with them. She glanced around the glade to find their intruder. When seeing Trevor, happiness burst in her chest. He leaned against a tree, his arms folded, as he watched her and the twins.

"Is this what you do the very day you are given a new dress?"

Oh good heavens. How could she forget such a thing? Quickly, she jumped to her feet and brushed the grass from her dress, noticing a grass stain already. "Forgive me, Your Grace, I wasn't thinking—"

"No need to apologize." He moved away from the tree, coming toward her. "I found it delightful to watch you play with Adam and Amanda." He switched his attention to the twins. "Are you enjoying yourself with Miss Louisa?"

"Yes, Papa," they chimed together.

Trevor motioned his hand toward the grass. "Please continue your game. Do not let me stop you."

She grinned and strode closer to him. "Why don't we continue the game with you, *Papa.*" She glanced at the children. "Does that sound fun?"

The twins cheered and jumped around their father, their cherubic faces red with excitement. Trevor laughed, reached down and tickled them. Louisa loved watching him play with the twins since she'd never seen him do this before. Such a lovely scene with Trevor looking cheerful and enjoying himself.

When the twins pushed him to the ground, Louisa fell to her knees and joined the tickling—Adam, Amanda, and then Trevor. When his gaze met hers, his eyes sparkled.

"Oh, Your Grace. What fun we are having." She sighed and pulled away.

He also sat up. "Indeed we are."

"It does my heart good to see you this way." She glanced at Adam and tousled his hair. "When Adam laughs, he looks just like you."

Trevor's laughing stopped suddenly, and she met his wide eyes. For a moment his expression flashed anger, but then quickly changed to confusion.

"Your Grace? Did I say something wrong?"

Deep in her heart she hoped she hadn't messed up—again. But what else could explain the sudden change in his countenance?

Chapter Nineteen

SHOCK VIBRATED THROUGH Trevor's brain, numbing him for a brief moment. He couldn't possibly have heard Louisa correctly.

"What?" He glanced from her to Adam, then back to Louisa.

"Did… did I say something wrong? Are you feeling well?" She leaned closer and touched his forehead. Her gaze narrowed from worry. "You lost the color in your face."

"You think Adam looks… like me?"

Louisa blinked as confusion wrinkled her forehead and around her eyes. Of course she wouldn't know he doubted her opinion, and at this point, he wasn't about to explain why. Trevor didn't need her pity.

"Of course he does," she said, pulling Adam beside her as she studied his face. "He might not have your hair or eye color, but his nose slopes like yours does—" she ran her finger along the angle of Adam's nose—"and his lips are shaped like yours."

She smiled at Adam, making him giggle, before meeting Trevor's hard stare. He loved watching how tender she was with the twins.

"Not only that," she continued, "but when you both laugh, your eyes twinkle the same way—like stars glimmering in a cloudless night's sky. And…" she scooted closer to Trevor— "when you laugh hard enough, both of you have a cute little dimple right here." She stroked the skin on Trevor's chin where he knew his dimple flashed on occasion.

When she moved her hand away, he slowly lifted his finger to the spot she'd just left. Louisa's touch was so sweet. So warm. He loved the way she touched him. He had since the first day they met.

"In fact," she said, taking Amanda and pulling her closer, "once in a while Amanda's dimple makes its debut, but not as often as Adam's." She smiled wide and stroked the little girl's chin.

Trevor remained silent as he studied the twins. Could Louisa be correct? He'd never thought the children looked anything like him. They took more after their mother. Yet now that Louisa had made him think about the similarities…

Good heavens. Now that Trevor could actually see the boy's features, Adam bore a striking resemblance to Trey when he was a small child.

Realization pounded in Trevor's head, along with the extra flow of blood heading to his brain. The guilt-stricken throb started in his skull and churned his stomach. Could he have been wrong all this time?

Trevor jumped to his feet and stumbled backward, rubbing his temple as guilt knocked so hard he feared it would create another hole in his head.

"Your Grace," Louisa gasped as she lunged for him, still on her knees. "What's wrong?"

"I—I—I need some time to myself to think. Please excuse me." He turned away and hurried up the hill toward the manor, praying Louisa wouldn't come after him and beg for an explanation.

Memories from when the children were born rushed through the cobwebs of his mind, and his headache grew. When the doctor had allowed Trevor into Gwen's room that glorious day he learned he'd become a father of twins, his wife had been propped up against the headboard, holding the most beautiful children he'd ever seen. The image was as clear now as it had been that day. She gazed upon the twins with love in her eyes. His mother chatted happily, cooing over the babes, pointing out how much they looked like Trevor when he was born. Suddenly Gwen's countenance changed and the loving emotion in her eyes disappeared. Trevor remembered wondering why she'd had such a dark, forlorn look on her face as if she'd longed for something she could never have.

Now he knew why. She *had* wanted Adam and Amanda to be Putney's children.

Joy burst in Trevor's chest as he ran into the house and straight for his study. He shoved the doors closed behind him, then hurried to the liquor tray for a glass of brandy to help relieve the pain in his head. Swallowing the amber liquid was hard because of the lump in his throat. Tears burned in his eyes that had nothing to do with the liquor.

He caught his reflection in the mirror and turned to fully gaze at himself. Shame washed over him. Guilt gnawed at his gut like a terminal disease for the way he'd treated *his* children when he doubted their parentage. He'd withdrawn himself from them after their mother had died, when he should have been closer to them, and comforting them for their loss.

Sinking into the nearest chair, he allowed the tears to fall. He'd gone from being the most loving father—to the worst. What kind of deranged father abandons his children in their time of need? Adam and Amanda couldn't possibly have understood what was going on during that time, or why they couldn't see their mother again.

He gulped down the rest of the brandy, nearly scalding his throat. He pushed the sting aside. He deserved the pain—and more for what he did to his wonderful children.

My children!

Taking a deep breath, he wiped his eyes and gazed toward the window. He had to get ahold of his emotions. Soon. He couldn't allow another moment to pass by without holding his beautiful twins and telling them how much their father loved them.

One way or another, he'd make up for the time he'd spent away from them.

PLAYING OUTSIDE WITH the children had worn them out. And worn Louisa out as well.

She escorted the twins toward the house, keeping an eye on the very door Trevor had walked through not more than a half hour ago. He hadn't returned, and her heart ached with worry. What could she have possibly done to anger him this time?

Both Adam and Amanda held her hand as they entered the house. Louisa listened carefully for Trevor's voice, but the closer they strolled to the stairs and she couldn't hear his baritone voice, the lower her hopes sank.

Mrs. Smythe bustled out from one of the rooms, smiling wide as her gaze moved from Louisa to the twins. "Oh, what a lovely picture you make standing together holding hands." She stroked her palm across each of the two-year-olds' heads, making them giggle. "And you, Miss Louisa, I do believe you have found something you are good at."

Chuckling, Louisa nodded. "Indeed, I have. I love caring for these children."

"And it shows." Mrs. Smythe winked, then turned to leave.

"Mrs. Smythe, could I have a moment with you after I put the children down for their nap?"

"Of course, my dear. I shall wait a half hour then come to the nursery."

"I would very much appreciate it." Louisa led the children up the stairs and toward their room, still on the lookout for Trevor— but not seeing him.

Once inside, she helped Amanda off with her dress. The little sweetheart kept yawning, her eyes drooping with fatigue.

"Miss Weesa?"

Louisa grinned at the way the girl said her name. "Yes, my dear."

"You stay fur-evow?"

"For-ever?" Louisa pronounced slower for Amanda. "I certainly hope so. It is my wish, and I pray your father allows me to stay."

She gave the darling girl a hug and tucked her into bed. When she turned to do the same for Adam, he'd fallen asleep on his bed—still clothed. Smiling, Louisa gently removed his shoes and covered him with a blanket before settling herself in the rocking chair between the two beds.

The smile remained on her face for a few minutes as she pondered how wonderful she'd felt since taking on this new responsibility. Indeed, she loved caring for the twins. Her memory hadn't given her any more flashbacks, but she received the feeling that she hadn't been married and had her own family. At least she hoped that was true. Nonetheless, she felt as if she had wanted children of her own, and being the twins' nurse would certainly fill a void in her life.

The creaking of the floor outside the nursery door alerted Louisa of a visitor. The door cracked open and Mrs. Smythe peeked her head inside. Quietly, Louisa left the rocking chair and stepped outside the room, softly closing the door behind her.

"I thank you for meeting with me, Mrs. Smythe." Louisa motioned to the next room—which was hers—before moving in that direction. "Shall we meet in here for a moment? I want our conversation to be private."

"Of course, my dear." The older woman nodded and followed.

As Louisa closed the door behind them, she took a deep breath for courage. What she was about to ask might not be right, but she just had to know.

She turned, faced the housekeeper, and smiled. "Something happened not too long ago with his lordship, and left me quite confused."

As she explained what happened with the children, the housekeeper's happy expression changed. Gradually, worried lines appeared in the older woman's forehead, around her eyes, and especially around her frown.

"So you can see," Louisa continued, "why I'm worried I did—or said—something wrong." She shook her head. "He looked so confused, and amazed at the same time when I pointed out the similarities between him and the twins. Then to leave like that without any explanation." She heaved a breath. "You can probably imagine my worry since I have made so many mistakes since His Grace has taken me in."

Mrs. Smythe's frown deepened as she shook her head. "Oh, that poor man."

"Please," Louisa placed her hand on the other woman's arm. "I must know—for my own state of mind."

"I really should not say. His lordship does not condone gossip."

"This isn't gossip, Mrs. Smythe. Not if it is what you know, and not if it will affect my ability to care for those adorable children."

The housekeeper released a pent-up sigh as she twisted her apron in her fingers. "Lady Kenbridge—the duke's deceased wife—had been carrying on with another man before and especially after she married Lord Kenbridge."

Louisa gasped and slapped her hand over her mouth. *This* she had not expected at all.

"Nobody knew for the longest time," Mrs. Smythe continued, "until the nursemaid caught them. She was let go the next day, but not without saying something to his lordship first." She shook her head. "I don't know what exactly happened, but later that day is when Lady Kenbridge was trampled by a horse and died. Something snapped inside the duke, and he was never the same after that. Before this, he had been the most attentive father any child would want to have, but after the death of his wife, he grew distant. Rarely did he visit the nursery to spend time with those children."

Louisa couldn't believe any of this, not that she thought the housekeeper had made up the story, but because Louisa couldn't understand why any woman would not stay faithful to a man like Trevor. "Oh, this is such a dreadful, heart-wrenching story, Mrs. Smythe. Do you think he suspected the children were not his?"

"Indeed I do," the housekeeper whispered.

"That would explain why he acted so surprised at what I said earlier."

"Yes, that does make sense." Mrs. Smythe smiled. "But you are correct, you know. Those adorable children look a lot like the duke. He has just not been able to see it due to the circumstances surrounding his wife's infidelity."

"I certainly understand that." Louisa rubbed her forehead. "That poor man, indeed. My heart just breaks for what he had to endure."

"As does mine." Mrs. Smythe touched Louisa's forearm. "Now please do not tell anyone of this. That is spreading gossip, which the master abhors."

"I shall not say a word. I thank you for confiding in me." Louisa smiled.

She sneaked back into the nursery and to the rocking chair without disturbing the children. Closing her eyes, she sighed heavily. Poor Trevor. How could any man be expected to tolerate such treatment from his wife? He must have been so confused. So heartbroken. So untrusting. She didn't blame him if he never trusted another woman again.

A pain pierced her chest, and she gasped. Head throbbing with uncertainty, she sat up and looked toward the door. What if... Oh, dear heavens, what if he didn't trust her? What if there was something in her past that could destroy her position here at the estate? Macgregor was certainly someone to be feared, but would he ever harm her now?

Taking deep breaths, she massaged her head, hoping to alleviate the pressure. No matter what happened after she regained her memory, she *must* be honest with Trevor. That was the only way she could keep him and the twins in her life.

But thinking it and doing it sounded impossible. What if she had not been an honest person in her past? Trevor would never forgive her.

Chapter Twenty

TREVOR NOW WALKED with a bounce in his step. Happiness flourished in his chest as he headed for the nursery the next day. Spending time with the children was foremost on his mind. Seeing Louisa came in at a close second.

He didn't know at what point he'd begun to have tender feelings for her, but each day, these feelings expanded, and although he still hesitated to think of the *L* word, he did care for her and couldn't imagine what his life would be like without seeing her on a daily basis. She had opened his eyes to many things since that first day, and it surprised him even now as to how blind he'd been. How foolish. But no more. He now had the courage to become the man he'd always wanted to be.

Trusting.

Loving.

And understanding.

Reaching the nursery, he stopped and smoothed his palms down his waistcoat and adjusted his cravat before softly opening the door. Thankfully, the twins were awake. Louisa sat on the floor in back of Amanda as she brushed *his daughter's*—how he loved thinking this now—hair. All three of them looked up at him, and all three smiled.

"Am I interrupting something?" he asked.

"Of course not, Your Grace. Do not be silly." Louisa tied the ribbon in Amanda's hair and stood. "You are very welcome to come in the nursery any time you please."

"What I would like to do right now," he said, bending and scooping up his children, "is to take my favorite people on a drive with me."

At first, the expressions on Adam and Amanda's face were of fright, but as soon as he settled them in each arm, they grinned and hugged him tight. Tears stung his eyes, but he blinked to keep them away. Now was not the time to become so emotional. In private was when he'd do this, but definitely not in front of Louisa or his children.

He looked at her and winked. "Does that sound pleasing to you?"

"You… you wish me to go riding with you?"

"Of course. You are the children's nursemaid, are you not?"

She chuckled. "Yes, I am."

"Then collect the wraps and I shall summon the carriage."

He set the twins down and they scampered to find their wraps. Louisa stood still, her gaze didn't waver as she looked upon him with a face glowing with happiness. Stepping closer, he dropped his eyes to her parted lips. More than anything he wanted to take her in his arms and kiss her. But since they were in front of the children, he didn't dare show such affection toward a servant.

He cupped the side of her face, and she snuggled against his palm, closing her eyes. The peaceful expression on her face made her look like an angel. How could he resist something so beautiful? So tempting?

Plain and simple, he couldn't.

He dropped his lips to hers, brushing them ever so softly across her mouth. A gasp sprang from her first, then ended with a moan as she wrapped her arms around his middle.

This kiss was as uplifting as their last had been, and he wanted to devour her fully. Fortunately, the giggles of his children stopped him from going any farther. He broke the kiss, but didn't pull away. Instead he rested his forehead against her. Breathing in her rose scent, he was content to stay this way for a moment longer.

"What was that for?" she asked.

"For… for being so wonderful."

She hiccupped a laugh. "No, Your Grace, *you* are the one who is wonderful."

"Trevor—if you please."

She smiled and sighed. "Trevor."

He rubbed his cheek against hers before placing one last kiss on her mouth. "Now, perhaps I should leave so you can ready the children." He stepped closer to the door. "I fear if I stay any longer I will be tempted to hold you longer."

Louisa's cheeks turned an adorable pink. "I shall have them ready very soon."

"Splendid." He winked, turned, and hurried out of the room.

He practically skipped down the stairs, whistling… something he hadn't done in quite a long time. The servants stopped and looked at him with wide eyes and grins. Apparently they noticed his new attitude as well. He chuckled and loved the newfound emotion expanding inside his chest.

Finally, he would feel like he had his very own family.

Ten minutes later, they were all settled in the opened landau and heading toward their destination. Louisa sat across from him by Amanda, and Adam sat next to Trevor. Excitement beamed on the twins' glowing faces. They pointed and laughed at the lovely landscape. It surprised him how much they knew, but when they started naming flowers, it shocked him even more. By the conversation between Louisa and the children, he concluded *she* had taught them. Her eyes danced with happiness as she helped them pronounce the flowers' names.

Green Park was first on Trevor's agenda for this afternoon, mainly so his children could see the animals, pet them, and perhaps get a cup of fresh milk. As a youngster, his mother had taken him here. Never his father, though. Trevor's sire was too busy sleeping off his nocturnal activities.

As Trevor walked through the park beside Louisa, each child held one of their hands. Not many people were out this afternoon, but the few who were gave Trevor judgmental stares—especially when noticing how closely he walked beside Louisa. Anger rose inside him and he wanted to tell them to mind their own business. Even Louisa fidgeted as if uncomfortable, but she said nothing. He didn't want anything to ruin their outing, so he put his anger behind him and continued with their walk.

Louisa helped the children name each animal, then she asked Adam and Amanda what sound each animal made. It amazed him how intelligent the twins were which of course made him puff his chest, proud of his children's accomplishments at such a young age.

After their walk through Green Park, he took them to Bond Street. The streets were much busier, but he brought them here because he wanted to purchase a gift for the children. As much as he wanted to get Louisa something special, he knew that wouldn't be proper... and the gossip circles would stir to life with that tidbit.

The driver stopped the landau and opened the door for Trevor. Once he was out, he turned and helped the children down, then reached a hand for Louisa. As before, her cheeks reddened, and she shyly looked away, but allowed his assistance. Immediately, Adam grasped Trevor's hand and Amanda the other. This time when they walked, Louisa walked a few steps behind. He really wanted her by his side, but knew it was best this way.

As they passed a shop window filled with pastries, Adam pulled away and stopped in front, pressing his nose to the glass. Trevor grinned. He recalled doing this very thing when he was a lad.

Amanda released his hand and stood by her brother, admiring the tarts in the window. "Papa?" she asked. "Peez, have one?"

"Of course, my dear."

He glanced at Louisa to ask if she would like a pastry, but she wasn't looking toward the window. Instead, she focused on something behind him. Instead of the shy smile he'd watched for the past little while, a suspicious frown tugged on her lips.

Just as he turned to see what bothered her, another person bumped into him, making him stumble. "Forgive me for not seeing—" he began to say, but the vagabond didn't stop.

Louisa gasped and jumped in the stranger's path. As the young lad skirted around to avoid her, Louisa's hand slipped in the boy's pocket quick as a flash. The vagabond pushed her shoulder, aiming his glare right at her, opened his mouth to speak, but then stopped. Wide eyes stared at Louisa for a few seconds, before the lad sprinted into a run.

Shock washed over Trevor as he witnessed the scene. Her movement was so quick—so precise—he wondered if he'd actually seen what he had.

Louisa stood still, staring at the object in her hand. Her face void of color.

"What in heaven's name—" he snapped, but then noticed what she held out to him. *My pocket watch?* He dug inside his pocket—the same place he always kept his watch—but it wasn't there. Words choked in his throat. *The thief.*

"Your Grace," Louisa said in a shaky voice. "I could not allow him to steal from you." She handed him the watch.

Still in shock, he shook his head. "How did you know he was stealing from me?"

"I..." She turned her head and stared at the direction the lad had run. "I saw him take your watch, and I knew I had to get it back."

"But, Louisa," Trevor stepped closer. "You took my watch right out of his pocket and he didn't even notice."

She blinked in bewilderment. "I know."

"How..." Trevor shook his head. Her wide eyes and colorless face told him this had been a mystery to her as well.

"Well," he said, expelling his breath, "shall we venture into the shop and get some pastries for our drive home?"

Nodding, she folded her shaking arms. "Yes. That is a splendid idea." She hurried to the twins and held their hands.

Trevor opened the door for the three before entering the shop. His mind whirled with unanswered questions but more with the fear that he *knew* what the answers were all along. By Louisa's quick actions as she retrieved his watch, Trevor now realized what her past had been. The realization left a bitter taste in his mouth that no pastry would be able to remove.

Chapter Twenty-One

RICHARD MACGREGOR SAT behind his desk and tallied—again—the totals for the week. Irritated by the figures on the columns before him, he growled and smacked his fist against the table. His income had depleted greatly since Louisa had left without a trace, and until he could find her and bring her back, his profits would continue to plummet.

None of the children who worked for him had been able to tell him what happened to her. The last thing they knew, she had gone into Mayfair to pickpocket a gent she'd been studying for a while, then never returned. Richard had checked the gaols from here to London, but she hadn't been arrested. If he didn't find her soon, Lord Blankenship would withdraw his offer to pay for Louisa's more *passionate* talents.

Changing her into a prostitute would double Richard's coffers, mayhap even triple them. Louisa had always been a lovely young girl, and as she reached her adult years, she became even lovelier. He had wanted to take her for his lover a few times, but business always came first, and having her remain a virgin would make him a lot of money.

From the outer room the door slammed, and scrambling footsteps rushed in Richard's direction. He stood and moved away from his desk just as David rushed into the room. The lad—in his twelfth year—huffed and puffed as if out of breath.

"I… saw… her."

Richard shook his head. "Let it out, boy. What are ye blubberin' about?"

David took a deep breath and exhaled slowly. He moistened his lips. "I saw Louisa."

Grasping David by the shoulders, Richard peered into the boy's wide eyes. "Ye'd better not be lyin' to me."

"I'm not, sir. I saw her plain as day." He took another deep breath. "She was dressed different, though—like a servant for those uppity lords and ladies."

Aghast, Richard released the boy as if his clothes were on fire. "Are ye certain?"

"Aye—with the Duke of Kenbridge, she was."

"What in the blazes was she doin' with a duke?"

"I dunno, sir, but I suspect she was watching his children."

"His *children?*" Richard shook his head. "She was playin' the part of nursemaid?"

"Aye."

Richard paced the room like a caged tiger, his mind spinning. Why would any lord of the realm want to hire a vagabond to be his servant? Unless… He stopped and stared out the window. Did the lord want her for other reasons—those reasons that happen after dark in a private room between a man and woman?

Anger filled Richard and he clenched his hands. If that were the case, she would not bring a good price from Lord Blankenship. In fact, the older gent might not even be interested in paying so handsomely for the chit.

He spun and faced David. "What did she do when she saw ye? What did she say?"

The lad shook his head. "It was the strangest thing, sir. She stared right at me but acted as if she didn't know who I was."

"Hmm…" Richard scratched his chin. "Very interestin', indeed. Makes me wonder what kind of game she plays with the Duke of Kenbridge. Clearly, she has led the man to believe she is someone else. No lord in his right mind would hire such a person as a servant."

"Aye, sir. I thought the same."

"So give me what you'd picked from the uppity lord." Richard held out his hand, palm up.

David dug through his tattered coat, searching for the item. The longer the lad searched, the more panic filled his expression.

"Well, where is it? Hand it over."

"I… I don't have it, sir." David's voice trembled.

"Ye don't *have* it? Where, pray tell, could it have gone?"

Suddenly the boy's movements stopped and he scowled. "Louisa took it from me."

"What makes ye think that?"

"She jumped in front of me as I was getting away. She surprised me, and I hesitated. Ye knows how quick her hands are. She probably took it right outta my pocket."

Richard rolled his eyes. Aye, his best thief would have done that, and nobody would have felt a thing. "Well, because of yer foolish hesitation, ye will go without food tonight. Now get out of here before I decide to give ye a harsher punishment. Ye disgust me and I don't want to see yer face again tonight."

David's sad eyes filled with tears. "Aye, sir," he muttered before turning and leaving.

Incompetent idiots, all of them.

His skull throbbed with a headache and he walked back to his desk and picked up his flask of ale. The liquor burned as it slid down his throat, which he enjoyed because usually it kept him alert. Most of the time, anyway. And he needed help right now. How could he get that girl back so he could make more money? Never in his life did he think he'd be sitting on top of the world, but Louisa brought many talents with her—which is why he could *not* lose her.

His last meeting with Percy Featherspoon had been an eye-opener, indeed. Richard had learned many things—one being that the man's own niece was blackmailing him—the very same chit Richard used to blackmail Percy with.

Chuckling, Richard lifted the drink to his lips. Poor Featherspoon had it coming both ways. The man was a fool for punishment, to be sure. But threatening Featherspoon to take his niece and make her Richard's mistress was the very thing that kept Percy working for him.

Richard sat in his chair and stared at the amounts he'd added earlier. He shook his head. One way or another, he needed to bring Louisa back. But how? Featherspoon had promised to keep looking for the girl—for his own purposes, of course. Unfortunately, she couldn't be found. But now…

His mind came to a screeching halt. David said she'd been with the Duke of Kenbridge. Although Richard did not know where the gent lived, he was quite certain finding a lord would be easy work. By the end of the week, Richard would have Louisa back in his clutches.

Louisa sat on her bed, staring into the shadowed room. Knees pulled to her chest, she gently rocked back and forth as her mind recalled what happened today in front of the pastry shop. She'd acted on instinct—without thinking of the consequences. All she knew was that Trevor was being robbed and she had to stop it.

When she ran in front of that boy, she didn't question her actions. She didn't think of why she slipped her hand in his coat pocket so quickly and pulled out Trevor's watch.

Now she thought about her actions, and she didn't like them one bit.

I'm a thief. Or at least she *was* a thief.

How else would she know what to do at that precise moment? How else could she have accomplished taking the watch back without the boy even knowing it? And that boy…

Squeezing her eyes closed, she took a deep breath. Louisa only remembered bits and pieces about her past, but when she'd met his stare for that brief second, she *knew* he'd been an acquaintance at one time in her life. She knew it like the sun would rise tomorrow.

And Trevor had suspected as well.

His attitude after that incident had changed drastically. On the drive back to the estate, he hardly said five words to her. Rarely did he even look her way. He focused primarily on the children, but his tone of voice had changed for the worse.

A tear slipped down her cheek as the pain in her chest tightened.

She turned in her bed and slipped under the covers. The single candle on the stand by her bed burned low. She didn't have the strength to lean up and blow it out. Instead, she closed her eyes and tried to remember her past.

Why couldn't she remember? She groaned and slammed her fist into the mattress. What was blocking it from coming forth?

Silently she prayed for help. For a miracle. For *anything* that would help her remember.

On the edge of sleep, the foggy mist in her brain parted and she saw herself sitting in a room on the floor, on a barren bedroll. Other children different ages were with her. She was young— mayhap eleven or twelve. They all wore tattered clothes that hung on their unwashed bodies.

A chill filled Louisa's chest as she remembered the confusion swimming in her head, the loneliness that consumed her, and especially the fear of her dire situation.

From the other room a child screamed as a man's strong voice boomed so loud it shook the walls. She—and the others—tried to cover their ears, but to no avail. The beatings of the child still echoed through the house like a soulful mourn.

Anger filled Louisa. Why didn't anyone stop this madman? But... she was a little older than the others, so perhaps she should set an example.

Finding courage she didn't think she possessed, she jumped to her feet and ran to the other room. A large, burly man stood with his back to her, his hand raised over his head as he held a whip. On the floor, a boy—perhaps in his sixth or seventh year—lay without a shirt. His bareback marked horribly with bloody wounds.

"Stop this instant," she shouted.

Slowly, the man turned and faced her. Shadows danced across his evil expression, but his bushy eyebrows were dominant, as was his large nose and wart on his cheek. The word— warlock—passed through her mind. Or was this man Satan himself?

The lad lay whimpering, his body shaking uncontrollably. Her heart broke for the helpless child, and she fell beside him, carefully gathering him in her arms.

"Look what you have done," she snapped at the man, meeting his glare head-on.

The man snickered. "When did ye decide to play Mother Hen?"

"When I could not stand hearing his cries any longer."

"This is not yer business."

"Why are you whipping him? What did he do to you?"

The man belched a laugh and his alcoholic breath filled the air. "He did not bring me what I asked for."

"He's new. You cannot blame him for not knowing how to steal. In fact, I shall teach him. But for the love of God, stop beating him!"

He shook his head, his smile widening. "And what if ye cannot teach the fool? What if ye fail?"

"Then..." Panic filled her and she gazed down into the lad's teary eyes. "Then I shall take his punishment."

"No," the boy whispered as more tears fell.

The man grasped her arm and yanked her to her feet. His dark glare pierced right through her. "Ye ready to take on such a challenge?"

"Indeed, I am." She lifted her stubborn chin.

"Ye have a week to train him. That's all."

Nodding, she pulled away from the man and helped the boy off the floor and back to his bedroll. "What is your name?"

"D—D—David," he muttered.

Gasping, Louisa was brought back to the present and jumped out of bed. Her body shook from the recent memory. David. The boy who tried to pick Trevor's pocket was named David. And...

she trained him.

She groaned and covered her face with her hands. Her eyes stung with tears and dread filled her chest. She had been the burly man's best thief. None of the other children could measure up to her. She made Macgregor a lot of money.

Macgregor!

That was the person who'd been whipping David.

Oh, how horrible. She must tell Trevor.

But she couldn't.

She shook her head, arguing with herself. She must tell him what she remembered. She didn't want him to accuse her of lying to him. If he turned her out on the street then she would accept her fate. But she could not lie to the man she had fallen in love with.

Before she could change her mind, she threw on her wrapper, slid her feet into slippers, then hurried out of the room. The evening was late, but she prayed Trevor would still be awake. She didn't dare check his room, so she went to his study to see if by chance he was there.

She knocked quietly on the closed door before slowly pushing it open. A low fire burned in the hearth, but that was the only light in the room—dim as it was. His scent filled the air around her and brought back those memories she had shared with him, kissing him, holding him, and falling in love. She feared all of that would end soon. When he heard what kind of person she'd been, he would toss her out in the street—and rightly so. But hopefully, he'd let her explain first.

Entering the room, she took soft steps, scanning the premises. No sign of Trevor. Yet, the fire still burned, and an empty glass sat on his desk. She moved closer and picked it up, sniffing inside. Brandy. He'd been here not long ago.

From behind, the floor creaked. She jumped and spun around, falling back against the desk. Trevor stood just inside the door holding a full bottle of brandy. Gone was his waistcoat and cravat, and his shirt was opened at the throat. Eyes, wide with surprise, peered her way as his attention moved over her from head to toe.

"Louisa? What in the blazes are you doing up this late at night?"

"I—I need to speak with you."

His gaze narrowed on her, ambling forward with quick strides. "You have been crying." He set the bottle on his desk before cupping her face. "What's amiss?"

Tenderness glowed in his worried eyes, and she tried not to cry from happiness, reminding herself that his attitude would certainly change when she confessed the truth.

She held his warm hands, not wanting them to leave her cheeks, but knowing she couldn't cuddle against them forever. "I remembered something tonight."

He slipped his arm around her and led her to the sofa. "Tell me." Sitting beside her, he took hold of her cold hands.

"Oh, Trevor. I fear what I have to say is very upsetting."

"Yes, I can see it on your face. But please tell me."

Nodding, she swallowed to moisten her throat. "Earlier today when I stopped that thief, I realized I knew him from somewhere, but I couldn't recall exactly where."

Trevor's body stiffened, but thankfully, he didn't pull his hands away.

"Tonight I remembered where I met him."

"Where?" he asked in a whisper.

"Do you remember the name Macgregor?"

"Yes, you had mentioned him once."

"I still don't recall everything I should, but I know he gathered children—orphans—to come work for him. He taught these children to steal from wealthy people."

"Pickpockets?"

"Yes." She swept her tongue across her dry lips before continuing. "The boy who took your watch... his name is David."

"He knew you as well?"

She gave a small nod. "Yes. I was also one of the children who worked for Macgregor."

Slowly, Trevor removed his hand and raked his fingers through his hair. His stubbled jaw tightened. A vein in his neck stood out more than she'd seen it before. Inwardly, she shriveled and died. He was withdrawing from her and she didn't know how to keep it from happening. As much as she wanted to return to the way they'd been this morning, that was now just a memory she would always cherish.

"Trevor," she quickly continued, "when I remembered this, I knew I had to come tell you immediately. I don't want to hold anything back from you."

"I appreciate your honesty."

His words were too clipped. His tone too harsh. The urge to cry was so strong, but she held back the tears even though it physically hurt her body to do so. The past had taught her to expect pain and heartache. She must sit and await her punishment.

"Was that all you remembered?" he asked, closing his eyes as he rubbed his forehead.

"Pretty much. However, I do know that I was Macgregor's best. It was my duty to teach the newcomers. David had been new, and I taught him."

"That certainly explains a lot, Louisa." Trevor blew out a pent-up breath before moving off the settee.

She remained still, giving him time to think. Silently, she prayed for strength—but most of all, she prayed he'd forgive her. She wanted him to understand and not blame her.

He walked to his desk and poured another full glass of brandy. Without saying a word, he tipped the drink to his lips and gulped it down quickly, grimacing after he'd swallowed. He walked to the hearth, leaned his bent arm against the stone, and stared into the smoldering fire. The wood popping as it broke apart was the only sound in the room.

She waited for what seemed like an eternity for him to say something. Anything. And the longer the silence stretched, the more her heart died. She should leave and return to her room, but she didn't dare make a sound. Giving Trevor time to think was the best thing to do right now, even if it meant sitting very still and biting her tongue.

What could he possibly be thinking right now? Not moving, he stared into the fire as if all of his answers were buried somewhere in the ashes and would magically swirl up from the grate and make themselves known.

Although obviously upset, Trevor was still so very handsome. She could stare at him forever but knew she'd never be allowed that chance of touching heaven. Or of having a love so pure, so unconditional, that nothing would ever worry her again… where peace filled her always.

Louisa's eyes drooped and she blinked hard to keep exhaustion from overtaking her to where she couldn't keep them open. Just as she thought all hope was lost of staying awake, Trevor turned and looked at her. She snapped to attention, ready for the final verdict.

Chapter Twenty-Two

A THIEF. AND an accomplished one, at that.

Fog filled Trevor's mind, and try as he might, he couldn't completely unscramble his confusion. He'd gotten to know the loving, kind, and wonderful woman inside. Being a thief shouldn't matter.

Yet it did.

How did she get to that low point in her life? By now, he was convinced her parents were of noble birth. So how could she have turned out with such a vice?

Trevor convinced himself he need not worry. Louisa was living a better life now. She would never return to her past—even when she finally regained her memory. She would want to stay with him and care for his twins.

Expelling his breath, he pushed his fingers through his hair. She sat straight on his sofa and stared at him with wide, frightened eyes.

"Forgive me for being caught up in my thoughts and ignoring you," he said.

Slowly, she shook her head. "No need to apologize. I understand why you are so quiet. With the declaration I made of being a thief, I expected you to come to some conclusion about tossing me out and ending my employment."

"Louisa, I cannot possibly blame you for being a thief. I'm

quite certain you were forced into this kind of life."

A rush of air escaped her mouth and her shoulders sagged.

"What brought you to this circumstance is most confusing," he continued, "and until your memory fully returns, we shall never know why a woman of such quality—as yourself—was brought to a horrid lowly point in your life."

Tears swam in her eyes, but through the sheen, he detected gratitude. "Louisa, we will work past this stumbling block which has been thrown in our path, and we will come out the victors."

"Indeed, we shall," she said with a choked voice.

"Am I correct to assume you have not stolen from me?"

"You are correct. I have never stolen from you."

"I doubt you ever will."

"Rest assured, Your Grace, I would never do such a thing. Why would I bite the hand that feeds me?"

He strolled to the sofa, took her cold hands in his, and helped her stand. A tear slipped down her cheek, and he brushed it with his thumb. "This, I know, my dear. Although you were a thief, you are not any longer. Instead, you are a nursemaid for my children who adore and love you. I can't ask for more."

Nodding, her bottom lip trembled and she smiled. "I shall do my best to make you proud, Your Grace."

He leaned in closer and whispered, "Louisa, please say my name."

"Trevor," she sighed and closed her eyes.

She looked so lovely with a happy expression and tears streaking down her cheeks, and full lips just waiting to be kissed long and hard. How he wanted to do that and nothing else for the rest of his life. Seeing the happiness radiating from her face made his heart heavy with an emotion he was not ready to analyze.

"Thank you," she said again softly, looking at him. "Thank you for believing in me."

"How can I not believe in you, my dear? Since I brought you to my home, you have showed me—and the others—what a wonderful, caring person you really are. Your actions do not lie when they are done selflessly." He brushed away a few more tears.

"No, Trevor. You are the one who is so wonderful... so giving." She lifted a hand and cupped his face. "I love your generous heart. I love your kind spirit. I love..."

His heart skipped a beat, wanting to know—praying to know—if she felt the same. "You love... what?"

She took a deep breath. "God help me, but I cannot stop myself from falling in love with you, Trevor."

Happiness burst in his chest. He wrapped his arms around her, pulling her to him as he captured her mouth with his, which she met with urgency. Love blossomed inside him, and as much as he fought it, he enjoyed the newfound feeling. Not once during his marriage to Gwen had he felt such a glorious emotion that made him want to jump for joy and cheer for everyone to hear.

Still, he didn't dare admit aloud he returned her love—didn't dare hope for fear this new feeling would be snatched away from him like most things in his life that he'd cared for.

Keeping her in his arms, he lowered them to the sofa as he continued to kiss her. He angled them against the cushions more comfortably while he told her with his mouth and hands how he felt. He stroked her back, arms, and neck, knowing if she didn't stop him soon, he might never stop. Yet, as she touched him—so sweet, so loving—he knew she would not be the first one to stop.

Once again, passion was in control. He didn't mind, not really, yet he knew if they continued, he'd certainly want to take things further. He couldn't. She was a mere servant, and until he knew her parentage, he couldn't make love to her no matter how much he wanted to.

As he slowed the kiss, he stroked her hair and neck, then trailed his lips down her slender throat. She arched, making it easier access. Skin so soft and tantalizing was an addiction to his lips.

When he grudgingly pulled away, her eyes flitted open and her stare met his. He hadn't realized until now that he'd pushed her back to where she nearly lay beneath him on the sofa. And how could he forget she was in her nightrail and wrapper?

Smiling, she swiped back the hair that had fallen over his forehead. More than anything, he wanted to gaze into her lovely eyes so full of passion and feel her tender, sweet touch… forever.

"My dearest Louisa, I do believe we should stop for now. Don't you?"

Dazed and breathless, she nodded. "Indeed, I think you are correct."

"I'm very relieved you came to see me tonight. I fear I had been in turmoil since our outing, and I didn't know what to do." He kissed her lips again, but briefly. "You have eased my mind considerably, and I can now sleep peacefully. And happily."

"As can I."

Although he didn't want to move away from the soft comfort of her body cuddled so close to his, he forced himself to stand. She took his hand and lifted herself off the sofa until she stood in front of him.

"Good night, my wonderful, sweet man." She smiled.

"And sleep tight, my lovely lady." He kissed her one last time before walking her to the door. From that point, he watched her leave down the hall, her nightrail and wrapper swishing against her legs. He longed for the time she would regain her memory so he would know exactly how to act around her, and whether or not to fully give her his heart.

LOUISA COULDN'T BELIEVE the good fortune that had fallen at her feet of late. Thankfully, she didn't recall a lot about her past, but her life was finally happy. Complete. If she never regained her memory, she would be satisfied with that, as long as Trevor and the twins were forever in her life.

Perhaps she shouldn't have told him she loved him last night, but she couldn't stop the words from flowing. She did love him, and she'd never experienced such an emotion before—that she knew about, anyway. Yet her heart told her this was the first time.

Today when she played with the children outside, Trevor joined them. Louisa made up silly little games, which made everyone laugh. She noticed that some of the servants stepped out of the house—or from the stables—to watch. Wide smiles stretched across their faces, which lightened Louisa's heart. Acceptance finally filled her soul as it never had before.

She loved the closeness she shared with Trevor, and it made her feel like she finally had a family. Her heart sank a fraction of an inch. She did love Trevor and his children, but would he ever want to marry someone like her? Would he ever want the children to have a mother who had been a thief?

Hopefully, he wouldn't judge her for her past mistakes and love her and *want* her to be in his life as his wife.

After they ate the midday meal and the twins took a nap, Trevor surprised them all by announcing another trip into Town. Today they rode in the landau, but closed the top. This time, Louisa didn't experience the judgmental stares as she had before. Trevor and the children played little games during their drive, and it did her heart glad to see Trevor bonding so closely with the children.

When the vehicle stopped in front of Astley's Amphitheatre, Louisa's heart leapt. The New Royal Circus was in town.

In a flash, a memory sprang forward. She remembered holding her mother's hand as she and an older cousin excitedly chattered about the circus while walking toward the structure. Louisa was probably in her seventh or eighth year, yet the memory was so clear. The steps separating her from the circus were many and her mother practically had to run beside Louisa to keep up the pace. Music played. Children cheered. Merchants sold pastries and other tasty treats for the children.

Louisa drew in a deep breath and placed her hand on Trevor's arm before he exited the landau. When his eyes met hers, she smiled. "I have been here before."

His eyebrows lifted in surprise. "You remember?"

"Yes. I was young. My parents brought me and my older cousin here."

Trevor swung toward her and grasped her gloved hands. "You remember having a cousin?"

She nodded. "I can picture them right now, like it was yesterday." Excitement hammered in her chest and she tightened her fingers with his. "Trevor, I can vision my parents. Papa was dressed in the same fashion as you, and my mother was adorned in a lovely lavender day dress. My cousin was about to enter Eton."

A rush of air escaped his mouth mere moments before he brought her hands to his lips and kissed. "This is a wonderful discovery, Louisa."

"I think so. The more I remember my past, the more I think my parents were indeed of Quality."

"I'm sure they were, my dear."

Trevor climbed down then helped Louisa and the twins. She held on to the twins' hands as they made their way toward the building. Groups of people littered the street and on the stairs. Louisa glanced from one to the other, taking in as many faces as she could, hoping to find some recognition. Instead, everyone looked like a stranger. Were her parents and cousin still alive? Then again, she doubted they were since she had to resort to thieving just to eat. Still, she prayed there was some extended family out there whom she could find.

The closer she came to the building, a strange—almost ee-rie—feeling rushed over her like a dark cloud of doom. Someone watched her, she could *feel* it, but there were too many people for her to see which one could be keeping an eye on her. Perhaps her mind played tricks on her or her memory. Had something bad happened a long time ago when she was here last?

Putting aside the uncomfortable feelings, she followed Trevor inside the building.

MY, MY... WHAT *do we have here?*

A malicious grin tugged on Macgregor's mouth as he watched Louisa scurry inside, holding on to two little children. If David hadn't told Macgregor about the little twit living with Lord Kenbridge, Richard wouldn't have taken a second glance when he saw the lord climbing out of his landau. And Richard certainly wouldn't have studied the nursemaid closely to see if this was his long-lost pupil, either.

Richard chuckled low as he filled his pipe. He slid the end into his mouth, lit it, and inhaled the tobacco. Louisa no longer looked like the little ragamuffin he'd taken under his wing all those years ago, but instead like a real lady—even wearing nice clothes. He didn't know if the woman had been compromised, and to find out, he'd have to study her and the duke a little closer. Richard wouldn't waste his time thinking of another way for the girl to make him money until he knew for certain.

Taking slow steps, he stayed behind a group of noblemen and their wives as they strolled toward the amphitheatre. Merchants tried to sway him into purchasing their wares, but Richard flipped his hand in the air, silently dismissing them. This evening, his mind would be on one thing. He wouldn't rest until he understood what Louisa was doing.

Once inside, he scanned the seats, looking for her. It took him a few minutes with as many people who were in his way, but he finally caught sight of her sitting prim and proper next to the duke and his children. Richard hurried toward them, but kept far enough away so she wouldn't see him. He found a seat that would be perfect while spying. If she kept her gaze on the stage— which he supposed she would, due to the entertainment—she would never know he was here. Watching. Waiting for the right moment to pounce like a tiger on its prey.

The show began, and Louisa's eyes danced nearly as much as the children who sat by her. Richard snickered. Although she had a woman's body, right now she appeared much younger by the way she laughed and clapped. But of course she'd react this way. Her childhood had been snatched away when Featherspoon kidnapped her then sold her.

Richard had never seen her look so happy, but it didn't matter. He needed her back. Now. The children he had working for him didn't bring in as much as Louisa had. Yet, as he watched her with the duke and his children as if they were the most important people in England, Richard understood that getting her back into his fold would be more difficult than he'd planned. She was now a grown woman and had tasted her independence if only for a short time. Naturally, she'd fight him, but he must not allow her to win.

Forcing her was an option, but the little tart was a handful when upset… and upset she would be when he finally brought her back to his house. Things would be different after that. She would not have any ambition to steal for him, even if he threatened to turn her into an older gent's mistress. No, Richard had to think of another means of convincing Louisa to do his bidding. But what?

A cheer rose through the crowd, startling Richard. He glanced at the stage just in time to see the lion tamer pull his head from the lion's mouth—unharmed. Richard switched his attention back to Louisa and the duke's children who were now jumping in their seats, clapping. Louisa hugged each one, her eyes glistening with tenderness. When she looked at the duke, a different expression lit her face. Indeed, the girl was in love. Richard shrugged. Regardless, that would end shortly if he had anything to do with it. And of course, he would have *everything* to do with it when she came back.

Suddenly, an idea jolted through him, almost knocking him from his seat. He hitched a breath as his mind swirled quickly to formulate a plan. Now he knew how to make Miss Hamilton bend to his will. Blackmail. Obviously, she loved those children and the duke. If she wanted to spare their lives, she would obey Richard and jump when he snapped his fingers.

Ease spread through him, relaxing his worry. He would have her in his grasp very soon.

Louisa leaned over and chatted with the duke for a few moments before the gent dropped some coins in her hand. She stood and sauntered toward the back of the building by the merchants.

Excitement grew inside Richard as he quickly followed, pushing people aside so he wouldn't lose her. Finally, he closed in behind her. He shoved a few people out of his way who tossed scowls at him.

Louisa purchased a bag of roasted nuts, and then turned to leave. Richard blocked her path.

"Please forgive me—" she said before her eyes lifted to his.

"Good evenin', my dear Louisa Hamilton. What a pleasure it is to see ye after all this time." He grinned. "Did ye miss me?"

Her eyes widened, and her face paled. The bag of peanuts fell to the ground.

Chapter Twenty-Three

A NUMBING COOLNESS spread through Louisa as if she stood up to her neck in frigid waters. It was disconcerting to feel this way when she knew she wasn't even close to a pond, but in a crowded building where people closed in all around her. All sounds disappeared and all she could hear was the man's voice in front of her. His dark, beady eyes pierced right through to her soul, and havoc trembled in her head. Her mind spun out of control, and she feared if she closed her eyes she would fall to the ground in an unconscious heap.

Loud voices from her past nagged at her, pulling her deeper into the recesses of her memory. She knew this man. Knew how he treated his friends—and especially the children who worked for him. Knew his forms of punishments if he didn't approve of what the children brought in from their daily working routines.

Richard Macgregor!

In a rush, she recalled being with him in a room, begging for him to stop whipping her. On her knees, she'd clutched his overcoat, pleading with him for forgiveness. Again. Just like the several times before.

Horrified, she now remembered that he hadn't listened to her pleas. Instead, he allowed his anger to guide his hand as he brought down the leather whip across her bare back....

A low chuckle came from his throat, bringing her from her

nightmare. "I see ye didn't miss me at all, Louisa. That makes me sad."

Shivers of disgust clawed through her and she wanted to gag. Although she remembered more about her past, there was still quite a bit she didn't know. But from the images that wouldn't leave her mind now, it was no wonder she had hidden them away.

"Macgregor," she whispered.

"In the flesh." He mocked a bow. "And my dear Louisa, ye have come up in the world, I see." His gaze swept over her. "I must admit ye look more like a lady now than ye did before."

Trembling, she nodded. "I—I am no longer a thief."

"Yes, I see that." He motioned his head back toward the stage. "I'm very surprised to see ye with a duke, however." Macgregor leaned in closer. "Does he know about yer past?"

Tears stung Louisa's eyes, but she refused to shed them, even as frightened as this man made her. "Yes, he knows."

He arched a bushy eyebrow. "And he's still keepin' ye on as his servant?"

"Yes."

"Hmm… What a very trustin' fellow, don't ye agree?"

"Indeed, he is."

"And I suppose he's a very generous man."

She nodded as fear grew inside her. By the evil glint in this man's eyes, what he had in store for her was something she would not like. There was no way Macgregor could make her return to his den of thieves, but his mind was plotting. She knew it, yet couldn't stop it.

Swallowing the lump in her throat, she took a deep breath, preparing to move past him. "If you will excuse me, I must get back—"

He blocked her with his arm. "One minute, I beg of ye." The corners of his mouth lifted in an evil sneer. "I suppose ye are enjoyin' yer position in the duke's household and that ye enjoy carin' for his children."

Louisa scowled. "We have no more to discuss, Macgregor. I'm no longer in your employ. I'm a grown woman and have found another home. Please leave me alone." She marched past him, but he grasped her elbow, stopping her once again.

"Before ye leave," he said, his voice nearly growling, "there is one thing I need ye to do for me before I consider ye out of my employ."

"Impossible. I will not do anything for you ever again." She ground out each word all the while fear pumped through her blood. This man was dangerous. Although she couldn't recall everything about him, she did know he was not a man who could be trusted.

"Oh, I think ye will, Miss Louisa." He leaned closer. "The Dowager Duchess of Kenbridge is filthy rich. On the occasions I've had the privilege to see her, I've noticed how she flaunts her jewelry. All I want is some of those jewels."

Louisa gasped and yanked her arm away. "If you think I'll lower myself to steal from that wonderful lady, think again."

"You *will*, especially if ye have a care for the safety of her grandchildren."

Fright immobilized Louisa. Even her mind refused to think of a way to get out of this situation. How dare he threaten to harm those adorable children. By refusing him, she would put the twins in danger.

"And if ye even think to tell the duke, I will harm him as well. In fact," Macgregor scratched his ear, "the duke might be the first one I hurt."

Panicked, she pulled on his sleeve. Tears pricked her eyes. "No. You cannot hurt them. They have done nothing to you."

"Louisa, my dear, all I'm asking for is a couple of necklaces."

Dread of the worst kind spread through her, knowing there was only one decision to make. "That is all?"

"Of course. A few of her necklaces and brooches will be worth much. But make certain these necklaces are decorated with colorful gems. I want only the best." He stroked his fingers down her cheek. "And I *know* ye can tell which ones will be more expensive."

"Yes, I can," she muttered.

"That's my girl. Do this one last thing for me and I shall never bother ye again."

Louisa didn't dare ask him to give her his word, only because she didn't trust him to stick to his promise. "How soon do you want me to do this?"

"Tomorrow?"

She shook her head. "That cannot be done. I will not even be at the dowager's house until week after next for a gathering she is having with her friends and family."

He nodded. "I suppose that will fit in with my plans."

"How will I find you to hand over the jewels?"

"I will find a way to be at the dowager's party. Watch for me." He winked, turned, and sauntered away as if he owned the world.

Frustration shook every bone in her body, and she didn't know whether to scream or cry. She'd do neither, since it would draw attention. In order to keep Trevor and the twins safe, she must steal from the dowager. And not tell a single soul.

On shaky legs, she crept back to Trevor and his children. She bumped into people on her way, not having the strength to apologize. Her heavy heart ached, and her head throbbed with indecision. But she couldn't back out now. She *must* do as Macgregor wanted.

When Trevor finally looked at her, his smile disappeared, and his face creased in worry. His concern for her welfare was evident in his kind eyes. She fought back the tears, but her fight was useless as she sat beside him.

"Louisa, what's wrong?"

As much as she wanted to confide in him, she didn't dare. Macgregor would certainly follow through with his threat. She loved Trevor too much to have any harm come to him—especially the way Macgregor tortured his victims.

"I—I have a headache."

"Louisa, it's more than that. I can see it on your pale face. Something is greatly troubling you."

"I—I—I remembered something."

His eyes widened. "What?"

"I saw someone I had known when I lived as a thief. Seeing this man brought back memories I had rather not ponder upon."

He slipped his arm around her shoulders. "Let's collect our things and we shall return home, posthaste."

"I would like that, my lord."

Although she was supposed to be caring for the children, Trevor was the one who helped the twins with their cloaks and led them through the throng of people who stood in their way as they hurried to their vehicle. With each step toward the landau, doom lurked like a dark cloud in Louisa's mind and heart. Stealing the jewels would turn her back into a thief, and in doing so, her life with Trevor slowly disappeared before her eyes. Things would never be the same again.

TREVOR PACED THE floor in his study, waiting for Louisa to put the children to bed. During the ride home, Louisa had been on the verge of tears. When he urged her to tell him what happened, all she would say was she recognized someone from her past and remembered a bad experience. She didn't want to talk about it in front of the children, and he agreed, especially with as upset as Louisa was.

But now as he waited for her to put the children to bed and come to his study, his patience wore thin. Very thin. He could still see her pale face, and especially her eyes void of tender emotion. Fright had consumed her and literally taken over her whole being. She had stared out the window of the landau on the drive home, only a shell of the woman he knew.

The grandfather clock in the hallway chimed ten o'clock. *Where is she?*

Expelling a pent-up breath, Trevor raked his fingers through his hair and marched to the study's opened door. The household was turning in for the night, and he surmised only a few servants were awake now.

He couldn't stand to wait any longer. Louisa should have been down by now. Obviously, she had chosen to stay in her room. Well, he couldn't rest tonight until he knew what she'd remembered.

Trevor bounded up the stairs two at a time. His long strides ate up the floor until he stood in front of her room. He knocked softly. Behind the door, shuffling feet creaked the floor, moving closer to the wooden barrier between them.

"Louisa, it's me. Let me in so we can talk." Just as his knock, he kept his voice quiet.

She didn't answer, although he knew she stood at the door because of her shadow on the floor from the space underneath. The seconds that ticked by seemed so long.

"Please, Louisa."

Finally she opened the door. Her puffy, red eyes drew his immediate attention. His heart broke, and he wanted to take her in his arms and soothe her fears.

"I don't feel well," she whispered, her voice cracking.

"I can see that, my dear." He walked inside and closed the door. "But I don't want you to be alone, either."

Without waiting for an invitation, he pulled her in his arms and brought her head to his chest. Her body shook with silent sobs as she clutched his waistcoat. Helplessness washed over him. If he could take away her pain, he would. If only he could help her regain her memory, he would do that as well. She shouldn't have to suffer.

Once her sobs diminished, he pulled her toward the two-seat sofa and they sat. He wouldn't let go of her even though she tried to pull away.

"Tell me what happened," he said.

She wiped her eyes. "When I went to get the roasted peanuts, I saw..." She swallowed noisily then looked at him. "I saw someone from my past... when I was a thief."

"Someone like David?"

"Yes."

"Then what happened?"

"I was so stunned, Trevor. I couldn't think. I just stood and stared." Her voice rose and her body trembled.

"Shhh..." He swiped his thumb under her eyes to dry her tears. "Calm down and tell me what else happened."

She took a deep breath. "When I realized how I knew him, my memory opened and I saw him in a room with me while I was being... whipped." Tears filled her eyes again. "I'd begged Macgregor not to punish me. I pleaded for his forgiveness, but he continued to whip me, laughing the whole time."

Trevor gnashed his teeth and held Louisa tight again. He'd kill that man if it was the last thing he'd do. Macgregor deserved his fate.

Kissing her forehead, Trevor cuddled her closer. "I'm so sorry you had to remember that. It is no wonder your mind chose to block that part of your life."

"Yes, that is what I thought as well."

He withdrew slightly, only enough to lift her chin so she would look at him. Her eyes swam with huge tears. Seeing her this way tore him apart inside. Beyond anything, he wanted to take away her pain, and his. He kissed above each eye, then her nose, before finally kissing her lips. He hoped she'd allow him to comfort her this way.

But when she pulled back, he realized his wish went unheard.

"Trevor, I need to have time to think about everything. Thank you for listening to me, but I really need to be alone."

He nodded. "Just remember I'm here for you. I will protect you at all times. Your past is where it should be now—in the past. Let it stay there. You have a new life here with me."

Her lips quaked, but she didn't say anything.

As he left her room, his heart grew heavier. Hopefully, she'd not have any more horrid memories. Then again, with the life she'd lived, there were probably many more terrible experiences just waiting to be revealed.

Chapter Twenty-Four

"THERE IS A bet going here in White's," Lord Hawthorne said cheerfully as he aimed his focus on Tristan, "that the police will not be able to discover who killed Lord Hollingsworth."

Trevor and his brothers sat at a table, and looked up as Dominic approached. Trevor silently groaned, wishing Hawthorne had stayed away. Yet, it seemed since the marquess and Trey were good friends, they always were seen together.

Quickly, before he could say anything condemning about Dominic's statement, Trevor tossed down his brandy in one gulp. The drink burned his throat and stung his eyes.

"What do you mean, my good man?" Trey asked.

Dominic pulled a chair from another table to join the brothers. "I have it on good authority that Lord Hollingsworth had many enemies."

Tristan tilted back his head and laughed heartily. "I would think so, Hawthorne. As crooked and deceitful as that lord was, I would imagine half of London would want to cut the lord's throat." He lifted his glass of whiskey, then drank it. "Put me down in the book for one thousand pounds. This will be an easy bet to win."

"I'll bet one thousand as well," Trey said, laughing.

"From what I have heard," Dominic continued, "the police

are baffled. They have many suspicions, but nothing conclusive." He grinned at Tristan. "Perhaps you won't need a good solicitor after all."

"You are correct there." Tristan nodded. "They cannot get me on this one. I did not kill the man, although the thought had crossed my mind often enough."

"Yours, along with many other blokes," Trey added.

"Which is why bets are being added in the book." Hawthorne swung his gaze at Trevor and nodded. "And I'm very happy to see you here with your brothers. I have some news for you as well."

Trevor really didn't want to hear what his brother's friend had to say. He really didn't care, for that matter. All that had been going through his mind since he brought Louisa and the children back from the circus was the way she'd acted. The way Louisa still acted now three days later.

Like she'd seen a ghost.

Like she was frightened of her own shadow.

But mostly, she had withdrawn from him, and the confusion inside him from her mysterious actions tore him apart more than he wanted to admit. Heaven help him, but he'd fallen madly in love with the woman, and he never wanted that happiness to end. So why did Trevor feel as if it was indeed ending?

"What kind of news?" he asked anyway.

"The other day, as I talked to Lord Talbot, I discovered his youngest daughter drowned about six years ago." Dominic leaned on the table, closer to Trevor. "The girl's body was never found. The girl would have been Louisa's age."

Trevor's interest perked a bit. "What was her name?"

"I cannot recall right now. We were into our cups a bit more than we should have been—"

"Just tell me, man. Was her name Louisa?"

Dominic frowned. "I don't believe so. But that doesn't mean she's not the same girl."

Irritated, Trevor slapped the table. "Hawthorne, how can you think such a thing?"

"Hear me out." Dominic raised his hand. "We have already surmised that something dreadful happened in Louisa's past. What if Louisa is not her real name, but the name given to her by her guardian or the person who raised her for six years?"

Trevor opened his mouth to rebut the marquess's theory, but the mere suggestion had him pausing in curiosity. If Louisa couldn't recall her past, how did she know Louisa wasn't her real name? He hated to admit it, but Hawthorne just might be correct with this assumption.

"You know I'm right." Dominic grinned wide.

"Do not start fluffing your feathers like a proud peacock just yet, Hawthorne," Trevor ground out. "There are still things that we must discover which would be similar to Louisa's life. Did you ask Lord Talbot what his daughter looked like? Or her exact age?"

"Do we even know Louisa's exact age?" Trey cut in. "We assume she's in her early twenties, but Trevor, you must admit, when you first saw her, you thought she was much younger."

"That's because of her thin frame," Trevor argued. "She's filled out since that first day. She does not resemble a half-starved child any longer."

Dominic shook his head. "The point I'm trying to make is because of her memory loss, that poor woman does not really know how old she is, either. For all we know, she might be Lord Talbot's daughter."

"Or Lord Danvers's," Trey added.

"Or," Trevor said as anger filled him, "Louisa could be the Duke of Devonshire's illegitimate daughter for all we know."

Dominic rolled his eyes. "You are *not* humorous, old man."

Trevor bunched his hands, wanting to wallop Hawthorne… and enjoy doing it. "So it seems we are all on a goose chase. We know Louisa was born from Quality parents, but because Louisa might not be her real name, and we are not certain of her true age, finding her past is out of our reach."

Silence stretched around the table as each man seemed lost in his own thoughts. All of this nonsense annoyed Trevor, but what confused him even more was knowing they might never learn Louisa's true identity. What if she never regained her memory?

Trevor loved her, but would he dare go against Society's rules and ask her to become his wife? Would marrying Louisa only bring ridicule to her and his children? He definitely could not put his family through that. If only the *ton* knew her like Trevor knew her, they'd see she was not just a mere servant. In fact, in ways she was better mannered than Gwen had been.

"I have an idea," Tristan said, breaking the silence.

Trevor glanced at the middle Worthington brother. "What is that?"

Tristan remained leaning back in his chair with his arms folded across his chest. "In the next few days, we ask around. We gather a list of those friends and acquaintances that had a daughter, sister, or grandchild disappear who could be Louisa's age. Then we turn this list in to Mother to invite to her weekend party. If any of these people are Louisa's family, she will recognize them, I hope."

Trey slapped his older brother on the shoulder. "Tristan, you are brilliant. Mother has been hounding me for names of people she could invite, and now I shall be able to help her." He glanced at the other men around the table. "We shall all be able to help."

Hawthorne and Tristan lifted their glass in a mock salute before drinking down the liquid.

Trevor pushed away from the table and stood. "Best of luck, men. Please ask around without giving away the real reason we want to know. In case Louisa is not who we think she is, I do not wish rumors to fly. Is that understood?"

"Perfectly." Dominic smiled. Trey and Tristan also acknowledged with a nod.

"Now, if you will excuse me. I have other matters to attend to." Trevor turned and stepped away, moving toward the door. But just as he reached the exit, another lord entered and nearly collided with Trevor.

When he recognized the lord, he bunched his hands by his sides. *Viscount Putney.* The very man he couldn't wait to speak with.

TREVOR ANTICIPATED SOME kind of reaction from the viscount. They stood staring at each other as if waiting for someone to draw their sword first. Finally, Putney's face hardened into a scowl, and his cheeks grew as red as his hair.

The viscount appeared as upset over their chance meeting as Trevor. "Putney, might I have a minute?"

The viscount lifted his arrogant nose as if he meant to snub Trevor. "Actually, Your Grace, I do have other business—"

"It will only take a minute, I assure you."

Putney's glare grew hotter as if he meant to burn holes through Trevor with his eyes. After a few awkward moments passed, the other man nodded.

Motioning toward another room, Trevor said, "Let us speak in here where it's more private."

"I agree."

Right away, a servant hurried to their side. "May I get you a drink, my lords?"

Trevor flipped his hand in a dismissal wave. "I think now is not the time—"

"But I would like a brandy," Putney quickly replied.

The servant gave a nod, turned and left the room.

Taking a deep breath, Trevor tried to calm his anger toward the other man. "Putney, I will make this short and to the point."

"I wish you would, Your Grace."

"Fine. You should know that Adam and Amanda are not your children," Trevor said softly.

The viscount's eyes widened before a dark scowl claimed his face. "How can you be so certain? The last I saw of them their hair had a trace of red, which makes them my offspring."

"I beg to differ. My mother has a trace of red in her hair as well. But of late, I have come to notice how much the twins resemble me." Trevor smiled as happiness filled his chest. This always happened when he thought of his beautiful children. "Their noses and mouths are the same shape as mine, and when they smile, they have a dimple in the same spot as I do. Adam even resembles Trey when he was a boy. Indeed, they are *my* children and not yours." He straightened just a little prouder and lifted his chin higher than before.

Putney's eyes misted and he blinked quickly. Sadness etched on his face even though he tried to look unaffected. Trevor almost felt sorry for him. Almost, but not quite. Did that make him a bad person because he didn't care about Putney's feelings? After all, Trevor wanted to believe he was a caring, understanding man even when it came to men who were in love with Gwen.

The viscount blew out a ragged breath. "Then I feel sorry for those poor children to have you as a father. I'm just happy to know I was the one who held their mother's love."

Trevor silently reprimanded himself for having second thoughts about the other man's feelings. "Well, Putney, at least she was able to have some happiness in her life since all she brought to mine was misery." He bowed. "Good day," he snapped before leaving the room and hurrying out through the door.

Maybe now the viscount would leave him alone. Trevor didn't want to admit that every time he saw that man, he remembered Gwen in Putney's arms that time in the stable. Her betrayal had hurt so much Trevor had actually wanted her dead. At the time, his injured pride had wanted revenge. Still, it was hard for him not to think he'd killed her. Perhaps he'd never be able to free the burden of guilt weighing heavily on his mind. But at least now he could rest easier, knowing the children were his.

Not far up the road, his landau sat parked waiting for him. Instead of waiting for the vehicle to be brought around, Trevor decided to walk. The weather was nice this early in the evening, and since he didn't have any pressing appointments, taking a small walk would do his mind good.

As long as he didn't think about Louisa.

But how could he not? Since bringing her into his home, he couldn't get her off his mind. And ever since he realized he loved her, all he wanted to do was hold her and talk about their future. He really didn't care about her past. Not anymore. She had been a thief, but he knew it wasn't by choice. A person like Louisa would have been forced to live in such a vile way to survive. Circumstances in her life had led her down the wrong pathway to a man like Macgregor. A man Trevor would like to meet face-to-face just so he could give the beast the beating he deserved for whipping Louisa like he'd done.

From the corner of his eyes, a lad—perhaps in his twelfth year or so—stood against a tree, trying his hardest not to act like he watched Trevor closely. Because of what happened with David, Trevor knew to be wary of pickpockets. And this boy was too suspicious.

Trevor slowed as he walked by the boy, almost hoping the vagabond would try to steal. As Trevor passed, he was almost disappointed when the lad didn't even try.

But when shuffling footsteps snuck behind him, Trevor wanted to grin. He'd teach this vagabond a lesson.

Just as the footsteps quickened and the boy brushed by him, Trevor snatched the boy's arm, stopping his hand as it began its descent into Trevor's pocket.

He glared into the vagabond's wide eyes. "I would not attempt that if I were you."

Color left the boy's dirty face quickly and he struggled to pull away. "Please, m'lord. Don't turn me in. I'm hungry, is all. I need money for food."

Trevor's heart twisted upon hearing the lad's plea, and he couldn't help but imagine Louisa when she was younger and doing this. The day he'd hit her with his vehicle, she'd look so much like this boy—ratted hair, tattered overcoat, fingerless gloves. "Where are your parents?"

"I… don't have any, m'lord."

"Who do you work for?"

"Pardon me?" Confusion creased the boy's forehead and narrowed eyes.

"Do you work for Macgregor?" Trevor demanded, not wanting to play any more games. The vagabond's face lost even more color—if that were possible—and Trevor knew he'd received his answer. "I will let you go on one condition."

The lad gulped and nodded slowly. "What is that?"

"You tell me where I can find Macgregor."

"Oh, no… no, m'lord. I cannot do that. If he ever found out—" Tears welled in his eyes. "I'd rather go to the gaol, m'lord."

Chapter Twenty-Five

ONCE AGAIN, TREVOR'S heart twisted for this frightened child. No wonder Louisa was such an emotional mess now. Macgregor was torturing poor, defenseless children, and someone needed to stop the man. Trevor was determined to be *that* person.

"If you will just tell me where Macgregor is, I will see to it that he never hurts you again."

The lad shook his head. "You don't know him like I do. He's smart, and he's dangerous."

"Yes, I'm aware of that. I know a woman who used to work for him. By chance, do you remember Louisa?"

The boy's eyes darted around, as if looking for someone. Trevor also scanned the area, wondering if another vagabond might be lurking about. When he didn't see anyone, he looked back at the boy whose eyes were wider than before.

"Aye, I know Louisa."

Trevor's heartbeat picked up a notch. Kneeling in front of the boy, he grasped both—very thin—shoulders. "Please tell me what you know about her. She's lost some of her memory, and I'm trying to help her get it back. Any information you have will be helpful."

"Well, I don't know…"

"I shall give you some food," Trevor added quickly then

nodded toward his landau. "I will take you wherever you want to go. Please help me. Help Louisa."

He couldn't believe he'd been reduced to begging, but right now he didn't enjoy feeling helpless when it came to that special woman.

"Aye, I can tell you a little."

Trevor jumped to his feet and escorted the boy toward the landau. His footman opened the door. Trevor instructed his driver to take them posthaste to the bakery. After Trevor and the boy climbed inside, the footman closed the door.

"What is your name?" Trevor asked.

"Norman Boyd, m'lord."

"How old are you?"

"I'm in my thirteenth year."

Trevor's stomach lurched. What happened in this young boy's life to make him want to work for a man like Macgregor? "How long have you been stealing?"

"For three years now."

"You say you don't have parents. Did they die?"

Nodding, the boy's gaze dropped to his lap as he twisted his fingers. "Aye. In a house fire."

"Why are you not in an orphanage or living with relatives?"

"No relatives, and the orphanage didn't want me, m'lord."

How odd. "Please explain. How could the orphanage not want you?"

Norman looked up, frowning. "The man who had come to take me out of school after my parents died, told me that."

"Was Macgregor this man?"

"No. But after a few days, the man who took care of me, sold me to Macgregor."

"*Sold* you?"

"Aye."

How utterly ridiculous. But then, Trevor didn't know the ways of this class of people. "Tell me all you can about Louisa?"

Just as Norman opened his mouth, the vehicle stopped. Trevor glanced out the window and noticed they were in front of a bakery. Once the footman opened the door, Trevor jumped down with the boy and walked into the shop. He purchased whatever the lad wanted—which was quite a bit. Trevor smiled, remembering when Louisa ate so heartily as if she hadn't eaten for months. His heart twisted again, and with it came anger. Macgregor needed to be stopped immediately.

After they climbed back in the landau, the boy stuffed his face with pastries. If Norman had any manners before, he definitely didn't have them now. Although Trevor didn't want the lad to speak with his mouth full of food, Trevor wanted to know what Norman knew about Louisa.

"Will you now tell me how you know Louisa?"

"Aye," he garbled and wiped the cuff of his sleeve across his mouth. "She worked for Macgregor. She was his best."

"Why? Because she could steal more?"

"That, and because she was so quick, none of her victims knew she was stealing from them."

Trevor nodded. "Continue."

"Macgregor favored Louisa because she taught the rest of us how to steal. And, I think he liked her because she was pretty."

Trevor gnashed his teeth. He prayed that man hadn't touched her in an improper manner. The mere idea had bile rising to his throat. "Do you know anything about her past? How she came to be with Macgregor?"

Norman shook his head. "All I knows is her family died, too."

Trevor's heart dropped. "All of them?"

"Aye. And the man who got her from her boarding school sold her to Macgregor."

Curiosity niggled its way into Trevor's mind. Louisa's story sounded very similar to Norman's. "Do you know if she knew this man?"

Norman shrugged. "A few times I heard her mention he was her friend's uncle."

"Did she say his name?"

"Not that I heard."

Trevor leaned closer. "What about the man who sold you to Macgregor? What was his name?"

"Percy Featherspoon," Norman said before taking a big bite from a pastry.

The name didn't sound familiar, but at least Trevor could have the man investigated. "Where did you live with Mr. Featherspoon?"

"In Scotland."

"Very interesting." Trevor scratched his chin. "Can you tell me anymore about Louisa? When she used to work for Macgregor?"

"I don't know. Macgregor's children don't talk very much. We see each other in the morning before we leave to work the streets, and we return late at night, very tired."

"Think, Norman. Tell me anything that might help Louisa get her memory back."

The lad was quiet for a few moments as he munched on his food. Finally, he lifted his wide eyes to Trevor.

"I remember Macgregor was having her do bad things."

Trevor's chest tightened, not knowing if he really wanted to hear this. "What sort of things?"

"Louisa was one of the oldest, and Macgregor trained the older ones to do more than just steal."

"Go on."

Norman shrugged. "He wanted Louisa to find more children and bring them to him."

Trevor lost his breath, either that or his heart had stopped beating. "Are you talking about kidnapping?"

"Aye—kidnapping."

"How... how did Louisa do this?"

"I don't know, m'lord. I just know that she would be gone for a few days and when she returned, she had a new child with her. Macgregor was very happy with her work. He said Louisa was very good with children."

A quick shaft of fear entered Trevor. Would Louisa take his twins away? No, he reasoned, they were too young. If his chest continued to tighten, he would not be able to endure the pain. He swallowed, moistening his suddenly dry throat. "What else did she do for Macgregor?"

Norman finished the last bite and wiped his mouth on his sleeve again. "Well, there was this other thing, but I don't know if it really happened."

By the way the lad cringed and hung his head, Trevor could tell it wasn't good. Did he really want to know? What could be worse than kidnapping children for Macgregor's torture pleasure? But even if he wished he hadn't started this conversation, he still opened his mouth and asked, "What is it?"

"I'd heard..." He heaved a deep breath. "I heard she killed someone for Macgregor. One day he was upset when Thomas didn't bring any profits for the day. Thomas wasn't very good at stealing. Anyway, Macgregor made Louisa take Thomas away... and kill him."

Oh Lord, no! Trevor's stomach lurched, and he feared he'd empty it right on his lap.

"She returned the next day and said she took care of it for Macgregor." Norman shrugged. "We all suspected she had killed Thomas."

"Did she actually *say* she killed the boy?"

"No, just that she *took care of him* for Macgregor."

Tilting his head back against the wall, Trevor inhaled deep breaths, trying to clear his mind and calm his stomach. This couldn't be right. The woman he'd known since running her over with his landau, was *not* capable of murder. She wasn't even capable of kidnapping children. She'd been the one who watched the twins so carefully when they were with Mrs. Jacobs. Louisa had been nothing but attentive and loving to Adam and Amanda.

Yet, was this how she was able to coax the other children away from their families and bring them to Macgregor?

Pain throbbed in his head, making his confusion greater. His heart told him not to believe, but there was that niggle of doubt knocking inside his subconscious that wouldn't leave. He wanted to believe the best of her because he loved her. The woman he'd come to know could not possibly have done all those terrible things. Because her past was still unknown, perhaps she could have done these horrid acts in able to survive Macgregor.

"M'lord? Can I leave now?"

Trevor looked back at the lad. "Leave? Do you really want to return to Macgregor and a life of thieving?"

"Where else would I go? I have no home. No family."

"But what if Macgregor and this Featherspoon fellow have lied to you all this time? What if your family is alive and wondering where you have been these past three years?"

Tears filled the boy's eyes and his bottom lip quivered. "I would love to believe that, m'lord. But I don't dare."

"Who were your parents?"

"My father was Baron Grisham."

Trevor nodded. "Do you remember where you lived?"

"Aye." Norman's face brightened. "I know it's quite a way's away, but will you take me there?"

"Yes, I will. I want to know if you were kidnapped or if your parents had indeed died."

Color bloomed on Norman's cheeks and excitement danced in his brown eyes as he explained where he had lived. Trevor leaned over and opened the door to instruct the driver where to go. Although it was several hours away, the ride would be worth it.

The first part of the drive, the boy chattered like a bird, talking about his home and family. At times Trevor wished the boy would stop, but then realized this kept him from thinking about Louisa… from thinking the worst in her.

Finally, an hour later, Norman fell asleep. Exhaustion settled over Trevor, but he refused to close his eyes. Picturing Louisa as a vagabond and doing what Norman had told him she had done, were not good images to have.

What worried him more than anything was having her regain her memory, only to discover she had been a bad person—that she had done all the things Norman told him about. Could Trevor still allow her to be in his home, caring for his children knowing she had done this? And, could he still love her and want her for his wife?

He must find Percy Featherspoon and get more answers.

When the vehicle slowed, Trevor peered out the window. Night had fallen over them, but up ahead stood a home all lit up. The half-moon helped to guide them as well.

"Norman," he said, reaching over and shaking the lad. "Wake up. I think we have arrived."

The boy stretched and yawned, then blinked with sleepy eyes. He scanned the inside of the landau as confusion crossed his features. When he met Trevor's gaze, it only took a moment before recognition struck and Norman smiled.

"Are we home?"

"I certainly hope so."

The boy scrambled to the window and pressed his nose against the glass. When the house came into view, Norman gasped. Shaking his head, he pulled back and looked at Trevor with teary eyes.

"That cannot be right. I was told the house burned down— that my family was in the house."

"Is that your home?" Trevor asked.

"Aye."

Hope budded in Trevor's chest, and he prayed he would be able to reunite the boy with his family.

When the vehicle stopped, Trevor and Norman climbed out. Trevor walked ahead of the lad, but with the boy's hurried steps, Trevor had to quicken his step. He stopped in front of the front door and pulled the bell.

Norman sniffed and wiped his moist eyes. "I don't under-stand, m'lord."

"We shall discover what really happened, I assure you."

The door opened and Trevor greeted the butler. "Pardon me for calling at such a late hour. I'm the Duke of Kenbridge, and I need to speak with Baron Grisham, if you please."

The butler bowed. "Good evening, Your Grace. What can I tell the baron is your purpose here?"

"He's alive?" Norman's voice rose and he pushed past Trevor and stood in front of the butler. "Is my father alive?"

Disgust painted the servant's face as he gazed down at the lad. "I beg your pardon—"

"Tillis, it's me. Norman."

The butler gasped. His mouth dropped open as he clutched the boy's shoulders to look at his face closer. "Oh my… It *is* you."

Trevor blew out a grateful breath, relieved his instincts had been correct. His heart lightened as Norman hugged the butler, then ran into the house calling for his parents. Happy and surprised shrieks came from the family as they gathered around Norman, crying and holding the boy.

Smiling, Trevor was glad he was able to find the boy's family. But would he ever find Louisa's? And if he could, would he discover he'd been wrong to assume she'd been the terrible person Norman had told him about?

Chapter Twenty-Six

L OUISA AWOKE EARLY in the morning with a stretch and a
yawn. She hadn't slept well last night, mainly because Trevor
had been gone all day and she feared the worst. The more she
remembered about her past—and told him about it—the more he
withdrew.

Then again, she'd been withdrawing just as much. She wasn't
naïve enough to believe that he'd marry her and they would live
happily-ever-after as in some fairytales she'd read to the children.
She'd done too much in her past; made too many mistakes, and
Trevor had every right to throw her out of his home and never
see her again.

Rubbing tired eyes, she climbed out of bed. She doubted the
twins would be up this early, but she still needed to get herself
ready for the day.

Although she loved those children dearly, they deserved
better than her as their nursemaid. They deserved a woman who
hadn't stolen from wealthy people—and turned around and
taught other children to do the same. They deserved better than a
nursemaid who was seriously contemplating stealing their
grandmother's jewels.

Dejected, Louisa slugged on weary legs to the water basin
and splashed water on her face, hoping it would bring her mind
awake so she could think of a way out of this turmoil. But by the

time she finished dressing, she hadn't thought of anything that would help her dire situation.

With a heavy heart, she knew there was only one choice to make. She must force her memory to return. If she could do that, perhaps she'd know where to go when she left Trevor and the twins. Tears pricked her eyes and a lump formed in her throat. She didn't want to leave, and thinking about that day was almost unbearable, but she could *not* have Macgregor torturing them, either. When that man made a promise of punishment, he always followed through.

She hurried out of her room and checked on the twins who were still asleep. It wasn't healthy to stand beside their beds, watching them this way, because the pain in her heart grew and she wanted to cry and hold them tight. She'd do neither.

Quietly, Louisa left their room and searched through the house until she found Mrs. Smythe. The housekeeper was in the kitchen talking with some of the staff. When the older woman saw Louisa, she smiled.

"Good morning, Louisa. I have been hearing good things about you lately."

Although Louisa didn't want to know—or care—happiness still lifted her heart, if only slightly. "I'm pleased to hear such a compliment." She swallowed and stepped closer. "Mrs. Smythe, could I have a word with you? In private?"

"Indeed, my dear." The older woman excused herself from the others and stepped into the dining room. "What is it?"

Taking a deep breath, Louisa twisted her hands against her middle and prayed she could convince the other woman for help. "I have had some confusing memories of late, and I feel I need to force myself to remember. I need to return to the place I had been when Lord Kenbridge hit me with his curricle."

Worry etched the housekeeper's brow as she patted Louisa's hands. "Are you certain this will help?"

"I'm hoping it will, which is why I need your assistance. First, I need to have someone care for the twins while I'm gone."

Mrs. Smythe nodded. "I will fetch my niece, Horatia. She has helped Mrs. Jacobs from time to time."

"Thank you, Mrs. Smythe. That would be most kind."

"What else is it that you need?"

"Well," Louisa hesitated, clutching her fingers until they turned white, "I need to know where exactly I was when His Grace hit me."

The housekeeper frowned. "I don't know the exact location, but I do know where the wooded area is located."

"That would be wonderful."

As Mrs. Smythe explained to Louisa, apprehension grew in her chest. From the terrible memories she'd discovered already, she didn't think she wanted to know more. Yet, she must. This was the only way to help Trevor and his children.

"Thank you again, Mrs. Smythe. I truly don't know what I would do without your help."

The kind woman smiled. "I'm just happy I can be of some assistance."

"Before I leave, I must tell His Grace where I'm going."

Mrs. Smythe shook her head. "He's already left the house."

Surprised, Louisa hitched a breath. "This early? He arrived home late last night."

"We all thought the same. But whatever he's doing, he's determined." She grinned. "That's the way he's always been."

"Well, I suppose I can write him a note to let him know where I'm going."

"Not to worry, Louisa. I shall tell him upon his return."

She sighed with relief. "Bless you, Mrs. Smythe. You have been a godsend."

Louisa hugged the housekeeper before making her way back up the stairs to her room to fetch her cloak and bonnet. Nervousness shook through her body as she shrugged on her outer garment, tied the ribbons of her bonnet, and left the house.

A small wind blew from the east, but if she stayed in the sun, she wouldn't get cold. As she walked past the stable, she debated whether or not to take one of Trevor's fine horses, but in the end, she didn't. The walk would do her good, and hopefully, the fresh air would rejuvenate her memory.

From the few things she had remembered, she must have had a normal childhood with loving parents and a friend she could rely on—and cry with. But sometime after the age of twelve, something must have happened that landed her in Macgregor's devious clutches. She supposed her family must have died, but she still needed answers.

The chirping birds lightened her heart slightly the more she walked. Peacefulness settled in her mind as she glanced over God's beautiful land. Closing her eyes, she smiled. She must have come from a family who strongly believed in God, because she knew without a doubt, He would help her along life's journey.

She sighed and opened her eyes. Unfortunately, she was having major stepping stones in her journey now. The Lord wouldn't give her challenges she couldn't handle, but He must think highly of her now to believe she could handle these trials.

As she walked by a fruit tree orchard, she picked a couple cherries before continuing on her way. To keep herself busy, she tried to expand on the memories of Macgregor that she'd had thus far. Even if she didn't want to think of how frightened she'd been in his presence, she *must* remember everything about him.

Slowly, bits and pieces from her past with him emerged. She recalled the first time she ever picked a gent's pocket and took his watch. That night, she'd cried herself to sleep on her bedroll. Those times she didn't want to steal, Macgregor punished her by not feeding her. In misery, she had to watch the other children as they ate. Emotions surfaced, and she remembered wanting to die several times.

Once while she was teaching her friend, David, they had discussed running away from Macgregor. But talking about it was as far as they had planned. Neither of them had homes except for with Macgregor. If only the orphanages would have taken them.

Louisa stopped suddenly as a thought invaded her mind. *Why would the orphanages not take them?*

Closing her eyes again, she rubbed the throb starting in her forehead. Something on the tip of her memory wanted to break through. She just knew it. Orphanages usually took children who didn't have a family. So why did she think she—or David—couldn't go to one?

The distant rumble of a carriage coming up the road pulled Louisa from her thoughts. She quickly moved aside so she wouldn't get hit. As she stood against a large oak, she plopped a few more cherries into her mouth, waiting for the conveyance to pass so she could continue her trek.

The large coach swayed as it neared. There was something familiar about the black and gold painted vehicle with the driver on top. But it wasn't until Louisa saw the lady riding inside and the coat of arms painted on the door that her heart hammered wildly. Why did the coach seem familiar? And pray, why did the woman inside look like someone Louisa should know?

Louisa pulled away from the oak tree and followed after the coach, even though it moved faster than she did. Concentrating on the woman who looked about her own age or slightly older, Louisa tried to figure out why the lady seemed so familiar.

Finally, another memory parted through the fog clouding her mind. Louisa stopped and focused.

Eliza Watson. The dearest friend Louisa had in school. Red ringlets framed the girl's round face, and contrasted greatly with her pink cheeks right after they'd chased each other playing favorite childhood games.

Louisa and Eliza collapsed in a grassy field, laughing. In the distance, the other girls in their school class played another game.

Just like it all happened yesterday, the scene opened wider in Louisa's mind.

Sitting in the grass, Louisa laughed at something Eliza just said. Out of the corner of her eyes, a tall, thin man strode toward them.

"It's my uncle." Eliza jumped up and ran to him. They hugged and

chatted for a brief moment before Eliza turned back, her eyes full of tears.

Something wasn't right. Eliza always had a chipper attitude and rarely ever frowned.

"Louisa." Eliza's voice broke.

Heart pounding in worry, Louisa slowly stood and held her hands out for her friend to take. "What's wrong?" She switched her gaze to the tall man who wore a forlorn expression.

"Louisa, this is my uncle, Mr. Featherspoon," Eliza whispered.

Louisa curtsied. "A pleasure to meet you."

"Miss Louisa, I fear I have come with disheartening news." The man's Adam's apple bounced. "It's about your family."

"What's wrong with my family?"

He shook his head and rubbed his sad eyes. "I'm sorry to inform you that there was a fire in your home. Your family perished in the burning house, I'm afraid."

Ice-cold shock vibrated through her as emptiness filled her chest. No! This couldn't be right. "There... there was a fire?"

"Yes, Miss Louisa," Mr. Featherspoon answered. "Early this morning. Not one person in the house survived."

"D—dead? My family is d—dead?"

The older man nodded. Eliza clutched Louisa's cold hands. She tried to focus on her friend, but her vision blurred with tears.

"Oh, Louisa." Eliza wrapped her arms around Louisa in a tight hug. "I'm so sorry. But you need not worry. My uncle will take care of you."

"No... no." Louisa pushed her friend away. "I cannot believe this. They are not dead. They are alive, I can feel it."

Confused, she turned and ran—nowhere in particular—just needed to get away to absorb the news Mr. Featherspoon had delivered.

Her family couldn't be dead. They couldn't have burned in a fire. Their servants were not that careless. Nothing made sense, and she couldn't possibly take this man's word even if he was the uncle of her friend. Images of her family perishing in scorching flames, screaming in agony, and crying out for help, brought more tears to Louisa's eyes and made her limbs weak, and frigid cold. In fact, her whole body felt cold, and weary like wet rags.

Off in the distance she heard her friend's frantic voice. "Louisa, get out of the water. Don't go another step. It's too deep."

Slowly, Louisa sank to her knees in the water she didn't remember entering. Her cloak tugged her in further until the water covered her face. Closing her eyes, she didn't care.

A man's arm wrapped around her and yanked her out of the water. Dazed, Louisa didn't speak as Eliza pulled off the wet cloak and wrapped Louisa in her uncle's overcoat.

"Louisa, my dear. Do not fear. I shall be here. Always. My uncle will take good care of you."

Louisa wiped her tears, her heart still aching because of the memory. Her family had died. But the question still remained, who were they?

Looking down the road, she forged ahead, determined to catch up with that coach. Eliza, her childhood friend was in that vehicle, and Louisa would find her.

TREVOR JUMPED OFF his horse, and gazed upon the meager cottage before him. Shutters were broken, and the place needed a good painting. Weeds took over the yard, and made Trevor wonder if anyone really lived here.

After spending a few hours this morning asking around, he was given the information he sought, which led him to this run-down cottage. Now, he just prayed he'd receive some answers while he was here.

He climbed the four broken-down steps to the front door and rapped hard. Perhaps the occupant would still be asleep, but Trevor didn't care. He hadn't come all this way to be put off.

No noise came from inside, so Trevor pounded on the door again. Finally, feet shuffled on the floor mere moments before the door creaked open. A man, perhaps in his late fifties, squinted against the sunlight falling upon Trevor.

"Pardon me for coming at this early hour," he explained, "but

I am in desperate need of finding Mr. Percy Featherspoon. I was told he lived here."

"What do you want with him?" the man barked with a slight slur.

Trevor peered closer into the man's glassy eyes, and took a whiff of the strong alcohol scent enveloping him. This must be him. After all, Trevor had been told the man was constantly foxed. "I have some questions to ask. Are you Mr. Featherspoon? My informants gave me a description of the man, and from what I can see, you resemble him quite a bit."

Shaking his head, the man pushed his fingers through his thinning crop of graying brown hair. "It's very early—"

"Indeed it is, but I have traveled a long way." Trevor reached in his pocket and withdrew a moneybag filled with coins and shook it. Upon hearing the clicking of the coins, the other man's eyes widened—just as Trevor had been told they would when offering money. "I beg you. Please answer some questions, and I shall make the time worthwhile."

"What is your name?" Featherspoon inquired.

"Trevor Worthington, the Duke of Kenbridge."

The man's eyes widened even more and he stumbled backward to open the door. "Please come in, Your Grace."

Upon entering, Trevor could see the furnishings once had been of fine quality. Not now. Most of the chairs were either broken, or the fabric was soiled and barren. The wooden floor held no rugs. And chips of paint from the walls were noticeably visible. Apparently, the man had fallen on bad times. Regardless, Trevor didn't want to sit on anything the man had to offer.

"Forgive me for the mess," the man muttered. "I wasn't expecting company."

"I don't plan on staying long, I assure you. I just need some answers." Trevor folded his arms. "Are you indeed Featherspoon?"

"Yes."

"Did you used to live in Scotland?"

"I have another house there, yes."

"What occupation is it that you do, may I ask?"

"I… um, well, you see, my lord, I take in orphaned children and place them in other homes."

"How very interesting. Tell me, Featherspoon, how do you know these children are orphans? Have you firsthand knowledge their families are dead?"

"Indeed, I do."

"So how is it," Trevor said as he slowly circled the older man, "that Norman Boyd's family is still alive? I assume you remember Norman Boyd from three years ago?" The man slowly nodded. "Splendid. Now I want to know why you told the boy his family had died in a house fire when that was false information."

At first Featherspoon's eyes widened in panic, then his face reddened. "What are you accusing me of, Your Grace?"

"I'm accusing you of lying. I stumbled across a vagabond yesterday by the name of Norman Boyd. He explained you were the one who told him about the demise of his parents before taking him to Scotland. Yet, when the boy told me where his family had lived, I took him there and they were alive. Even the house you had told him burned down, still stood." He stepped closer, not taking his stare off the older man. "So now I wonder why you lied to him."

Featherspoon huffed and squared his shoulders. "I did not lie, my lord."

"Then please tell me why I was able to reunite Norman with his family last evening, after being separated from them for three long, miserable years."

"Apparently, I had gotten the wrong information about the boy."

"From whom do you get your information, may I ask?"

"From… from the local constable, of course."

"Do you work directly through one man?"

"Of course not. I work through many."

Trevor scratched his chin, not removing his eyes from the

pathetic creature in front of him. "Tell me, do you remember assisting a lovely girl by the name of Louisa several years passed? Apparently, her family had died in a house fire, similar to the story you gave Norman."

Featherspoon waved an unsteady hand through the air before stumbling toward a half empty bottle of whiskey sitting on the table. "I'll have you know, my lord, that I help several... *many* children a year. I do not recall anyone by the name of Louisa." He grasped the liquor with an unsteady hand, placed the bottle to his lips and drank.

"She is probably in her twentieth year now." Trevor growled and clutched the man's shirt, pulling the man's attention back to Trevor instead of the bottle. "You had better start remembering or I will not give you a shilling of what's in the coin bag."

A bead of sweat formed on the man's face and he gulped. "I faintly recall a girl by the name of Louisa, but I do think her family really died."

Trevor tightened his fingers in Featherspoon's shirt and glared. "And how am I to trust your word when you gave Norman false information?"

"I—I—I don't know what to tell you, my lord."

"The truth! That's what I want."

"I don't remember." Featherspoon shook his head.

Cussing under his breath, Trevor pushed the man away. Featherspoon fell to the floor, landing on his buttocks. The bottle dropped out of his hands and rolled, liquid spilling in its journey.

Trevor expelled a pent-up breath as he scrubbed his face. Pacing the floor, his mind scrambled to think of other things to ask. Then again, the man lied. How would Trevor ever know the truth?

He stopped in front of Featherspoon still on the floor. "How much does Macgregor pay you for these children?"

Within seconds, the color of the man's skin changed from an angry red to a panicked white. "Macgregor?"

"You heard me," Trevor snarled in aggravation. "Norman

told me you *sold* him to Macgregor. Even Louisa had worked for the lout." He reached down and grasped the lapels of the man's waistcoat and jerked him to a standing position. "You cannot lie to me about Macgregor. I know you sold children to Satan's spawn."

"Macgregor knew I couldn't possibly find all the children a good home. He assured me he would help."

Trevor shook his head. "I don't believe that for one moment. You knew what kind of man Macgregor was. You knew what kind of life those children would have."

"No… no. You must believe me. I didn't have a choice."

"Why? Was Macgregor blackmailing you?"

"I—I—I…"

"Tell me," Trevor barked.

Featherspoon broke down and sobbed like the pathetic— foxed—man he was. Trevor dropped him back on the floor. Standing over him, he rubbed his forehead as the man curled up and cried like a babe. Trevor was helpless, and he hated feeling this way. But apparently, shaking the man and making threats weren't going to do a thing.

"Tell me one more thing," Trevor said a little more calmly. "Where can I find him? If you are not man enough to put a stop to the man's sick ways of raising children, then I will. I am *not* afraid of Macgregor."

"I—I don't know." Featherspoon sniffed and wiped his nose on his shirtsleeve. "Macgregor never stays in one place for very long. He could be anywhere—even back in Scotland for all I know."

"He's here in England, I assure you. I have come across three members of his band of thieves already."

The blubbering fool wouldn't answer Trevor. Featherspoon kept shaking his head and saying he didn't know. Perhaps this was not the best time to talk with the man since he was sick with the morning effects from his drinking spree. However, Trevor wondered if he could catch Featherspoon sober at all.

"When your memory clears," Trevor told him, "locate me and we shall do business. I'll pay well to find this man." He turned and marched out of the house, more frustrated now than when he'd entered.

He mounted his horse, but before riding away, glanced around the barren land. If Macgregor paid Featherspoon for each child, where did the money go? No, there had to be more to the story. Obviously, Featherspoon was not getting paid well, which meant Macgregor was blackmailing.

Trevor peered back at the small rundown cottage. He needed to somehow make Featherspoon believe that he would help him—that Macgregor needed to be put out of business immediately.

Clicking his tongue against the roof of his mouth, he urged his horse forward. But after moving a short distance, he heard Featherspoon's shout. Quickly, Trevor stopped his horse, and spun around toward the house. Featherspoon stood on the porch holding a pistol. The wicked glint in the other man's eyes caused Trevor to hitch a breath.

I'm a dead man.

Chapter Twenty-Seven

S LOWLY, TREVOR LIFTED his hands in the air. "Featherspoon, I'm unarmed. Do you really wish to shoot an unarmed man? If you shoot me, you will no longer have honor and your bad name will follow you forever."

"I don't need trouble," the man shouted from the steps. "You, my lord, are trouble."

"I beg to differ. All I want is to find answers for my friend, Louisa. She needs to know about her past. As soon as I get these answers, I will leave you alone."

"Louisa was a problem, and that subject should be dropped. Her past is not worth looking into, I assure you."

Featherspoon's confusing words made Trevor want to curse—and shake the man senseless. But for now, Trevor needed to talk him out of firing his pistol. "If you will allow me, I can help you. I suspect you are in trouble, and I think I can assist you in some way."

"You cannot help me. Nobody can." He swayed a little, then quickly steadied himself.

"Please let me try." Slowly, Trevor dismounted and took careful steps toward the man pointing the pistol.

"Stay right where you are," Featherspoon shouted.

Trevor inhaled deeply, praying he could convince this man to put the weapon down. "All I want is to know about Louisa. What is her last name? Where did she come from?" He shrugged. "That's all the information I'm after."

Tears gathered in the man's eyes. "It did not happen the way it was supposed to. I was promised money. I was never paid."

"If money is what you seek, I can pay you. Please tell me what I want to know, and I will happily give you money for your assistance."

Featherspoon shook his head. "People have told me that for so long, I refuse to believe it. My life is controlled, and I cannot stop it."

"Is Macgregor the one controlling you?" Trevor paused for an answer, but the man continued to shake his head. "If he is, I can stop him. I will give you back the control you lost."

"It's useless. Useless…"

"Tell me, Mr. Featherspoon, do you take children from wealthy families and sell them to Macgregor?"

"Yes."

Trevor's heart lightened. Finally, he was getting somewhere. "Did Louisa come from noble parents?"

"Yes."

"Do you recall their title?"

"D—D—doesn't matter now."

Inward, Trevor growled. *So close…* "I beg you, Mr. Featherspoon. Help me and I shall help you."

The other man's expression wavered from sadness to confusion, before his face grew red and he glared Trevor's way. His aim became steadier as he pointed the pistol.

"It's too late now, Your Grace. Too late for all of us."

Trevor's heart dropped. The perplexed man was going to pull the trigger. *Lord, help me!*

Suddenly, a loud thud rang through the air. Featherspoon's body jerked. His eyes rolled back in his head and he collapsed. Behind him stood a boy—perhaps in his tenth year—holding a large piece of wood. The boy resembled the vagabonds Trevor had seen lately, except this one was a little cleaner.

"F—f—forgive me, sir, but I couldn't allow him to shoot you." The boy wiped his moist eyes.

"Who are you?" Trevor strolled closer, still hesitant.

"Isaac, sir. Isaac Dickson."

"Are you related to Featherspoon?"

The boy shook his head and his eyes filled quickly with tears. "No. One week ago, he told me… told me my family…"

"Burned in a house fire?"

Isaac nodded and swiped at his eyes again. "I believed him, but after hearing what you said…" He sniffed.

Trevor motioned the boy from off the porch. "I will take you to your family if you wish. I don't believe they are dead."

The boy flew down the steps and ran to Trevor, burying his face in Trevor's coat. "I don't either."

He patted Isaac's head, studying Mr. Featherspoon. Blood gushed out the back of his head. The man's skin was deathly white. Trevor pushed the boy away and hurried to the porch. Turning Featherspoon over, Trevor checked to see if the man was alive. His chest did not rise or fall. Trevor laid his head on the man's chest. No heartbeat.

"D—did I kill him?" Isaac asked in a squeaky voice.

"Not to worry. You did the right thing." Trevor met the boy's panicked eyes. "I assure you, the law will not punish you. This man was very bad and had kidnapped many children."

"He told me I would live with a man named Macgregor soon."

"No, Isaac. I will not allow that to happen." He stood and moved down the steps toward the boy. "Let us take you home and I will see that Featherspoon has a proper burial." He led the way to his horse, but then stopped and glanced back at the cottage. "Are there any more children in there?"

"No. Just me."

Trevor mounted, then lifted the boy behind him. As he rode away, his heart lifted—if only slightly. At least he knew Louisa's parents were of Quality, and he *knew* they were not dead. This trip hadn't been wasted after all. Yet, he still wasn't any closer to finding out who she really was. He prayed that the weekend party his mother would have would spark something in Louisa's memory and open a way to her past.

LOUISA'S SIDES HURT with exertion, but she pushed herself in the direction the coach had taken. No other roads had veered off the path, and she prayed she'd reach the vehicle's destination soon. She neared the wooded area where Mrs. Smythe had told her she'd been hit. Slowing her footsteps, she glanced around the area, hoping to remember something.

Nothing looked familiar. Yet…

Breathing slower, she closed her eyes and concentrated. It was as if a memory tried to break through, but everything was dark. It was night. Only a sliver of a moon lit her way. She was running—fast—searching for someone.

Confusion had clouded her mind as she ran. Pain twisted her heart.

She'd just been to a house…

Louisa gasped and opened her eyes. There was a house near-by. She *knew* if she went to this place she'd remember something.

Once again, she ran, not caring if her legs were weak or her body hurt. She pushed herself, knowing this was where she'd remember.

Up ahead the road forked. Her mind told her to take the road going left. She ran harder. Excitement beat in her head, as her subconscious told her this was the way.

Her childhood friend, Eliza must live this way. Perhaps that's why she felt so connected to the area. Through the trees, smoke from chimneys rose above the leaves. She pushed herself faster until the house was in full view.

Then she stopped and fell to her knees.

Home.

The gray, two-story house was exactly as it had been in the brief memories she had. A two-step porch, small flower garden, and the golden-cased knockers on the double doors were still the same.

Confusion filled her as dark clouds of doubt hung in her memory. She couldn't possibly be remembering correctly, when only earlier she recalled the moment she was told her family died in a house fire. Yet, the house still stood—the very same as she remembered from years past.

Gradually, thoughts formed in her mind, memories blended to create a story. For seven years, she'd been told she was an orphan, but the day she was hit by Trevor's curricle, she had seen her cousin—her betrothed—and followed him home. Here. To this very spot. She had wanted to see if her parents were still alive, so snuck closer to the window only to have two servants escort her to the tall iron gate.

These gates. She slid her hands over the cold iron, remembering vividly. She had wanted to find the constable... anyone who would remember her and take her to Frank. But in her confused state of mind, she ran into the road, not seeing or hearing Trevor's curricle coming her way.

She closed her eyes and constrained her forehead against the iron gate as tears streamed down her face. All those years... all those miserable, horrible years with Macgregor... she had actually had family. And where was Eliza's uncle? Why hadn't he taken care of Louisa as her friend had promised? Why had he sold her to Macgregor?

Voices coming from the house alerted Louisa and she blinked her teary eyes to focus. Eliza walked out of the house with an older woman. A sob caught in Louisa's throat and she slapped her hand to her mouth. *Mother.*

Painful sobs shook through Louisa's body. She was unable to call out or even move. She needed to make her mother aware of her presence, but didn't know how. They must have thought *her* dead all those years as well. Why else would they not have come for her? And why…

She glared at her friend, hate and anger welling in Louisa's chest. Why was Eliza chatting with a woman she was told had died? Had Eliza known all this time? But she must. Eliza knew Mr. Featherspoon had taken Louisa to Scotland. Why hadn't her friend told her parents?

Anger grew inside her like a fire spreading quickly through her limbs and gave her the strength to stand. Whether Eliza wanted this or not, Louisa was going to find out the truth. Now.

She reached for the latch on the gate, but someone's large hand grasped her shoulder, turning her around. Evil eyes pierced straight through her as the man slowly shook his head.

"I would not do that if I were ye," Macgregor said.

She was too upset to be afraid. Besides, her family was so close now, this man shouldn't frighten her any longer. "My memory has returned, Mr. Macgregor. I have a family, and I'm no longer yours."

He shrugged and folded his beefy arms. "I still have need for ye, my sweet Louisa, which means ye are still mine."

"Are you insane? My family lives here—the very family Mr. Featherspoon told me had perished in a fire. Mr. Macgregor, you no longer have rein over me, now get out of my sight." She swung back to the gate, but once again, he stopped her. This time his hand on her arm squeezed painfully tight and she cried out, pulling away.

"Ye were always a daydreamer, Louisa. Ye never believed yer family had died even after we proved it." He tsked and shook his head.

"You never proved a thing."

"As much as ye want to have a family, ye never will. I'm yer only family… me and the other children."

"You are wrong. Mr. Featherspoon lied to me. He lied to you." She motioned her head toward the manor. "This is my family. Now let me be!"

The evil man's gaze darted back and forth between her and

the house. With narrowed eyes, he scratched his head as if in deep thought. Louisa didn't like his calculating expression at all.

"Even if this was yer family as ye proclaim, the bargain we made still stands. However I'll add another juicy tidbit to our deal. If ye do *not* get me the dowager's jewels, not only will I harm the duke and his children, but the people who live at this place as well. In fact, I'm wonderin' right now how I could get ye to steal from them. They look as if they have fat pockets, don't ye think?" He stepped closer, his gaze delving deep into hers. "Ye know I will follow through with my threats. One more week is all I ask. Ye get me those jewels, or those ye love—and whoever lives here—will die the fiery death ye had been told about all those years ago."

Her stomach churned and she clutched her middle. What had she done? But more than that, how could she get out of this? The truth was she couldn't. He was serious, and she knew not to go against him or else someone ended up hurt... or dead.

"If ye tell *anyone* about this, I shall torture ye as ye have never been tortured before." He ran the pad of his thumb along her bottom lip. "I'm almost hopin' ye go against me. I have somethin' very excitin' and pleasurable planned for us, my dear."

She turned her face away as bile rose to her throat. "I will do as you ask and steal the dowager's jewels," she whispered brokenly. "But that's all."

"What about the family that lives here?" He glanced at the manor again.

Her heart crumpled even more. "You were right. I don't know them. I was just daydreaming about having a real family again."

"Good girl." Softly, he patted her cheek. "Now, come with me and I shall get ye out of here."

Dejectedly, she followed, her heart breaking with each step as he led her to his horse. Her life was over one way or another. If she didn't do as he said, he'd seriously hurt everyone she loved. If she did as he instructed, they would all hate and disown her because of her thievery.

He offered his hand to help her into his curricle, but she brushed it aside and climbed in by herself. Once he sat next to her and urged the horse into a trot, she dared take a glance back at her family's estate. Nobody had noticed her. Although sadness filled her, she was grateful they hadn't. Macgregor would have indeed harmed them.

"Why have you been watching me?" she asked, her voice rose in anger.

"Because I know how badly ye want to break free of me, and I could not possibly allow that to happen until after ye have stolen the jewels." He glanced her way with an arched eyebrow. "And my first instincts were correct."

Louisa blew out a gush of air and rubbed her forehead. "I will get the jewels for you."

"Of course ye will."

Macgregor whistled a lively tune, which gnawed on her nerves. They rode for a few minutes as questions swam in her head. Although she remembered her past now, there were still things she wanted to know. When she lived with Macgregor, she rarely voiced her opinion or even spoke to the man. He had frightened her beyond belief. But now... Now she had more courage, it seemed.

"Why did Mr. Featherspoon sell me to you?"

His whistling stopped and he peered her way. "Because we have a bargain, him and I. He delivers children to my doorstep, and I keep the law away from him."

"The law?" She blinked tired eyes. "I would think the law would be searching for you."

"No. He does the kidnappin', not I."

"Is that why the law is looking for him? Because they suspect him of kidnapping?"

"That and more. Although a drunk, he is a clever man and does not leave traces of his wrong doin's."

"So my real family...they don't believe I was kidnapped?"

"Not at all."

"Then what do they think happened to me?"

"If they are still alive, they would have been told ye drowned, my dear."

She forced a laugh. "I don't think my family would believe that. They knew I could swim."

Macgregor looked her way again. "Not when yer cloak was found in the river."

"And who, pray tell, found my cloak?"

"The teacher at yer school."

Louisa pieced together everything that happened the day she'd heard about her family dying. This did not make sense at all. "What about my friend, Eliza? She knew I didn't drown. She was there with me when her uncle gave me the sad news."

Macgregor tilted his head back and laughed. His yellow and brown teeth were coated with food particles, and she wanted to gag.

"Oh, my dear Louisa. Yer startin' to see things clearly, already. Do I really need to tell ye?"

"I don't understand. Why would my good friend lie to my family about my death… and lie to me about her uncle?"

He shrugged and focused back on the road. "That ye will have to ask her. The deal she made was with Featherspoon, not me."

"But you must know something."

He chuckled. "What they did was none of my concern. The children I have purchased are the only things that matter right now."

She folded her arms tightly across her chest and scowled. "My family is alive, and one day I *will* find them."

"Oh, my naïve Louisa. There is one thing ye do not understand yet."

"Then enlighten me."

"If yer family is alive and ye happen to find them, they will not want ye any longer. Their precious little girl has turned into a common thief." Tsking, he shook his head. "Nobody will want ye after ye take the dowager's jewels. *Nobody*... but me."

Tears stung her eyes as her heart finished breaking. Although she didn't want to admit it, Macgregor was correct. Nobody would want her—not her family, and especially not Trevor.

Her life as she knew it had turned into a hellish nightmare.

Chapter Twenty-Eight

W*HERE IS THAT man?*

Richard Macgregor paced the small amount of floor space in his office, glancing out the window every minute as he passed. It had been two hours now since he'd taken Louisa back to the duke's estate, and the first place Macgregor went after that was to meet Percy Featherspoon at the office. That man had promised Macgregor another child. Today.

Richard stopped in front of the window. Outside, the street was busy with hackneys creeping down the road and couples leisurely strolling in the early afternoon as if they didn't have a care in the world. The imps who worked for him were out in their assigned spots, watching for the best moment to pick some gent's pocket or snatch a lady's wrist purse.

Because Richard had nothing to do at this particular moment but wait for Featherspoon, irritation for the man's tardiness grew by leaps and bounds. Already, Richard wanted to throttle the man, and when given the chance, he'd surely follow through with his instincts.

Grumbling, he raked his fingers through his hair. It wasn't like Featherspoon to be this late. Something must have happened.

Richard's heartbeat paused as his mind took a different direction. Could Percy have been discovered by the police and taken to the gaol? Or perhaps that insipid niece of Featherspoon's had the man dancing around her selfish demands once again. The woman was almost as crafty as Richard, himself.

He scratched his ear. Perhaps it was now time to meet the young lady face-to-face. For years, he'd known about her hold on Featherspoon, which was the very key that kept the worthless man working for Richard. He'd threatened Featherspoon many times to take Miss Eliza Watson and teach her how to work the streets. Perhaps now was the time to follow through with the threat. Of course, the girl was past the age he needed, but she would serve him well as a harlot—just as Louisa would eventually.

After hurrying out of his office and locking the door, he took fast steps to his steed and mounted. There was no time to waste since he was losing daylight fast. Thankfully, he'd known about Miss Watson's life through Featherspoon, and if Richard didn't act quickly, the young maiden would soon be the wife to Lord Wellesley. Richard could not let that happen now. But first, he must find Featherspoon and drag him along in order to be formally introduced to Miss Watson.

Kicking his heels into the horse's belly, he urged the animal faster toward Featherspoon's pitiful home. If that man didn't drink himself into oblivion every day, he might wonder why Richard did not pay him well.

He chuckled. Once again, he enjoyed being in control and making people bend to *his* will.

As he neared the meager cottage of his colleague, a long wagon, two carriages, and several horses stood vacated in front. Curious, Richard slowed his steed and crept closer. All the occupants of these vehicles clustered near the front porch. A fancy-dressed young lady stood out amongst a handful of working men, with the girl's maid lingering close by. A man—who Richard had tried his best to avoid—asked the young lady questions. When she turned and Richard saw her face, recognition struck like a blow to the forehead.

Miss Watson.

Yet why was she talking to the local constable?

Panic clutched Richard's heart. Featherspoon's niece must have ratted out her uncle.

Gritting his teeth, Richard pulled his horse to a halt. He'd like nothing better than to get his hands on that girl and teach her what happens when people cross him.

Another movement drew his attention to the porch as two men lifted a body draped in a blanket and carried it to the wagon. Eliza held a white lacey handkerchief to her mouth as the men moved the covered body past her. Hesitantly, she touched the blanket only to quickly withdraw her hand.

Oh good heavens... That body was Featherspoon. Richard knew it. How did the poor man end up dead?

Richard backed his horse into the trees so as not to be spotted. His mind twirled with questions. With Featherspoon dead, where would Richard get his children? And speaking of children... where was the one Percy had promised Richard? He scanned the surroundings again, but didn't see a young lad.

Within minutes, the wagon started on its way, and the constable and two men quickly followed. Richard waited until they rode past before he rode up the drive. Miss Watson and her maid were climbing in their curricle. The blue gown she wore and the white bonnet and matching shawl seemed vaguely familiar. He knew he'd seen Eliza earlier today, but where?

Suddenly, it hit him. He'd seen Eliza at the same house Louisa had been in front of, daydreaming. Pieces of the puzzle started fitting together, and he grinned like a child on Christmas. The house Louisa had been looking at *had* been her true family's house. Eliza was soon to be Lady Wellesley—and Frank Hamilton lived with the Earl of Danvers.

In the early years after Richard had purchased Louisa, she mentioned her friend—the one whose uncle had took her after her family had died. Chuckling, Richard shook his head. What would Louisa think if she knew her school friend was marrying into the family?

As Richard rode closer to the two women sitting in the vehicle, Eliza's gaze fell upon him. He bowed slightly and smiled. "Good afternoon."

"Is there something I can help you with?" she asked in a sweet honey-toned voice.

"I have come to visit my friend, Mr. Featherspoon."

Frowning, Eliza shook her head. "You are too late. My uncle died earlier. His body was just taken to the morgue, in fact."

Gasping, Richard acted shocked over the news. "How terrible. Do ye know how he died?"

"He was murdered. Someone hit him on the back of the head with a thick piece of wood."

He shook his head. "Such terrible news, indeed."

Eliza's gaze swept over him slowly. Disgust gradually appeared on her expression. "Pardon me, but may I ask your name?"

"Certainly." He jumped off his horse and bowed again. "I'm Mr. Macgregor."

Her eyes widened for a split second. Even the color in her cheeks disappeared. Indeed, she had heard of him.

Her throat constricted as she lifted her chin. "Well, I'm sorry we had to meet under such dire circumstances, but I must be on my way home to inform my family of my uncle's passing."

She flipped the reins to urge the horse forward, but Richard grasped the harness and stopped the animal. "One moment more." He waited for her reaction and was pleased when a hint of fear crept across her face.

"I really need to return home, Mr. Macgregor."

"As I'm certain ye do, but what I have to say will only take a moment, I assure ye."

"Please hurry then."

He stepped closer to her side of the vehicle. Eliza's back stiffened and she held the reins so tight her knuckles turned white. Beside her, the maid appeared just as frightened as she scooted closer to Eliza.

"Miss Watson, I know ye know who I am and about the relationship I had with yer uncle."

"I—I fear I do not know what you are referring to."

"There's no need to lie, Miss Watson. Yer uncle spoke of ye quite often and I feel I know ye well." He flipped his hand. "But because of the untimely death of yer uncle, I'm afraid I will now have to find someone to replace him as my business partner."

She didn't speak, just stared intently into his eyes.

He continued, "It wasn't until a few minutes ago, when I realized who the fortunate person would be to take his place."

She licked her lips. "Who?"

He smiled wide. "Miss Watson, I believe ye are the perfect person to take over where yer uncle left off."

The maid gasped and placed her hand over her mouth. Eliza laughed, but it sounded forced. "Mr. Macgregor, I do not think—"

"Because if ye don't," he quickly went on, "I will allow yer friend, Louisa, to meet the family she thought died in a fire six years ago—and especially, the friend who created the lie."

Finally, the color in her face finished fading. He knew he had her now.

"Mr. Macgregor," she said with a shaky voice, "I really have no idea what you are talking about."

"Indeed you do, Miss Watson."

"Please move out of my way or I shall run you over." She shouted a command to the horse and flicked the reins again.

"I shall give you twenty-four hours to decide," he called loudly as the curricle rode off.

Rubbing his hands together, he snickered as he walked toward his horse. His plans were unfolding nicely. Once again—after a few weeks of uncertainty—he had control of his life.

THE SUN DIPPED low in the horizon, bringing shades of pink to the sky. Trevor rode his steed hard as he headed back to the house before dusk settled over the land. Anticipation drummed inside of him with each pound from the horse's hooves. He couldn't wait to tell Louisa what he'd discovered. Hopefully, she'd be overjoyed, and maybe she could even remember something about her past—anything that would lead them back to the identity of her family.

He had now helped two boys whom Featherspoon had told were orphans, but Trevor found the families and reunited them. Certainly, this would be happy news for Louisa's situation.

He hadn't seen her in a couple of days, and although he'd been kept busy, he missed watching her care for his children. He missed her smile, her infectious laugh, and her dreamy gaze when she looked at him. Another thing he longed for was feeling the warmth of her soft body while in his arms, and the sweetness of her tender touch. And heaven help him, he missed the desire stirring inside of him whenever they kissed.

More than anything he wanted to help Louisa discover her past. He wanted her family to be alive. She might be the Danvers' daughter, but if that were the case, then she'd be engaged to Lord Wellesley. Although, the man was within weeks of marrying another. It didn't matter. Trevor loved Louisa and he knew she returned his affection, and everything else could be worked out.

He reached the manor just as the sun disappeared and night's shadows took over. After dismounting and tossing the reins to the groomsman, Trevor darted up the steps and hurried inside his house. Hobbs came out of the parlor and greeted him with a bow.

"Welcome home, Your Grace."

He smiled. "Hobbs, have you seen Miss Louisa and my children?"

"I believe they finished their dinner not long ago and are now in the nursery."

"Splendid." Trevor nodded. "I shall go see them right away."

Taking the stairs two at a time, he sprinted toward the nursery, anxious to see his children—but especially Louisa. He reached the door and paused, taking a deep breath. He didn't want to appear like he'd run the whole way.

Slowly, he opened the door and peeked inside. Louisa sat on a chair with the twins on her lap, reading them a bedtime story. The children—already in their night clothes—focused on the pictures, but every so often looked up at Louisa with spellbound expressions.

A grin stole across Trevor's face. The love Adam and Amanda had for her shone in their eyes. Trevor's heart melted. He knew how the twins felt since he had had the same emotions inside him for quite some time.

When he lifted his gaze to peer into Louisa's face… His heart dropped. Something was wrong. Dreadfully wrong. Gone was the sparkle he enjoyed watching dance in her eyes. Gone was the beautiful smile that lit her face. Even the tone of her voice seemed forlorn.

Although she'd been distant since their trip to the circus, the way she looked today was so very different. As if there was nothing inside her—no energy, no happiness. Nothing. As if despair had taken over and left only a shell of a woman.

He needed to speak with her, but couldn't have the children around because he was certain Louisa would become emotional and that would only upset Adam and Amanda. Quietly, he pulled the door closed then went in search of Mrs. Smythe. He found her in the kitchen and motioned for her to step into the dining room.

"Good evening, Your Grace," she said after leaving the kitchen. "It is a pleasure to see you home early today knowing how busy you have been."

"Indeed, Mrs. Smythe, I have been quite busy. Could you go upstairs and ask Miss Louisa to come to my study? I need to speak with her posthaste."

She nodded. "She just returned home herself a half hour ago."

"She did?"

"Yes. This morning she needed to go to the place where you hit her with your curricle to see if she could force her memory to return."

"And? Did it return?"

Frowning, the housekeeper shook her head. "I don't believe so, Your Grace. Miss Louisa has been very quiet and is keeping to herself."

"It sounds like I definitely need to speak with her, then."

"Shall I watch the children until you are finished with her?"

"If you will, I shall appreciate your thoughtfulness."

"Very well."

He hurried into his study, closed the door, and poured himself a drink. As he paced the floor, he shrugged out of his overcoat, content to wear just his waistcoat over his shirt. A small fire had already been burning in the hearth, which warmed the room considerably. Nice and cozy. Just the way he liked it.

It took about ten minutes, but soon a knock came upon the door. "Come in."

The door opened, and Louisa entered. Her sad expression tugged at his heart. He'd do anything to make her happy again.

"You wanted to see me, Your Grace?"

"Yes. Please close the door."

She did as instructed, then walked closer. "Have I done something that displeases you?"

"Indeed you have, Louisa." Slowly, he stepped toward her, stopping mere inches in front. "You didn't say my name." He smiled.

She returned a smile, but it seemed as if she struggled to make her lips curve upward. Her eyes didn't twinkle like they used to, either. "Forgive me, Trevor. I have been out of sorts of late."

He cupped her shoulders, his thumbs rubbing circles on her arms. "I realize this, Louisa. You have been distant ever since the circus. Please, let me help you."

"If only you could."

"Mrs. Smythe tells me you went to the place where I hit you to see if your memory would return."

She nodded, but didn't say anything.

"I'm assuming by your silence that your memory has not returned."

Tears glistened in her eyes as she pulled away from him and moved to the hearth. "Oh, Trevor. Sometimes I feel as if I will never get my life back."

Her body trembled slightly, so he stepped behind her and slipped his arms around her waist, pulling her against him. "You don't need your life back, my dear. You have a new life here."

She stroked his arms and laid the back of her head against his chest. "I know I do, I just wish..." She breathed deeply, then released it in a gush.

"Louisa, these past couple of days I have discovered some things about your past."

Her body stiffened. "What have you discovered?"

"Your family might be alive," he whispered in her ear.

She turned in his arms and faced him. He kept his arms around her waist, not wanting her to leave.

"Are you certain?" she asked.

He nodded. "I met a boy who had worked with you under Macgregor's control. I discovered this boy was told his family died in a house fire. The next day I met another boy who was about to be sold to Macgregor, and his story mirrored the other. Because of the coincidence, I decided to find out what really happened. I found each boy's family—alive."

"But how is all this related to my situation?"

Trevor sighed heavily and sat on the edge of his desk, pulling her in a more intimate position toward him. "Each boy talked about a man who'd told them about their family's death. Mr. Percy Featherspoon."

He waited for any kind of recognition—a memory to emerge or anything. Her face remained blank. "This name doesn't sound familiar to you at all?"

She shrugged.

"Please, Louisa. Try to remember. This is vital to my discovery."

She closed her eyes. During the few silent moments, he took advantage of admiring her features. Lovely, long lashes, perky little nose, kissable lips. Beautiful blonde hair he loved to stroke when she left it down. Skin so flawless, and so soft. On impulse, he lifted his knuckles and gently brushed them across her cheek. Louisa's eyes flew open, but she didn't pull away.

"I—I think I remember a man by this name. I recall he was my friend's uncle."

Confusion washed over him and he crinkled his brow. "Your friend's uncle, you say? Do you remember your friend's name?"

Her head moved slowly in a nod. "Eliza."

"Your memory is returning. In time you shall remember everything."

"I pray you are correct."

"From the information I collect, Mr. Featherspoon was the man responsible for kidnapping children and selling them to Mr. Macgregor."

Her eyes widened, but she didn't speak. He continued, "I found Mr. Featherspoon yesterday and spoke with the man."

She gasped and clutched his hands. "Indeed? What did he say?"

"At first he acted as if he didn't kidnap children, but that he took orphans in and found them homes. However, I pointed out the boy I had talked with and found his family alive." He rubbed his fingers across hers. "I kept questioning him about you. What I found out was that you *were* born of nobility."

Tears glistened in her eyes. "Did he say who my parents were?"

"Unfortunately, no. The man met his Maker quicker than I would have liked."

"He died? How?"

"One of the children he had recently kidnapped crushed Mr.

Featherspoon's skull. The boy had been listening to us and snuck up behind his kidnapper and killed him."

A deep breath expelled from her mouth. "I have to admit, how relieved I am to hear that. Too bad the same fate could not come to Macgregor any time soon."

"If I have my way, it will."

A few more tears slid down her cheeks and he swiped them away with his thumb.

"If only I could believe that, but I know Macgregor, Trevor. He is a calculating, evil man. You do not want to cross him. Even now I fear for your life because you have been asking questions about him."

"Shhh…" He pulled her against his chest, resting her head just under his chin. "No need to fear, my love. I shall protect you. Always."

He kissed her forehead, his lips lingering. How could he help it? Kissing this woman became an addiction to him—one that he never wanted to leave. She lifted her head. Her moist eyes tore at his heart, and the frightened, empty look in her eyes worried him.

"Trevor, you are the most thoughtful person I have ever met. I feel so safe in your arms. I just wish I could feel that even when we are apart. Then, and only then, shall I truly feel safe."

He smiled and kissed the tip of her nose. "If I could keep you in my arms all the time, I would. You are constantly in my thoughts and in my heart." He cupped the side of her face. "Louisa, I'm completely in love—"

She cut off his words when she lifted her mouth to his, silencing him. The kiss was so very sweet, yet there seemed to be desperation to her actions that he couldn't explain. She grasped his shirt, opening her mouth as she deepened the kiss.

Explosions shot through him, and he enfolded her in his arms tighter, meeting her demanding kisses. The palms of her hands wandered over his chest, then up his shoulders before she linked her fingers around his neck, bringing her even closer. He loved the way she caressed him. He loved the way he felt more like a man in her presence than he'd ever felt while married to Gwen.

He moved his hands over Louisa's back, touching her everywhere, not resting in any particular area. Desires built inside him, hotter than before. Images of coupling with her as man and wife floated through his head, and he wanted more than anything to fulfill these dreams.

Her mouth left his as she trailed her lips over his chin and down his neck while her fingers plucked at his cravat then loosened the buttons on his waistcoat. His heart flip-flopped, knowing she wanted what he did. Because his thoughts were in pure bliss right now, thinking rationally was not an option. Feeling—and loving—were uppermost in his mind.

Searching for the buttons on her gown, he frantically ran his hands over her back. When the tips of his fingers brushed across the first barrier, he fumbled to unlatch her dress. One button came loose, then a second. His heart pounded crazily against his chest, threatening to crack a rib or two.

Before he could get the third released, a knock came upon his door. Louisa froze in his arms.

He didn't want to let her go. He wouldn't. "Now is not the time. I'm busy," he called out.

"Your Grace, there is an urgent visitor here for you," Hobbs said loudly.

Grumbling, Trevor rested his face in the crook of Louisa's neck. Deep breaths to calm himself were not helping at this particular moment, however.

Louisa kissed the side of his face before pulling away. Swollen, red lips were evident of the ardent passionate attention he'd given her. Desire still clung to her expression when she smiled.

"I believe you should see what is so important."

"You are more important." He reached for her to bring her back into his arms, but she withdrew further to the corner of the room.

Blowing out a frustrated breath, he raked his fingers through his hair and stomped to the door. Although irritated over the untimely appearance of his butler, what he and Louisa had been doing was not proper. He loved her and wanted to show her how much, but it wouldn't have been right to do that until *after* they were married.

Trevor stopped at the door and paused a moment to collect his wits before cracking open the door just enough to see his butler. "What is so urgent?"

"Forgive me, Your Grace, but Lord Hawthorne is in the sitting room with an urgent message for you. He implored me to find you posthaste."

Trevor wanted to throttle his brother's friend for disrupting Trevor's intimate moment, but as his mind cleared, he realized Dominic just might have discovered something important to Louisa's past. "Tell Lord Hawthorne I shall be in momentarily."

"I shall, Your Grace."

After closing the door, Trevor rushed through adjusting his cravat into place. Louisa stood facing a window. The buttons on her gown were already fastened. As he passed his overcoat lying on the sofa, he picked it up and shrugged into it, making his way toward Louisa.

"My love, please forgive me—"

She faced him and shook her head. "There is nothing to forgive. I need to return to the nursery to put the children to bed." She helped him by fastening the buttons of his waistcoat and straightening his cravat. "We shall finish this later." She smiled, but not fully.

"Indeed, we shall, my love." He kissed her once more on the lips before quitting the room, making sure he closed the door behind him.

When he entered the sitting room, Dominic paced in front of the wide hearth, taking long strides. He stopped and fixed his gaze on Trevor.

"We do not have a moment to lose," Lord Hawthorne said, marching toward Trevor.

"What is going on?"

"Your mother is having a small dinner party tonight. Trey and Judith were invited along with the Earl and Countess of Danvers and their nephew, Lord Wellesley and his fiancée, Miss Watson."

Confused, Trevor shook his head. "Why is this so urgent?"

"Because, my good man, your mother is a meddlesome dowager. Surely you realize that. If she were to say the wrong thing to the Danvers about Louisa…"

Trevor cursed. "By Jove, you are right, Hawthorne. We must get there immediately."

As Trevor hurried toward the front door, he prayed his mother wouldn't give any information to the Danverses, or if she did, that Trey would be able to smooth things over. One way or another, Louisa's name could *not* be dragged through the gossip mills, especially when he would ask her to marry him. Soon.

Chapter Twenty-Nine

TREVOR RUSHED INTO his mother's house with Lord Hawthorne on his heels. Bentley, the dowager's butler, greeted them inside the door.

"Your Grace," he said, bowing, "what a surprise it is to see you. The dowager has a few visitors here for her dinner party—"

"This I know, Bentley," Trevor grumbled. "And I hope she forgives Lord Hawthorne and me for barging in on her guests."

The lanky butler nodded. "Should I set extra plates at the table for you?"

"Yes, please."

"Your mother and her guests are still in the sitting room."

"Splendid." Trevor tried to smile under the duress. "We will show ourselves in, if you don't mind." He didn't wait for the butler to answer, but led Dominic toward the sitting room.

When Trevor entered, the Earl of Danvers and Wellesley stood near the hearth visiting with Trey, while Judith, the countess, and Miss Watson sat on the sofa near the dowager. The ladies were adorned in beautiful silks and lace, and the men looked as dignified as any gentleman would at a Society function.

Trevor studied the countess a little closer this time. It had been many years since he'd had the opportunity to speak with her, and now he wanted to know if she resembled his Louisa in any way. All he could see of her now was the side of her face. It appeared the women shared the same nose and oval face. Perhaps this was Louisa's long-lost mother after all.

At first nobody noticed him or Lord Hawthorne, but soon, Trey's gaze lifted and his eyes widened.

"Kenbridge, Hawthorne. What a pleasant surprise." Trey smiled and moved away from the other men. "I did not know the two of you were invited to Mother's dinner party."

A gasp tore from the dowager, which directed Trevor's attention toward her. "Mother, please forgive me for interrupting your gathering." He stepped to her chair, bent and kissed her cheek, then moved to his sister-in-law and kissed her hand. "Judith, you are lovelier than ever. Motherhood looks good on you." He winked.

She chuckled. "Always the charmer, my dear brother-in-law."

"Oh, no. Your loving husband obtained that title quite a while ago."

The group laughed.

Trevor bowed to the earl who now stood by his wife. "Good evening, Danvers. It is good to see you again."

"As you, Kenbridge." The earl returned a bow.

"Oh, Trevor." His mother stood. "I—I had no idea you were coming. I should have Bentley set two more places at the table."

"Already done." Trevor gave his mother a wink then turned to the others. "Please, excuse my interruption. I fear my appearance is most untimely. I hope you don't mind conversing with a boring lord such as myself."

"Nonsense," his mother said, flipping her hand.

"It is always a pleasure to converse with you." Countess Danvers grinned.

Trevor looked at Wellesley and nodded. "It is good to see you again."

"Your Grace," Wellesley began, "may I introduce my fiancée to you? This is Miss Eliza Watson." He motioned his hand toward the young woman.

"Nice to meet you, Miss Watson."

She curtsied. "It's a pleasure to make your acquaintance, Your Grace."

Eliza. Trevor knew he'd heard that name recently. As his mind scrambled to remember, Louisa's voice echoed through his head. *I recall Featherspoon was my friend's uncle. Eliza was my friend from school...*

Shock punched him in the stomach and he sucked in a quick breath. He'd wondered for a while if Louisa's parents were the Danverses, and now as he gazed upon the countess closer this time, he realized her amazing eyes were as beautiful and green as Louisa's. Hope sprang in his chest, making it hard to breathe.

Something didn't make sense and Trevor's head pounded with confusion. If Eliza's uncle was Featherspoon, then she would have known Louisa didn't drown as Wellesley had mentioned when referring to his cousin the other day.

"Miss Watson, forgive me for speaking out of turn, but I think I might know your family."

Her face brightened. "Indeed?"

"Do you have an uncle by the name of Percy Featherspoon?"

Her face paled and eyes widened. "Umm... Well, yes, but my family disowned my mother's brother many years ago."

"Oh, then I apologize for bringing up the uncomfortable topic."

She laughed, which sounded forced. "You did not know. There is nothing to apologize for."

At that moment, Bentley walked in and announced dinner.

Trevor offered his arm to his mother, who took it graciously. Following them were Trey and Judith, the earl and countess, Wellesley and Miss Watson, and bringing in the rear strolled Lord Hawthorne. Once everyone had been seated, Trey started the conversation by asking about the welfare of Trevor's twins. Deep inside, he knew his younger brother was slowly getting around to the subject of Louisa.

"Thank you for asking," Trevor said before taking a sip of his wine. "My children are flourishing well in their studies. Even better than before. Just recently, I have had to replace their nursemaid."

"Mrs. Jacobs?" Judith asked.

"Yes. The older lady had been treating my children poorly. If not for a woman I had recently met, I would have never known about Mrs. Jacobs's unforgiveable cruelness."

"Oh, dear," Countess of Danvers gasped. "I pray your children were not harmed."

"Not to worry, my lady. The twins are too young and will not remember anything in a few years."

"I must confess," Dominic added as the servants brought in the first course, "I have met the new nursemaid, and she is an angel sent right from heaven. Adam and Amanda adore her."

"How lovely." The countess smiled as she picked up her spoon. "It is always wonderful to have such a person to care for our children."

"Indeed it is." Trevor nodded.

Trey turned to the countess. "I trust you had a similar nursemaid for your child?"

The older woman's cheeks darkened in a blush. "I did, although I probably spent more time with Elizabeth than the nurse."

Trevor paused in thought, not wanting to voice his opinion yet. If Louisa was indeed the Danvers' daughter, why would she go by another name?

"Forgive me, Lady Danvers," Judith began, "but who is Elizabeth?"

"My daughter." Sadness clouded the older woman's eyes. "She died when she was in her twelfth year."

Judith frowned. "Accept my apologies for not knowing."

"I thank you." The countess looked to her husband and squeezed his hand. "It was a difficult time, but we muddled through the heartache together." She turned her focus to Eliza. "And Miss Watson was a godsend to us during that hard time. She had been Elizabeth's close friend in school."

Wellesley reached his hand and patted Eliza's.

Trevor bunched his hands under the table. What was going on? Frustration pounded through him almost as fast as it had when he couldn't get the right answers from Featherspoon. If Eliza was such a close friend, and her uncle was the one who kidnapped Louisa, wouldn't Miss Watson know?

"How fortunate for you to know Elizabeth," Trevor said as politely as he could before eating a spoonful of soup.

Smiling, Miss Watson didn't say anything. Although Trevor could tell the young woman soaked in the attention well.

He quickly continued before anyone else spoke next. "And by the time you and Lord Wellesley start having children, I'm certain my nursemaid will be available to work for you." He shrugged. "By that time, my children would be in need of a governess."

"But Kenbridge," Lord Hawthorne interrupted. "I'm certain *Louisa*—" he said louder—"would love to be the twins' governess as well."

Miss Watson's spoon hit the porcelain bowl, drawing everyone's attention to her. Suddenly, the pinkness Trevor had noticed in her cheeks only a few moments earlier had disappeared and her skin took on a paler color. There was even a slight shake to the young woman's hands.

"Oh, my dear. Are you all right?" the dowager asked.

"I… um, yes, I'm fine."

"You will have to forgive her," Wellesley said quickly, patting his fiancée's hand again. "Miss Watson has a bittersweet fondness for the name Louisa. For about seven years, the whole family has felt this way."

Miss Watson grasped his hand and tightened her fingers. Wordlessly, she shook her head as she aimed her glare at Wellesley. But it seemed the man didn't notice her silent plea as Trevor had.

"How so?" Dominic asked.

"Miss Watson never called my cousin by her Christian name,

Elizabeth. Eliza always referred to my cousin as Louisa."

Excitement shot through Trevor, but he tried not to show it. He swung his gaze to Trey and Dominic, who looked as elated as Trevor felt.

"Why is that, I wonder?" the dowager asked, who looked remarkably at ease and calm.

The countess chuckled. "Elizabeth thought hers and Eliza's name were too much alike, so my daughter went by her middle name, Louisa."

"What an odd coincidence," Trevor's mother added.

"Why do you say that?" the countess inquired of the dowager before taking another sip of her soup.

"Just that my son's nursemaid is named Louisa, and we think she was separated from her family a long time ago."

Knowing his mother wasn't tactfully trying to squeeze in the information, Trevor quickly covered his mother's hand with his. "Now, Mother. I do not think your guests want to hear about my nursemaid's memory loss."

"Memory loss, you say?" the earl asked in an anxious voice.

"Oh, yes." The dowager nodded to the earl before looking back at Trevor. "Go ahead, dear. Tell them about how Louisa cannot remember anything about her past."

"I would like to know." The countess leaned forward in her chair, her eyes resting on Trevor.

"As you wish." He took a deep breath. "Approximately a month ago, I was riding home from a dinner party, when someone ran out in front of me from the shadows of the trees." Not daring to go into much detail especially about Macgregor or stating the man's name, Trevor explained about how he came to meet Louisa, and how she couldn't remember anything. "The fascinating thing about all of this is that out of the few things she can remember, one of them is being raised by parents of Quality."

"Fascinating indeed." The earl nodded. "How old is this young woman?"

Trevor shrugged. "I wish I knew. The poor woman does not

even remember. But if I can calculate, I would say she was..." He looked at Eliza. "Probably around Miss Watson's age. She is a lovely woman with beautiful blonde hair, and the most amazing green eyes..."

Miss Watson groaned and fell against Wellesley in a swoon. Those around her jumped to assist. Although Trevor stood, he didn't rush to the woman's side. Even from where he sat, he could tell it was all an act. Indeed, this woman knew something, and he was certain the truth would not be pleasant for Louisa—or the Danverses—to hear.

After a few minutes of everyone fussing over Miss Watson, the earl shook his head and gazed at the dowager. "I fear we must cut our evening short. Miss Watson has been out of sorts all evening—even before we came. I think we should get her home."

"I agree." Trevor's mother frowned. "This poor girl needs to rest."

"Indeed, she does." Wellesley lifted Miss Watson in his arms as she groaned and placed her hand over her eyes.

As Trey and Dominic assisted the women out to their carriages. Elation rushed through Trevor. The truth of Louisa's past would be out soon, but not soon enough. He couldn't rush things with the Danverses, but tonight when he returned home, he would certainly ask Louisa to be his wife.

LOUISA PACED HER bedroom floor, wringing her hands like she would wet rags. Her body felt as limp, as well. She'd overheard Trevor and Lord Hawthorne discussing their plans for the evening. Thankfully, they had not closed the door and she'd heard their conversation clearly. Of course it didn't help that she snuck toward the room to listen, anyway.

Dread grew in a lump at the pit of her belly the longer she thought about Trevor and Lord Hawthorne's conversation.

Trevor would know the truth soon enough, which was what Louisa wanted. But she first wanted Macgregor taken care of so he would leave the ones she loved alone.

Her dream of being happy for the rest of her life with Trevor and his children fizzled quickly, leaving a gaping hole in her heart. All she had now were memories of their times together to cherish.

She'd watched him and Lord Hawthorne leave atop their horses not more than ten minutes ago. Praying Trevor would forgive her for what she was about to do, she rushed to her closet and located the maid's uniform she had worn when she first started working for Trevor.

It didn't take her long to change, and she threw on her black cloak and bonnet before leaving the room. She crept down the servants' stairs and out the back door. By now, Trevor and Lord Hawthorne would have arrived at the dowager's estate, the very same place Louisa planned to go.

But for very different reasons.

Night had fallen completely, and the half-moon didn't leave Louisa much light. She couldn't complain. She was used to sneaking around in the dark. She'd been an expert at this for six years and had hated every minute.

Getting a horse was a little more difficult, but soon she pulled a mare out of the stable, mounted, and was on her way. The small wind tugged at her bonnet, threatening to remove the hat, but she didn't care.

Tears stung her eyes, but she refused to cry. Showing emotion would do her no good. As much as she hated returning to her former life, she must. Trevor and the twins meant more to her than anything, and she couldn't allow Macgregor to harm them.

Even if it meant stealing the dowager's jewels.

Tonight while wrapped in Trevor's arms, it had been heaven. She never wanted to leave. When he had told her he'd loved her, she had tried to stop the words by pressing her mouth to his.

Hearing those three little words had been a dream come true, but then reality sank in, dragging her down like a boulder to the bottom of the ocean, she knew now that their love could never be. Once he discovered her past—and what she was going to do tonight—he would never want her for his wife. Her chest ached when she thought of a life without him and the twins, but it was something she would have to sacrifice in order to keep them safe.

Not only that, her parents were better off not knowing about her past mistakes. All those terrible things she did while working for Macgregor. None of it could be forgiven, and she knew not to ask. It was better that her parents believed she had drowned.

And Eliza…

May Eliza rot in *hell* for what she had put Louisa through!

Louisa knew not why her so-called friend had done this to her, but eventually Louisa would find out and make Eliza pay dearly for all those lost years.

Thankfully, Mr. Featherspoon's life had ended and he would have to explain himself come judgment day. And one day when all of this was over and she knew those she loved were not going to be harmed by Macgregor, she would find a way to send *that evil man* to meet his Maker, as well.

When Louisa came upon the dowager's estate, she slowed the mare until she reached the back door to the servant's quarters. She dismounted then crept inside the house. The kitchen sounded busy, so she avoided going near that room. Voices came from the dining room, and when she heard Trevor, her heart pitter-pattered. Having these kinds of feelings was not healthy, but she would always treasure the way she felt whenever he was around.

It wasn't hard to find the backstairs, so she hurried up toward the dowager's chambers. The manor was grand—although not as lovely as Trevor's. Still, Louisa found the double doors leading into the dowager duchess's room easily enough. A low fire in the hearth gave her light, and as she crept into another room, the lamps were turned low as well. The dowager had plenty of lovely things decorating her walls.

Louisa unfastened her bonnet and laid it on a chair. Sadness grew inside her for what she was about to do, and she said a silent prayer the Lord would forgive her because she knew for certain Trevor would not.

The first thing she found were empty satchels that Louisa knew dowagers liked to carry with them when they were out in public. These would help Louisa to carry the jewels and hopefully hide them better when she left the manor.

Once she located the jewelry boxes, Louisa stared, unable to move. So many lovely necklaces that were costly. So many rings, and brooches, and watches. If Macgregor even realized the dowager had this many pieces of jewelry, he'd have all of his children stealing from her constantly.

With a shaky hand, she picked up the closest necklace, heavy with rubies and diamonds. *I cannot do this,* her heart screamed, but reason told her she *must.* It was as if an invisible hand tried to snatch the item back in a game of tug-of-war, but soon she brought it to the satchel and dropped it inside. Tears burned her eyes and grief burdened her already achy chest as she shoved two more necklaces in the small bag.

Several voices in her head grew louder and clashed, some encouraging her to take the jewels, others begging her not to. The vision of Trevor's handsome face formed in her mind. He smiled at her; lovingly caressed her cheek, and tenderly kissed her with so much emotion. Then she saw the twins. Their cherubic faces looking at her for help as Ms. Jacobs made them march, and then their expressions glowed when Louisa became their nursemaid. Trevor and his children trusted her. Completely. Without question.

"I cannot do this," she muttered. "I will *not* do this!"

Wearily, she leaned against the dresser. She was not Louisa Hamilton the thief. Not any longer. She could not steal from the people she loved. There had to be another way to stop Macgregor. He wasn't expecting these pieces of jewelry for a few more days. Surely, if she confessed to Trevor, he would be able to help her. Between the two of them—and perhaps his brother and Lord Hawthorne—they could come up with a solution to the problem. Would Macgregor really know she had told Trevor? The evil man couldn't spy on her every moment of the day.

Feeling better about her decision, she placed her hand back inside the satchel to withdraw the necklaces, but a noise from the other room startled her. She jumped and turned toward the sound. A man stood at the door.

Trevor.

Her heart sank, and her knees shook. Standing in the door-way, his narrowed eyes switched from her to the jewels in her hand. A frown marred his handsome face as sadness and distrust deepened his gaze.

"Trevor, this is not what it looks like."

"It looks like you are stealing from my mother."

She placed the jewels on the dresser and hurried to him. "Trevor, please, let me explain," she begged, clutching his overcoat.

Disgust deepened his expression as he peeled her hands away from his body as if she were a diseased leper.

"What could you possibly explain? Here I am, trying desperately to find your past while you are sneaking around behind my back and stealing from us."

Her heart broke and tears streamed down her eyes, blurring her vision. "No, Trevor. You don't understand. Macgregor made me—"

"Indeed, I'm certain he did." He pushed past her and lifted the jewels, letting them spill between his fingers back into the satchel. "Take these to Macgregor and go back to his band of thieves." He shoved the bag in her hands. "And tell him he's done a fabulous job turning a lady into a criminal. You are certainly the *best* thief—and deceiver—I have ever come across." Trevor took a deep breath. "Now please leave this house before my mother sees what you have done, because it would surely break her heart as it has mine."

Louisa fell to her knees and clutched his trouser leg. "No. Please listen to me. Don't do this, Trevor—"

"And do *not* call me that name ever again." He pushed her away. "Leave now before I summon the police and have you arrested like I should have done the first time I met you."

Her world crumpled down around her worse than she could have ever imagined. Sobbing, she lifted herself off the floor and fled out the door as fast as her unsteady legs could carry her.

Chapter Thirty

RICHARD MACGREGOR SAT at his desk inside his tiny office, reading the missive that had just been delivered. He grinned and wanted to shout with happiness. Things couldn't have gone any better if he'd planned them himself. Then again, mayhap he had planned it without really knowing.

Of course he had. Chuckling, he glanced at the letter in his hand.

Mr. Macgregor. I have thought over the brief conversation we had outside my uncle's home yesterday, and I have come to a decision. I will take over where my uncle left off only on one condition. You must take care of Louisa Hamilton. Six years ago my uncle promised he would not harm my friend but take her far away so her family would never see her again. Now I find she is back and her family is becoming suspicious. I still do not want my schoolmate harmed, but please take her far away from London as quickly as possible. Once this has been resolved, I will find children to work for you as my uncle had. Meet me outside the front steps of the hospital tonight at seven so we can discuss this agreement. Regards, Miss Eliza Watson.

Smiling, Richard pulled away from the desk and gazed out of the window. The evening shadows played in the dark corners of the unlit streets as people scurried inside buildings or to their carriages. Fortune shined upon him for the first time in weeks. Things were coming together nicely. Soon Louisa would be in his grasp once again and doing his bidding as always. He would keep the two women away from each other, because he did not plan on sending Louisa away as Miss Watson had requested. His brilliant pupil was much too valuable for that. But now he knew how to blackmail both women to get his way.

Shuffling footsteps grew louder coming from the other room. Richard turned as David ran in, huffing from exhaustion. Moisture dampened his dirty brow and made hair stick to his skin.

"What are ye doin' here? Yer supposed to be at the Kenbridge estate watching Louisa."

"I have come from there because I discovered something."

"What have ye discovered?" Richard barked.

"'Tis not good news, I fear."

Richard grumbled and stepped closer. "Tell me."

"I kept an eye on the estate just as you'd asked, and I crept closer to the stables to hear anything noteworthy." The scraggly boy shook his head. "'Tis not good, I tell ye."

"Out with it before I whip ye."

"Louisa… she has left the manor." David took in a ragged breath, still wheezing. "From what I've gathered, the duke let her go."

"*Let her go?*" Richard shouted as he grabbed the scrawny boy's shoulders. "What do ye mean? The duke was in love with her. Why did he let her go?"

"I don't know, sir. That's just what I heard."

"Then ye heard wrong."

David shook his head. "No, I didn't, because I also heard the duke talking to one of his friends."

"What did they say?"

"The duke said he didn't want to see Louisa's face ever again—or he'd summon the police and have her arrested. Apparently, he caught her stealin' his mother's jewels. He was pretty upset, I tell ye."

Richard grinned. His plan was working better than he thought. "Splendid."

"I also heard…" David said softer with a touch of confusion in his throat.

"What?"

"I heard something about Mr. Featherspoon. I heard he'd kidnapped us from our families and told them we were dead." He took a hesitant step forward, blinking back tears as his lips quivered as if he would cry at any moment. "Is this true? Is my family really alive?"

"Of course it's not true."

"But I heard the duke tell his friend about two boys he'd helped. Norman was one of them."

"I have no way of knowin' if Featherspoon lied to ye or not. But it doesn't matter because now ye work for me," Richard snapped and pushed David toward the door. "Now get out there and find Louisa. If ye see the others, tell them this is urgent. I need her found and brought to me tonight or ye'll all go without food for a week."

"Yes, sir." David sniffed and ran out the door into the street.

Richard shrugged on his coat, then plopped a hat on his head as he walked outside. He had a meeting with a pretty lady he wasn't about to miss. Now with Louisa missing, it would be easier for him to convince Eliza her friend was *taken care of*.

He whistled and walked with a bounce in his step. Louisa would not stay away for long, he was certain. He didn't know what exactly happened between her and the duke, but the girl was in love with Kenbridge, and because she wanted him and his children safe, she would bring Richard the jewels she'd taken.

Come to think of it, he'd brainwashed all of his children quite well. Of course, he only did what came natural to him. He'd been orphaned at a young age and learned the art of picking pockets and lying his way through life. The older he grew, the more he learned about how to manipulate people. Now he was very good at it. The best, in fact.

The wind became stronger the closer he came to the hospital. A spring storm was definitely brewing, and there weren't as many large buildings around this area to block the wind. He bundled his coat around his neck a little tighter and hurried. He always tried to walk in the shadows, especially at night, to keep hidden. If spotted by a policeman, they'd recognize Richard right away. Being this close to Town made it harder to earn a living because the police knew Macgregor well. Yet this was the perfect time to be around London because of the season and all of Society's functions happening around them. Once the season was over, Macgregor would pack up his miscreants and leave for a little while.

Across the street, two policemen trolled the area. Macgregor lowered his hat on his forehead and cast his gaze to the ground, hurrying his footsteps even more. The other two men laughed, and their voices echoed through the street. Thankfully, they hadn't looked Richard's way. And with any luck, they would keep on walking and not even notice Richard.

But although they didn't glance at him, Richard still felt like someone watched him. Closely. Slowing, he searched the nearly empty street to find the source of the eerie feeling running amok through him. Too many shadows. Too many noises from the wind beating on the windows and walls.

He turned a corner, only one block away from the hospital. It was nearly seven. Miss Watson would probably be waiting for him by now.

From a nearby alleyway, a cat screeched. Richard jumped, and then chuckled at being so skittish tonight. Even if the police were after him—and several enemies wanted Richard dead—he would never get caught. His children feared him too much to go against him. And the police… Well, Richard could slip from them easy enough just as he'd done for several years.

Quick footsteps pounded behind him. He reached for the knife he always kept in his coat pocket for protection. *Gone.* Grumbling, he walked faster, his mind twirling as he tried to remember where he'd put the weapon. He never took his out of his pocket unless it was to use it on someone. But he hadn't had to threaten anyone with it for weeks.

Now was *not* the time to panic. Neither was it the time for someone to threaten him since he could not protect himself.

He just needed to turn the corner up a little ways and he'd be within shouting distance of the hospital. Up ahead, there were more streetlamps lighting the way as well.

Macgregor.

His name whispered with the wind as it blew against his face. Ridiculous. The wind wouldn't say his name… But someone had.

He stopped, swung quickly around, hoping to catch whoever followed him. The street remained empty.

Macgregor.

There it was again. He jerked toward the sound coming from a different direction. Something wasn't right, and he didn't like the spooky feeling crawling up his spine.

Nearby, hurried footsteps crunched on the road, coming closer by the second. He couldn't be frightened. He was *never* frightened. People were afraid of him, not the other way around.

"Who goes there?" he shouted then heard his question echoed. "This is ludicrous." He grumbled and turned back toward his destination.

As he passed an alleyway, a woman cloaked in brown and black rags, rushed out and grasped his arm. "Please, govna, I beg ye for some money. I'm starvin' and need to feed me fam'ly."

Gagging, he pushed her away. Her stench of raw onions and fresh urine was more than he could stand. "Leave me alone, ye old crow."

She reached for him again, and he stumbled over his feet to get away, bumping into someone else. Suddenly, a sharp pain pierced his back, cutting through his clothes and slicing his skin. Fiery agony blazed through his body as his shirt dampened quickly from his blood. He jerked around to see who had stabbed him, but all he could see in the shadows was a hand holding *his* missing knife coated with his own blood.

The pain became unbearable, and he collapsed to his knees. Coldness seeped through him like liquid pouring through his veins. Each breath he took became more difficult until he couldn't breathe at all. Quickly, his vision turned black.

TREVOR SAT AT the breakfast table, staring at his plate of untouched food. For three days he hadn't had any ambition to do anything, let alone eat. Since finding Louisa stealing from his mother, he had locked himself in his home, refused visitors, stayed in his chambers more than he should, and turned away the offer of playing with his children.

Everywhere he looked, he saw Louisa. In the brief time she'd spent in his household, she had turned everything around. Even his servants had smiled more. That was before she left, of course. Before… he bade her to leave and never return.

The sorrow in his heart was, at times, more than he could bear. Gwen's death had never crushed him as much. Now he wondered how he could go on. He'd given his whole heart to Louisa, and for the first time in a long while, he believed in love and trust, only to have her show him that love and trust didn't belong in his life.

He'd lain awake at night, trying hard not to remember her smile and the way she stared dreamily into his eyes. Desperately, he tried not to think of kissing her and the way she'd melted into his arms. He tried not to recall the way his children loved to be around her and the way she made them laugh. The way she'd made *him* laugh.

He wouldn't allow his emotions to get the best of him. He refused to cry, although a few times when he'd drift off to sleep only to awaken to find his pillow damp.

"Your Grace"—Hobbs walked in with a package in his

hands—"this just came for you."

Trevor's frown deepened. "Who brought it?"

"It was from a courier, my lord."

Hobbs set the package on the table then laid the newspaper beside it. "And here is your daily paper. Is there anything else you need now?"

"Not right now, thank you."

The butler nodded and quit the room. Trevor stared at the small package, having no idea who would have given him this— or why. He really didn't feel like opening it, but curiosity nudged him enough to move his plate aside and slide the package in front of him. Quickly, he tore off the paper just to get it over and done with.

Lying inside was his mother's satchel with the necklaces Louisa had taken three nights ago.

His throat choked with emotion and his eyes became misty. Shaking his head slowly, he told himself he would not let this affect him. Using his finger, he moved the necklaces around, noticing a paper underneath. He pulled out the paper and opened it up. Beautiful handwriting slightly slanted lined the page. The date on the letter was yesterday.

My Dearest, Since you would not let me explain the other night, I have decided to write you a missive—if only for my own state of mind. I pray you read what I have to say. What I wanted to tell you the other night was that although I had originally started to take the jewels, I had changed my mind and was putting them back when you caught me. Before this had happened—the day I had left to see if I could force my memory to return—I did remember what happened. I remembered everything about my life and especially the day I ran in front of your vehicle. I had found my family that day, but before I could tell them, Macgregor stopped me and threatened to harm them, and especially you and the twins, if I didn't steal your mother's jewels. Believe me when I say, I did not want to, but I also know Macgregor would have hurt you, so I had no choice.

When you walked in on me, I had changed my mind and was coming to tell you the truth to see if you could help me find a way to stop him. Not to worry, though. I will find a way to stop him. Maybe then I will be able to forgive myself for all the terrible things I have done while in Macgregor's employ. And mayhap one day you will soon come to forgive me, which is the thing I want the most. Please do not let my family know I'm alive. One day I will feel confident enough to tell them the truth, but until then, I cannot forgive myself for everything I have done in the past. Give the twins a kiss from me and tell them I love and miss them. Yours Always, Elizabeth Louisa Hamilton.

Tears blurred his vision and he quickly blinked them away. What was wrong with him? Could he really believe what she wrote? Had she indeed tried to save his life by stealing his mother's jewels for Macgregor?

Deep in his heart, he believed her. Yet the things he'd heard about her from those other children who had worked for Macgregor made Trevor doubt she was so sweet and innocent.

Groaning, he buried his face in his hands, resting his elbows on the table. His head throbbed with indecision. So maybe she had been a thief, but while she was with him, she brought love, laughter and happiness back into his home. His children loved her. He had loved her.

Curse him, he loved her even now.

Expelling a deep breath, he straightened in his chair. His gaze fell to the opened newspaper. In bold letters the article announced, *Notorious Thief, Richard Macgregor, Found Dead—Stabbed in Alleyway.*

Trevor gasped and picked up the newspaper to read more. He scanned the article quickly, then read through it once more to try to make sense of what happened. Macgregor was dead. Murdered. But the paper didn't sound like the police were diligently looking for his killer. Why would they when Macgregor had been a wanted criminal for years?

Then a name jumped out at him. Miss Eliza Watson. Trevor

quickly read on. She'd been in front of the hospital that night with her maid and saw a man stabbed down the street, and running away was a woman.

A woman? Why would a woman want to kill Macgregor? Trevor chuckled, knowing he had wanted to strangle the man a time or two. Even Louisa had motive…

Louisa.

Trevor jumped up, knocking his chair over. Had she killed Macgregor? Although Trevor didn't blame her, would the police see it the way Trevor had?

She needed help. His heart could hear her crying through the letter. Indeed, she was alone and helpless, and she did need his help. Louisa also needed her family's help. She'd asked him in her letter not to tell her parents, but Trevor felt he had to. They needed to know, didn't they?

"Hobbs, have my horse brought around," Trevor barked as he hurried out of the dining room, marching toward the front door. "Never mind, I shall do it myself."

He opened the door, ready to rush out, but stopped quickly. A gentleman and a younger boy stood at Trevor's doorstep.

"Oh, forgive me for almost running you over," he quickly apologized. "I am in a hurry and—"

"Lord Kenbridge?" a small voice asked.

Trevor lowered his gaze back to the boy. He didn't recognize the lad at first, but then the eyes and smile looked familiar.

"It's me, Norman Boyd." He pointed to the man standing beside him. "And this is my father, Baron Grisham."

Trevor blinked several times. The boy looked entirely different all cleaned up, like a gentleman's son.

Trevor smiled. "What a pleasant surprise."

"Forgive us for coming unannounced," the baron began, "but Norman said he needed to speak with you."

"Forgive me, I'm in a hurry," Trevor told them, but then motioned for them to come inside, "but I do have a few minutes to visit since my horse has not yet been saddled."

"This will only take a moment, Your Grace," Norman said. His expression suddenly changed as a frown claimed his face. "I want to apologize, my lord. That day you caught me, I was told to lie to you."

Trevor shook his head. "Lie to me? By whom?"

"Macgregor. He told me to watch you and try to pick your pocket, but he wanted me to get caught, and when I did, I was to lie to you." Norman took a deep breath after his hurried speech.

Folding his arms across his chest, Trevor nodded. "Pray, please tell me what you lied about."

"About Louisa. Those things I told you were a lie." He shrugged. "Well, most of it, anyway. Louisa was Macgregor's best pupil, and she did teach us how to steal, but…" He licked his lips then swallowed hard. "She never did kidnap any children and she never did kill anyone. That was the lie."

Relief poured through Trevor from the boy's admission. Although it upset him to think the lad lied to him, which created doubt in his mind about Louisa, Trevor did understand why Norman did it. Macgregor had all of the children frightened to death.

"Do you forgive me, Your Grace?" Norman asked with a sincere voice.

"Of course, I do." Trevor ruffled the boy's hair and smiled. "Thank you for letting me know. This has worried me since you told me." He looked up at the baron. "And thank you for bringing him."

"You are very welcome, Your Grace."

The man turned with his son and started out the door, but Trevor quickly stopped them. "One more thing, if you don't mind."

Baron Grisham arched his eyebrows. "What is it?"

"If we had never discovered that Norman had been kidnapped, would you have wanted to find your child even though he may have been in a band of thieves for several years and was considered a criminal?"

Tears filled the older man's eyes. "I wanted my son back. It didn't matter to me what he'd done. I just wanted him back with the family who loved him."

This was the answer Trevor wanted to hear. "I thank you, Baron Grisham. Have a pleasant day."

If Trevor's daughter had been kidnapped, he would move heaven and earth to try to find her, just as he knew Louisa's father would.

And that was exactly what Trevor planned to do. Whether it took moving the heaven and earth, he *would* find her.

Chapter Thirty-One

S HIVERING, LOUISA HUDDLED in the corner of a stall wrapped in a horse blanket. In those six years she practically lived on the streets working for Macgregor, she knew where to go to keep warm and where she could find food to steal. Her memory had returned completely now, and she knew exactly what to do in whatever situation she was placed in. It was as if she'd never left and spent a whole month being loved by two adorable children and one very handsome and kindhearted man.

Sickness rolled in her stomach, but not from lack of food this time. Instead, disgust for the life she now lived—because of her wrong decisions—weighed her down and made her miserable.

The weather had turned chilly today. At least she had a warmer dress to wear instead of the rags she'd been in when Trevor had hit her with his curricle. And the cloak and bonnet she had on when he kicked her out of his mother's house were her only possessions. Still, they were much better than what she'd been accustomed to for six very long and miserable years.

A noise from the front of the stable brought her alert. Fear crept upon her, making her heart thump wildly. She couldn't be discovered hiding in the stable. She didn't want anyone to catch her. Instead, she wanted to surprise Eliza Watson whenever her childhood friend left the house.

Slowly, Louisa rose and peeked over the stall. Whistling, a

groomsman walked around the carriage, preparing it for travel. For the first time in three days, hope grew inside of her. She prayed Eliza would be the one needing the vehicle this morning so that Louisa would get her chance to speak with her former friend.

Going without seeing Trevor or the twins for so long had put Louisa in a melancholy mood, and she couldn't stand to be miserable any longer. She was determined to formulate a plan and stop Macgregor, along with confronting her childhood friend before making an appearance to her family. Living like this was destroying her heart, and she refused to take this abuse even one more minute.

"Mornin' Joe." Another stable hand walked up to help the groomsman.

"Good morning."

He ran his hands over his wide middle. "Who needs the carriage today?"

"Miss Eliza. Who else in this miserable family wants us to wait on them hand and foot?"

Surprise flipped through Louisa, and she quickly covered her mouth before a laugh escaped. Obviously, the servants did not approve of their mistress.

The stable hand shook his head, his long black hair slapped against his neck. "Honestly, I cannot wait until she marries. Good riddance to the spoiled chit, I say."

"And I would say the same." The groomsman nodded in agreement. "The sooner she becomes Lady Wellesley, the better for us all."

Louisa gasped and sank down the wall. Eliza… engaged to Frank?

As children she and Eliza were inseparable and Eliza was always over at Louisa's house. When they became older, Louisa realized her friend had an infatuation with Frank. By this time, Louisa and Frank had become betrothed, and not wanting to go against the wishes of her parents, she didn't argue with their decision. Secretly, however, she had wished Frank would rebut the betrothal and marry someone else. Somebody more his age, or prettier, or even wealthier—anything, but wanting to marry her. Eliza had been starry-eyed whenever Frank was around, and Louisa had wondered if Frank was interested in her friend.

One day she'd asked him, praying that he found Eliza better suited for him. Instead, he'd rolled his eyes and flipped his hands in the air. "She's too chubby for me," he'd said.

From what Louisa had seen of her old friend yesterday, the years had been kind to Eliza. She'd lost her baby fat, thank heavens. So perhaps that was why Frank changed his mind.

"Where is Miss High-and-Mighty off to this early in the morning?" the younger man asked the groomsman.

"I don't know for certain, but I heard her telling the butler she had to visit with the policeman about that man's death the other day."

"Oh, that Macgregor fellow—the thief from Seven Dials?"

Louisa gasped again, and slapped her hand over her mouth. *Macgregor? Dead?* Cautiously, she slid back up the wall to peek at the two servants.

"Aye. The same fellow." The groomsman shook his head. "It makes no sense to me. Miss Eliza says she saw the man stabbed while she was coming out of the hospital that night. Yet…"

Pausing, the tall man took a quick look around, probably searching for anyone who would overhear. Thankfully, he didn't see Louisa.

"What was she doing at the hospital?" the groomsman continued in a lower voice. "She has never gone there before."

"Do you think she's lying?"

"I do." The groomsman scrubbed his unshaven chin. "She did take the carriage that night, and indeed she went into the hospital, but she never once mentioned why she was there. Not only that, but when I saw her come out of the hospital, the police had already been summoned to the commotion happening down the street. I do not think she saw any stabbing at all because the killer would have already taken off by that time."

"Very interesting, indeed." The stable hand nodded.

Louisa thought the same thing. *Interesting...* So what was Eliza up to this time? Whose life was she trying to destroy? Of course Louisa still wanted to know why her childhood friend ruined her life when they had been such good friends.

"Well, I had better take the carriage around to the front now and wait for her to come out." The taller man adjusted his hat before buttoning his overcoat.

As the groomsman drove the carriage out, Louisa snuck out of the stall and quickly ducked in the next one. She listened close for any noise that she'd been discovered. After a moment of silence, she hurried to the next stall, and continued the pattern until she reached the doors. Thankfully Eliza's family didn't have many servants, because it made sneaking easier than Louisa had planned.

The carriage was now stopped in front of the house. Nobody stood around waiting, except for the groomsman and he sat atop in the driver's seat, his attention turned the other way. On quiet feet, Louisa crept to the carriage, opened the door, and as gently as she could, climbed inside.

Just as she closed the door, the vehicle moved as the groomsman jumped down. Panicked, her heart stalled. He must have felt her climbing in.

"Good morning, Miss Eliza," the man called out.

Louisa expelled a relieved breath and huddled on the seat in the corner. The curtains were pulled down, giving the box very little light. Although, when the door opened, she would certainly be noticed.

"Please take me to the police headquarters. They are expecting me."

"As you wish, Miss Eliza."

Louisa held her breath. The door opened and Eliza climbed in, her head down as she focused on stepping inside without tangling her gown and cloak—a habit most ladies did when entering a vehicle.

Before Eliza was completely in her seat, the door closed.

Blinking—probably adjusting her eyes to the semi-darkness—Eliza scanned the inside the box until she spotted the unknown person in the carriage. "Oh!" Eliza shrieked.

Immediately, Louisa jumped next to the other woman on the seat and covered her mouth. "Say one more word and I swear I shall snap your neck in two with my bare hands. Do not think I won't, either." Louisa hated to sound so threatening, when she would never follow through with the promise. Hopefully, Eliza didn't realize this.

The other woman calmed quickly as she narrowed her gaze. "L-L-Louisa?"

Louisa slowly released her hold. "Strange how you would think that, considering I am supposed to be dead. Something—I might add—you have known about since your uncle kidnapped me."

Even through the shadows, Louisa could tell when the other woman's face lost color. Betrayal crushed Louisa, and she wanted to cry in fury, but she'd give her so-called friend time to explain before lashing out her own anger.

"I—I thought you were dead," Eliza muttered.

"Indeed? When did this happen? We exchanged letters for two months before your uncle sold me to a man who was Satan's own child. Yet my family had heard I had drowned at the girl's school—the very school we had attended together until the day your uncle came."

Eliza shook her head. "Honestly, Louisa. I didn't know."

"You lie!" Louisa grasped the other woman's shoulders and shook her hard. "Tell me the truth for once in your miserable life."

"Beg pardon," Eliza snapped as she pushed Louisa away. "If you are assuming that I do not speak the truth, then you are sadly mistaken."

"No, you are the sad person in this situation, Eliza. Because you convinced yourself that your lies are in fact the truth, and in doing so, you ruin people's lives."

Eliza huffed. "I don't have to take this abuse from you. Leave my carriage this instant."

"Not until I get some answers." Anger pumped through Louisa stronger than it had ever done before. She wanted to cause physical harm to this woman, when she'd never experienced such fierce anger before. The newfound feeling frightened her.

"Well, I don't know what you want me to say, especially if you will not believe a word of it."

Shaking her head, Louisa sat back in the seat and folded her arms. "Why do you hate me so? What did you think to gain from sending me to hell and telling my family I had died?"

Eliza stared at Louisa in silence. Only the clip-clop of the horse's hooves and the rattle of the carriage were heard. Malice darkened Eliza's expression and slowly she bunched her hands into fists on her lap.

"You had everything a young girl could ever want," Eliza spat. "And you flaunted it in front of others."

"I did not."

"Your parents spoiled you and treated you as if you were the queen herself. And I—I had *nothing*."

"Eliza, what are you talking about? Your parents saw to your comfort just as mine did for me."

"No. My father was a drunk and gambled away our money. My paternal grandmother was the one paying for my schooling. I knew once I was out of school, no man would want me for his bride because I would not have a dowry to give him. I was not as pretty as you. You have no idea how badly I wanted to be you."

"Eliza? What does any of this have to do with having your uncle kidnap me?"

"Because *I* wanted to be your parents' daughter. *I* wanted to be the one betrothed to Frank—a boy I had loved for many years. But I knew it would not happen unless you were dead. I didn't want you dead, but I wanted you to disappear. I once caught my uncle kidnapping a child, and I threatened to inform my family of his crimes. Uncle Percy had fallen out of the good graces of my family, and he was desperate to be reclaimed, and he begged me not to turn him in. He told me he would do *anything* for me. That was when I realized he could kidnap you and take you far away. I would tell everyone you had drowned in the river. Then and only then could I take your place in your family's heart. It took time, of course, but now they look upon *me* as their daughter. Not you."

Louisa hadn't realized she'd been crying until a tear trickled down her cheek. "If you had only said something to me back then, I know my family would have helped you."

"Not when I wanted Frank as my husband and I couldn't because you were betrothed to him. It was after you had told me your parents had betrothed you to him when I started planning your disappearance. I'm sorry you were sold to Macgregor because I had not planned for that to happen. However, I am not sorry about everything else I did. Frank and I are to be married next week, and you are *not* going to stop it."

Louisa held up her hands in defeat. "Oh, believe me. I will not stop it at all. I don't love Frank. I never did. You can have him. All I want is my family—and home. I want my *real* life back."

"Well, I honestly don't know how you can do that without the truth coming out. If Frank and your parents discover it was me all along..." She waved a hand in the air. "Impossible. It cannot work, Louisa. You cannot reenter your life now. Not when everything is finally falling into place for me."

Was the kind of anger pumping through her now what criminals experienced before they committed a crime? Yet the hatred inside Louisa ran hot—fiery hot—and she had no wish to cool it any time soon.

Louisa lashed out and struck the other woman across the face, then grasped her thin shoulders for a hard shake. "Just try to stop me. I will *not* let you win."

For a split second, Eliza's eyes widened in panic, then a devilish grin spread across her face. "I beg to differ, my friend. I *will* stop you." She lifted her hand which now clutched a knife. "Release me at once or I will surely use this to protect myself."

Keeping her eyes on the knife, Louisa slowly backed away. Why in heaven's name did Eliza have a weapon on her person? A knife—in fact—that looked vaguely familiar… "Where did you get that? Is that not Mr. Macgregor's hunting knife?"

Eliza laughed with a wicked grate to her voice. "My, my… I'm surprised at you, Louisa. You know so much about Macgregor." She tilted her head to the side. "I heard you were Macgregor's *best*. Does that mean he made you his whore, too?"

"How dare you! I would not allow *that man* to touch me in such a vile way. I would have killed him if he had."

"Well, what do you know—your wish came true. Now the man is dead, and you can take the credit."

Louisa shook her head. "What are you talking about?"

Just then the carriage rolled to a stop and Eliza took a quick glance out the window. Her smile widened when she met Louisa's stare.

"You shall find out in a moment, my dear friend." She reached for the door and opened it, climbing out backward. Once her feet hit the ground, she motioned with the knife. "Come down."

Panic settled in Louisa's chest. Something was not right. She didn't dare comply with the other woman's wishes, yet did she have a choice?"

"Miss Watson? What is going on?" a voice asked from behind Eliza.

"Oh, Constable Oxley. I'm so happy you are here. I was accosted in my own carriage by this vagabond, and thankfully, I was able to get the weapon away from her to protect myself." Eliza pointed inside the carriage. "I have found Mr. Macgregor's killer. She is a madwoman, I tell you, and completely insane."

Dread poured over Louisa as the man and two other policemen rushed toward her, pointing their swords at her. At this particular moment, she did not know how to fix this. Perhaps this was her destiny after all.

Chapter Thirty-Two

TREVOR HURRIED INTO White's where he'd been told Trey and Dominic were spending their leisurely afternoon. Other lords greeted Trevor, and he nodded to be polite, but never replied. After searching through two rooms, he found Trey and Dominic playing cards with three other men.

Slowing his pace, Trevor strolled to the table so as not to draw any attention to himself. He waited patiently—though he wanted to drag the two out of this room by their ears—until the card game ended and a winner was announced. Trevor sighed in relief.

"Kenbridge, my good man," Dominic said cheerfully. "Would you enjoy playing the next game with us?"

"No, I do not wish to join. What I would like, instead, is to talk with you and my brother. In private, if at all possible."

Hawthorne and Trey traded glances before they pushed away from the table and muttered excuses to the others. Trevor led them out of the room and into another more private.

"You are out of sorts again today, aren't you?" Trey asked.

"Actually yes, but for different reasons this time." Trevor walked to the window and glanced outside but didn't really see anything. There was too much on his mind to concentrate on other things. "I need your help." He looked back at the other two. "I need to find Louisa."

Both men gaped—their eyes widened.

Trey shook his head. "You are not talking rationally, my brother. Are you not the one who told her to leave the other night?"

"Indeed, I did, but I was wrong. Dreadfully wrong." He handed the letter to them and waited for them to read it. When they both looked up, surprise registered on their faces even more than before.

"She really is the Danvers' daughter," Hawthorne muttered.

"Yes, she is. But what is worse, is that Macgregor was stabbed in an alleyway last night." Trevor shoved the newspaper at them. "I'm worried Louisa will get blamed for killing the man."

"No, it could not have been her." Trey skimmed the article. "She would not do that, but even if she did, I would not judge her."

"Not me, either," Dominic quickly added.

"Another thing that worries me is the witness who claims to have seen a woman running away from the stabbing." Trevor pointed to the newspaper. "I don't trust Miss Watson. Her actions the other night at Mother's dinner party proved she is hiding something."

Dominic grumbled and slammed his fist against a chair. "I feel the same frustration, Your Grace. What is it that you wish us to do?"

"Somehow we have to find her and protect her. She cannot go to the gaol for a crime she did not commit."

Pushing his fingers through his black hair, Trey walked to a chair and sat. "What about her family? Should they know?"

"She does not wish them to know," Dominic argued as he flipped his finger against the letter.

"I debated over this issue as well," Trevor said. "I think I know why Louisa doesn't want them to know—because of her criminal past."

"A past she had no control over." Dominic huffed.

"I agree, but she is not thinking that way." Trevor shook his head. "I believe her family would want to know if she was in danger so they could help."

"Will Louisa be put out with you for telling her family?" Trey asked.

Trevor shrugged. "That is a chance I will have to take. Right now, I fear for her safety." He switched his attention between Trey and Dominic. "Are you with me?"

"Always." Trey stood.

"Right beside you, Your Grace." Dominic nodded. "I will do anything to help that poor woman."

Trevor scowled and pointed his finger toward his brother's best friend. "Do not think about charming her, do you understand?"

A grin stretched across Hawthorne's mouth. "I promise not to seduce her, just as long as you admit you are in love with her."

"Augh!" Trevor threw his hands in the air. He couldn't count how many times he wanted to punch the insolent lord in the face but resisted. "Fine. I shall admit it now. I love her. I have loved her almost from the first day I brought her to my home. There. Are you satisfied?"

Trey chuckled and patted his brother's back. "No need to get so upset, Trevor. Hawthorne and I knew you were in love with her all this time. We were just waiting for you to admit it."

Mumbling curses, Trevor swung around and marched toward the front door. A smile tried to tug at his lips, but he refused to allow the other two lords to see how uncomfortable this made him. Admitting he had such feelings for a woman—since he'd never had them before—was new to him and he wished Hawthorne and his brother hadn't witnessed his weakness.

Nonetheless, Trevor did love her and he'd do anything to help her.

Trey caught up to Trevor and tugged on his sleeve. He stopped and faced his youngest brother. A smirk played across Trey's face. "Not to worry, my dear brother." Trey grinned. "Hawthorne knows how to make the Worthington men confess things they don't normally do. If not for Nic, I would not have admitted to loving Judith."

Trevor arched a brow. "Indeed?"

"Oh yes. Nic even went as far as to kiss her—in front of me, no less."

A chuckle sprang to Trevor's throat. "I can believe that. But if he tries that on Louisa, I swear I will call him out."

"Oh, I'm quite certain Hawthorne will not do that to Louisa. Or to you. Nic knows me well, which is why he attempted to make me jealous." He shrugged. "It worked like a charm."

"Good." Trevor turned and hurried out the front door as a servant ran to fetch the horses.

Hawthorne stopped beside Trevor and nudged his arm. "Are we going to talk to the Danverses now?"

"Yes."

"I wish we knew more about Miss Watson. I, too, don't feel she is being entirely honest."

Trevor glanced at Nic. "Well, considering her uncle is the very man who kidnapped Louisa, I think that right there will give the Danverses enough doubt to start questioning her as well."

"Good thinking, brother." Trey nodded.

The servant brought the horses around, and each man grasped the reins. Just as Trevor mounted, another horseman rode up to them and stopped quickly. The dust around them puffed into thick clouds, and the wind didn't assist matters any, either.

As the dust cloud cleared, Trevor recognized the rider. "Tristan. It is good to see you this afternoon."

"Trevor, I'm glad I caught you. I was just at the gaol, and—"

"You were at the gaol?" Trevor's voice rose. "Why? What happened? Do I need to hire my solicitor to represent you?" He shook his head. "I cannot believe they think you guilty of Hollingsworth's death."

"Trevor, that's not why I was there. But as I was leaving, the police were bringing in a prisoner." Tristan leaned over and touched Trevor's arm. "They have arrested Louisa."

Trevor's heart cried out and buzzed through his already pounding head. His chest ached as panic surged through him. He glanced at Trey and Hawthorne, whose angry expressions mirrored the way Trevor felt.

"Go tell the Danverses," Trevor instructed. "It's extremely crucial for me to talk with Louisa now." He turned to Tristan. "Will you help me?"

"Yes. What do you wish me do to?"

"Find Miss Watson. She is behind this somehow. I need to know."

Tristan shrugged. "I can help you with that one already. Miss Watson was the one who turned Louisa in to the authorities."

Trevor's curses mixed loudly with Trey and Dominic's. "All right, so the woman is more vindictive than we thought. I shall ride to the gaol immediately. Hopefully Louisa can shed some light on this."

Trey and Dominic kicked their horses into a run as Tristan followed. With a heavy heart, Trevor rode toward the gaol, knowing not what he would find, or even if Louisa would speak to him. He had been wrong to judge her so quickly the other night and he would always be sorrowful for his actions. But right now he must make amends by finding Macgregor's true killer.

He rode his horse hard, only stopping when he reached the building. Quickly, he dismounted and threw his reins to a servant boy who hurried over to assist. Trevor's long strides ate up the distance between him and the gaol until he walked inside. Many people milled about, and he turned to the first policeman he found.

"Please, sir. I need to speak with the magistrate or governor of the facility," Trevor demanded.

"Neither are here at the moment. How may I assist you?"

"I am the Duke of Kenbridge, and I heard you brought in a prisoner. A woman by the name of Louisa Hamilton. I would like to see her, please."

The other man arched a gray bushy eyebrow. "Why, may I ask?"

"Because she works for me, and I think she is innocent. I will hire my solicitor if I must, but she will not be sent to the gallows for something she did not do."

"I shall allow you to see her, but only for a few minutes." The jailer turned and walked down a long hall.

The stench of unwashed bodies and rotten food had Trevor gagging. He withdrew a handkerchief from his pocket and lifted it to his nose. "Has her trial been set yet?"

"No, it has not," the man told him over his shoulder. "Perhaps tomorrow when Magistrate Templeton arrives."

Trevor could not let Louisa stay in this godforsaken place overnight. There had to be some way to get her released.

As he passed the rooms lining tightly along the way, he noticed the damp walls and floors. Mice scampered across the floor as if they owned the building. Bile rose to Trevor's throat. These conditions were not tolerable. He must get Louisa out—even if he had to sneak her out.

The jailer stopped at a door and withdrew a set of brass keys, Trevor peered into the small window. Sitting on a cot facing the wall with her black cloak wrapped around her was the woman he loved completely. Her hair flowed long over her shoulders and back and much too tangled for his liking. Her appearance almost reminded him of when he had brought her home, the only difference being her clothes were not tattered. His heart wrenched with sorrow.

As the jailer unlocked the door, Louisa turned her head toward the opening with widened eyes. The man took one step inside. "You have a visitor." Then he backed out and motioned for Trevor to enter. Taking a deep breath, Trevor walked in.

Chapter Thirty-Three

L OUISA BLINKED, NOT once but several times to clear her vision. The man she never thought she'd see again stood just inside her prison; a room so small it barely had space for a cot—if that was what this thing she sat upon was called. She'd had a better bed while working for Macgregor.

Seeing Trevor standing there made her heart leap, but she didn't dare get too anxious and hope Trevor was here to save her. Then again, his expression wasn't one of anger. Instead, sadness and regret laced his eyes and his frown.

"T—Tre… Your Grace?" There was a catch in her voice, and she wished it hadn't sounded so helpless.

"Louisa," he said taking a step closer. "This is wrong. So wrong."

All right, so maybe he wasn't here to save her. "Indeed, it is."

His gaze jumped around the room, not resting on anything for a few awkward moments until it reached her eyes then stopped.

"Oh, Louisa. This is my fault. All of it." He rushed to her, knelt on one knee, and grasped her cold hands.

Still not believing any of this was happening, Louisa blinked again, but this time it was to stop her tears from building. Her efforts were wasted when liquid streamed down her face. She shook her head. "You shouldn't kneel on the floor. God only knows what vermin has been on this ground." She pulled his hands to help him up, but he was unmovable.

"My dearest, Louisa, I know you didn't kill Macgregor, although I would not have blamed you if you had. There were several times I wanted to relieve your suffering by ending that man's life." Trevor rubbed his thumbs over her knuckles.

"I—I—" Her voice choked and she swallowed hard to help move the lump of emotion stuck in her throat. "I didn't kill him."

"I know, my dear, which is why I'm here. I want to help you any way I can."

"You cannot." She shook her head. "My childhood friend, Miss Eliza Watson, has created a lie that only festers and grows larger. I have no way to cease her stories, and I cannot prove my innocence." She sniffed. "I am destined for the gallows, I fear."

"No! I forbid it." Trevor's voice rose. "There must be a way out of this nightmare. I cannot let this happen to you. My life has changed so drastically since you entered, and I cannot imagine my future without you in it." He wrapped his arms around her, pulling her close.

A soapy, yet woodsy scent enveloped her and she wanted to close her eyes and pretend she was back in his home living out her dream. But his clean smell reminded her where she'd been for the past few days as reality shook her to her senses.

"No." She pushed him away. "I have been sleeping in a stable, wrapped in a horse blanket. Your Grace, you should not be so personal with me holding me so close, and you should definitely *not* be here."

He withdrew, his eyes narrowed and lips turned downward as he stared into her eyes. "Don't you want me here, Louisa?"

Her heart lurched again. "That's not what I said."

"I know it is not, but I still expect you to answer my question from your heart."

Dropping her attention to his cravat, her bottom lip trembled. She fought the turbulent emotions spinning through her, especially when all she wanted to do was cry like a baby. "Your

Grace, as much as I want my fairytale dream to come true, I know it is impossible. I have lived as a vagabond—a criminal—for six years. Your children deserve so much better than a woman who used to steal just so she could eat a decent meal. You deserve better than a woman who has lived on the streets wearing tattered clothes and who rarely bathed."

He lifted her chin with his fingers until she met his warm, blue gaze. "My children deserve someone who shows them love and who will take the time to play with them and teach them. They deserve someone who loves them unconditionally. I deserve a woman who makes me laugh and whom I want to be with every moment of the day. I deserve a woman who makes me happy, and makes me feel loved more than I have ever felt before." With both hands, he cupped her face. "We don't care that you were a vagabond and picked pockets because we know why you did it. Your experience has made you the strong woman you are today. We don't want anyone else. The children deserve *you*. And I want no other woman than the one I'm looking at now. You are the one for me, Louisa. You are the woman I love... the woman I *want* to love and make happy for the rest of our lives."

She couldn't hold back any longer. Closing her eyes, she buried her face in his neck and cried. Happiness burst inside her, yet at the same time, agony gripped her chest, making it hard to breathe. How could they ever become happy when she would be dragged to the gallows for murdering Macgregor any day now?

"Oh, Trevor." She sniffed. "I dare not dream of a life with you and the twins. It's impossible. Especially now."

He kissed the side of her head. "It's not impossible. My brothers and Lord Hawthorne are helping me. One way or another we will force Miss Watson to confess."

Louisa lifted her head to look at him. Smiling, he wiped her tears with the pads of his thumbs. "Trevor, do you honestly believe she is going to confess after all these many years? She has worked hard to get where she is, and she isn't going to let anything stop her from becoming a nobleman's wife. She's lied to so many people, especially my parents, and even if they knew I was alive, I fear they would not condone the kind of life I've led. They would not understand—or forgive—all the despicable things I have done."

"But I have." He kissed her lips briefly. "Do you not think your parents are as understanding as I? Believe me when I tell you, they will be. More so, in fact. I was the one who doubted you when I witnessed you taking my mother's jewels. If I had been more understanding—and forgiving—I would have allowed you to explain instead of sending you out on the street." His smile disappeared as sadness dulled his eyes. "If I had been more understanding, you would not be sitting here right now. Can you ever forgive me?"

The irony of the situation made her laugh, even though there was little humor to be found in her situation. "Oh, Trevor. You are such a gem. Is it any wonder I love you so much?" She swept her gaze over his handsome face. "There is nothing to forgive. You have been my deliverer all along. I adore you, and I always will."

From behind Trevor, the prison guard cleared his throat loudly. Inwardly, Louisa cringed. How could she have forgotten they had company?

"My lord, your time is over," the guard said gruffly.

Trevor pulled her into his arms again and kissed her. Although the kiss was not as passionate as she'd experienced from him before, she still felt all the emotion—and love—he had. In a small way, it comforted her to know he cared so much. And he'd help her.

Grudgingly, she pulled away. "I love you," she whispered.

"I love you." Smiling, he stood. "Keep believing good shall overcome all things."

She nodded. "I will." But as he walked out of the room and the door was closed and locked, it was hard not to let despair come over her once again. Her life had been one hurdle of disappointment after another, and now that her dream was within reach, she knew it would be hopelessly snatched away from her.

TREVOR NEVER THOUGHT he would be able to get in to see Lord and Lady Danvers since Trevor's brothers and Dominic were not successful earlier today since the Danverses were out. But finally, Trevor was given an appointment to meet with them. Time was not passing fast enough. Each minute that ticked by made his heart cry with anguish. Louisa shouldn't have to be punished by staying in that flea-infested room, and he would do anything to get her out. *Anything.*

Being idle was not a good way to pass time, and so after leaving the gaol, Trevor rode through the streets of London searching for something that might assist him in releasing Louisa. He even scoured the area where Macgregor was reported to have been killed. The good Lord must have had His hand in Louisa's fate, because Trevor had stumbled across something that indeed would help Miss Watson confess. But now he needed to calm himself and not do anything rash in order for his plan to go smoothly.

"It's time."

Trey's voice pulled Trevor from his thoughts as he looked upon his younger brother. Both brothers stood by Lord Hawthorne near the door to Trevor's study, preparing to leave. All three looked so refined in their best as if they were ready to attend a lavish ball. Instead of the pleasantries that come with Society's function, this evening their main purpose was to inform the Danverses about their long-lost daughter, and force Miss Watson to tell the truth.

Trevor heaved a heavy sigh, nodded, and hurried outside to his waiting horse.

The men rode in silence, which was a good thing because then Trevor could collect his thoughts, and pray like he'd never prayed before. This had to work. He couldn't bear thinking of the woman he loved going to the gallows and hanged for a crime she didn't commit.

They reached the manor, dismounted, and strode up the porch to the door. Trevor knocked and within seconds, the butler answered. Dressed respectfully in burgundy-and-black attire, the butler represented the House of Danvers well.

Trevor acknowledged the servant with a nod. "Good evening. I'm the Duke of Kenbridge, and I am here to see Lord and Lady Danvers, along with my brothers and Lord Hawthorne."

"Please come in, Your Grace." The butler bowed. "They are waiting for you in the sitting room."

When Trevor entered the room, Lord and Lady Danvers stood, as well as their nephew, Lord Wellesely. They all bowed to each other. Trevor was relieved to see Miss Watson absent this time. Then again, how could he get the girl to confess if she wasn't here?

"Your Grace," the earl began, "what an honor it is to have you in our home."

"I thank you, Danvers. It is an honor to be here."

The earl motioned to the couches. "Please sit and we'll call for refreshments."

Trevor situated himself on the chair. "I want to say how disappointed I was that my mother's dinner party ended so suddenly the other evening. I had hoped to get to know you all better. I trust Miss Watson is feeling better?"

Their hosts nodded, but it was Wellesley who leaned forward on his seat. "She is doing much better, thank you. In fact, her attitude has changed for the better within a day's time."

I'm certain it has. Trevor forced himself to smile. "I'm relieved to hear this. I was hoping to see her tonight and express my concern for her welfare."

"Actually," Lady Danvers said, "Miss Watson is expected for

dinner tonight. She should be arriving soon, I believe."

Thank you, Lord. Trevor's smile was not forced this time. "Splendid. I look forward to our visit with her." His brothers and Hawthorne nodded in agreement. "But until then, I would like to address a very delicate and emotional topic if you don't mind."

"What is it?" Lord Danvers asked in a worried tone.

Trevor glanced at his brothers, who gave him a reassuring nod. "The other night at my mother's dinner party—" Trevor switched his attention to the hosts—"when we were discussing my friend's memory loss, I believe we might have stumbled across something that affects you all."

Lady Danvers twisted her hands in her lap. "The young lady whose name is Louisa?"

"Yes, the very same." Trevor took a deep breath. "This poor lady had been told when she was twelve years of age that her parents were killed in a house fire, then she was immediately taken to Scotland and in the care of her friend's uncle. From that point, she was sold to a man who hired young children to work for him—as pickpockets."

The Danverses gasped, and Wellesley's jaw tightened as he bunched his hands into fists.

Trevor continued, "Just recently, Louisa and the gang of thieves were brought to London. This is where I ran her over and nearly killed her. She had lost her memory from the accident, but during the weeks afterward, we realized she had been raised by parents of Quality. My mother met the young woman and realized she resembled Lady Danvers quite a bit with her beautiful green eyes."

When he looked at the countess, her eyes watered. Trevor went on. "I didn't dare hope she was your lost daughter until I had real proof. The other day, Louisa returned to the place where I had hit her with my curricle, in hopes of forcing her memory to return. It had." He paused and licked his lips, but when he opened his mouth to finish, hurried footsteps pounded on the floor in the hallway just as Miss Watson flung open the door and rushed inside the room. All eyes turned toward hers.

"Oh, forgive me for being late and intruding upon your guests." Patting her ringlets into place, she smiled politely and sashayed toward Wellesley.

"Eliza, please sit," Wellesley snapped. "You interrupted the duke, who had come to tell us some interesting news."

Miss Watson's face hardened as she threw daggers Trevor's way. She didn't say a word but sat next to Wellesley.

"Please continue, Your Grace," the earl urged. "What did your friend remember?"

Taking a deep breath, Trevor silently prayed everything would go according to his plan. It must. Louisa's life was at stake. "Louisa remembers her identity now, and realized that for six years she had been lied to." He moistened his throat. "She remembers being raised Elizabeth Louisa Hamilton. Your daughter."

Gasps ricocheted around the room accompanied by Lady Danvers's sobs as she covered her face. The earl stared wide eyed at Trevor as he slipped his arm around his wife's shoulders. Wellesley's face turned white, and Miss Watson's face reddened.

"How can this be?" Wellesley muttered.

Trevor shrugged. "Apparently, Louisa was kidnapped by a man named Mr. Percy Featherspoon."

A different set of gasps exploded, this time sounding accusing. Both the Danvers and Frank pinned their glares at Eliza.

"That is your uncle," Wellesley exclaimed.

The little deceiver must have gained control of her emotions as Eliza feigned a surprised expression toward Trevor. "You must be insane. My uncle kidnapped my dearest friend?" She switched her focus to the Danverses and her fiancé. "My family knew Uncle Featherspoon was unethical at times and a swindler, but we had no idea he was kidnapping children."

The earl jumped to his feet. "Your Grace, you must take us to Louisa at once. We want to know what happened… We want to know if she is all right."

"Therein lies the problem," Hawthorne said, then met Trevor's eyes.

Trevor nodded. "Lord and Lady Danvers, early this morning Louisa was arrested for murdering the very man who she worked for—the man who taught her to steal and made her live like a vagabond for six years."

"Augh," Lady Danvers groaned as her face turned whiter.

Miss Watson tried to appear helpful as she rushed to the older woman's side and fanned her face.

"However," Trevor continued, "I *know* she is innocent."

"As do I." Trey stood.

"And I." Tristan nodded and rose by his brother.

"And I know she's not guilty, as well," Dominic acknowledged.

"For this very reason," Trevor continued, "I am here at your home now, Lord Danvers. Your daughter might be hanged for something she didn't do. I need your help. I will take you to see her tonight, if you wish."

"But what if she is not who she says?" Miss Watson lifted her voice above the others. "How do you know this woman is not an imposter?"

As Trevor prepared his reply, his brothers and Dominic chuckled.

"Miss Watson," Tristan began, "all you have to do is look at Louisa to know she is her mother's daughter."

"If you knew her as we do," Trey added, "you would know Louisa is incapable of deceit."

"But you said she'd lived as a thief for six years. Good heavens, she was under the care of the notorious criminal, Mr. Macgregor. Knowing that tells me not to trust this woman."

"Tell me, Miss Watson," Dominic said, walking closer as he looked at her with a critical eye, "where did you hear such a thing? You were not privy to the conversation we had a moment ago before you arrived, which means you could not have possibly heard what we said. And the other evening while at the dowager duchess's home when the duke spoke about Louisa, he not once mentioned Macgregor's name." He scratched his chin. "So now I'm curious to how you know about this man."

Excitement shot through Trevor, and he could have hugged Hawthorne if it were proper. Instead, he gave his brother's friend a nod of approval and glared at Miss Watson. "Lord Hawthorne is correct. I am also anxious to hear how you know about this Macgregor fellow."

The young woman's eyes widened as they darted from person to person around the room, her face losing color by the second. She forced a laugh. "I must have heard it somewhere. Why else would I know?" She shrugged. "Perhaps I heard my uncle speak of this vile man."

"That does not make any sense, either, Miss Watson." Trey stepped closer. "At my mother's dinner party, you clearly stated your family had not spoken to your uncle in years."

The Earl of Danvers waved his hands through the air. "Please forgive me, but can we discuss this at a later time? If my daughter is in the gaol, I want to get her released immediately."

"Do you know how?" Trevor asked quickly.

The earl gave him a sharp nod. "Magistrate Templeton is a cousin. We know each other well. He'll listen to me and help, I assure you."

Trevor swept his hand, motioning toward the door. "Come then. Let's be on our way. There isn't a moment to lose."

Lord Danvers marched to the foyer and barked orders to the servants. Within seconds, the cloaks were fetched while the vehicle was being prepared. Miss Watson scurried from one person to another, muttering lies about her not knowing about Featherspoon's activities. From what Trevor could tell, her desperate pleas were being ignored by the Danverses and Frank.

Once they were all ready, Trevor, his brothers and Hawthorne walked to the front door—being held open by the butler— and hurried to their horses while the others made their way to the carriage. Before anyone could climb in, a squeaky voice called out in the night.

"Miss Watson."

Everyone stopped and looked at the vagabond rushing to Eliza's side. The young woman gasped, and pushed the boy away.

"Leave me, you vermin."

"Miss Watson, it's me, David. Don't ye remember? I'm the one who helped ye the other night."

"You… have the wrong… person," she stammered as she tried to urge the Danverses and Wellesley into the coach.

Trevor left his horse and came closer to the lad. "You. Boy. What business do you have with Miss Watson?"

David faced Trevor and lowered his gaze to his worn, brown shoes. "Sir, I need to talk to her. She promised me money for helping her the other night, and I came to collect."

Chapter Thirty-Four

TREVOR HITCHED AN excited breath. Things couldn't have worked out better if he planned them himself. Although he was the one who found David earlier this afternoon and paid him to come confront Eliza. Inwardly, he grinned.

"Liar," Miss Watson shrieked, then tugged on Frank's sleeve. "Please, if you love me, you will make that boy leave."

Wellesley arched a distrustful eye. "What makes you think I *love* you? The only reason I'm marrying you is because my uncle and aunt wanted me to."

"Oh!" Eliza slapped a hand over her mouth as tears filled her eyes. "You cannot mean it."

"Believe me, I do."

Trey stepped forward and touched the vagabond on the arm. "What is your name, boy?"

"David."

"David, what kind of help did you give Miss Watson the other evening?"

"She wanted me to steal Mr. Macgregor's favorite knife and bring it to her. She said she was going to put an end to his thieving and blackmailing career." The boy shrugged. "I was more than happy to comply since I recently learned that my parents were still alive and he knew it."

"Nooo..." Eliza sobbed into her hands. "He's lying, I tell

you."

Frank tightened his hand on Eliza's elbow. "Let us confront Louisa and see what the *real* story is." He glanced at the Danverses. "Forgive me aunt and uncle, but I have wondered about Eliza's story from the first time I heard she saw Louisa drown. And recently, I have caught her in lies. I cannot trust her, and I certainly cannot marry her."

The earl nodded. "We shall discuss this further, but for now, I want to find my daughter."

Trevor, his brothers, and Hawthorne mounted as the Danverses climbed in their vehicle. Trey allowed David to ride on his horse.

The journey to the gaol seemed longer, Trevor noticed. But maybe it was because the truth would finally be discovered. He pushed his steed faster, knowing he'd arrive quicker than the others. It didn't matter. He wanted to see Louisa again and hold her in his arms and never let her go.

Thirty minutes later, he arrived, and quickly dismounted. He hurried inside and found a jailer. "Is Magistrate Templeton here?"

"No, my lord. He is home with his family."

"Then I suggest you send someone over right away to fetch him and bring him here. Miss Louisa Hamilton—who has been accused of murdering Mr. Macgregor—is innocent, and my brothers and the Danverses are bringing the true murderer here at any moment."

When the guard stood still not looking like he was going to move, Trevor shouted, "Now man. If you value your position in this facility, you will move quickly."

The jailer hastened his step and hurried out the door. Trevor knew not everyone would fit inside Louisa's room, but if they could prove her innocence now, the guards would release her. Trevor wanted to run to her room and tell her not to worry, but didn't dare. Not yet.

Soon the Danvers' carriage arrived—Miss Watson still sobbing and mumbling her innocence—and not long after that,

Magistrate Templeton arrived, appearing irate. Between Trevor, his brothers, and Lord Danvers, they explained the story to the magistrate before allowing David to tell his story.

When the magistrate gave orders to release Louisa and lock up Miss Watson, Trevor's heart sang with happiness. His brothers and Dominic clapped Trevor on his shoulders. Lady Danvers kept wiping her wet eyes. The earl's stern expression wavered while he comforted his wife.

During the wait, Trevor paced the hallway in the front part of the building, anxious about seeing Louisa again. He wouldn't hold back his feelings for her—even in front of her parents. Lord Wellesley stepped away from the Danverses and cautiously walked to Trevor. He stopped and waited to see what Wellesley wanted.

The man sighed heavily and ran his fingers through his blond hair. "Is she really the Danvers' daughter?" he asked in a low tone.

"Yes."

"Are you aware"—his Adam's apple bobbed—"that we are betrothed?"

Trevor's heartbeat stalled for a split-second. He had heard this, but forgotten. It didn't matter. Contracts could be broken, and Trevor would see that this one was dissolved immediately. "Are you aware I'm in love with her?"

Frank nodded. "That is why I decided to speak with you."

"Then I must tell you she is in love with me, as well."

Frank grinned. "Splendid."

Shocked, Trevor shook his head slowly. "Why are you excited about this news?"

"Because I'm in love with another woman. I didn't want to marry Elizabeth, but the contract was signed before I could stop it. When we thought Elizabeth had drowned, my aunt and uncle wanted me to marry Eliza. I couldn't disappoint them, so I agreed—grudgingly."

Trevor touched Frank's arm. "Then you need to tell Lord and

Lady Danvers about your young woman and how much you love her. They will understand, I assure you."

"Thank you, Your Grace. Our talk has relieved me greatly."

"As it has me." Trevor nodded.

From down the corridor, the footsteps echoed. The hall was dark, only the lamp held by the jailer could be seen. The group clustered together; watched and waited.

LOUISA DIDN'T KNOW how Trevor did it, but she'd spend the rest of her life thanking him. When the jailer had told her she was free, she didn't quite believe him—until he threw Eliza in the room and locked the door. Eliza's eyes shot fiery daggers toward Louisa as her childhood friend shouted curses toward the jailer and even a few threats directed Louisa's way.

The jailer couldn't walk fast enough, and although Louisa's body was weary with fatigue and loss of nourishment, she still kept up beside him. Yet as they neared the entryway and she recognized the people standing by Trevor, her heart sank. At first anger shot through her, knowing he was the one who had brought her parents. But the longer she studied their expressions, the more she could see they had not blamed her as she'd feared.

Her mother stood beside her father, trembling as tears poured from her eyes. When Louisa was within speaking distance, she broke into a run and right into the open arms of her parents. She cried against her mother as her father's strong arms wrapped around both of them.

"I'm so sorry," she uttered in between sobs.

"There, there," her father comforted with a hoarse voice.

"I didn't know. I promise I didn't." Louisa shook her head.

Mother stroked Louisa's ratted hair as if it were more precious than silk. "How could you, my dear?"

Louisa lifted her head and stared into her mother's watery

eyes. "Can you ever forgive me?" She looked at her father. "Can you forget that I stayed alive by picking pockets and stealing?"

"We have already forgotten," her father assured.

Magistrate Templeton placed his hand on the earl's shoulder. "You should return home and rest now."

"Thank you for your help," her father told his cousin.

"I'm happy that I was able to assist in the matter." The magistrate nodded.

Louisa turned with her parents to leave, when she noticed Trevor. Kind and patient Trevor, who stood against the wall waiting for her. His handsome face smiled at her so lovingly she wanted to cry all over again.

Pulling away from her parents, she stepped toward him. He met her halfway and took her in his arms. She buried her face in his chest and breathed in his masculine scent, the woodsy smell she'd always loved.

"Thank you," she mumbled against his clothes.

His large palms drew circles on her back. "No, I thank *you* for forgiving me," he whispered.

She raised her head and looked at him. "For what?"

"For not trusting you in the first place."

"I don't blame you." She smiled.

He motioned his head toward her family. "I will let you return home with them, but only if you promise I can come visit you tomorrow."

"Absolutely."

He placed a small kiss on her forehead then pushed her toward her parents. Before she reached them, she gave a hug to Trey, Tristan, and Dominic, thanking them for their help.

As she walked out of the building, she glanced once more at Trevor. He mouthed the words, *I love you.* Her heart burst as tears clouded her eyes. Finally, she could dream of having a fairytale life with him.

Epilogue

L OUISA STROLLED THROUGH her mother's flower garden, her fingertips gently grazing the soft petals of the roses. The vibrant blooms were just as she remembered them from her childhood, but somehow now they seemed even more beautiful, more alive. Everything had changed in the last two months, yet it all felt so perfectly right.

Across the lawn, the joyful laughter of the twins drifted toward her, carried on the warm afternoon breeze. She turned to see Adam and Amanda—*her* children now—chasing each other in playful abandon. A smile spread across her face.

It was hard to believe how much her life had transformed since marrying Trevor. Just two months ago, she had been unsure of her future, uncertain if happiness like this could ever be hers. But now, being called *Mother* by the twins, hearing their laughter, and sharing her days and nights with a loving, handsome husband had brought her a joy she never knew was possible. Her life had taken on new meaning, richer and fuller than she had ever dreamed, and every moment felt like a gift she would treasure forever.

Louisa's heart swelled with happiness as she watched her parents laughing and playing with the twins, embracing their new roles as doting grandparents. Seeing them all together, united in joy, filled her with a deep sense of peace she hadn't thought possible. Coming back into their lives had brought her a kind of fulfillment she had never dared to hope for, especially after spending the last six years surviving as a thief and beggar. She had been lost for so long, but now, little by little, the painful memories of Macgregor's cruelty had begun to fade, replaced by the warmth and love Trevor and the twins brought to her days.

Her nightmares no longer held the same power over her. Instead, they were dissolving into shadows as new, sweeter dreams took their place. Dreams of family, of a future filled with love and hope.

She smiled softly as she thought of the day she and Trevor married—just two weeks after her release from gaol. It had been the most beautiful wedding she could have ever imagined, more than she believed she deserved after the life she'd led. Yet here she was, standing in the garden of her childhood, surrounded by love, her heart filled with gratitude.

Sighing contentedly, she looked up at the vast, clear blue sky and whispered a prayer of thanks. *Thank you, Lord, for bringing me Trevor.*

Louisa continued her walk through the flower garden, surrounded by the gentle rustling of leaves and the soft fragrance of roses, a peaceful solitude settling over her. She quietly thanked the Lord again for all He had given her—her family, her freedom, and the life she never thought she'd have. After so many years of hardship, the woman who had tormented her, Eliza, was no longer a threat. Last week, Louisa had learned that Eliza had been hanged for her crimes, a final chapter closed in the saga of her past.

But even with that weight lifted, Louisa's thoughts lingered on the children who had suffered under Macgregor's cruelty. She had spent time helping them find their way home, tracking down the families who feared they'd lost their sons and daughters forever. Most were reunited, though some were true orphans. Louisa's heart ached for those few, but she was determined to help them find the happiness and peace that now filled her own life. If she could have her second chance, so could they.

The sudden pounding of hooves shattered the stillness of the garden, and she turned swiftly toward the sound. Her husband rode up quickly, his horse skidding to a halt before he dismounted in one fluid motion. She stood still, watching him as he approached, her heart fluttering as his grin widened with every step.

When he finally reached her, he swept her into his arms, lifting her off the ground as though she weighed nothing at all. Louisa laughed, wrapping her arms around his neck, her heart swelling with joy as she felt his warmth and strength envelop her. In his embrace, the world felt safe and complete.

She gazed into his dreamy blue eyes. "What is this all about?"

"I missed you."

"Trevor, I fear you are teasing me. Your brothers and Lord Hawthorne were supposed to keep you busy at White's, since you hardly get out anymore."

He shook his head. "I was completely bored, my dear, and could not wait to return to the arms of my beautiful wife."

"Your brothers are going to think you are neglecting them."

"No they will not think that way. In fact, Trey cannot stay away from Judith for very long, either. I think Tristan and Dominic are contemplating finding themselves wives as well."

She ran her fingers through her husband's glorious, thick black hair. "I do love you, and I'm happy you are here."

"Are you ready to go home?" He waggled his eyebrows suggestively.

"Heavens no. We would have to leave the twins with my parents, and they would for certain know what we were up to."

Tilting back his head, he laughed heartily. "Oh, my dear wife. Your parents will not fault us at all for wanting to be alone any chance we can get." He set her down until her feet touched the ground before kissing her.

After the kiss ended, she sighed and leaned her head on his chest. "Indeed, my wonderful husband, you are correct. We will certainly need to find more time to be together, especially now."

He withdrew only enough for her to look at him again. "And why is that?"

"Because in seven or so months, we will be making an addition to the family."

"We will? I thought you had found homes for all of Macgregor's children."

"Oh, I have. Although I am seriously thinking about starting a home for orphaned children. A *good* place that will teach the children what they need to learn… what they will miss from not having parents."

He nodded. "That is an excellent idea, my love. I will support you, as long as you don't plan on being there every day and all day. The twins and I still need you desperately."

"Oh, I will not spend my time there. I only want to get a center started. Besides, I have other plans for my family now."

A grin stretched his mouth. "What kind of plans?"

"I told you. I am going to add to our household size."

Trevor's breath hitched as his eyes widened. "A… baby? We are going to have a baby?"

"Of course, my dear husband. What did you think I was talking about?"

Trevor let out a joyful whoop, lifting her effortlessly into the air once more, spinning them both in a circle of shared laughter and pure delight. As he set her gently back on the ground, his lips found hers in a deep, passionate kiss. Louisa responded without hesitation, pouring all the love and gratitude she felt for him into that single, intimate moment. The kiss was a reflection of everything they had endured and all the happiness they had found together.

Her heart raced, as it always did when he was near, his touch igniting a fire within her. Trevor had a way of making her feel truly alive—he had from the very beginning. In his arms, she wasn't just a woman who had survived a painful past; she was a woman cherished, desired, and loved beyond measure. Every time he held her, every kiss, reminded her that she was no longer broken, but whole, because of the love they shared.

Trevor broke the kiss and rested his forehead against hers. "Oh, Louisa. I never thought I could be this happy. When I married Gwen and there was no love between us, I thought I was destined for a loveless life. But you entered and brought laughter into my world. You showed me what it's like to be loved. Indeed, you have made my life complete, and I thank you."

She snuggled her cheek against his. "I assure you, I will try to make you happy every moment of our lives."

"You already do." He winked.

The End

About the Author

Marie Higgins is an award-winning, best-selling author of clean romance novels that melt your heart and have you falling in love over and over again. Since 2010, she's published over 100 heartwarming, on-the-edge-of-your-seat romances. She's broadened her readership by writing mystery/suspense, humor, time-travel, and paranormal, along with her love for historical romances. Her readers have dubbed her "Queen of Tease" because of her twists and unexpected endings.

Website – www.authormariehiggins.com
Facebook – facebook.com/marie.higgins.7543
TikTok – tiktok.com/@author.mariehiggins
Instagram – instagram.com/author.mariehiggins
Bookbub – bookbub.com/authors/marie-higgins
Twitter – @mariehigginsxox